IN THE SHADOW OF
AGATHA
CHRISTIE

IN THE SHADOW OF
AGATHA
CHRISTIE

CLASSIC CRIME FICTION BY
FORGOTTEN FEMALE WRITERS:
1850–1917

EDITED BY LESLIE S. KLINGER

PEGASUS CRIME

NEW YORK LONDON

IN THE SHADOW OF AGATHA CHRISTIE

Pegasus Books Ltd.
148 W 37th Street, 13th Floor
New York, NY 10018

First Pegasus Books cloth edition January 2018

Interior design by Maria Fernandez

Library of Congress Cataloging-in-Publication Data is available.

ISBN: 978-1-68177-630-9

10 9 8 7 6 5 4 3 2 1

Printed in the United States of America
Distributed by W. W. Norton & Company
www.pegasusbooks.us

"What a woman—oh, what a woman!"

—The King of Bohemia, in "A Scandal in Bohemia"

by Arthur Conan Doyle

CONTENTS

INTRODUCTION

LESLIE S. KLINGER

xi

THE ADVOCATE'S WEDDING DAY

CATHERINE CROWE

1

THE SQUIRE'S STORY

ELIZABETH CLEGHORN GASKELL

15

TRACES OF CRIME

MARY FORTUNE

33

MR. FURBUSH

HARRIET PRESCOTT SPOFFORD

47

MRS. TODHETLEY'S EARRINGS

ELLEN WOOD

59

CATCHING A BURGLAR

ELIZABETH CORBETT

87

THE GHOST OF FOUNTAIN LANE

C. L. PIRKIS

99

THE STATEMENT OF JARED JOHNSON

GERALDINE BONNER

123

POINT IN MORALS

ELLEN GLASGOW

139

THE BLOOD-RED CROSS

L. T. MEADE AND ROBERT EUSTACE

155

THE REGENT'S PARK MURDER

BARONESS ORCZY

181

THE CASE OF THE REGISTERED LETTER

AUGUSTA GRONER

197

THE WINNING SEQUENCE

M. E. BRADDON

233

MISSING: PAGE THIRTEEN

ANNA KATHARINE GREEN

247

THE ADVENTURE OF THE CLOTHES-LINE

CAROLYN WELLS

285

JURY OF HER PEERS

SUSAN GLASPELL

297

BIBLIOGRAPHY

321

ACKNOWLEDGMENTS

325

ABOUT THE EDITOR

327

INTRODUCTION

A gatha Christie is undoubtedly the world's best-selling mystery author, hailed as the "Queen of Crime," with sales in the billions and more translations than any other author. Her books, according to her estate, have outsold any other than the Bible and Shakespeare. Christie burst onto the literary scene in 1920, with *The Mysterious Affair at Styles*, introducing the Belgian detective Hercule Poirot; her last novel was published in 1976, a career longer than even Conan Doyle's forty-year span. The indefatigable Miss Marple, who starred in Christie's last book, first appeared in 1927. Yet as late as 1929, Dorothy Sayers, in her classic introduction to the 1929 *Omnibus of Crime*, could write, "But the really brilliant woman detective has yet to be created." And prior to Christie, only Anna Katharine Green, discussed below, had achieved any real recognition as a crime writer.

In the nineteenth century, Arthur Conan Doyle dominated the genre, along with William Godwin, Eugène Vidoc, Edgar Allan Poe, Émile Gaboriau, Fergus Hume, and Wilkie Collins—all notably male. It is also the common view that in the nineteenth century, crime writing was a spasmodic enterprise, with occasional bursts of popularity of the mystery stories of Poe or Gaboriau, but not really established until the overwhelming success of Sherlock Holmes in the 1890s.* But there were earlier notable contributions to the genre, by women writers in England, the United States, Australia, and Europe, throughout the period from 1850 to 1890, and even after Holmes came to predominate the model of the detective, women writers were traveling different roads.

Crime writing was not an invention of the nineteenth century. Bruce Cassiday, in *Roots of Detection: The Art of Deduction before Sherlock Holmes* (1983), includes examples of deductive reasoning applied to crime from Herodotus, the apocryphal Scriptures, *The Arabian Nights*, Voltaire's *Zadig*, E. T. Hoffmann, and Edward Bulwer-Lytton. In America, sermons often told horrifying tales of crimes and repentant criminals. Gothic novels were populated with mysterious deaths and terrifying villains, and the widely sold Newgate Calendars focused on crimes, criminals, and their capture. However, stories of detection did not flourish until mid-century, with the rise of the professional police force.

The first great writer of tales of criminal detection was the Frenchman Eugène Vidocq (1775–1857), whose memoirs and novels found a ready audience. Vidocq, a reformed criminal, was appointed in 1813 to be the first head of the Sûreté Nationale, the outgrowth of an informal detective force created by Vidocq and adopted by Napoleon as a supplement to the police. His 1828 memoirs recounted his adventures in the detection and capture of criminals, often involving disguises and wild flights. Later books told of his criminal career, and sensational novels published under his name (probably written by others) capitalized on his reputation as a bold detective.

While Vidocq's stories captivated the public, they were hardly original tales of detective fiction. The first great purveyor of *fictional* stories about a detective was Edgar Allan Poe (1809–1849), whose Chevalier Auguste Dupin set the standard for a generation to come. The cerebral Dupin first

---

* Sayers herself expressed this view in *Omnibus of Crime*, though she does mention Anna Katharine Green's Violet Strange (see p. 247, below) and Baroness Orczy's Lady Molly (see below, p. 181) in a footnote.

appeared in Poe's short story "Murders in the Rue Morgue" (1841). At the same time, Poe introduced another staple of detective fiction, the partner and chronicler (nameless in Poe's tales) who is less intelligent than the detective but serves as a sounding board for the detective's brilliant deductions. In each of the three Dupin stories (the other two are "The Mystery of Marie Rogêt" [1842] and "The Purloined Letter" [1844], the detective outwits the police and shows them to be ineffective crime fighters and problem solvers. Yet Poe apparently lost interest in the notion, and his detective "series" ended in 1844.

Another Frenchman, Emile Gaboriau, created the detective known as Monsieur Lecoq, drawing heavily on Vidocq as his model. First appearing in *L'ffaire Lerouge* (1866), Lecoq was a minor police detective who rose to fame in six cases, appearing between 1866 and 1880. Although Sherlock Holmes describes Lecoq as a "miserable bungler," Gaboriau's works were immensely popular, and Fergus Hume, English author of the best-selling detective novel of the nineteenth century *The Mystery of a Hansom Cab* (1886), which sold over 500,000 copies worldwide, explained that Gaboriau's financial success inspired his own work.

Memoirs of police officers and detectives were another important stream of stories. *Richmond; or, Scenes in the Life of a Bow Street Officer: Drawn Up from His Private Memoranda*, published anonymously in 1827, purported to be true tales of criminal detection (though now thought to be largely fictional). Also in England, "Waters's" *Recollections of a Detective Police-Officer* appeared in 1856, and *Revelations of a Lady Detective* in 1864.* James M'Govan's *Brought to Bay, or Experiences of a City Detective*, which was issued by the Edinburgh Publishing Company in 1878, was a great success, leading to two more volumes of these (fictional) stories of an Edinburgh detective.

---

* The latter book was published anonymously, and based on an erroneous auction catalog, Ellery Queen claimed that the book first appeared in 1861 under the title *Experiences of a Lady Detective*, its author was "Anonyma," the author/principal character of a series of shilling shockers, and the 1864 *Revelations* volume was a sequel. However, Queen later corrected this claim, clarifying that the book was *reissued* in 1884 with a subtitle of "Experiences of a Lady Detective," causing the confusion. Most scholars now identify the author as William Stephens (or Stevens) Hayward (1835–1870), who frequently wrote books for the *Revelations* publisher George Vickers.

In America, *Detective Sketches [by a New York Detective]* appeared in 1881 in the format of a "dime novel." These were cheap, pulp editions, usually published anonymously or by fictitious authors, first popularized in England as "shilling shockers" or "penny dreadfuls," featuring highwaymen, pirates, and other criminals, ghosts, vampires (*Varney the Vampyre* first seeing the light of day, so to speak, in this format), and other shocking subjects. Ellery Queen estimates that between 1860 and 1928, more than six thousand different detective dime novels were published in the United States, including female detectives such as Lady Bess, Lizzie Lasher (the Red Weasel), and Lucilla Lynx.

In England, criminals and detectives peopled Charles Dickens's tales as well. While not widely regarded as an author of detective fiction, Dickens created Inspector Bucket, the first significant detective in English literature. When Bucket appeared in *Bleak House* (1852–1853), he became the prototype of the official representative of the police department: honest, diligent, stolid, and confident, albeit not very colorful, dramatic, or exciting. Wilkie Collins, author of two of the greatest novels of suspense of the nineteenth century, *The Woman in White* (1860) and *The Moonstone* (1868), contributed a similar character, Sergeant Cuff, who appears in *The Moonstone*. Cuff is known as the finest police detective in England, who solves his cases with perseverance and energy, rather than genius. Sadly, after *The Moonstone*, he is not heard from again.

The first female detective probably was Mrs. G. in *The Female Detective* (1864) by Andrew J. Forrester Jr.* However, the first female *crime writer* is probably the British writer Caroline Clive, whose novel *Paul Ferroll* (1855), published under the pseudonym "V.," is clearly a murder mystery, albeit one without a detective figure. Spoiler alert: Twenty years

---

* The critic Stephen Knight has suggested that "Andrew Forrester" is the same "Mrs. Forrester" who wrote a romance novel *Fair Women* in 1867 and is likely to be a woman who concealed her gender to write in two genres. *Crime Fiction 1800–2000: Detection, Death, Diversity* (Basingstoke, Hampshire: Palgrave MacMillan, 2004). However, in the 2010 edition of his book, now titled *Crime Fiction since 1800: Detection, Death, Diversity*, Knight seems to have abandoned this suggestion, positing instead that "Andrew Forrester" was two brothers, John and Daniel, who were engaged in investigative work. Knight's original view is adopted in Watson, Kate, *Women Writing Crime Fiction, 1860–1880: Fourteen American, British and Australian Authors* (Jefferson, NC: McFarland & Company (2012).

after the murder, the title character, whose wife was the victim, admits to the killing. Clive (1801–1873) also wrote a handful of short stories, a half-dozen volumes of poetry, and some other novels, including a "prequel" to *Paul Ferroll* in which she explored the husband's motives, but none achieved the success of her first venture into crime writing.

In America, the New England–based Harriet Prescott Spofford began to write stories about women in contemporary American society. The author of hundreds of stories, essays, poems, and children's tales, she also began to focus on crime writing. Her first crime story was "In a Cellar," published in 1859, which she submitted under an assumed name, causing the editors to think that it was a translation of Dumas or Balzac. In "Mr. Furbush" (1865), included in this volume, she created the first "series" detective character. Furbush appears again in "In the Maguerriwock" (1868). However, after this story, Spofford apparently bowed to the public's demand for more realistic narratives and returned to writing New England sketches.

Oline Keese was the penname of Caroline Woolmer Leakey (1827–1881), an Australian gentlewoman whose novel *The Broad Arrow* (1859) is the first depiction of convict oppression and brutality in Van Diemen's Land (Tasmania), focusing on the plight of a woman, Maida Gwynnham, who has been wrongly convicted. It precedes by fifteen years the better-known *For the Term of His Natural Life* by Marcus Clarke, also set in Tasmania and also telling the story of an innocent character. While Leakey's novel is full of Christian righteousness, it is also indignant about the corrupt and corrupting convict system. Leakey also wrote moral tales but with no crime element.

Although Ellen Davitt (ca. 1812–1879) only wrote for three years, 1865 to 1868, she was a significant contributor to Australian crime writing. Educated in England, she relocated to Victoria in the 1850s. Davitt was the elder sister of Anthony Trollope's wife, though she never spoke of the connection. Her novel *Force and Fraud* was serialized in the *Australian Journal* in 1865, and that journal also published her novel-length serials "Black Sheep: A Tale of Australian Life" and "Uncle Vincent; or Love and Hatred," subtitled "A Romance of Modern Times." Her last serial was "The Wreck of Atalanta, which appeared in the *Journal* in 1867. *Force and Fraud* is the first murder mystery published in Australia and the first "whodunnit," drawing on the developing genre of British mystery fiction. However, there is no detective figure, and the police fare badly in Davitt's view. Perhaps as a result and certainly in part by reason of its Australian setting, it was largely ignored outside Australia.

Elizabeth Gaskell (1810–1865) was a close friend of Charlotte Brontë and therefore quite naturally became her biographer. Gaskell produced seven novels, four novella, and over forty short stories, and the longer works generally focused on historical, domestic, and social themes. In her short fiction, however, she anonymously wrote sensationalized, Gothic stories. Gaskell was certainly interested in cirme writing: She was enthusiastic about and recommended Caroline Clive's *Paul, Ferroll* and her novella "Dark Night's Work" (1863) and her novel *Mary Barton* (1848) both incoprorate crime. Her story "The Grey Woman" (1861) also includes crime, though it can hardly be called crime writing, but "Disappearances" (1851) is listed in Barzun and Taylor's *Catalogue of Crime* as is "The Squire's Tale," included in this volume.

Although well-known later in her career as a prolific author of "sensation" fiction, Mary Elizabeth Braddon (1835–1915) also wrote an important crime novel, *The Trail of the Serpent* (1860). Originally titled *Three Times Dead; or, The Secret of the Heath*, it focuses on Jabez North (Emphraim East in the original verison), a criminal who changes his identity three times, and Mr. Peters, a unrelenting but highly unusual police detective. She also incorporated crime into some of her better-known work: Richard Audley functions as a detective in her well-remembered *Lady Audley's Secret* (1862), and *Eleanor's Victory* (1863) also includes a proto-detective. Although Braddon would never identify herself as a "crime writer," her fiction did much to advance the genre.

Mrs. Henry (Ellen) Wood (1814–1887) began publishing her novel *East Lynne* in the same year as Braddon's *Trail of the Serpent*. Wood's story included crime elements, though no detective, but in 1862, her novel *Mrs. Halliburton's Troubles* featured police detective Sergeant Delves. In addition to dozens of novels, Wood penned six volumes of stories about Johnny Ludlow, a young man who lives in a rural community. All of the stories appeared in the *Argosy* magazine, which Wood owned and edited. Many of the stories feature crimes of all types, and Johnny is an unusually observant lad, though certainly not a detective. The first Ludlow story was published in 1868, and over the next 23 years, 89 more tales appeared. The first series was collected in 1874, and the stories were not identified as written by Wood, perhaps because she wanted to conceal that virtually the entire contents of some *Argosy* issues were from her pen. The secret was concealed until the second series appeared in collected form in 1880. Very popular at their inception, as the mystery genre developed in England, by 1885, when the third collection of Ludlow tales was published, their style was being left behind. "[T]hese chronicles of petty crime and misadventure at the best but painted photographs which do not deserve the name of works of art," wrote the *Saturday Review*. Nonetheless, the stories were an important transition to the stylized detection of the era of Sherlock Holmes.

An American writer not normally associated with crime writing is Louisa May Alcott (1832–1888). However, between 1863 and 1869, primarily under the name A. M. Barnard, she wrote a number of lesser-known shorter works—she referred to them as her "blood-and-thunder" stories— with themes including drug use, ghosts, violence, revenge, murder, insanity, and mental abberations. Though little remembered, her best-known are "Pauline's Passion and Punishment" (1863), "The Abbot's Ghost" (1866), "Behind a Mask" (1866), "Long Fatal Love Chase" (1866), and "The Mysterious Key" (1867). With the success of *Little Women* in 1868, however, she abandoned the genre.

In 1866–1867, the first crime novel written by a woman in America was published, *The Dead Letter: An American Romance*.* Its author was the remarkable Metta Victoria Fuller Victor (1831–1885), writing under the name of "Seely Regester." Victor had written and would continue to write dozens of other works, including novels, short stories, dime novels, poetry, and housewives' manuals that included boys' adventures, westerns, juvenile fiction, and humor. For purposes of this survey, most noteworthy were her two other tales written under "Seely Regester," a novel titled *The Figure Eight; or, The Mystery of Meredith Place* (serialized in *The Illuminated*

---

* Catherine Ross Nickerson goes further, crediting Victor as "the first writer, male or female, to produce full-length detective novels in the United States." Introduction, *The Dead Letter and The Figure Eight* by Metta Fuller Victor (Durham, NC: Duke University Press, 2003).

Western World, 1869) and "The Skeleton at the Banquet."[*] All of these fea-tured detectives: In *The Dead Letter*, there is both a police detective, Mr. Burton, and an amateur, Richard Redfield (who is training to be a lawyer). In *The Figure Eight* and "The Skeleton at the Banquet," the detectives are amateurs. *The Dead Letter* was published both as a serial dime novel and in book form, and it was successful enough to be pirated by *Cassell's Magazine* and reprinted in England in 1866–1867. Kate Watson concludes that Victor's work "both contributed to and made possible that of her more famous sister-in-crime, Anna Katharine Green."[†]

Mary Fortune, who touchingly styled herself "Waif Wander" on some of her fiction, was the most prolific female crime writer of the nineteenth century. Born in Ireland, she moved to Canada with her father and mar-ried Joseph Fortune in 1851. Nothing is known of his fate, but Mary Fortune migrated with her father to Australia in 1855, where three years later she married a mounted trooper, Percy Rollo Brett. She began to write, and her first stories appeared in 1865 as part of the "Memoirs of an Australian Police Officer" series, thus predating the work of Metta Victor. Michael Sims, in *The Dead Witness: A Connoisseur's Guide to Victorian Detective Stories*,[‡] terms Fortune the author of "the first known detective story written by a woman." In 1868, Fortune initiated the "Detective's Album" casebook series, eventually including over 500 stories, written between 1868 and 1908. All of her stories were published anonymously or pseudonymously during her lifetime, and it was not until 1987 that a scholar, Lucy Sussex, with the aid of a collector, John Kinmont Moir, identified the body of her work. Fortune, assesses Kate Watson, "was an innovative writer who challenged literary, generic and gender boundaries and conventions. . . . [S]he was genuinely ground-breaking, producing narratives which can with confidence be called crime and detective fiction."[§]

---

[*] The story first appeared in the anthology *Stories and Sketches by Our Best Authors* (Boston: Lee and Shepard, 1867).

[†] *Women Writing Crime Fiction, 1860–1880*, p. 117.

[‡] New York: Walker & Company, 2012, p. 179.

[§] *Women Writing Crime Fiction, 1860–1880*, p. 184.

With the exception of Edgar Allan Poe, Anna Katharine Green (1846–1935) is the best-known American writer of mystery fiction before Mary Roberts Rinehart, whose 1908 novel *The Circular Staircase* became the fountainhead of an enormous body of modern American crime writers. Rinehart herself acknowledged Green as her direct ancestor: When it came to selecting a publisher to which to submit *The Circular Staircase*, Rinehart stated that she merely looked at who had published Green's latest work. Michael Sims, in *The Dead Witness*, credits Green as the first woman to write a "full-fledged" detective novel, discounting Metta Fuller Victor's *The Dead Letter* as dependent on the psychic visions of the detective's young daughter—"thus rejecting the underlying rational basis of detection."[*] Green, the daughter of a lawyer, wrote *The Leavenworth Case* (featuring New York police detective Ebenezer Gryce) after college, though it was not published until 1878. It was an instant bestseller and led to another twenty-eight mystery novels, countless short stories, and books in other genres. Though Gryce was the lead detective in three novels, it was the character of Amelia Butterworth, a nosy society spinster, that was her great innovation—Butterworth was undoubtedly the inspiration for Agatha Christie's Miss Marple. Green also can be credited as inspiring the Nancy Drew series of girls' mysteries: Her young society debutante, Violet Strange, appeared in a series of nine stories (one is included in this volume), solving crimes in order to earn enough money to support a disinherited sister.

Mrs. George (Elizabeth) Corbett (1846–1930) is a fascinating English writer. Many of her books were written in serial form and are currently unavailable. Initially, Corbett was regarded as a mystery writer, ranked as high as Conan Doyle. Her novels *The Missing Note* (1881) and *Pharisees Unveiled: The Adventures of an Amateur Detective* (1889) set this tone, though the latter is more science fiction than mystery, about a doctor who develops an invisibility potion. Today, Corbett is best remembered for her feminist novel *New Amazonia: A Foretaste of the Future* (1889). However, she also wrote the important crime novel *When the Sea Gives Up Its Dead* (1894), featuring a young woman, Annie Cory, who is an able amateur detective seeking to clear the reputation of her man. In the course of her detection,

---

[*] *The Dead Witness*, p. xxvii.

she works in disguise, including dressing as a man (in the manner of Doyle's Irene Adler). This book may well be the first appearance of a female detective written by a woman. Corbett also wrote short stories, and her volume *Secrets of a Private Inquiry Office,* published in 1890, collects fifteen tales of Bob White, one of the co-owners of the Bell & White Agency; his partner, the narrator, who is an man named Bell (no first name given); and a silent partner whom they term "Jones," irrelevant to this matter. Corbett wrote additional stories about the agency, but their publication history is confused, and no copies of collections of these stories is extant.

With the success of writers like Anna Katharine Green in America, L. T. Meade, C. L. Pirkis, the Baroness Orczy, and Mrs. George Corbett in England, and Mary Fortune (albeit anonymously) in Australia, the sluice gates were finally open for women crime writers.

Women who followed them, such as Mignon Eberhart, Patricia Wentworth, Dorothy Sayers, and of course Agatha Christie would not have thrived without the bold, fearless work of their predecessors, and the genre would be much poorer for their absence. Today, women are an irremovable part of the tapestry of mystery fiction. So, while Agatha Christie may still reign as the "Queen of Crime," it is important to remember that she did not ascend that throne except on the shoulders of women who came before her, too many of whom have been lost in her shadow.

—Leslie S. Klinger

IN THE SHADOW OF
AGATHA CHRISTIE

Catherine Crowe (1800–1876) was an English playwright, author, and poet, who also wrote for children. Her novel Adventures of Susan Hopley; or Circumstantial Evidence, *first published in 1841 and later republished with the subtitle "Adventures of a Maid Servant," is one of the earliest crime novels. Originally published anonymously, it became a highly successful stage play. The titular heroine discovers a murder and skillfully sifts the evidence and discovers the criminal, qualifying her as probably the first female detective. Crowe also wrote many short stories, and her most popular book was* Night-Side of Nature *(1848), a collection of stories of the supernatural. The following, combining a crime and a revengeful spirit, first appeared in the magazine* Household Words *for June 22, 1850, without identification of the author.*

THE ADVOCATE'S
WEDDING DAY

CATHERINE CROWE

Antoine de Chaulieu was the son of a poor gentleman of Normandy, with a long genealogy, a short rent-roll, and a large family. Jacques Rollet was the son of a brewer, who did not know who his grandfather was; but he had a long purse, and only two children. As these youths flourished in the early days of liberty, equality, and fraternity* and were near neighbors, they naturally hated each other. Their enmity commenced at school, where the delicate and refined De Chaulieu, being the only *gentilhomme*† amongst the scholars, was the favorite of the master (who was a

---

* That is, in the early days of the French Revolution (which first exploded in 1789).

† Gentleman.

bit of an aristocrat in his heart), although he was about the worst dressed boy in the establishment, and never had a sou to spend; whilst Jacques Rollet, sturdy and rough, with smart clothes and plenty of money, got flogged six days in the week, ostensibly for being stupid and not learning his lessons,—which he did not,—but in reality for constantly quarrelling with and insulting De Chaulieu, who had not strength to cope with him.

When they left the academy, the feud continued in all its vigor, and was fostered by a thousand little circumstances, arising out of the state of the times, till a separation ensued, in consequence of an aunt of Antoine de Chaulieu's undertaking the expense of sending him to Paris to study the law, and of maintaining him there during the necessary period.

With the progress of events came some degree of reaction in favor of birth and nobility; and then Antoine, who had passed for the bar, began to hold up his head, and endeavor to push his fortunes; but fate seemed against him. He felt certain that if he possessed any gift in the world, it was that of eloquence, but he could get no cause to plead; and his aunt dying inopportunely, first his resources failed, and then his health. He had no sooner returned to his home than, to complicate his difficulties completely, he fell in love with Miss Natalie de Bellefonds, who had just returned from Paris, where she had been completing her education. To expatiate on the perfections of Mademoiselle Natalie would be a waste of ink and paper; it is sufficient to say that she really was a very charming girl, with a fortune which, though not large, would have been a most desirable addition to De Chaulieu, who had nothing. Neither was the fair Natalie indisposed to listen to his addresses; but her father could not be expected to countenance the suit of a gentleman, however well-born, who had not a ten-sous piece in the world, and whose prospects were a blank.

Whilst the ambitious and love-sick barrister was thus pining in unwelcome obscurity, his old acquaintance, Jacques Rollet, had been acquiring an undesirable notoriety. There was nothing really bad in Jacques; but having been bred up a democrat, with a hatred of the nobility, he could not easily accommodate his rough humor to treat them with civility when it was no longer safe to insult them. The liberties he allowed himself whenever circumstances brought him into contact with the higher classes of society,

4

had led him into many scrapes, out of which his father's money had in one way or another released him; but that source of safety had now failed. Old Rollet, having been too busy with the affairs of the nation to attend to his business, had died insolvent, leaving his son with nothing but his own wits to help him out of future difficulties; and it was not long before their exercise was called for.

Claudine Rollet, his sister, who was a very pretty girl, had attracted the attention of Mademoiselle de Bellefonds's brother, Alphonse; and as he paid her more attention than from such a quarter was agreeable to Jacques, the young men had had more than one quarrel on the subject, on which occasion they had each, characteristically, given vent to their enmity, the one in contemptuous monosyllables, and the other in a volley of insulting words. But Claudine had another lover, more nearly of her own condition of life; this was Claperon, the deputy-governor of the Rouen jail, with whom she had made acquaintance during one or two compulsory visits paid by her brother to that functionary. Claudine, who was a bit of a coquette, though she did not altogether reject his suit, gave him little encouragement, so that, betwixt hopes and fears and doubts and jealousies, poor Claperon led a very uneasy kind of life.

Affairs had been for some time in this position, when, one fine morning, Alphonse de Bellefonds was not to be found in his chamber when his servant went to call him; neither had his bed been slept in. He had been observed to go out rather late on the previous evening, but whether he had returned nobody could tell. He had not appeared at supper, but that was too ordinary an event to awaken suspicion; and little alarm was excited till several hours had elapsed, when inquiries were instituted and a search commenced, which terminated in the discovery of his body, a good deal mangled, lying at the bottom of a pond which had belonged to the old brewery.

Before any investigation had been made, every person had jumped to the conclusion that the young man had been murdered, and that Jacques Rollet was the assassin. There was a strong presumption in favor of that opinion, which further perquisitions* tended to confirm. Only the day before, Jacques had been heard to threaten Monsieur de Bellefonds with speedy vengeance.

---

* Searches.

On the fatal evening, Alphonse and Claudine had been seen together in the neighborhood of the now dismantled brewery; and as Jacques, betwixt poverty and democracy, was in bad odor with the respectable part of society, it was not easy for him to bring witnesses to character or to prove an unexceptionable *alibi*. As for the Bellefonds and De Chaulieus, and the aristocracy in general, they entertained no doubt of his guilt; and finally, the magistrates coming to the same opinion, Jacques Rollet was committed for trial at the next assizes, and as a testimony of good-will, Antoine de Chaulieu was selected by the injured family to conduct the prosecution.

Here, at last, was the opportunity he had sighed for. So interesting a case, too, furnishing such ample occasion for passion, pathos, indignation! And how eminently fortunate that the speech which he set himself with ardor to prepare would be delivered in the presence of the father and brother of his mistress, and perhaps of the lady herself. The evidence against Jacques, it is true, was altogether presumptive; there was no proof whatever that he had committed the crime; and for his own part, he stoutly denied it. But Antoine de Chaulieu entertained no doubt of his guilt, and the speech he composed was certainly well calculated to carry that conviction into the bosom of others. It was of the highest importance to his own reputation that he should procure a verdict, and he confidently assured the afflicted and enraged family of the victim that their vengeance should be satisfied.

Under these circumstances, could anything be more unwelcome than a piece of intelligence that was privately conveyed to him late on the evening before the trial was to come on, which tended strongly to exculpate the prisoner, without indicating any other person as the criminal. Here was an opportunity lost. The first step of the ladder on which he was to rise to fame, fortune, and a wife was slipping from under his feet.

Of course so interesting a trial was anticipated with great eagerness by the public; the court was crowded with all the beauty and fashion of Rouen, and amongst the rest, doubly interesting in her mourning, sat the fair Natalie, accompanied by her family.

The young advocate's heart beat high; he felt himself inspired by the occasion; and although Jacques Rollet persisted in asserting his innocence, founding his defence chiefly on circumstances which were strongly corroborated by the information that had reached De Chaulieu the preceding evening, he was nevertheless convicted.

In spite of the very strong doubts he privately entertained respecting the justice of the verdict, even De Chaulieu himself, in the first flush of success, amidst a crowd of congratulating friends and the approving smiles of his mistress, felt gratified and happy; his speech had, for the time being, not only convinced others but himself; warmed with his own eloquence, he believed what he said. But when the glow was over, and he found himself alone, he did not feel so comfortable. A latent doubt of Rollet's guilt now pressed strongly on his mind, and he felt that the blood of the innocent would be on his head. It was true there was yet time to save the life of the prisoner; but to admit Jacques innocent, was to take the glory out of his own speech, and turn the sting of his argument against himself. Besides, if he produced the witness who had secretly given him the information, he should be self-condemned, for he could not conceal that he had been aware of the circumstance before the trial.

Matters having gone so far, therefore, it was necessary that Jacques Rollet should die; and so the affair took its course; and early one morning the guillotine was erected in the courtyard of the gaol, three criminals ascended the scaffold, and three heads fell into the basket, which were presently afterward, with the trunks that had been attached to them, buried in a corner of the cemetery.

Antoine de Chaulieu was now fairly started in his career, and his success was as rapid as the first step toward it had been tardy. He took a pretty apartment in the Hôtel Marbœuf, Rue Grange Batelière, and in a short time was looked upon as one of the most rising young advocates in Paris. His success in one line brought him success in another; he was soon a favorite in society, and an object of interest to speculating mothers; but his affections still adhered to his old love, Natalie de Bellefonds, whose family now gave their assent to the match,—at least prospectively,—a circumstance which furnished such additional incentive to his exertions, that in about two years from his first brilliant speech he was in a sufficiently flourishing condition to offer the young lady a suitable home.

In anticipation of the happy event, he engaged and furnished a suite of apartments in the Rue de Helder; and as it was necessary that the bride should come to Paris to provide her trousseau, it was agreed that the wedding should take place there, instead of at Bellefonds, as had been first projected,—an arrangement the more desirable, that a press of business rendered Monsieur de Chaulieu's absence from Paris inconvenient.

Brides and bridegrooms in France, except of the very high classes, are not much in the habit of making those honeymoon excursions so universal in this country. A day spent in visiting Versailles, or St. Cloud, or even the public places of the city, is generally all that precedes the settling down into the habits of daily life. In the present instance, St. Denis was selected, from the circumstance of Natalie's having a younger sister at school there, and also because she had a particular desire to see the Abbey.

The wedding was to take place on a Thursday; and on the Wednesday evening, having spent some hours most agreeably with Natalie, Antoine de Chaulieu returned to spend his last night in his bachelor apartments. His wardrobe and other small possessions had already been packed up, and sent to his future home; and there was nothing left in his room now but his new wedding suit, which he inspected with considerable satisfaction before he undressed and lay down to sleep.

Sleep, however, was somewhat slow to visit him, and the clock had struck one before he closed his eyes. When he opened them again, it was broad daylight, and his first thought was, had he overslept himself? He sat up in bed to look at the clock, which was exactly opposite; and as he did so, in the large mirror over the fireplace, he perceived a figure standing behind him. As the dilated eyes met his own, he saw it was the face of Jacques Rollet. Overcome with horror, he sank back on his pillow, and it was some minutes before he ventured to look again in that direction; when he did so, the figure had disappeared.

The sudden revulsion of feeling which such a vision was calculated to occasion in a man elate with joy may be conceived. For some time after the death of his former foe, he had been visited by not infrequent twinges of conscience; but of late, borne along by success and the hurry of Parisian life, these unpleasant remembrances had grown rarer, till at length they had faded away altogether. Nothing had been further from his thoughts than Jacques Rollet when he closed his eyes on the preceding night, or when he opened them to that sun which was to shine on what he expected to be the happiest day of his life. Where were the high-strung nerves now, the elastic frame, the bounding heart?

Heavily and slowly he arose from his bed, for it was time to do so; and with a trembling hand and quivering knees he went through the processes of the toilet, gashing his cheek with the razor, and spilling the water over his well-polished boots. When he was dressed, scarcely venturing to cast a glance in the mirror as he passed it, he quitted the room and descended the stairs, taking the key of the door with him, for the purpose of leaving it with the porter; the man, however, being absent, he laid it on the table in his lodge, and with a relaxed hand and languid step he proceeded to the carriage which quickly conveyed him to the church, where he was met by Natalie and her friends.

How difficult it was now to look happy, with that pallid face and extinguished eye!

"How pale you are! Has anything happened? You are surely ill?" were the exclamations that assailed him on all sides.

He tried to carry the thing off as well as he could, but he felt that the movements he would have wished to appear alert were only convulsive, and that the smiles with which he attempted to relax his features were but distorted grimaces. However, the church was not the place for further inquiries; and whilst Natalie gently pressed his hand in token of sympathy, they advanced to the altar, and the ceremony was performed; after which they stepped into the carriages waiting at the door, and drove to the apartments of Madame de Bellefonds, where an elegant *déjeuner** was prepared.

"What ails you, my dear husband?" inquired Natalie, as soon as they were alone.

"Nothing, love," he replied; "nothing, I assure you, but a restless night and a little overwork, in order that I might have today free to enjoy my happiness."

"Are you quite sure? Is there nothing else?"

"Nothing, indeed, and pray don't take notice of it; it only makes me worse."

---

* Lunch.

Natalie was not deceived, but she saw that what he said was true,—notice made him worse; so she contented herself with observing him quietly and saying nothing; but as he felt she was observing him, she might almost better have spoken; words are often less embarrassing things than too curious eyes.

When they reached Madame de Bellefonds' he had the same sort of scrutiny to undergo, till he grew quite impatient under it, and betrayed a degree of temper altogether unusual with him. Then everybody looked astonished; some whispered their remarks, and others expressed them by their wondering eyes, till his brow knit, and his pallid cheeks became flushed with anger.

Neither could he divert attention by eating; his parched mouth would not allow him to swallow anything but liquids, of which he indulged in copious libations; and it was an exceeding relief to him when the carriage which was to convey them to St. Denis, being announced, furnished an excuse for hastily leaving the table.

Looking at his watch, he declared it was late; and Natalie, who saw how eager he was to be gone, threw her shawl over her shoulders, and bidding her friends good morning they hurried away.

It was a fine sunny day in June; and as they drove along the crowded boulevards and through the Porte St. Denis, the young bride and bridegroom, to avoid each other's eyes, affected to be gazing out of the windows; but when they reached that part of the road where there was nothing but trees on each side, they felt it necessary to draw in their heads, and make an attempt at conversation.

De Chaulieu put his arm round his wife's waist, and tried to rouse himself from his depression; but it had by this time so reacted upon her, that she could not respond to his efforts; and thus the conversation languished, till both felt glad when they reached their destination, which would, at all events, furnish them something to talk about.

Having quitted the carriage and ordered a dinner at the Hôtel de l'Abbaye, the young couple proceeded to visit Mademoiselle de Bellefonds, who was overjoyed to see her sister and new brother-in-law, and doubly so when she found that they had obtained permission to take her out to spend the afternoon with them.

As there is little to be seen at St. Denis but the Abbey, on quitting that part of it devoted to education, they proceeded to visit the church with its various objects of interest; and as De Chaulieu's thoughts were now forced into another direction, his cheerfulness began insensibly to return. Natalie looked so beautiful, too, and the affection betwixt the two young sisters was so pleasant to behold! And they spent a couple of hours wandering about with Hortense, who was almost as well informed as the Suisse, till the brazen doors were open which admitted them to the royal vault.

Satisfied at length with what they had seen, they began to think of returning to the inn, the more especially as De Chaulieu, who had not eaten a morsel of food since the previous evening, confessed to being hungry; so they directed their steps to the door, lingering here and there as they went to inspect a monument or a painting, when happening to turn his head aside to see if his wife, who had stopped to take a last look at the tomb of King Dagobert, was following, he beheld with horror the face of Jacques Rollet appearing from behind a column. At the same instant his wife joined him and took his arm, inquiring if he was not very much delighted with what he had seen. He attempted to say yes, but the word died upon his lips; and staggering out of the door, he alleged that a sudden faintness had overcome him.

They conducted him to the hotel, but Natalie now became seriously alarmed; and well she might. His complexion looked ghastly, his limbs shook, and his features bore an expression of indescribable horror and anguish. What could be the meaning of so extraordinary a change in the gay, witty, prosperous De Chaulieu, who, till that morning, seemed not to have a care in the world? For, plead illness as he might, she felt certain, from the expression of his features, that his sufferings were not of the body, but of the mind; and unable to imagine any reason for such extraordinary manifestations, of which she had never before seen a symptom, but a sudden aversion to herself, and regret for the step he had taken, her pride took the alarm, and, concealing the distress she really felt, she began to assume a haughty and reserved manner toward him, which he naturally interpreted into an evidence of anger and contempt.

The dinner was placed upon the table, but De Chaulieu's appetite, of which he had lately boasted, was quite gone; nor was his wife better able to eat. The young sister alone did justice to the repast; but although the bridegroom could not eat, he could swallow champagne in such copious draughts that erelong the terror and remorse which the apparition of Jacques Rollet had awakened in his breast were drowned in intoxication.

Amazed and indignant, poor Natalie sat silently observing this elect of her heart, till, overcome with disappointment and grief, she quitted the room with her sister, and retired to another apartment, where she gave free vent to her feelings in tears.

After passing a couple of hours in confidences and lamentations, they recollected that the hours of liberty, granted as an especial favor to Mademoiselle Hortense, had expired; but ashamed to exhibit her husband in his present condition to the eyes of strangers, Natalie prepared to reconduct her to the Maison Royal herself. Looking into the dining-room as they passed, they saw De Chaulieu lying on a sofa, fast asleep, in which state he continued when his wife returned. At length the driver of their carriage begged to know if monsieur and madame were ready to return to Paris, and it became necessary to arouse him.

The transitory effects of the champagne had now subsided; but when De Chaulieu recollected what had happened, nothing could exceed his shame and mortification. So engrossing, indeed, were these sensations, that they quite overpowered his previous ones, and, in his present vexation, he for the moment forgot his fears. He knelt at his wife's feet, begged her pardon a thousand times, swore that he adored her, and declared that the illness and the effect of the wine had been purely the consequences of fasting and overwork.

It was not the easiest thing in the world to reassure a woman whose pride, affection, and taste had been so severely wounded; but Natalie tried to believe, or to appear to do so, and a sort of reconciliation ensued, not quite sincere on the part of the wife, and very humbling on the part of the husband. Under these circumstances it was impossible that he should recover his spirits or facility of manner; his gayety was forced, his tenderness constrained; his heart was heavy within him; and ever and anon the source whence all this disappointment and woe had sprung would recur to his perplexed and tortured mind.

Thus mutually pained and distrustful, they returned to Paris, which they reached about nine o'clock. In spite of her depression, Natalie, who had not seen her new apartments, felt some curiosity about them, whilst De

Chaulieu anticipated a triumph in exhibiting the elegant home he had prepared for her. With some alacrity, therefore, they stepped out of the carriage, the gates of the hotel were thrown open, the *concierge* rang the bell which announced to the servants that their master and mistress had arrived; and whilst these domestics appeared above, holding lights over the balusters, Natalie, followed by her husband, ascended the stairs.

But when they reached the landing-place of the first flight, they saw the figure of a man standing in a corner, as if to make way for them. The flash from above fell upon his face, and again Antoine de Chaulieu recognized the features of Jacques Rollet.

From the circumstance of his wife preceding him, the figure was not observed by De Chaulieu till he was lifting his foot to place it on the top stair: the sudden shock caused him to miss the step, and without uttering a sound, he fell back, and never stopped until he reached the stones at the bottom.

The screams of Natalie brought the concierge from below and the maids from above, and an attempt was made to raise the unfortunate man from the ground; but with cries of anguish he besought them to desist.

"Let me," he said, "die here. O God! what a dreadful vengeance is thine! Natalie, Natalie," he exclaimed to his wife, who was kneeling beside him, "to win fame, and fortune, and yourself, I committed a dreadful crime. With lying words I argued away the life of a fellow-creature, whom, whilst I uttered them, I half believed to be innocent; and now, when I have attained all I desired and reached the summit of my hopes, the Almighty has sent him back upon the earth to blast me with the sight. Three times this day—three times this day! Again! Again! Again!" And as he spoke, his wild and dilated eyes fixed themselves on one of the individuals that surrounded him.

"He is delirious," said they.

"No," said the stranger, "what he says is true enough, at least in part." And, bending over the expiring man, he added, "May Heaven forgive you, Antoine de Chaulieu! I am no apparition, but the veritable Jacques Rollet, who was saved by one who well knew my innocence. I may name him, for he is beyond the reach of the law now: it was Claperon, the jailer, who, in a fit of jealousy, had himself killed Alphonse de Bellefonds."

"But—but there were three," gasped Antoine.

"Yes, a miserable idiot, who had been so long in confinement for a murder that he was forgotten by the authorities, was substituted for me. At length I obtained, through the assistance of my sister, the position of *concierge* in the Hôtel Marbœuf, in the Rue Grange Bateliere. I entered on my new place yesterday evening, and was desired to awaken the gentleman on the third floor at seven o'clock. When I entered the room to do so, you were asleep; but before I had time to speak, you awoke, and I recognized your features in the glass. Knowing that I could not vindicate my innocence if you chose to seize me, I fled, and seeing an omnibus starting for St. Denis, I got on it with a vague idea of getting on to Calais and crossing the Channel to England. But having only a franc or two in my pocket, or indeed in the world, I did not know how to procure the means of going forward; and whilst I was lounging about the place, forming first one plan and then another, I saw you in the church, and, concluding that you were in pursuit of me, I thought the best way of eluding your vigilance was to make my way back to Paris as fast as I could; so I set off instantly, and walked all the way; but having no money to pay my night's lodging, I came here to borrow a couple of livres of my sister Claudine, who is a *brodeuse** and resides au *cinquième*."†

"Thank Heaven!" exclaimed the dying man, "that sin is off my soul. Natalie, dear wife, farewell! Forgive—forgive all."

These were the last words he uttered; the priest, who had been summoned in haste, held up the cross before his failing sight; a few strong convulsions shook the poor bruised and mangled frame; and then all was still.

---

* An embroiderer.

† On the fifth floor (or in the fifth apartment).

Elizabeth Cleghorn Gaskell (1810–1865), popularly known as Mrs. Gaskell, was influenced by Jane Austen and in mid-life became a prolific English novelist and short story writer. Her novels generally focus on the lives of women caught up in the Industrial Revolution, and she penned a popular biography of Charlotte Brontë. Despite extensive critical praise in the nineteenth century, her writing has generally been relegated to the dustbin of history. Many of her short stories incorporated crimes or gothic, supernatural, or sensational elements and were published anonymously, perhaps because she was concerned that such works would affect sales of her more conventional novels. The following, which appeared in Household Words *for Christmas 1853, is told by an anonymous "squire" about small-town life and recounts how an "old maid" and a magistrate came to identify a cold-blooded murderer.*

THE SQUIRE'S STORY

ELIZABETH CLEGHORN GASKELL

I n the year 1769 the little town of Barford was thrown into a state of
great excitement by the intelligence that a gentleman (and quite the
gentleman, said the landlord of the George Inn) had been looking at
Mr. Clavering's old house. This house was neither in the town nor in the
country. It stood on the outskirts of Barford, on the roadside leading to
Derby. The last occupant had been a Mr. Clavering—a Northumberland
gentleman of good family—who had come to live in Barford while he was
but a younger son; but when some elder branches of the family died, he
had returned to take possession of the family estate. The house of which I
speak was called the White House, from its being covered with a greyish
kind of stucco. It had a good garden to the back, and Mr. Clavering had
built capital stables, with what were then considered the latest improvements. The point of good stabling was expected to let the house, as it was

in a hunting county; otherwise it had few recommendation. There were many bedrooms; some entered through others, even to the number of five, leading one beyond the other; several sitting-rooms of the small and poky* kind, wainscoted round with wood, and then painted a heavy slate colour; one good dining-room, and a drawing-room over it, both looking into the garden, with pleasant bow-windows.

Such was the accommodation offered by the White House. It did not seem to be very tempting to strangers, though the good people of Barford rather piqued themselves on it, as the largest house in the town; and as a house in which townspeople and county people had often met at Mr. Clavering's friendly dinners. To appreciate this circumstance of pleasant recollection, you should have lived some years in a little country town, surrounded by gentlemen's seats. You would then understand how a bow or a courtesy from a member of a county family elevates the individuals who receive it almost as much, in their own eyes, as the pair of blue garters fringed with silver did Mr. Bickerstaff's ward. They trip lightly on air for a whole day afterwards. Now Mr. Clavering was gone, where could town and county mingle?

I mention these things that you may have an idea of the desirability of the letting of the White House in the Barfordites' imagination; and to make the mixture thick and slab,† you must add for yourselves the bustle, the mystery, and the importance which every little event either causes or assumes in a small town; and then, perhaps, it will be no wonder to you that twenty ragged little urchins accompanied the gentleman aforesaid to the door of the White House; and that, although he was above an hour inspecting it, under the auspices of Mr. Jones, the agent's clerk, thirty more had joined themselves on to the wondering crowd before his exit, and awaited such crumbs of intelligence as they could gather before they were threatened or whipped out of hearing distance. Presently, out came the gentleman and the lawyer's clerk. The latter was speaking as he followed the former over the threshold. The gentleman was tall, well-dressed, handsome; but there was a sinister cold look in his quick-glancing, light blue eye, which a keen observer

---

* Uncomfortably small and crowded.

† Thick and viscous.

might not have liked. There were no keen observers among the boys, and ill-conditioned gaping girls. But they stood too near; inconveniently close; and the gentleman, lifting up his right hand, in which he carried a short riding-whip, dealt one or two sharp blows to the nearest, with a look of savage enjoyment on his face as they moved away whimpering and crying. An instant after, his expression of countenance had changed.

"Here!" said he, drawing out a handful of money, partly silver, partly copper, and throwing it into the midst of them. "Scramble for it! fight it out, my lads! come this afternoon, at three, to the George, and I'll throw you out some more." So the boys hurrahed for him as he walked off with the agent's clerk. He chuckled to himself, as over a pleasant thought. "I'll have some fun with those lads," he said; "I'll teach 'em to come prowling and prying about me. I'll tell you what I'll do. I'll make the money so hot in the fire-shovel that it shall burn their fingers. You come and see the faces and the howling. I shall be very glad if you will dine with me at two; and by that time I may have made up my mind respecting the house."

Mr. Jones, the agent's clerk, agreed to come to the George at two, but, somehow, he had a distaste for his entertainer. Mr. Jones would not like to have said, even to himself, that a man with a purse full of money, who kept many horses, and spoke familiarly of noblemen—above all, who thought of taking the White House—could be anything but a gentleman; but still the uneasy wonder as to who this Mr. Robinson Higgins could be, filled the clerk's mind long after Mr. Higgins, Mr. Higgins's servants and Mr. Higgins's stud had taken possession of the White House.

The White House was re-stuccoed (this time of a pale yellow colour), and put into thorough repair by the accommodating and delighted landlord; while his tenant seemed inclined to spend any amount of money on internal decorations, which were showy and effective in their character, enough to make the White House a nine days' wonder to the good people of Barford. The slate-colored paints became pink, and were picked out with gold; the old-fashioned banisters were replaced by newly gilt ones; but, above all, the stables were a sight to be see. Since the days of the Roman Emperor never was there such provision made for the care, the comfort, and the health of horses. But every one said it was no wonder, when they were led through Barford, covered up to their eyes, but curving their arched and delicate necks, and prancing with short high steps, in repressed eagerness. Only one groom came with them; yet they required the care of three men. Mr. Higgins, however, preferred engaging two lads out of Barford; and Barford highly approved of his preference. Not only was it kind and thoughtful to give employment to the lounging lads themselves, but they were receiving such a training in Mr. Higgins's stables as might fit them for Doncaster or Newmarket. The district of Derbyshire in which Barford was situated was too close to Leicestershire not to support a hunt and a pack of hounds. The master of the hounds was a certain Sir Harry Manley, who was *aut* a huntsman *aut nullus.** He measured a man by the length of his fork,† not by the expression of his countenance, or the shape of his head. But as Sir Harry was wont to observe, there was such a thing as too long a fork, so his approbation was withheld until he had seen a man on horseback; and if his seat there was square and easy, his hand light, and his courage good, Sir Harry hailed him as a brother.

Mr. Higgins attended the first meet of the season, not as a subscriber but as an amateur. The Barford huntsmen piqued themselves on their bold riding; and their knowledge of the country came by nature; yet this new strange man, whom nobody knew, was in at the death,‡ sitting on his horse, both well breathed and calm, without a hair turned on the sleek skin of the latter, supremely addressing the old huntsman as he hacked off the tail of the fox; and he, the old man, who was testy even under Sir Harry's slightest rebuke, and flew out on any other member of the hunt that dared to utter a word against his sixty years' experience as stable-boy, groom, poacher, and what not—he, old Isaac Wormeley, was meekly listening to the wisdom of this stranger, only now and then giving one of his quick, up-turning, cunning glances, not unlike the sharp o'er-canny looks of the poor deceased Reynard, round whom the hounds were howling, unadmonished by the short whip, which was now tucked into Wormeley's well-worn pocket. When Sir Harry rode into the copse—full of dead brushwood and wet tangled grass—and

---

* This means "either a huntsman or nothing."

† This refers to the length of a rider's legs, the lower part of the rider's body.

‡ That is, the capture of the fox in the fox hunt.

was followed by the members of the hunt, as one by one they cantered past, Mr. Higgins took off his cap and bowed—half deferentially, half insolently—with a lurking smile in the corner of his eye at the discomfited looks of one or two of the laggards. "A famous run, sir," said Sir Harry. "The first time you have hunted in our country; but I hope we shall see you often."

"I hope to become a member of the hunt, sir," said Mr. Higgins.

"Most happy—proud, I am sure, to receive so daring a rider among us. You took the Copper-gate, I fancy; while some of our friends here"— scowling at one or two cowards by way of finishing his speech. "Allow me to introduce myself—master of the hounds." He fumbled in his waistcoat pocket for the card on which his name was formally inscribed. "Some of our friends here are kind enough to come home with me to dinner; might I ask for the honour?"

"My name is Higgins," replied the stranger, bowing low. "I am only lately come to occupy the White House at Barford, and I have not as yet presented my letters of introduction."

"Hang it!" replied Sir Harry; "a man with a seat like yours, and that good brush in your hand, might ride up to any door in the county (I'm a Leicestershire man!), and be a welcome guest. Mr. Higgins, I shall be proud to become better acquainted with you over my dinner-table."

Mr. Higgins knew pretty well how to improve the acquaintance thus begun. He could sing a good song, tell a good story and was well up in practical jokes; with plenty of that keen worldly sense, which seems like an instinct in some men, and which in this case taught him on whom he might play off such jokes, with impunity from their resentment, and with a security of applause from the more boisterous, vehement or prosperous. At the end of twelve months Mr. Robinson Higgins was, out-and-out, the most popular member of the Barford hunt; had beaten all the others by a couple of lengths, as his first patron, Sir Harry, observed one evening, when they were just leaving the dinner-table of an old hunting squire in the neighbourhood.

"Because you know," said Squire Hearn, holding Sir Harry by the button—"I mean, you see, this young spark is looking sweet upon Catherine; and she's a good girl, and will have ten thousand pounds down, the day she's married, by her mother's will; and, excuse me, Sir Harry, but I should not like my girl to throw herself away."

Though Sir Harry had a long ride before him, and but the early and short light of a new moon to take it in, his kind heart was so much touched by Squire Hearn's trembling, tearful anxiety, that he stopped and turned back into the dining-room to say, with more asseverations than I care to give,—

"My good Squire, I may say, I know that man pretty well by this time; and a better fellow never existed. If I had twenty daughters he should have the pick of them."

Squire Hearn never thought of asking the grounds for his old friend's opinion of Mr. Higgins; it had been given with too much earnestness for any doubts to cross the old man's mind as to the possibility of its not being well founded. Mr. Hearn was not a doubter, or a thinker, or suspicious by nature; it was simply his love for Catherine, his only daughter, that prompted his anxiety in this case; and, after what Sir Harry had said, the old man could totter with an easy mind, though not with very steady legs, into the drawing-room, where his bonny, blushing daughter Catherine and Mr. Higgins stood close together on the hearth-rug; he whispering, she listening with downcast eyes. She looked so happy, so like her dead mother had looked when the squire was a young man, that all his thought was how to please her most. His son and heir was about to be married, and bring his wife to live with the squire; Barford and the White House were not distant an hour's ride; and, even as these thoughts passed through his mind, he asked Mr. Higgins if he could stay all night—the young moon was already set—the roads would be dark—and Catherine looked up with a pretty anxiety, which, however, had not much doubt in it, for the answer.

With every encouragement of this kind from the old squire, it took everybody rather by surprise when, one morning, it was discovered that Miss Catherine Hearn was missing; and when, according to the usual fashion in such cases, a note was found, saying that she had eloped with the man of her heart, and gone to Gretna Green, no one could imagine why she could not quietly have stopped at home and been married in the parish church. She had always been a romantic, sentimental girl; very pretty and very affectionate, and very much spoiled, and very much wanting in common sense. Her indulgent father was deeply hurt at this want of confidence in his never-varying affection; but when his son came, hot with indignation from the baronet's (his future father-in-law's house, where every form of law and of ceremony was to accompany his own impending marriage), Squire Hearn pleaded the cause of the young couple with imploring cogency, and protested that it was a piece of spirit in his daughter, which he admired and was proud of. However, it ended with Mr. Nathaniel Hearn's declaring that he and his wife would have nothing to do with his sister and her husband. "Wait till you've seen him, Nat!" said the old Squire, trembling with his distressful anticipations of family discord. "He's an excuse for any girl. Only ask Sir Harry's opinion of him." "Confound Sir Harry! So that a man sits his horse well, Sir Harry cares nothing about anything else. Who is this man—this fellow? Where does he come from? What are his means? Who are his family?"

"He comes from the south—Surrey or Somersetshire, I forget which; and he pays his way well and liberally. There's not a tradesman in Barford but says he cares no more for money than for water; he spends like a prince, Nat. I don't know who his family are, but he seals with a coat of arms, which may tell you if you want to know; and he goes regularly to collect his rents from his estates in the south. Oh, Nat! if you would but be friendly, I should be as well pleased with Kitty's marriage as any father in the county."

Mr. Nathaniel Hearn gloomed, and muttered an oath or two to himself. The poor old father was reaping the consequences of his weak indulgence to his two children. Mr. and Mrs. Nathaniel Hearn kept apart from Catherine and her husband; and Squire Hearn durst never ask them to Levison Hall, though it was his own house. Indeed, he stole away as if he were a culprit whenever he went to visit the White House; and if he passed a night there, he was fain to equivocate when he returned home the next day; an equivocation which was well interpreted by the surly, proud Nathaniel. But the younger Mr. and Mrs. Hearn were the only people who did not visit at the White House. Mr. and Mrs. Higgins were decidedly more popular than their brother and sister-in-law. She made a very pretty, sweet-tempered hostess, and her education had not been such as to make her intolerant of any want of refinement in the associates who gathered round her husband. She had gentle smiles for townspeople as well as county people; and unconsciously played an admirable second in her husband's project of making himself universally popular.

But there is some one to make ill-natured remarks, and draw ill-natured conclusions from very simple premises, in every place; and in Barford this bird of ill-omen was a Miss Pratt. She did not hunt—so Mr. Higgins's admirable riding did not call out her admiration. She did not drink—so the well-selected wines, so lavishly dispensed among his guests, could never mollify Miss Pratt. She could not bear comic songs, or buffo* stories—so, in that way, her approbation was impregnable. And these three secrets of popularity constituted Mr. Higgins's great charm. Miss Pratt sat and watched. Her face looked immovably grave at the end of any of Mr. Higgins's best stories; but there was a keen, needle-like glance of her unwinking little eyes, which Mr. Higgins felt rather than saw, and which made him shiver, even on a hot day, when it fell upon him. Miss Pratt was a Dissenter, and, to propitiate this female Mordecai, Mr. Higgins asked the Dissenting minister whose services she attended, to dinner; kept himself and his company in good order; gave a handsome donation to the poor of the chapel. All in vain—Miss Pratt stirred not a muscle more of her face towards graciousness; and Mr. Higgins was conscious that, in spite of all his open efforts to captivate Mr. Davis, there was a secret influence on the other side, throwing in doubts and suspicions, and evil interpretations of all he said or did. Miss Pratt, the little, plain old maid, living on eighty pounds a year, was the thorn in the popular Mr. Higgins's side, although she had never spoken one uncivil word to him; indeed, on the contrary, had treated him with a stiff and elaborate civility.

The thorn—the grief to Mrs. Higgins was this. They had no children! Oh! how she would stand and envy the careless, busy motion of half a dozen children; and then, when observed, move on with a deep, deep sigh of yearning regret. But it was as well.

It was noticed that Mr. Higgins was remarkably careful of his health. He ate, drank, took exercise, rested, by some secret rules of his own; occasionally bursting into an excess, it is true, but only on rare occasions—such as

---

* Vulgarly comic.

when he returned from visiting his estates in the south, and collecting his rents. That unusual exertion and fatigue—for there were no stage-coaches within forty miles of Barford, and he, like most country gentlemen of that day, would have preferred riding if there had been—seemed to require some strange excess to compensate for it; and rumours went through the town that he shut himself up, and drank enormously for some days after his return. But no one was admitted to these orgies.

One day—they remembered it well afterwards—the hounds met not far from the town; and the fox was found in a part of the wild heath, which was beginning to be enclosed by a few of the more wealthy townspeople, who were desirous of building themselves houses rather more in the country than those they had hitherto lived in. Among these, the principal was a Mr. Dudgeon, the attorney of Barford, and the agent for all the county families about. The firm of Dudgeon had managed the leases, the marriage-settlements, and the wills, of the neighbourhood for generations. Mr. Dudgeon's father had the responsibility of collecting the landowners' rents just as the present Mr. Dudgeon had at the time of which I speak: and as his son and his son's son have done since. Their business was an hereditary estate to them; and with something of the old feudal feeling was mixed a kind of proud humility at their position towards the squires whose family secrets they had mastered, and the mysteries of whose fortunes and estates were better known to the Messrs. Dudgeon than to themselves.

Mr. John Dudgeon had built himself a house on Wildbury Heath; a mere cottage as he called it: but though only two stories high, it spread out far and wide, and workpeople from Derby had been sent for on purpose to make the inside as complete as possible. The gardens too were exquisite in arrangement, if not very extensive; and not a flower was grown in them but of the rarest species. It must have been somewhat of a mortification to the owner of this dainty place when, on the day of which I speak, the fox, after a long race, during which he had described a circle of many miles, took refuge in the garden; but Mr. Dudgeon put a good face on the matter when a gentleman hunter, with the careless insolence of the squires of those days and that place, rode across the velvet lawn, and tapping at the window of the dining-room with his whip-handle, asked permission—no! that is not it—rather, informed Mr. Dudgeon of their intention—to enter his garden in a body, and have the fox unearthed. Mr. Dudgeon compelled himself to smile assent, with the grace of a masculine Griselda; and then he hastily gave orders to have all that the house afforded of provision set out for luncheon, guessing rightly enough that a six hours' run would give even homely fare an acceptable welcome. He bore without wincing the entrance of the dirty boots into his exquisitely clean rooms; he only felt grateful for the care with which Mr. Higgins strode about, laboriously and noiselessly moving on the tip of his toes, as he reconnoitred the rooms with a curious eye.

"I'm going to build a house myself, Dudgeon; and, upon my word, I don't think I could take a better model than yours."

"Oh! my poor cottage would be too small to afford any hints for such a house as you would wish to build, Mr. Higgins," replied Mr. Dudgeon, gently rubbing his hands nevertheless at the compliment.

"Not at all! not at all! Let me see. You have dining-room, drawing-room—" he hesitated, and Mr. Dudgeon filled up the blank as he expected.

"Four sitting-rooms and the bedrooms. But allow me to show you over the house. I confess I took some pains in arranging it, and, though far smaller than what you would require, it may, nevertheless, afford you some hints."

So they left the eating gentlemen with their mouths and their plates quite full, and the scent of the fox overpowering that of the hasty rashers of ham; and they carefully inspected all the ground-floor rooms. The Mr. Dudgeon said,—

"If you are not tired, Mr. Higgins—it is rather my hobby, so you must pull me up if you are—we will go upstairs, and I will show you my sanctum."

Mr. Dudgeon's sanctum was the centre room, over the porch, which formed a balcony, and which was carefully filled with choice flowers in pots. Inside, there were all kinds of elegant contrivances for hiding the real strength of all the boxes and chests required by the particular nature of Mr. Dudgeon's business: for although his office was in Barford, he kept (as he informed Mr. Higgins) what was the most valuable here, as being safer than an office which was locked up and left every night. But, as Mr. Higgins reminded him with a sly poke in the side, when next they met, his own house was not over-secure. A fortnight after the gentlemen of the

Barford hunt lunched there, Mr. Dudgeon's strong-box, in his sanctum upstairs, with the mysterious spring-bolt to the window invented by himself, and the secret of which was only known to the inventor and a few of his most intimate friends, to whom he had proudly shown it; this strong-box, containing the collected Christmas rents of half a dozen landlords (there was then no bank nearer than Derby), was rifled; and the secretly rich Mr. Dudgeon had to stop his agent in his purchases of paintings by Flemish artists, because the money was required to make good the missing rents.

The Dogberries and Verges* of those days were quite incapable of obtaining any clue to the robber or robbers; and though one or two vagrants were taken up and brought before Mr. Dunover and Mr. Higgins, the magistrates who usually attended in the court-room at Barford, there was no evidence brought against them, and after a couple of nights' durance in the lock-ups they were set at liberty. But it became a standing joke with Mr. Higgins to ask Mr. Dudgeon, from time to time, whether he could recommend him a place of safety for his valuables; or, if he had made any more inventions lately for securing houses from robbers.

About two years after this time—about seven years after Mr. Higgins had been married—one Tuesday evening Mr. Davis was sitting reading the news in the coffee-room of the George Inn. He belonged to a club of gentlemen who met there occasionally to play at whist, to read what few newspapers and magazines were published in those days, to chat about the market at Derby, and prices all over the country. This Tuesday night it was a black frost; and few people were in the room. Mr. Davis was anxious to finish an article in the *Gentleman's Magazine*; indeed, he was making extracts from it, intending to answer it, and yet unable with his small income to purchase a copy. So he stayed late; it was past nine, and at ten o'clock the room was closed. But while he wrote, Mr. Higgins came in. He was pale and haggard with cold. Mr. Davis, who had had for some time sole possession of the fire, moved politely on one side, and handed to the new-comer the sole London newspaper which the room afforded. Mr. Higgins accepted it, and made some remark on the intense coldness of the weather; but Mr. Davis was too full of his article, and intended reply, to

---

* Comical members of the Town Watch in Shakespeare's *Much Ado About Nothing*.

fall into conversation readily. Mr. Higgins hitched his chair nearer to the fire, and put his feet on the fender, giving an audible shudder. He put the newspaper on one end of the table near him, and sat gazing into the red embers of the fire, crouching down over them as if his very marrow were chilled. At length he said,

"There is no account of the murder at Bath in that paper?" Mr. Davis, who had finished taking his notes, and was preparing to go, stopped short, and asked,—

"Has there been a murder at Bath? No! I have not seen anything of it—who was murdered?"

"Oh! it was a shocking, terrible murder!" said Mr. Higgins, not raising his look from the fire, but gazing on with his eyes dilated till the whites were seen all round them. "A terrible, terrible murder! I wonder what will become of the murderer? I can fancy the red glowing centre of that fire— look and see how infinitely distant it seems, and how the distance magnifies it into something awful and unquenchable."

"My dear sir, you are feverish; how you shake and shiver!" said Mr. Davis, thinking privately that his companion had symptoms of fever, and that he was wandering in his mind.

"Oh, no!" said Mr. Higgins. "I am not feverish. It is the night which is so cold." And for a time he talked with Mr. Davis about the article in the *Gentleman's Magazine*, for he was rather a reader himself, and could take more interest in Mr. Davis's pursuits than most of the people at Barford. At length it drew near to ten, and Mr. Davis rose up to go home to his lodgings.

"No, Davis, don't go. I want you here. We will have a bottle of port together, and that will put Saunders into good humour. I want to tell you about this murder," he continued, dropping his voice, and speaking hoarse and low. "She was an old woman, and he killed her, sitting reading her Bible by her own fireside!" He looked at Mr. Davis with a strange searching gaze, as if trying to find some sympathy in the horror which the idea presented to him.

"Who do you mean, my dear sir? What is this murder you are so full of? No one has been murdered here."

"No, you fool! I tell you it was in Bath!" said Mr. Higgins, with sudden passion; and then calming himself to most velvet-smoothness of manner, he laid his hand on Mr. Davis's knee, there, as they sat by the fire, and gently detaining him, began the narration of the crime he was so full of; but his voice and manner were constrained to a stony quietude: he never looked in Mr. Davis's face; once or twice, as Mr. Davis remembered afterwards, his grip tightened like a compressing vice.

"She lived in a small house in a quiet old-fashioned street, she and her maid. People said she was a good old woman; but for all that, she hoarded and hoarded, and never gave to the poor. Mr. Davis, it is wicked not to give to the poor—wicked—wicked, is it not? I always give to the poor, for once I read in the Bible that 'Charity covereth a multitude of sins.' The wicked old woman never gave, but hoarded her money, and saved, and saved. Some one heard of it; I say she threw temptation in his way, and God will punish her for it. And this man—or it might be a woman, who knows?—and this person—heard also that she went to church in the mornings, and her maid in the afternoons; and so, while the maid was at church, and the street and the house quite still, and the darkness of a winter afternoon coming on, she was nodding over the Bible—and that, mark you! is a sin, and one that God will avenge sooner or later,—and a step came in the dusk up the stair, and that person I told you of stood in the room. At first he—no! At first, it is supposed—for, you understand, all this is mere guess-work—it is supposed that he asked her civilly enough to give him her money, or to tell him where it was; but the old miser defied him, and would not ask for mercy and give up her keys, even when he threatened her, but looked him in the face as if he had been a baby.—Oh, God! Mr. Davis, I once dreamt when I was a little innocent boy that I should commit a crime like this, and I wakened up crying; and my mother comforted me—that is the reason I tremble so now—that and the cold, for it is very very cold!"

"But did he murder the old lady?" asked Mr. Davis. "I beg your pardon, sir, but I am interested by your story."

"Yes! He cut her throat; and there she lies yet in her quiet little parlour, with her face upturned and all ghastly white, in the middle of a pool of blood. Mr. Davis, this wine is no better than water; I must have some brandy!"

Mr. Davis was horror-struck by the story, which seemed to have fascinated him as much as it had done his companion.

"Have they got any clue to the murderer?" said he. Mr. Higgins drank down half a tumbler of raw brandy before he answered.

"No! No clue whatever. They will never be able to discover him; and I should not wonder, Mr. Davis—I should not wonder if he repented after all, and did bitter penance for his crime; and if so—will there be mercy for him at the last day?"

"God knows!" said Mr. Davis, with solemnity. "It is an awful story," continued he, rousing himself; "I hardly like to leave this warm light room and go out into the darkness after hearing it. But it must be done"—buttoning on his greatcoat—"I can only say I hope and trust they will find out the murderer and hang him. If you'll take my advice, Mr. Higgins, you'll have your bed warmed, and drink a treacle posset just the last thing; and, if you'll allow me, I'll send you my answer to Philologus before it goes up to old Urban."*

The next morning, Mr. Davis went to call on Miss Pratt, who was not very well; and, by way of being agreeable and entertaining, he related to her all he had heard the night before about the murder at Bath; and really he made a very pretty connected story out of it, and interested Miss Pratt very much in the fate of the old lady—partly because of a similarity in their situations; for she also privately hoarded money, and had but one servant, and stopped at home alone on Sunday afternoons to allow her servant to go to church.

"And when did all this happen?" she asked.

"I don't know if Mr. Higgins named the day; and yet I think it must have been on this very last Sunday."

"And to-day is Wednesday. Ill news travels fast."

"Yes, Mr. Higgins thought it might have been in the London newspaper."

"That it could never be. Where did Mr. Higgins learn all about it?"

"I don't know; I did not ask. I think he only came home yesterday: he had been south to collect his rents, somebody said."

Miss Pratt grunted. She used to vent her dislike and suspicions of Mr. Higgins in a grunt whenever his name was mentioned.

---

* "Philologus" was the pseudonym of an occasional correspondent to the *Gentleman's Magazine*. Sylvanus Urban was the magazine editor.

"Well, I shan't see you for some days. Godfred Merton has asked me to go and stay with him and his sister; and I think it will do me good. Besides," added she, "these winter evenings—and these murderers at large in the country—I don't quite like living with only Peggy to call to in case of need."

Miss Pratt went to stay with her cousin, Mr. Merton. He was an active magistrate, and enjoyed his reputation as such. One day he came in, having just received his letters.

"Bad account of the morals of your little town here, Jessy!" said he, touching one of his letters. "You've either a murderer among you, or some friend of a murderer. Here's a poor old lady at Bath had her throat cut last Sunday week; and I've a letter from the Home Office, asking to lend them my "very efficient aid," as they are pleased to call it, towards finding out the culprit. It seems he must have been thirsty, and of a comfortable jolly turn; for before going to his horrid work he tapped a barrel of ginger wine the old lady had set by to work; and he wrapped the spigot round with a piece of a letter taken out of his pocket, as may be supposed; and this piece of a letter was found afterwards; there are only these letters on the outside, "ns, Esq., -arford, -egworth," which some one has ingeniously made out to mean Barford, near Kegworth. On the other side there is some allusion to a race-horse, I conjecture, though the name is singular enough—Church-and-King-and-down-with-the-Rump."

Miss Pratt caught at this name immediately; it had hurt her feelings as a Dissenter only a few months ago, and she remembered it well.

"Mr. Nat Hearn has, or had (as I am speaking in the witness-box, as it were, I must take care of my tenses), a horse with that ridiculous name."

"Mr. Nat Hearn," repeated Mr. Merton, making a note of the intelligence; then he recurred to his letter from the Home Office again.

"There is also a piece of a small key, broken in the futile attempt to open a desk—well, well. Nothing more of consequence. The letter is what we must rely upon."

"Mr. Davis said that Mr. Higgins told him—" Miss Pratt began.

"Higgins!" exclaimed Mr. Merton, "ns. Is it Higgins, the blustering fellow that ran away with Nat Hearn's sister?"

"Yes!" said Miss Pratt. "But though he has never been a favourite of mine—"

"*ns*," repeated Mr. Merton. "It is too horrible to think of; a member of the hunt—kind old Squire Hearn's son-in-law! Who else have you in Barford with names that end in ns?"

"There's Jackson, and Higginson, and Blenkinsop, and Davis, and Jones. Cousin! One thing strikes me—how did Mr. Higgins know all about it to tell Mr. Davis on Tuesday what had happened on Sunday afternoon?"

There is no need to add much more. Those curious in lives of the highwayman may find the name of Higgins as conspicuous among those annals as that of Claude Duval. Kate Hearn's husband collected his rents on the highway, like many another gentleman of the day; but, having been unlucky in one or two of his adventures, and hearing exaggerated accounts of the hoarded wealth of the old lady at Bath, he was led on from robbery to murder, and was hung for his crime at Derby, in 1775.

He had not been an unkind husband; and his poor wife took lodgings in Derby to be near him in his last moments—his awful last moments. Her old father went with her everywhere but into her husband's cell; and wrung her heart by constantly accusing himself of having promoted her marriage with a man of whom he knew so little. He abdicated his squireship in favour of his son Nathaniel. Nat was prosperous, and the helpless silly father could be of no use to him; but to his widowed daughter the foolish fond old man was all in all; her knight, her protector, her companion, her most faithful loving companion. Only he ever declined assuming the office of her counsellor; shaking his head sadly, and saying,

"Ah! Kate, Kate! if I had had more wisdom to have advised thee better, thou need'st not have been an exile here in Brussels, shrinking from the sight of every English person as if they knew thy story."

I saw the White House not a month ago; it was to let, perhaps for the twentieth time since Mr. Higgins occupied it; but still the tradition goes in Barford that once upon a time a highwayman lived there, and amassed untold treasures; and that the ill-gotten wealth yet remains walled up in some unknown concealed chamber; but in what part of the house no one knows.

Will any of you become tenants, and try to find out this mysterious closet? I can furnish the exact address to any applicant who wishes for it.

Mary Helena Fortune (1833–1910) is sadly overlooked. An Australian, Fortune wrote more crime/detective fiction than any other women in the nineteenth century (over 500 stories) and was the first to write detective fiction specifically. Her first collection of short stories, The Detective's Album *(1871), precedes Anna Katharine Green's* The Leavenworth Case *by seven years. Her lack of fame is probably attributable to the anonymity which applied to all of her work. The following story, featuring an official police detective, first appeared in* The Australian Journal *for December 2, 1865, and, typically, her authorship was uncredited.*

TRACES OF CRIME

MARY FORTUNE

There are many who recollect full well the rush at Chinaman's Flat. It was in the height of its prosperity that an assault was committed upon a female of a character so diabolical in itself, as to have aroused the utmost anxiety in the public as well as in the police, to punish the perpetrator thereof.

The case was placed in my hands, and as it presented difficulties so great as to appear to an ordinary observer almost insurmountable, the overcoming of which was likely to gain approbation in the proper quarter, I gladly accepted the task.

I had little to go upon at first. One dark night, in a tent in the very centre of a crowded thoroughfare, a female had been preparing to retire to rest, her husband being in the habit of remaining at the public-house until a late hour, when a man with a crape mask who—must have gained an earlier entrance—seized her, and in the prosecution of a criminal offence, had injured and abused the unfortunate woman so much that her life was despaired of. Although there was a light burning at the time, the woman was barely able to describe his general appearance; he appeared to her like a German, had no whiskers, fair hair, was low in stature, and stoutly built.

With one important exception, that was all the information she was able to give me on the subject. The exception, however, was a good deal to a detective, and I hoped might prove an invaluable aid to me. During the struggle she had torn the arm of the flannel shirt he wore, and was under a decided impression that upon the upper part of the criminal's arm there was a small anchor and heart tattooed.

Now, I was well aware that in this colony to find a man with a tattooed arm was an everyday affair, especially on the diggings, where, I dare say, there is scarcely a person with who has not come in contact more than once or twice with half a dozen men tattooed in the style I speak of—the anchor or heart, or both, being a favourite figure with those gentlemen who are in favour of branding. However, the clue was worth something, and even without its aid, not more than a couple of weeks had elapsed when, with the assistance of the local police, I had traced a man bearing in appearance a general resemblance to the man who had committed the offence, to a digging about seven miles from Chinaman's Flat.

It is unnecessary that I should relate every particular as to how my suspicions were directed to this man, who did not live on Chinaman's Flat, and to all appearances, had not left the diggings where he was camped since he first commenced working there. I say to all appearances, for it was with a certain knowledge that he had been absent from his tent on the night of the outrage that I one evening trudged down the flat where his tent was pitched, with my swag on my back, and sat down on a log not far from where he had kindled a fire for culinary or other purposes.

These diggings I will call McAdam's. It was a large and flourishing goldfield, and on the flat where my man was camped there were several other tents grouped, so that it was nothing singular that I should look about for a couple of bushes, between which I might swing my little bit of canvas for the night.

After I had fastened up the rope, and thrown my tent over it in regular digger fashion, I broke down some bushes to form my bed, and having spread thereon my blankets, went up to my man—whom I shall in future call "Bill"—to request permission to boil my billy* on his fire.

It was willingly granted, and so I lighted my pipe and sat down to await the boiling of the water, determined if I could so manage it to get this suspected man to accept me as a mate before I lay down that night.

Bill was also engaged in smoking, and had not, of course, the slightest suspicion that in the rough, ordinary looking digger before him he was contemplating the "make-up" of a Victorian detective, who had already made himself slightly talked of among his comrades by one or two clever captures.

"Where did you come from, mate?" inquired Bill, as he puffed away leisurely at a cutty.†

"From Burnt Creek," I replied, "and a long enough road it is in such d— hot weather as this."

"Nothing doing at Burnt Creek?"

"Not a thing—the place is cooked."

"Are you in for a try here, then?" he asked, rather eagerly I thought.

"Well, I think so; is there any chance do you think?"

"Have you got a miner's right?" was his sudden question.

"I have," said I taking it out of my pocket, and handing the bit of parchment for his inspection.

"Are you a hatter?"‡ inquired Bill, as he returned the document.

"I am," was my reply.

"Well, if you have no objections then, I don't mind going mates with you—I've got a pretty fair prospect, and the ground's going to run rather deep for one man, I think."

"All right."

So here was the very thing I wanted, settled without the slightest trouble.

My object in wishing to go mates with this fellow will, I dare say, readily be perceived. I did not wish to risk my character for cuteness by arresting

---

* Tin can with a wire handle, used to boil tea or soup.

† Cutty pipe, a short pipe.

‡ Solitary miner.

my gentleman, without being sure that he was branded in the way described by the woman, and besides, in the close supervision which I should be able to keep over him while working together daily, heaven knows what might transpire as additional evidence against him, at least so I reasoned with myself; and it was with a partially relieved mind that I made my frugal supper, and made believe to turn in, fatigued, as I might be supposed to be, after my long tramp.

But I didn't turn in, not I. I had other objects in view, if one may be said to have an object in view on one of the darkest nights of a moonless week—for dark enough the night in question became, even before I had finished my supper, and made my apparent preparations for bed.

We were not camped far enough from the business part of the rush to be very quiet, there was plenty of noise—the nightly noise of a rich gold-field—came down our way, and even in some of the tents close to us, card-playing, and drinking, and singing, and laughing, were going on; so it was quite easy for me to steal unnoticed to the back of Bill's little tent, and, by the assistance of a small slit made in the calico by my knife, have a look at what my worthy was doing inside, for I was anxious to become acquainted with his habits, and, of course, determined to watch him as closely as ever I could.

Well, the first specimen I had of his customs was certainly a singular one, and was, it may be well believed, an exception to his general line of conduct. Diggers, or any other class of men, do not generally spend their evenings in cutting their shoes up into small morsels, and that was exactly what Bill was busily engaged in doing when I clapped my eye to the hole. He had already disposed of a good portion of the article when I commenced to watch him: the entire upper of a very muddy blucher boot lying upon his rough table in a small heap, and in the smallest pieces that one would suppose any person could have patience to cut up a dry, hard, old leather boot.

It was rather a puzzler to me this, and that Bill was doing such a thing simply to amuse himself was out of the question; indeed, without observing that he had the door of his tent closely fastened upon a warm evening, and that he started at the slightest sound, the instincts of an old detective would alone have convinced me that Bill had some great cause indeed to make away with those old boots; so I continued watching.

He had hacked away at the sole with an old but sharp butcher's knife, but it almost defied his attempts to separate it into pieces, and at length he gave it up in despair, and gathering up the small portions on the table, he swept them with the mutilated sole into his hat, and opening his tent door, went out.

I guessed very truly that he would make for the fire, and as it happened to be at the other side of a log from where I was hiding, I had a good opportunity of continuing my espial. He raked together the few embers that remained near the log, and flinging the pieces of leather thereon, retired once more into his tent, calculating, no doubt, that the hot ashes would soon scorch and twist them up, so as to defy recognition, while the fire he would build upon them in the morning would settle the matter most satisfactorily.

All this would have happened just so, no doubt, if I had not succeeded in scraping nearly every bit from the place where Bill had thrown them, so silently and quickly, that I was in the shelter of my slung tent with my prize and a burn or two on my fingers before he himself had had time to divest himself of his garments and blow out the light.

He did so very soon, however, and it was long before I could get asleep. I thought it over and over in all ways, and looked upon it in all lights that I could think of, and yet, always connecting this demolished boot with the case in the investigation of which I was engaged, I could not make it out at all.

Had we overlooked, with all our fancied acuteness, some clue which Bill feared we had possession of, to which this piecemeal boot was the key? And if so why had he remained so long without destroying it?

It was, as I said before, a regular puzzler to me, and my brain was positively weary when I at length dropped off to sleep.

Well, I worked for a week with Bill, and I can tell you it was work I didn't at all take to. The unaccustomed use of the pick and shovel played the very mischief with my hands; but, for fear of arousing the suspicions of my mate, I durst not complain, having only to endure in silence, or as our Scotch friends would put it, Grin and bide it. And the worst of it was, that I was gaining nothing—nothing whatever—by my unusual industry.

I had hoped that accidentally I should have got a sight of the anchor and heart, but I was day after day disappointed, for my mate was not very regular in his ablutions, and I had reckoned without my host in expecting that the very ordinary habit of a digger, namely, that of having a regular wash at least every Sunday, would be a good and certain one for exposing the brand.

But no, Bill allowed the Sunday to come and go, without once removing what I could observe was the flannel shirt, in which he had worked all the week; and then I began to swear at my own obtuseness— the fellow must be aware that his shirt was torn by the woman, of course he suspects that she may have seen the tattooing, and will take blessed good care not to expose it, mate or no mate, thought I; and then I called myself a donkey, and during the few following days, when I was trusting to the chapter of accidents, I was also deliberating on the to be or not to be of the question of arresting him at once, and chancing it. Saturday afternoon came again, and then the early knock-off time, and that sort of quarter holiday among the miners, namely, four o'clock, was hailed by me with the greatest relief, and it was with the full determination of never again setting foot in the cursed claim that I shouldered my pick and shovel and proceeded tentwards.

On my way I met a policeman, and received from him a concerted signal that I was wanted at the camp, and so telling Bill that I was going to see an old mate about some money that he owed me, I started at once.

"We've got something else in your line, mate," said my old chum, Joe Bennet, as I entered the camp, "and one which, I think, will be a regular poser for you. The body of a man has been found in Pipeclay Gully, and we can scarcely be justified by appearances in giving even a surmise as to how he came by his death."

"How do you mean?" I inquired. "Has he been dead so long?"

"About a fortnight, I dare say, but we have done absolutely nothing as yet. Knowing you were on the ground we have not even touched the body: will you come up at once?"

"Of course I will!" And after substituting the uniform of the force for the digger's costume, in which I was apparelled, in case of an encounter with my "mate," we went straight to "Pipeclay."

The body had been left in charge of one of the police, and was still lying, undisturbed in the position in which it had been discovered; not a soul was about, in fact, the gully had been rushed and abandoned, and bore not the slightest trace of man's handiwork, saving and except the miner's holes and their surrounding little eminences of pipeclay, from which the gully was named. And it was a veritable gully, running between two low ranges of hills, which hills were covered with an undergrowth of wattle and cherry trees, and scattered over with rocks and indications of quartz, which have, I dare say, been fully tried by this time.

Well, on the slope of one of the hills, where it amalgamated as it were with the level of the gully, and where the sinking had evidently been shallow, lay the body of the dead man. He was dressed in ordinary miner's fashion, and saving for the fact of a gun being by his side, one might have supposed that he had only given up his digging to lie down and die beside the hole near which he lay.

The hole, however, was full of water—quite full; indeed the water was sopping out on the ground around it, and that the hole was an old one was evident, by the crumbling edges around it, and the fragments of old branches that lay rotting in the water.

Close to this hole lay the body, the attitude strongly indicative of the last exertion during life having been that of crawling out of the water hole, in which indeed still remained part of the unfortunate man's leg. There was no hat on his head, and in spite of the considerable decay of the body, even an ordinary observer could not fail to notice a large fracture in the side of the head.

I examined the gun; it was a double-barrelled fowling piece, and one barrel had been discharged, while very apparent on the stock of the gun were blood marks, that even the late heavy rain had failed to erase. In the pockets of the dead man was nothing, save what any digger might carry— pipe and tobacco, a cheap knife, and a shilling or two, this was all; and so leaving the body to be removed by the police, I thoughtfully retraced my way to the camp.

Singularly enough, during my absence, a woman had been there, giving information about her husband, on account of whose absence she was becoming alarmed; and as the caution of the policeman on duty at the camp had prevented his giving her any idea of the fact of the dead body having been discovered that very day, I immediately went to the address which the woman had left, in order to discover, if possible, not only if it was the missing man, but also to gain any information that might be likely to put me upon the scent of the murderer, for that the man had been murdered I had not the slightest doubt.

Well, I succeeded in finding the woman, a young and decidedly good-looking Englishwoman of the lower class, and gained from her the following information:—

About a fortnight before, her husband, who had been indisposed, and in consequence not working for a day or two, had taken his gun one morning in order to amuse himself for an hour or two, as well as to have a look at the ranges near Pipeclay Gully, and do a little prospecting at the same time. He had not returned, but as he had suggested a possibility of visiting his brother who was digging about four miles off, she had not felt alarmed until upon communicating with the said brother she had become aware that her husband had never been there. From the description, I knew at once that the remains of the poor fellow lying in Pipeclay Gully were certainly those of the missing man, and with what care and delicacy I might possess I broke the tidings to the shocked wife, and after allowing her grief to have vent in a passion of tears, I tried to gain some clue to the likely perpetrator of the murder.

Had she any suspicions? I asked; was there any feud between her husband and any individual she could name?

At first she replied no, and then a sudden recollection appeared to strike her, and she said that some weeks ago a man had, during the absence of her husband, made advances to her, under the feigned supposition that she was an unmarried woman. In spite of her decidedly repellent manner, he had continued his attentions, until she, afraid of his impetuosity, had been obliged to call the attention of her husband to the matter, and he, of course feeling indignant, had threatened to shoot the intruder if he ever ventured near the place again.

The woman described this man to me, and it was with a violent whirl of emotional excitement, as one feels who is on the eve of a great discovery, that I hastened to the camp, which was close by.

It was barely half-past five o'clock, and in a few minutes I was on my way, with two or three other associates, to the scene of what I had no doubt had been a horrible murder. What my object was there was soon apparent. I had before tried the depth of the muddy water, and found it was scarcely four feet, and now we hastened to make use of the remaining light of a long summer's day in draining carefully the said hole.

I was repaid for the trouble, for in the muddy and deep sediment at the bottom we discovered a deeply imbedded blucher boot; and I dare say you will readily guess how my heart leaped up at the sight.

To old diggers, the task which followed was not a very great one; we had provided ourselves with a tub, etc., and washed every bit of the mud at the bottom of the hole. The only find we had, however, was a peculiar bit of wood, which, instead of rewarding us for our exertions by lying like gold at the bottom of the dish in which we turned off, insisted upon floating on the top of the very first tub, when it became loosened from its surrounding of clay.

It was a queer piece of wood, and eventually quite repaid us for any trouble we might have had in its capture. A segment of a circle it was, or rather a portion of a segment of a circle, being neither more nor less than a piece broken out of one of those old fashioned black wooden buttons, that are still to be seen on the monkey-jacket of many an Australian digger, as well as elsewhere.

Well, I fancied that I knew the identical button from whence had been broken this bit of wood, and that I could go and straightaway fit it into its place without the slightest trouble in the world—singular, was it not?—and as I carefully placed the piece in my pocket, I could not help thinking to myself, "Well, this does indeed and most truly look like the working of Providence."

There are many occasions when an apparent chance has effected the unravelling of a mystery, which but for the turning over of that particular page of fatality, might have remained a mystery to the day of judgment, in spite of the most strenuous and most able exertions. Mere human acumen would never have discovered the key to the secret's hieroglyphic, nor placed side by side the hidden links of a chain long enough and strong enough to tear the murderer from his fancied security, and hang him as high as

Haman. Such would almost appear to have been the case in the instance to which I am alluding, only that in place of ascribing the elucidation and the unravelling to that mythical power chance, the impulse of some inner man writes the word Providence.

I did not feel exactly like moralizing, however, when, after resuming my digger's "make-up," I walked towards the tent of the man I have called Bill. No; I felt more and deeper than any mere moralist could understand. The belief that a higher power had especially called out, and chosen, one of his own creatures to be the instrument of his retributive power, has, in our world's history, been the means of mighty evil, and I hope that not for an instant did such an idea take possession of me. I was not conscious of feeling that I had been chosen as a scourge and an instrument of earthly punishment; but I did feel that I was likely to be the means of cutting short the thread of a most unready fellow-mortal's life, and a solemn responsibility it is to bring home to one's self I can assure you.

The last flush of sunlight was fading low in the west when I reached our camping ground, and found Bill seated outside on a log, indulging in his usual pipe in the greying twilight.

I had, of course, determined upon arresting him at once, and had sent two policemen round to the back of our tents, in case of an attempted escape upon his part; and now, quite prepared, I sat down beside him; and, after feeling that the handcuffs were in their usual place in my belt, I lit my pipe and commenced to smoke also. My heart verily went pit-a-pat as I did so, for, long as I had been engaged in this sort of thing, I had not yet become callous either to the feelings of wretched criminal or the excitement attendant more or less upon every capture of the sort.

We smoked in silence for some minutes, and I was listening intently to hear the slightest intimation of the vicinity of my mates; at length Bill broke the silence. "Did you get your money?" he inquired.

"No," I replied, "but I think I will get it soon."

Silence again, and then withdrawing the pipe from my mouth and quietly knocking the ashes out of it on the log, I turned towards my mate and said.

"Bill, what made you murder that man in Pipeclay Gully?"

He did not reply, but I could see his face pale and whiten in the grey dim twilight, and at last stand out distinctly in the darkening like that of the dead man we found lying in the lonely gully.

It was so entirely unexpected that he was completely stunned: not the slightest idea had he that the body had ever been found, and it was on quite nerveless wrists that I locked the handcuffs, as my mates came up and took him in charge.

Rallying a little, he asked huskily, "Who said I did it?"

"No person," I replied, "but I know you did it."

Again he was silent, and did not contradict me, and so he was taken to the lock-up.

I was right about the broken button, and had often noticed it on an old jacket of Bill's. The piece fitted to a nicety; and the cut-up blucher! Verily, there was some powerful influence at work in the discovery of this murder, and again I repeat that no mere human wisdom could have accomplished it.

Bill, it would appear, thought so too, for expressing himself so to me, he made a full confession, not only of the murder, but also of the other offence, for the bringing home to him of which I had been so anxious.

When he found that the body of the unfortunate man had been discovered upon the surface, in the broad light of day, after he had left him dead in the bottom of the hole, he became superstitiously convinced that God himself had permitted the dead to leave his hiding place for the purpose of bringing the murderer to justice.

It is no unusual thing to find criminals of his class deeply impregnated with superstition, and Bill insisted to the last that the murdered man was quite dead when he had placed him in the hole, and where, in his anxiety to prevent the body from appearing above the surface, he had lost his boot in the mud, and was too fearful of discovery to remain to try and get it out.

Bill was convicted, sentenced to death, and hung; many other crimes of a similar nature to that which he had committed on Chinaman's Flat having been brought home to him by his own confession.

Harriet Prescott Spofford (1835–1921) was a New England-born and –educated woman whose writing used the gothic form to explore the lives of women in America. An outpouring of stories, poems, and children's fiction established her reputation, and she is best known for her 1860 story "Circumstance," which famously shocked Emily Dickinson. However, she also focused on crime writing, creating a fully formed scientific detective connected with the New York police. The first of these stories, published in Harper's Monthly *30 (Apr. 1865), established the sleuth's function as that of a camera lens, to observe with unflinching and meticulous particularity. His obsession with justice is blended here with a sympathetic view of women.*

MR. FURBUSH

HARRIET PRESCOTT SPOFFORD

I t is not very long since the community was startled by the report of an extraordinary murder that occurred at one of our fashionable hotels, under peculiar circumstances and in broad daylight, and without affording, as it appeared, the slightest clew to motive or murderer. Public curiosity, finding that nothing was likely to satisfy it, gradually dropped the matter, and as gradually it died out of the newspapers.

The person who was thus abruptly ushered from this world into the unknown region of the next was a young girl, some twenty summers old, and possessed of great personal charms. She was the heiress to a small fortune, a mere annuity, but had resided since her childhood with her guardian, the wealthy and generous Mr. Denbigh, who had always surrounded her with every luxury and elegance. When Mr. Denbigh married, he and his wife took their ward with them on the foreign tour they made, and the three had but just returned to America, residing temporarily at a hotel till their uptown mansion should be suitably prepared, when the sudden and terrible death of Miss Agatha More threw such a gloom over all their plans that the preparations were for a time abandoned, and Mr. Denbigh's energies were called upon to assist his wife in rallying from the low nervous fever into which she had been thrown and prostrated by this tragedy, when returning with her husband from a drive they had discovered it in all its horror.

Mr. Denbigh was himself greatly afflicted by the death of his ward and the fearful manner of it—she had been strangled in her own handkerchief—for besides the debt of affection he owed her as a child of a dear dead friend, long years of familiarity, her extreme loveliness, and the winning gentleness of her sweet and timid ways, had given her a deep and warm place in his heart. Of late she had been a little out of health, not recovering rapidly from the great exhaustion and weakness of severe seasickness, and he had been unremitting in his endeavors to promote her comfort and happiness; while in making ready their new abode, both he and his wife had paid such heed to the tastes and needs of Agatha, meaning, as Mr. Denbigh said, that it should be felt by her to be as much her own home as theirs, without any sense of obligation, that now the place without her seemed too much a desert ever to enter upon it again.

Mrs. Denbigh, moreover, must have felt sorely, it would seem, the loss of the gentle daily companion of three years; but even more than on her own account she appeared to resent the deed for the sake of her husband to whom she was so passionately devoted, and no sooner was she able to lift her head from its pillow once more than she interested herself with revengeful vigor in the proceedings that had been undertaken. Mr. Denbigh, personally, cared little to discover the perpetrator of the atrocious crime; he felt that no human justice of cord or gibbet could restore Agatha; but his wife, burdened with their bereavement and with her own weight of indignation, would not rest with the mystery unraveled. In the deepest mourning, discarding almost every ornament, impressing so upon them more deeply the emergencies of the case and commanding their sympathies, she was closeted every morning with the detectives of the police, sparing her husband as much of the painful duty as possible, as she would have walked over burning plowshares at a word from him.

It was at first supposed that the deed had been done for plunder, as various valuable jewels, gifts of the Denbighs, and heirlooms from Miss More's own mother, were discovered to be missing; but they afforded in themselves insufficient reason, and were subsequently discovered in a package picked up by one of the police themselves at a crossing of a crowded thoroughfare where they had apparently been purposely dropped. Neither did Miss More's lovers afford any clew to the miscreant; she had had several suitors and attendants, none of whom had Mr. Denbigh favored; and though Mrs. Denbigh had urged Agatha to regard young Elliot with kindness, Mr. Denbigh frowned, Agatha remained indifferent, and young Elliot, having taunted Mr. Denbigh with the assurance that since he countenanced none of Miss More's lovers it could be but from sinister intentions on his part, had withdrawn, vowing vengeance, and declaring that, since he could not have her, nobody else should. Still that was hardly murder. And the poor fellow was found, besides, to be in such a heartbroken state as to disarm suspicion. The only other accusation that could take shape and breath might have been directed toward Agatha's maid; but as she was able to prove that she was down in the laundry, and had remained there uninterruptedly from nine till one, while the occurrence had taken place between the hours of eleven and twelve in the morning, and as she had evidently nothing to gain and much to lose by it, that idea was also dismissed, though both young Elliot and the servant-maid remained under surveillance. Finally, in despair, the Denbighs abandoned the investigation, and departed to spend the winter in Madeira, returning in the spring to their city abode, whose adornment had been left to the tender mercies of the upholsterers, since they had themselves so completely lost interest in it.

Here the general course of the matter rested. One officer alone, Detective Furbush—a man of genteel proclivities, fond of fancy parties and the *haut ton,* curious in fine women and aristocratic defaulters and peculators— who had not at first been detailed upon the case, but had been interested in the reports of it, having become at last much in earnest about it, pursued it still, incidentally, on his own account and in a kind of amateur way. It seemed to him a fatal fascination, a predestination of events that kept his steps nearly always about the purlieus of the Margrand House.

---

* The fashionable elite.

One day that Detective Furbush had happened, in a spare hour, to take his little daughter into a photograph gallery, he lounged about a window while the child was undergoing the awful operation. Along the opposite side of the street from this window ran one end of the Margrand House, with its countless windows and projections. The Margrand House fronted on a square, one end of it running down this street, and always receiving, on its stone facings and adornments, the whole sheet of the noon sun. A thought suddenly occurred to Mr. Furbush. So as soon as the operator was at leisure he attacked him with the inquiry if there were any picture of that fine building, the Margrand House? To which the operator replied affirmatively, and showed him one taken from the square. "However," said the operator, "though it doesn't take in so much, and was only what this one window could do for itself, I call this a prettier picture," and he produced something which, having been taken at such a short focal distance, resembled the photographs of the rich architecture of some Venetian façade. "It was the morning of the Great Walden Celebration," continued the operator.

"What one?" asked Mr. Furbush.

"The Great Walden Celebration."

"Ah yes," responded Mr. Furbush, not letting the rest of his thought reach the air, running as it did, "that was the morning of the More murder."

"And we let one of the boys try his hand at the craft," resumed the operator, "there being nothing doing; and it was such a lively scene in the street below, narrow as it is. And, as was to be expected from him, the crowd and procession turned into dot and line, and the whole of that part of the building opposite came out as if it had sat for its picture."

"Exactly," said Mr. Furbush, as, rubbing his finger over his lips, he looked at the sheet on which the central portion of that side of the hotel, with its quaint windows and lintels and ornamentation were most minutely given. It was in that very portion of the house that Miss Agatha More's room had been situated; nay, so well was it all impressed upon him, that Mr. Furbush could tell the very window of the room in which she had met her cruel fate. Never was there such a coincidence, to Mr. Furbush's mind, before or since, never such an interposition of Providence; the day that an unknown hand had brought Agatha More to her doom, perhaps the very hour, the sun had made a revelation of that room's interior upon this sheet of sensitized paper, his Ithuriel's spear* had touched this shapeless darkness and turned it into form and truth. The Walden Celebration had defiled through the street and into the square, at a somewhat earlier hour than the supposed hour of the murder, since it was to see the procession from a more advantageous point of view that Mr. and Mrs. Denbigh had driven out, and while they were gone the terrible action was thought to have been committed. Still the window might have a secret of its own to tell even concerning that.

Straightway Mr. Furbush made a prize of the operator; and procuring, through channels always open to him, the strongest glasses and most accurate instruments, had the one chosen window in the picture magnified and photographed, remagnified and rephotographed, till under their powerful, careful, prolonged, and patient labor, a speck came into sight that would perhaps well reward them. Mr. Furbush strained his eyes over it; to him it was a spot of greater possibilities than the nebula in Orion. This little white unresolved cloud, again and again they subjected to the same process, and once more, as if a ghost had made apparition, it opened itself into an outline—into a substance—and they saw the fingers of a hand, a white hand, doubled, but pliant, strong, and shapely; a left hand, on its third finger wearing rings, one of which seemed at first a mere blot of light, but, gradually, as the rest, answering the spell of the camera, showed itself a central stone set with five points, each point consisting of smaller stones: the color of course could not be told; the form was that of a star. Held in the tight, fierce fingers of that clenched hand, between the pointed thumb and waxy knuckles, and one edge visible along the tips deep dinted into the thumb's side, was grasped an end of a laced handkerchief. Now the handkerchief of Agatha More, the instrument of her destruction, was always carried folded in the shape of its running knot in Mr. Furbush's great wallet, a large, laced, embroidered handkerchief; that this was its photograph he needed but a glance to rest assured. All the rest of the dark deed was hidden beyond the angle of light afforded by the window frame. And whosoever the murderer might be, Mr. Furbush said to himself with the pleasantry of the headsman, it was evident that the owner of this picture had a hand in it. And here he paid the photographer for his labors and bade him adieu.

---

* It was said that the touch of the spear of the angel Ithuriel would reveal any deceit.

Mr. Furbush was now, however, not much better off than he had been before. He had the hand that did the deed in his possession, to be sure, but to whose body was he to affix that hand, and how was he to do it? And in what did it differ from any other hand? In nothing but that fetter which made it his prisoner, that five-pointed star, that blot of light upon the third finger, above a wedding ring. A wedding ring—that would seem to prove the hand to be a woman's; the five-pointed glittering ring—that proved the woman to be no pauper. Worn above the wedding ring, it must be its guard, and was probably as inseparable as that. To identify that hand, to certify that ring, became the recreation of Mr. Furbush's days and nights, so much to the detriment of all his other business that he fell into sad disrepute thereby at the Bureau. Mr. Furbush became all at once a gay man, plunged into the dissipations of fashionable life; he had been there before, on similar necessity, and knew how to carry himself. His costume grew singularly correct, he handled his lorgnette at the Opera like a coxcomb of the first milk and water; he procured invitations to ball and party, and watched every lady who for the moment daintily ungloved herself; he was as constant at church as the sexton; he made a part of the beau monde. It was all in vain. And though Mr. Furbush carried the photograph in his breast pocket, ready at any moment to descend like the hand of the Inquisition upon its victim, he might as well have carried there a pardon to all concerned, for all the good it did him.

But the world goes round.

One starlit night Mr. Furbush, pursuing some scent of other affairs along the princely avenue with its rows of palaces, took in, as was his wont, with every wink, a whole scene to its last details. He saw the beggar on these steps shrink into shadow, the housemaid in that area listening to the beguiling voice of the footman-three-doors-off no longer keeping his distance; he saw, there, the gay scene offered by the bright balcony casement with its rich curtains still unclosed; he saw, yet beyond, the light streaming from between open doors down the shining steps at whose foot the carriage waited, while a gentleman at its door hurried, with a pleasant word, the stately woman who came down to enter it beside him. She came down slowly, Mr. Furbush noted, moving like a person whom organic difficulty of the heart indisposes to quick exertion; she was one of those whom Mr. Furbush called magnificent—great coils of blue-black hair, twisted with diamonds, wreathing her queenly head tiara-wise, her features having the firmness and the pallor of marble, her eyes rivaling the diamonds in their steady splendor. A heavy cloak of ermine wrapped her velvet attire, and she was buttoning a glove as she descended. She paused a moment under the carriage lamp, giving her husband the ungloved hand to help her in. The carriage light flashed upon it, and in that second of its lingering, Mr. Furbush saw, plainly as he saw the stars above him, on the third finger of that left hand, above the wedding ring, the circlet with its five-pointed star whose duplicate he carried.

Mr. Furbush was thunderstruck. Here was what he had sought for thrice a twelvemonth; and unexpectedly blundering upon it turned him into stone. When he recovered himself with an emphatic "Humph!" the carriage had rolled away and the doors were closed.

Mr. Furbush was not the man to lose opportunities. The business in hand might go to the dogs; tomorrow would answer as well for that as tonight; for this there was no time like the present. Fortified with an outside subordinate he demanded entrance into the mansion alone, and announcing his intention to await the arrival home of the master and mistress, made himself agreeable to the footman and butler in the upper hall till hour after hour pealing forth at last struck midnight as if they tolled a knell. The footman was asleep in his chair, the butler heard the mellifluous murmur of the visitor's voice by starts with a singing sensation as if his fingers were in his ears and out again momentarily. The wheels grated on the curb below, the horses hammered the pavement, the doors were flung apart, and the master and mistress of the house returned from the entertainments they had shared. She was a little paler, a little more magnificent, a little more imposing in her height and dignity than before; there was only one emotion, though, apparent through it all—that she valued her beauty and power only for its influence on the man beside her. Mr. Furbush's keen eye saw the quick heave and restless agitation that the heart kept up beneath the velvets, simply in the moment when her husband touched her hand helping her across the threshold, and saw the whole story of her eye as it rested that instant on his. He would have had the entire case at once—if he had not had it before.

"Mr. and Mrs. Denbigh," said he, approaching them then, "may I beg to see you alone for a few moments on a matter of importance?"

And in conformity with his request he was conducted, through other apartments, into a library, a place more secluded than they, a rather somber room, wainscoted all its lofty height in bookcases, and with here and there a glimmering bust. Mr. Denbigh himself turned up the gas and closed the door.

"Your business, Sir?" said he then to Mr. Furbush.

"My business, Sir, is more particularly with Mrs. Denbigh; although I desire your presence. I am a member of the police—"

Mrs. Denbigh, who yet stood with her hand laid passively along the back of a chair, slowly grasped the back till the glove that she wore with a quick crack ripped down the length of the finger, and the five-pointed ring protruded its sparkling face like the vicious head of a serpent.

"I am a member of the police," continued Mr. Furbush, quietly. "I have something in my possession which I desire Mrs. Denbigh to look at and see if it belong to her." Perhaps the woman breathed again. Whether she did or not he proceeded to open his great leathern wallet on the library table beneath the chandelier.

Mrs. Denbigh moved forward with her slow majesty, dragging her velvets heavily, and the cloak dropping from her shoulder.

"Queer subjects—women," thought Mr. Furbush. "Ah! You had more spring in you once. As handsome a thing as a leopard!"

But in spite of that calm deliberate step Mr. Furbush saw her heart fluttering there like a white dove in its nest. She did not speak, but waited a moment beside him. "Will you be so kind," said he, "as to remove your glove?"

She quietly did so. Perhaps wonderingly.

"Excuse me, madame," then continued he, lifting her hand as he spoke, doubling its cold fingers over one end of a running knot that a soiled handkerchief made, a laced embroidered handkerchief he had produced, and, powerless in his grasp, he laid hand and all—a white hand, doubled, but pliant, strong, and shapely, holding in its fingers, between the pointed thumb and waxy knuckles, the laced handkerchief's end, just an edge visible along the tips deep dinted into the thumb's side; and with the five-pointed ring burning its bale-fire above it, laid the hand and all on the table beside the photograph that he spread there.

"Is it yours?" said he.

A detective has perhaps no right to any pity; but for a moment Mr. Furbush would gladly have never heard of the More murder as he saw in the long, slow rise and fall of the bosom this woman's heart swing like a pendulum, a noiseless pendulum that ceases to vibrate. Her eyes wavered a moment between him and the table, then, as if caught and chained by something that compelled their gaze, glared at and protruded over the sight they saw beneath them. Her own hand—her own executioner. A long shudder shook her from head to foot. Iron nerve gave way, the white lips parted, she threw her head back and gasped; with one wild look toward her husband she turned from him as if she would have fled and fell dead upon the floor.

"Hunt's up," said Mr. Furbush to his subordinate, coming out an hour or two later, and the two found some congenial oyster-opener, while the Chief explained how he had gone to get his wife's spoons from the maid who had appropriated them and taken service elsewhere. Mr. Furbush made a night of it; but never soul longed for daylight as he did, he had a notion that he had scarcely less than murdered—himself; and good fellow as he must needs be abroad that night, indoors the next day he put his household in sackcloth and ashes.

You will not find Mr. Furbush's name on the list of detectives now. He has sickened of the business. He says there is too much night work. He has found a patron now—a wealthy one apparently. He has opened one of the largest and most elegant photographing establishments in the city; he was always fond of chemicals, he says. He has still, in an inner drawer, some singular but fast-fading likenesses of a hand, a clenched, murderous hand—among them not the one Mr. Denbigh burned. He has a few secrets appertaining to his profession, which no one else has yet obtained. Meanwhile it has never been exactly explained how the story of the ring found the light.

Perhaps it was in order that Mr. Furbush might never be convicted of compounding a felony!

Ellen (Mrs. Henry) Wood (1814–1887) published over 100 stories before her first novel, Danesbury House, *appeared, in 1860, the same year that Mary Elizabeth Braddon's first novel appeared. Both became enormously popular; Wood's next novel,* East Lynne (1860–1861), *a tale of crime and a seductive heroine, made her reputation. Many more tales of detection followed, but her crowning achievement was the creation of Johnny Ludlow, a young man with a detective's eye, who appeared in a series of tales from 1868 to 1891 that spanned six volumes. Her work has been hailed as the bridge from the sterility of Poe's Dupin to the flawed but fascinating Sherlock Holmes. The following story, collected in the third volume of "Johnny Ludlow" tales, first appeared in* The Argosy *(UK) for December 1873.*

MRS. TODHETLEY'S EARRINGS

ELLEN WOOD

Again we had been spending the Christmas at Crabb Cot. It was January weather, cold and bright, the sun above and the white snow on the ground. Mrs. Todhetley had been over to Timberdale Court, to the christening of Robert and Jane Ashton's baby: a year had gone by since their marriage. The mater went to represent Mrs. Coney, who was godmother. Jane was not strong enough to sit out a christening dinner, and that was to be given later. After some mid-day feasting, the party dispersed.

I went out to help Mrs. Todhetley from the carriage when she got back. The Squire was at Pershore for the day. It was only three o'clock, and the sun quite warm in spite of the snow.

"It is so fine, Johnny, that I think I'll walk to the school," she said, as she stepped down. "It may not be like this tomorrow, and I must see about those shirts."

The parish school was making Tod a set of new shirts; and some bother had arisen about them. Orders had been given for large plaits in front, when Tod suddenly announced that he would have the plaits small.

"Only—Can I go as I am?" cried Mrs. Todhetley, suddenly stopping in indecision, as she remembered her fine clothes: a silver-grey gown that shone like silver, white shawl of china crape, and befeathered bonnet.

"Why, yes, of course you can go as you are, good mother. And look all the nicer for it."

"I fear the children will stare! But then—if the shirts get made wrong! Well, will you go with me, Johnny?"

We reached the schoolhouse, I waiting outside while she went in. It was during that time of strike that I have told of before, when Eliza Hoar died of it. The strike was in full swing still; the men looked discontented, the women miserable, the children pinched.

"I don't know what in the world Joseph will say!" cried Mrs. Todhetley, as we were walking back. "Two of the shirts are finished with the large plaits. I ought to have seen about it earlier; but I did not think they would begin them quite so soon. We'll just step into Mrs. Coney's, Johnny, as we go home. I must tell her about the christening."

For Mrs. Coney was a prisoner from an attack of rheumatism. It had kept her from the festivity. She was asleep, however, when we got in: and Mr. Coney thought she had better not be disturbed, even for the news of the little grandson's christening, as she had lain awake all the past night in pain; so we left again.

"Why, Johnny! Who's that?"

Leaning against the gate of our house, in the red light of the setting sun, was an elderly woman, dark as a gipsy.

"A tramp," I whispered, noticing her poor clothes.

"Do you want anything, my good woman?" asked Mrs. Todhetley.

She was half kneeling in the snow, and lifted her face at the words: a sickly face, that somehow I liked now I saw it closer. Her tale was this. She had set out from her home, three miles off, to walk to Worcester, word having been sent her that her daughter, who was in service there, had met with an accident. She had not been strong of late, and a faintness came over her as she was passing the gate. But for leaning on it she must have fallen.

"You should go by train: you should not walk," said Mrs. Todhetley.

"I had not the money just by me, ma'am," she answered. "It 'ud cost two shillings or half-a-crown. My daughter sent word I was to take the train and she'd pay for it: but she did not send the money, and I'd not got it just handy."

"You live at Islip, you say. What is your name?"

"Nutt'n, ma'am," said the woman, in the local dialect. Which name I interpreted into Nutten; but Mrs. Todhetley thought she said Nutt.

"I think you are telling me the truth," said the mater, some hesitation in her voice, though. "If I were assured of it I would advance you half-a-crown for the journey."

"The good Lord above us knows that I'm telling it," returned the woman earnestly, turning her face full to the glow of the sun. "It's more than I could expect you to do, ma'am, and me a stranger; but I'd repay it faithfully."

Well, the upshot was that she got the half-crown lent her; and I ran in for a drop of warm ale. Molly shrieked out at me for it, refusing to believe that the mistress gave any such order, and saying she was not going to warm ale for parish tramps. So I got the ale and the tin, and warmed it myself. The woman was very grateful, drank it, and disappeared.

"Joseph, I am so very sorry! They have made two of your shirts, and the plaits are the large ones you say you don't like."

"Then they'll just unmake them," retorted Tod, in a temper.

We were sitting round the table at tea, Mrs. Todhetley having ordered some tea to be made while she went upstairs. She came down without her bonnet, and had changed her best gown for the one she mostly wore at home: it had two shades in it, and shone like the copper teakettle. The Squire was not expected home yet, and we were to dine an hour later than usual.

"That Miss Timmens is not worth her salt," fired Tod, helping himself to some thin bread-and-butter. "What business has she to go and make my shirts wrong?"

"I fear the fault lies with me, Joseph, not with Miss Timmens. I had given her the pattern shirt, which has large plaits, you know, before you said you would prefer—Oh, we hardly want the lamp yet, Thomas!" broke off the mater, as old Thomas came in with the lighted lamp.

"I'm sure we do, then," cried Tod. "I can't see which side's butter and which bread."

"And I, not thinking Miss Timmens would put them in hand at once, did not send to her as soon as you spoke, Joseph," went on the mater, as Thomas settled the lamp on the table. "I am very sorry, my dear; but it is only two. The rest shall be done as you wish."

Something, apart from the shirts, had put Tod out. I had seen it as soon as we got in. For one thing, he had meant to go to Pershore: and the pater, not knowing it, started without him.

"Let them unmake the two," growled Tod.

"But it would be a great pity, Joseph. They are very nicely done; the stitching's beautiful. I really don't think it will signify."

"*You* don't, perhaps. You may like odd things. A pig with one ear, for example."

"A what, Joseph?" she asked, not catching the last simile.

"I said a pig with one ear. No doubt you do like it. You are looking like one now, ma'am."

The words made me gaze at Mrs. Todhetley, for the tone bore some personal meaning, and then I saw what Tod meant: an earring was absent. The lamp-light shone on the flashing diamonds, the bright pink topaz of the one earring; but the other ear was bare and empty.

"You have lost one of your earrings, mother!"

She put her hands to her ears, and started up in alarm. These earrings were very valuable: they had been left to her, when she was a child, in some old lady's will, and constituted her chief possession in jewellery worth boasting of. Not once in a twelvemonth did she venture to put them on; but she had got them out today for the christening.

Whether it was that I had gazed at the earrings when I was a little fellow and sat in her lap, I don't know; but I never saw any that I liked so well. The pink topaz was in a long drop, the slender rim of gold that encircled it being set with diamonds. Mrs. Todhetley said they were worth fifty guineas: and perhaps they were. The glittering white of the diamonds round the pink was beautiful to look upon.

The house went into a commotion. Mrs. Todhetley made for her bedroom, to see whether the earring had dropped on the floor or was lodging inside her bonnet. She shook out her grey dress, hoping it had fallen amidst the folds. Hannah searched the stairs, candle in hand; the two children were made to stand in corners for fear they should tread on it. But the search came to nothing. It seemed clear enough that the earring was not in the house.

"Did you notice, Johnny, whether I had them both in my ears when we went to the school?" the mater asked.

No, I did not. I had seen them sparkling when she got out of the carriage, but had not noticed them after.

I went out to search the gardenpath that she had traversed, and the road over to the Coneys' farm. Tod helped me, forgetting his shirts and his temper. Old Coney said he remarked the earrings while Mrs. Todhetley was talking to him, and thought how beautiful they were. That is, he had remarked *one* of them; he was sure of that; and he thought if the other had been missing, its absence would have struck him. But that was just saying nothing; for he could not be certain that both were there.

"You may hunt till tomorrow morning, and get ten lanterns to it," cried Molly, in her tart way, meeting us by the baytree, as we went stooping up the path again: "but you'll be none the nearer finding it. That tramp got's the earring, Master Joe."

"What tramp?" demanded Tod, straightening himself.

"A tramp that Master Johnny there must needs give hot ale to," returned Molly. "*I* know what them tramps are worth. They'd pull rings out of ears with their own fingers, give 'em the chance: and perhaps this woman did, without the missis seeing her."

Tod turned to me for an explanation. I gave it, and he burst into a derisive laugh, meant for me and the mater. "To think we could be taken in by such a tale as that!" he cried: "we should never see tramp, or half-crown, or perhaps the earring again."

The Squire came home in the midst of the stir. He blustered a little, partly at the loss, chiefly at the encouragement of tramps, calling it astounding folly. Ordering Thomas to bring a lantern, he went stooping his old back down the path, and across to Coney's and back again; not believing any one had searched properly, and finally kicking the snow about.

"It's a pity this here snow's on the ground, sir," cried Thomas. "A little thing like an earring might easily slip into it in falling."

"Not a bit of it," growled the Squire. "That tramp has got the earring."

"I don't believe the tramp has," I stoutly said. "I don't think she was a tramp at all: and she seemed honest. I liked her face."

"There goes Johnny with his 'faces' again!" said the Squire, in laughing mockery; and Tod echoed it.

"It's a good thing you don't have to buy folks by their faces, Johnny; you'd get finely sold sometimes."

"And she had a true voice," I persisted, not choosing to be put down, also thinking it right to assert what was my conviction. "A voice you might trust without as much as looking at herself."

Well, the earring was not to be found; though the search continued more or less till bedtime, for every other minute somebody would be looking again on the carpets.

"It is not so much for the value I regret it," spoke Mrs. Todhetley, the tears rising in her meek eyes, "as for the old associations connected with it. I never had the earrings out but they brought back to me the remembrance of my girlhood's home."

Early in the morning I ran down to the schoolhouse. More snow had fallen in the night. The children were flocking in. Miss Timmens had not noticed the earrings at all, but several of the girls said they had. Strange to say, though, most of them could not say for certain whether they saw *both* the earrings: they thought they did; but there it ended. Just like old Coney!

"I am sure both of them were there," spoke up a nice, clean little girl, from a back form.

"What's that, Fanny Fairfax?" cried Miss Timmens, in her quick way. "Stand up. How are you sure of it?"

"Please governess, I saw them both," was the answer; and the child blushed like a peony as she stood up above the others and said it.

"Are you sure you did?"

"Yes, I'm quite sure, please, governess. I was looking which o' the two shined the most. 'Twas when the lady was stooping over the shirt, and the sun came in at the window."

"What did they look like?" asked Miss Timmens.

"They looked—" and there the young speaker came to a standstill.

"Come, Fanny Fairfax!" cried Miss Timmens, sharply. "What d'you stop for? I ask you what the earrings looked like. You must be able to tell if you saw them."

"They were red, please, governess, and had shining things round them like the ice when it glitters."

"She's right, Master Johnny," nodded Miss Timmens to me: "and she's a very correct child in general. I think she must have seen both of them."

I ran home with the news. They were at breakfast still.

"What a set of muffs the children must be, not to have taken better notice!" cried Tod. "Why, when I saw only the one earring in, it struck my eye at once."

"And for that reason it is almost sure that both of them were in at the schoolhouse," I rejoined. "The children did not particularly observe the two, but they would have remarked it directly had only one been in. Old Coney said the same."

"Ay: it's that tramp that has got it," said the Squire. "While your mother was talking to her, it must have slipped out of the ear, and she managed to secure it. Those tramps lay their hands on anything; nothing comes amiss to them; they are as bad as gipsies. I dare say this was a gipsy—dark as she was. I'll be off to Worcester and see the police: we'll soon have *her* found. You had better come with me, Johnny; you'll be able to describe her."

We went off without delay, caught a passing train, and were soon at Worcester and at the police station. The Squire asked for Sergeant Cripp: who came to him, and prepared to listen to his tale.

He began it in his impulsive way; saying outright that the earring had been stolen by a gipsy-tramp. I tried to say that it might have been only lost, but the pater scoffed at that, and told me to hold my tongue.

"And now, Cripp, what's to be done?" he demanded, not having given the sergeant an opportunity to put in a word edgeways. "We must get the earring back; it is of value, and much prized, apart from that, by Mrs. Todhetley. The woman must be found, you know."

"Yes, she must be found, agreed the sergeant. Can you give me a description of her?"

"Johnny—this young gentleman can," said the Squire, rubbing his brow with his yellow silk handkerchief, for he had put himself into a heat, in spite of the frosty atmosphere that surrounded us. "He was with Mrs. Todhetley when she talked to the woman."

"A thin woman of middle height, stooped a good deal, face pale and quiet, wrinkles on it, brown eyes," wrote the sergeant, taking down what I said. "Black poke bonnet, clean cap border, old red woollen shawl with the fringe torn off in places. Can't remember gown: except that it was dark and shabby."

"And, of course, sir, you've no clue to her name?" cried the sergeant, looking at me.

"Yes: she said it was Nutten—as I understood it; but Mrs. Todhetley thought she said Nutt." And I went on to relate the tale the woman told. Sergeant Cripp's lips extended themselves in a silent smile.

"It was well got up, that tale," said he, when I finished. "Just the thing to win over a warm-hearted lady."

"But she could not have halted at the gate, expecting to steal the earring?"

"Of course not. She was prowling about to see what she could steal, perhaps watching her opportunity to get into the house. The earring fell in her way, a more valuable prize than she expected, and she made off with it."

"You'll be able to hunt her up if she's in Worcester, Cripp," put in the pater. "Don't lose time."

"*If* she's in Worcester," returned Mr. Cripp, with emphasis. "She's about as likely to be in Worcester, Squire Todhetley, as I am to be at this present minute in Brummagem," he familiarly added. "After saying she was coming to Worcester, she'd strike off in the most opposite direction to it."

"Where on earth are we to look for her, then?" asked the pater, in commotion.

"Leave it to us, Squire. We'll try and track her. And—I hope—get back the earring."

"And about the advertisement for the newspapers, Cripp? We ought to put one in."

Sergeant Cripp twirled the pen in his fingers while he reflected. "I think, sir, we will let the advertisement alone for a day or two," he presently said. "Sometimes these advertisements do more harm than good: they put thieves on their guard."

"Do they? Well, I suppose they do."

"If the earring had been simply lost, then I should send an advertisement to the papers at once. But if it has been stolen by this tramp, and you appear to consider that point pretty conclusive—"

"Oh, quite conclusive," interrupted the pater. "She has that earring as sure as this is an umbrella in Johnny Ludlow's hand. Had it been dropped anywhere on the ground, we must have found it."

"Then we won't advertise it. At least not in tomorrow's papers," concluded Sergeant Cripp. And telling us to leave the matter entirely in his hands, he showed us out.

The Squire went up the street with his hands in his pockets, looking rather glum.

"I'm not sure that he's right about the advertisement, Johnny," he said at length. "I lay awake last night in bed, making up the wording of it in my own mind. Perhaps he knows best, though."

"I suppose he does, sir."

And he went on again, up one street, and down another, deep in thought.

"Let's see—we have nothing to do here today, have we, Johnny?"

"Except to get the pills made up. The mother said we were to be sure and not forget them."

"Oh, ay. And that's all the way down in Sidbury! Couldn't we as well get them made up by a druggist nearer?"

"But it is the Sidbury druggist who holds the prescription."

"What a bother! Well, lad, let us put our best leg foremost, for I want to catch the one o'clock train, if I can."

Barely had we reached Sidbury, when who should come swinging along the pavement but old Coney, in a rough white great-coat and top-boots. Not being market day, we were surprised to see him.

"I had to come in about some oats," he explained. And then the Squire told him of our visit to the place, and the sergeant's opinion about the advertisement.

"Cripp's wrong," said Coney, decisively. "Not advertise the earring!— why, it is the first step that ought to be taken."

"Well, so I thought," said the pater.

"The thing's not obliged to have been stolen, Squire; it may have been dropped out of the ear in the road, and picked up by some one. The offering of a reward might bring it back again."

"And I'll be shot if I don't do it," exclaimed the pater. "I can see as far through a millstone as Cripp can."

Turning into the Hare and Hounds, which was old Coney's inn, they sat down at a table, called for pen and ink, and began to draw out an advertisement between them. "Lost! An earring of great value, pink topaz and diamonds," wrote the Squire on a leaf of his pocket-book; and when he had got as far as that he looked up.

"Johnny, you go over to Eaton's for a sheet or two of writing-paper. We'll have it in all three of the newspapers. And look here, lad—you can run for the pills at the same time. Take care of the street slides. I nearly came down on one just now, you know."

When I got back with the paper and pills, the advertisement was finished. It concluded with an offer of £5 reward. Applications to be made to Mr. Sergeant Cripp, or to Squire Todhetley of Crabb Cot. And, leaving it at the offices of the *Herald*, *Journal*, and *Chronicle*, we returned home. It would appear on the next day, Saturday; to the edification, no doubt, of Sergeant Cripp.

"Any news of the earring?" was the Squire's first question when we got in.

"No, there was no news of it," Mrs. Todhetley answered. And she had sent Luke Macintosh over to the little hamlet, Islip; who reported when he came back that there was no Mrs. Nutt, or Nutten, known there.

"Just what I expected," observed the pater. "That woman was a thieving tramp, and she has the earring."

Saturday passed over, and Sunday came. When the Worcester paper arrived on Saturday morning the advertisement was in it as large as life, and the pater read it out to us. Friday and Saturday had been very dull, with storms of snow; on Sunday the sun shone again, and the air was crisp.

It was about three o'clock, and we were sitting at the dessert table cracking filberts, for on Sundays we always dined early, after morning service—when Thomas came in and said a stranger had called, and was asking if he could see Mrs. Todhetley. But the mater, putting a shawl over her head and cap, had just stepped over to sit a bit with sick Mrs. Coney.

"Who is it, Thomas?" asked the Squire. "A stranger! Tell him to send his name in."

"His name's Eccles, sir,"said Thomas, coming back again. "He comes, he says, from Sergeant Cripp."

"My goodness!—it must be about the earring," cried the Squire.

"That it is, sir," said old Thomas. "The first word he put to me was an inquiry whether you had heard news of it."

I followed the pater into the study. Tod did not leave his filberts. Standing by the fire was a tall, well-dressed man, with a black moustache and blue silk necktie. I think the Squire was a little taken aback at the fashionable appearance of the visitor. He had expected to see an ordinary policeman.

"Have you brought tidings of Mrs. Todhetley's earring?" began the pater, all in a flutter of eagerness.

"I beg a thousand pardons for intruding upon you on a Sunday," returned the stranger, cool and calm as a cucumber, "but the loss of an hour is sometimes most critical in these cases. I have the honour, I believe, of speaking to Squire Todhetley?"

The Squire nodded. "Am I mistaken in supposing that you come about the earring?" he reiterated. "I understood my servant to mention Sergeant Cripp. But—you do not, I presume, belong to the police force?"

"Only as a detective officer," was the answer, given with a taking smile. "A *private* officer," he added, putting a stress upon the word. "My name is Eccles."

"Take a seat, Mr. Eccles," said the Squire, sitting down himself, while I stood back by the window. "I do hope you have brought tidings of the earring."

"Yes—and no," replied Mr. Eccles, with another fascinating smile, as he unbuttoned his top-coat. "We think we have traced it; but we cannot yet be sure."

"And where is it?—who has it?" cried the Squire, eagerly.

"It is a very delicate matter, and requires delicate handling," observed the detective, after a slight pause. "For that reason I have come over today myself. Cripp did not choose to entrust it to one of his men."

"I am sure I am much obliged to him, and to you too," said the Squire, his face beaming. "Where is the earring?"

"Before I answer that question, will you be so kind as to relate to me, in a few concise words, the precise circumstances under which the earring was lost?"

The pater entered on the story, and I helped him. Mr. Eccles listened attentively.

"Exactly so," said he, when it was over. "Those are the facts Cripp gave me; but it was only secondhand, you see, and I preferred to hear them direct from yourselves. They serve to confirm our suspicion."

"But where is the earring?" repeated the pater.

"If it is where we believe it to be, it is in a gentleman's house at Worcester. At least he may be called a gentleman. He is a professional man: a lawyer, in fact. But I may not give names in the present stage of the affair."

"And how did the earring get into his house?" pursued the Squire, all aglow with interest.

"News reached us last evening," began Mr. Eccles, after searching in his pockets for something that he apparently could not find: perhaps a note-case—"reached us in a very singular way, too—that this gentleman had been making a small purchase of jewellery in the course of yesterday; had been making it in private, and did not wish it talked of. A travelling pedlar—that was the description we received—had come in contact with him and offered him an article for sale, which he, after some haggling, purchased. By dint of questioning, we discovered this article to be an earring: one earring, not a pair. Naturally Mr. Cripp's suspicion was at once aroused: he thought it might be the very self-same earring that you have lost. We consulted together, and the result is, I decided to come over and see you."

"I'd lay all I've got it is the earring!" exclaimed the Squire, in excitement. "The travelling pedlar that sold it must have been that woman tramp."

"Well, no," returned the detective, quietly. "It was a man. Her husband, perhaps; or some confederate of hers."

"No doubt of that! And how can we get back the earring?"

"We shall get it, sir, never fear; if it be the earring you have lost. But, as I have just observed, it is a matter that will require extreme delicacy and caution in the handling. First of all, we must assure ourselves beyond doubt that the earring *is* the one in question. To take any steps upon an uncertainty would not do: this gentleman might turn round upon us unpleasantly."

"Well, let him," cried the Squire.

The visitor smiled his candid smile again, and shook his head. "For instance, if, after taking means to obtain possession of the earring, we found it to be coral set with pearls, or opal set with emeralds, instead of a pink topaz with diamonds, we should not only look foolish ourselves, but draw down upon us the wrath of the present possessor."

"Is he a respectable man?" asked the pater. "I know most of the lawyers—"

"He stands high enough in the estimation of the town, but I have known him do some very dirty actions in his profession," interrupted Mr. Eccles, speaking rapidly. "With a man like him to deal with, we must necessarily be wary."

"Then what are you going to do?"

"The first step, Squire Todhetley, is to make ourselves sure that the earring is the one we are in quest of. With this view, I am here to request Mrs. Todhetley to allow me to see the fellow-earring. Cripp has organized a plan by which he believes we can get to see the one I have been telling you of; but it will be of no use our seeing it unless we can identify it."

"Of course not. By all means. Johnny, go over and ask your mother to come in," added the Squire, eagerly. "I'm sure I don't know where she keeps her things, and might look in her places for ever without finding it. Meanwhile, Mr. Eccles, can I offer you some refreshment? We have just dined off a beautiful sirloin of beef: it's partly cold now, but perhaps you won't mind that."

Mr. Eccles said he would take a little, as the Squire was so good as to offer it, for he had come off by the first train after morning service, and so lost his dinner. Taking my hat, I dashed open the dining-room door in passing. Tod was at the nuts still, Hugh and Lena on either side of him.

"I say, Tod, do you want to see a real live detective? There's one in the study."

Who should be seated in the Coneys' drawingroom, her bonnet and shawl on, and her veil nearly hiding her sad face, but Lucy Bird—Lucy Ashton that used to be. It always gave me a turn when I saw her: bringing up all kinds of ugly sorrows and troubles. I shook hands, and asked after Captain Bird.

She believed he was very well, she said, but she had been spending the time since yesterday at Timberdale Court with Robert and Jane. Today she had been dining with the Coneys—who were always kind to her, she added, with a sigh—and she was now about to go off to the station to take the train for Worcester.

The mater was in Mrs. Coney's bedroom with old Coney and Cole the doctor, who was paying his daily visit. One might have thought they were settling all the cases of rheumatism in the parish by the time they took over it. While I waited, I told Mrs. Bird about the earring and the present visit of Detective Eccles. Mrs. Todhetley came down in the midst of it; and lifted her hands at the prospect of facing a detective.

"Dear me! Is he anything dreadful to look at, Johnny? Very rough? Has he any handcuffs?"

It made me laugh. "He is a regular good-looking fellow—quite a gentleman. Tall and slender, and well-dressed: gold studs and a blue necktie. He has a ring on his finger and wears a black moustache."

Mrs. Bird suddenly lifted her head, and stared at me: perhaps the description surprised her. The mater seemed inclined to question my words; but she said nothing, and came away after bidding good-bye to Lucy.

"Keep up your heart, my dear," she whispered. "Things may grow brighter for you some time."

When I got back, Mr. Eccles had nearly finished the sirloin, some cheese, and a large tankard of ale. The Squire sat by, hospitably pressing him to take more, whenever his knife and fork gave signs of flagging. Tod stood looking on, his back against the mantelpiece. Mrs. Todhetley soon appeared with a little cardboard box, where the solitary earring was lying on a bed of wool.

Rising from the table, the detective carried the box to the window, and stood there examining the earring; first in the box, then out of it. He turned it about in his hand, and looked at it on all sides; it took him a good three minutes.

"Madam," said he, breaking the silence, "will you entrust this earring to us for a day or two? It will be under Sergeant Cripp's charge, and perfectly safe."

"Of course, of course," interposed the Squire, before any one could speak. "You are welcome to take it."

"You see, it is possible—indeed, most probable—that only one of us may be able to obtain sight of the other earring. Should it be Cripp, my having seen this one will be nearly useless to him. It is essential that he should see it also: and it will not do to waste time."

"Pray take charge of it, sir, said Mrs. Todhetley, mentally recalling what I had said of his errand to her and Lucy Bird. "I know it will be safe in your hands and Sergeant Cripp's. I am only too glad that there is a probability of the other one being found."

"And look here," added the Squire to Eccles, while the latter carefully wrapped the box in paper, and put it into his inner breast-pocket, "don't you and Cripp let that confounded gipsy escape. Have her up and punish her."

"Trust us for that," was the detective's answer, given with an emphatic nod. "*She is already as good as taken*, and her confederate also. There's not a doubt—I avow it to you—that the other earring is yours. We only wait to verify it."

And, with that, he buttoned his coat, and bowed himself out, the Squire himself attending him to the door.

"He is as much like a detective as I'm like a Dutchman," commented Tod. "At least, according to what have been all my previous notions of one. Live and learn."

"He seems quite a polished man, has quite the manners of society," added the mater. "I do hope he will get back my poor earring."

"Mother, is Lucy Bird in more trouble than usual?" I asked.

"She is no doubt in deep distress of some kind, Johnny. But she is never out of it. I wish Robert Ashton could induce her to leave that most worthless husband of hers!"

The Squire, after watching off the visitor, came in, rubbing his hands and looking as delighted as old Punch. He assumed that the earring was as good as restored, and was immensely taken with Mr. Eccles.

"A most intelligent, superior man," cried he. "I suppose he is what is called a gentleman-detective: he told me he had been to college. I'm sure it seems quite a condescension in him to work with Cripp and the rest."

And the whole of tea-time and all the way to church, the praises were being rung of Mr. Eccles. I'm not sure but that he was more to us that night than the sermon.

"I confess I feel mortified about that woman, though," confessed Mrs. Todhetley. "You heard him say that she was as good as taken: they must have traced the earring to her. I did think she was one to be trusted. How one may be deceived in people!"

"I'd have trusted her with a twenty-pound note, mother."

"Hark at Johnny!" cried Tod. "This will be a lesson for you, lad."

Monday morning. The Squire and Tod had gone over to South Crabb. Mrs. Todhetley sat at the window, adding up some bills, her nose red with the cold: and I was boxing Hugh's ears, for he was in one of his frightfully troublesome moods, when Molly came stealing in at the door, as covertly as if she had been committing murder.

"Ma'am! ma'am!—there's that tramp in the yard!"

"What?" cried the mater, turning round.

"I vow it's her; I know the old red shawl again," pursued Molly, with as much importance as though she had caught half the thieves in Christendom. "She turned into the yard as bold as brass; so I just slipped the bolt o' the door against her, and come away. You'll have her took up on the instant, ma'am, won't you?"

"But if she has come back, I don't think she can be guilty," cried Mrs. Todhetley, after a bewildered pause. "We had better see what she wants. What do you say, Johnny?"

"Why, of course we had. I'll go to her, as Molly's afraid."

Rushing out of hearing of Molly's vindictive answer, I went round through the snow to the yard, and found the woman meekly tapping at the kitchen-door—the old red shawl, and the black bonnet, and the white muslin cap border, all the same as before. Before I got quite up, the kitchen-door was cautiously drawn open, and Mrs. Todhetley looked out. The poor old woman dropped a curtsy and held out half-a-crown on the palm of her withered hand.

"I've made bold to call at the door to leave it, lady. And I can never thank you enough, ma'am," she added, the tears rising to her eyes; "my tongue would fail if I tried it. 'Tis not many as would have trusted a stranger; and, that, a poor body like me. I got over to Worcester quick and comfortable, ma'am, thanks to you, and found my daughter better nor I had hoped for."

The same feeling of reliance, of trust, arose within me as I saw her face and heard her voice and words. If this woman was what they had been fancying her, I'd never eat tarts again.

"Come in," said Mrs. Todhetley; and Molly, looking daggers as she heard it, approached her mistress with a whisper.

"Don't, ma'am. It's all a laid-out plan. She has heard that she's suspected, and brings back the half-crown, thinking to put us off the scent."

"Step this way," went on Mrs. Todhetley, giving no heed to Molly, except by a nod—and she took the woman into the little store-room where she kept her jam-pots and things, and bade her go to the fire.

"What did you tell me your name was," she asked, "when you were here on Friday?"

"Nutt'n, ma'am."

"Nutten," repeated the mater, glancing at me. "But I sent over to Islip, and no one there knew anything about you—they denied that any one of your name lived there."

"Why, how could they do that?" returned the woman, with every appearance of surprise. "They must have mistook somehow. I live in the little cottage, ma'am, by the dung-heap. I've lived there for five-and-twenty year, and brought up my children there, and never had parish pay."

"And gone always by the name of Nutten?"

"Not never by no other, ma'am. Why should I?"

Was she to be believed? There was the half-crown in Mrs. Todhetley's hand, and there was the honest wrinkled old face looking up at us openly. But, on the other side, there was the assertion of the Islip people; and there was the earring.

"What was the matter with your daughter, and in what part of Worcester does she live?" queried the mater.

"She's second servant to a family in Melcheapen Street, ma'am, minds the children and does the beds, and answers the door, and that. When I got there—and sick enough my heart felt all the way, thinking what the matter could be—I found that she had fell from the parlour window that she'd got outside to clean, and broke her arm and scarred her face, and frighted and shook herself finely. But thankful enough I was that 'twas no worse. Her father, ma'am, died of an accident, and I can never abear to hear tell of one."

"I—I lost an earring out of my ear that afternoon," said Mrs. Todhetley, plunging into the matter, but not without hesitation. "I think I must have lost it just about the time I was talking to you. Did you pick it up?"

"No, ma'am, I didn't. I should have gave it to you if I had."

"You did not carry it off with you, I suppose!" interrupted wrathful Molly; who had come in to get some eggs, under pretence that the batter-pudding was waiting for them.

And whether it was Molly's sharp and significant tone, or our silence and looks, I don't know; but the woman saw it all then, and what she was suspected of.

"Oh, ma'am, were you thinking that ill of me?"—and the hands shook as they were raised, and the white border seemed to lift itself from the horror-stricken face. "Did you think I could do so ill a turn, and after all the kindness showed me? The good Lord above knows I'm not a thief. Dear heart! I never set eyes, lady, on the thing you've lost."

"No, I am *sure* you didn't," I cried; "I said so all along. It might have dropped anywhere in the road."

"I never see it, nor touched it, sir," she reiterated, the tears raining down her cheeks. "Oh, ma'am, do believe me!"

Molly tossed her head as she went out with the eggs in her apron; but I would sooner have believed myself guilty than that poor woman. Mrs. Todhetley thought with me. She offered her some warm ale and a crust; but the old woman shook her head in refusal, and went off in a fit of crying.

"She knows no more of the earring than I know of it, mother."

"I feel sure she does not, Johnny."

"That Molly's getting unbearable. I wonder you don't send her away."

"She has her good points, dear," sighed Mrs. Todhetley. "Only think of her cooking! and of what a thrifty, careful manager she is!"

The Squire and Tod got home for lunch. Nothing could come up to their ridicule when they heard what had occurred, saying that the mother and I were two muffs, fit to go about the world in a caravan as specimens of credulity. Like Molly, they thought we ought to have secured the woman.

"But you see she was honest in the matter of the half-crown," debated Mrs. Todhetley, in her mild way. "She brought that back. It does not stand to reason that she would have dared to come within miles of the place, if she had taken the earring."

"Why, it's just the thing she would do," retorted the Squire, pacing about in a commotion. "Once she had got rid of the earring, she'd show up here to throw suspicion off herself. And she couldn't come without returning the half-crown: it must have gone nicely against the grain to return *that*."

And Mrs. Todhetley, the most easily swayed spirit in the world, began to veer round again like a weathercock, and fear we had been foolish.

"You should see her jagged-out old red shawl," cried Molly, triumphantly. "All the red a'most washed out of it, and the edges in tatters. *I* know a tramp when I sees one: and the worst of all tramps is them that do the tricks with clean hands and snow-white cap-borders."

The theme lasted us all the afternoon. I held my tongue, for it was of no use contending against the stream. It was getting dusk when Cole called in, on his way from the Coneys. The Squire laid the grievance before him, demanding whether he had ever heard of two people so simple as I and the mother.

"What did she say her name was?" asked Cole. "Nutten?—of Islip? Are you sure she did not say Norton?"

"She said Nutt'n. We interpreted it into Nutten."

"Yes, Johnny, that's how she would say it. I'll lay a guinea it's old Granny Norton."

"Granny Norton!" echoed the Squire. "She is respectable."

"Respectable, honest, upright as the day," replied Cole. "I have a great respect for old Mrs. Norton. She's very poor now; but she was not always so."

"She told us this morning that she lived in the cottage by the dung-heap, I put in."

"Exactly: she does so. And a nice dung-heap it is; the disgrace of Islip," added Cole.

"And you mean to say, Cole, that you know this woman—that she's not a tramp, but Mrs. Norton?" spoke the pater.

"I know Mrs. Norton of Islip," he answered. "I saw her pass my window this morning: she seemed to be coming from the railway-station. It was no tramp, Squire."

"How was she dressed?" asked Mrs. Todhetley.

"Dressed? Well, her shawl was red, and her bonnet black. I've never seen her dressed otherwise, when abroad, these ten years past."

"And—has she a daughter in service at Worcester?"

"Yes, I think so. Yes, I am sure so. It's Susan. Oh, it is the same person: you need not doubt it."

"Then what the deuce did Luke Macintosh mean by bringing word back from Islip that she was not known there?" fiercely demanded the Squire, turning to me.

"But Luke said he asked for her by the name of Nutt—Mrs. Nutt. I questioned him about it this afternoon, sir, and he said he understood Nutt to have been the name we gave him."

This was very unsatisfactory as far as the earring went. (And we ascertained later that poor Mrs. Norton *was* Mrs. Norton, and had been suspected wrongly.) For, failing the tramp view of the case, who could have sold the earring to the professional gentleman in Worcester?

"Cripp knows what he is about; never fear," observed the Squire. "Now that he has the case well in hand, he is sure to pull it successfully through."

"Yes, you may trust Cripp," said the doctor. "And I hope, Mrs. Todhetley, you will soon be gladdened by the sight of your earring again." And Cole went out, telling us we were going to have a thaw. Which we could have told him, for it had already set in, and the snow was melting rapidly.

❧

"To think that I should have done so stupid a thing. But I have been so flustered this morning by that parson and his nonsense that I hardly know what I'm about."

The speaker was Miss Timmens. She had come up in a passion, after twelve o'clock school. Not with us, or with her errand—which was to bring one of the new shirts to show, made after Tod's fancy—but with the young parson. Upon arriving and unfolding the said shirt, Miss Timmens found that she had brought the wrong shirt—one of those previously finished. The thaw had gone on so briskly in the night that this morning the roads were all mud and slop, and Miss Timmens had walked up in her pattens.

"He is enough to make a saint swear, with his absurdities and his rubbish," went on Miss Timmens, turning from the table where lay the unfolded shirt, and speaking of the new parson; between whom and herself hot war waged. "You'd never believe, ma'am, what he did this morning"—facing Mrs. Todhetley. "I had got the spelling-class up, and the rest of the girls were at their slates and copies, and that, when in he walked amidst the roomful. 'Miss Timmens,' says he to me, in the hearing of them all, 'I think these children should learn a little music. And perhaps a little drawing might not come amiss to those who have talent for it.' 'Oh yes, of course,' says I, hardly able to keep my temper, 'and a little dancing as well, and let 'em go out on the green daily and step their figures to a fife and tambourine!' 'There's nothing like education,' he goes on, staring hard at me, as if he hardly knew whether to take my words for jest or earnest; 'and it is well to unite, as far as we can, the ornamental with the useful, it makes life pleasanter. It is quite right to teach girls to hem dusters and darn stockings, but I think some fancy-work should be added to it: embroidery and the like.' 'Oh, you great baby!' I thought to myself, and did but just stop my tongue from saying it. 'Will embroidery and music and drawing help these girls to scour floors, and cook dinners, and wash petticoats?' I asked him. 'If I had a set of young ladies here, it would be right for them to learn accomplishments; but these girls are to be servants. And all I can say, sir, is, that if ever those new-fangled notions are introduced, you'll have to find another mistress, for I'll not stop to help in it. It would just lead many a girl to her ruin, sir; that's what it would do, whoever lives to see it.' Well, he went away with that, ma'am, but he had put my temper up—talking such dangerous nonsense before the girls, their ears all agape to listen!—and when twelve o'clock struck, I was not half through the spelling-class! Altogether, it's no wonder I brought away the wrong shirt."

Miss Timmens, her errand a failure, began folding up the shirt in a bustle, her thin face quite fiery with anger. Mrs. Todhetley shook her head; she did not approve of nonsensical notions for these poor peasant girls any more than did the rest of us.

"I'll bring up the right shirt this evening when school's over; and if it suits we'll get on with the rest," concluded Miss Timmens, making her exit with the parcel.

"What the world will come to later, Mr. Johnny, if these wild ideas get much ground, puzzles me to think of," resumed Miss Timmens, as I went with her, talking, along the garden-path. "We shall have no servants, sir; none. It does not stand to reason that a girl will work for her bread at menial offices when she has had fine notions instilled into her. Grammar, and geography, and history, and botany, and music, and singing, and fancy-work!—what good will they be of to her in making beds and cleaning saucepans? The upshot will be that they won't make beds and they won't clean saucepans; they'll be above it. The Lord protect 'em!—for I don't see what else will; or what will become of them. Or of the world, either, when it can get no servants. My goodness, Master Johnny! what's that? Surely it's the lost earring?"

Close to the roots of a small fir-tree it lay: the earring that had caused so much vexation and hunting. I picked it up: its pink topaz and diamonds shone brightly as ever in the sun, and were quite uninjured. Mrs. Todhetley remembered then, though it had slipped her memory before, that in coming indoors after the interview with the woman at the gate, she had stopped to shake this fir-tree, bowed down almost to breaking with its weight of snow. The earring must have fallen from her ear then into the snow, and been hidden by it.

Without giving himself time for a mouthful of lunch, the Squire tore away to the station through the mud, as fast as his legs would carry him, and thence to Worcester by train. What an unfortunate mistake it would be should that professional gentleman have been accused, who had bought something from the travelling pedlar!

"Well, Cripp, here's a fine discovery!" panted the Squire, as he went bursting into the police-station and to the presence of Sergeant Cripp. "The lost earring has turned up."

"I'm sure I am very glad to hear it," said the sergeant, facing round from a letter he was writing. "How has it been found?"

And the Squire told him how.

"It was not stolen at all, then?"

"Not at all, Cripp. And the poor creature we suspected of taking it proves to be a very respectable old body indeed, nothing of the tramp about her. You—you have not gone any lengths yet with that professional gentleman, I hope!" added the Squire, dropping his voice to a confidential tone.

Cripp paused for a minute, as if not understanding.

"We have not employed any professional man at all in the matter," said he; "have not thought of doing so."

"I don't mean that, Cripp. *You* know. The gentleman you suspected of having bought the earring."

Cripp stared. "I have not suspected any one."

"Goodness me! you need not be so cautious, Cripp," returned the Squire, somewhat nettled. "Eccles made a confidant of me. He told me all about it—except the name."

"What Eccles?" asked Cripp. "I really do not know what you are talking of, sir."

"What Eccles—why, your Eccles. Him you sent over to me on Sunday afternoon: a well-dressed, gentlemanly man, with a black moustache. Detective Eccles."

"I do not know any Detective Eccles."

"Dear me, my good man, you must be losing your memory!" retorted the Squire, in wrath. "He came straight to me from you on Sunday; you sent him off in haste without his dinner."

"Quite a mistake, sir," said the sergeant. "It was not I who sent him."

"Why, bless my heart and mind, Cripp, you'll be for telling me next the sun never shone! Where's your recollection gone to?"

"I hope my recollection is where it always has been, Squire. We must be at cross-purposes. I do not know any one of the name of Eccles, and I have not sent any one to you. As a proof that I could not have done it, I may tell you, sir, that I was summoned to Gloucester on business last Friday directly after I saw you, and did not get back here until this morning."

The Squire rubbed his face, whilst he revolved probabilities, and thought Cripp must be dreaming.

"He came direct from you—from yourself, Cripp; and he disclosed to me your reasons for hoping you had found the earring, and your doubts of the honesty of the man who had bought it—the lawyer, you remember. And he brought back the other earring to you that you might compare them."

"Eh—what?" cried Cripp, briskly. "Brought away the other earring, do you say, sir?"

"To be sure he did. What else did you send him for?"

"And he has not returned it to you?"

"Returned it! of course not. You hold it, don't you?"

"Then, Squire Todhetley, you have been cleverly robbed of this second earring," cried Cripp, quietly. "*Dodged* out of it, sir. The man who went over to you must have been a member of the swell-mob. Well-dressed, and a black moustache!"

"He was a college man, had been at Oxford," debated the unfortunate pater, sitting on a chair in awful doubt. "He told me so."

"You did not see him there, sir," said the sergeant, with a suppressed laugh. "I might tell you I had a duke for a grandmother; but it would be none nearer the fact."

"Mercy upon us all!" groaned the Squire. "What a mortification it will be if that other earring's gone! Don't you think some one in your station here may have sent him, if you were out yourself?"

"I will inquire, for your satisfaction, Squire Todhetley," said the sergeant, opening the door; "but I can answer for it beforehand that it will be useless."

It was as Cripp thought. Eccles was not known at the station, and no one had been sent to us.

"It all comes of that advertisement you put in, Squire," finished up Cripp, by way of consolation. "The swell-mob would not have known there was a valuable jewel missing but for that, or the address of those who had missed it."

The pater came home more crestfallen than a whipped schoolboy, after leaving stringent orders with Cripp and his men to track out the swindler. It was a blow to all of us.

"I said he looked as much like a detective as I'm like a Dutchman," quoth Tod.

"Well, it's frightfully mortifying," said the Squire.

"And the way he polished off that beef, and drank down the ale! I wonder he did not contrive to walk off with the silver tankard!"

"Be quiet, Joe! You are laughing, sir! Do you think it is a laughing matter?"

"Well, I don't know," said bold Tod. "It was cleverly done."

Up rose the pater in a passion. Vowing vengeance against the swindlers who went about the world, got up in good clothes and a moustache; and heartily promising the absent and unconscious Cripp to be down upon him if he did not speedily run the man to earth.

And that's how Mrs. Todhetley lost the other earring.

Mrs. George (Elizabeth) Corbett was an English writer of mysteries and feminist literature, at one point as highly regarded as Conan Doyle. In 1890, Corbett published a collection of fifteen short stories titled Secrets of a Private Inquiry Office, *in which a female detective named Dora plays a small part. She also apparently wrote a collection of stories titled* Adventures of a Lady Detective, *though no information is available about this work except that it is referred to in some advertisements for Corbett's other books. In 1891, Corbett published a series of ten stories in the* Leicester Chronicle *titled* Behind the Veil, or Revelations by a Lady Detective, *which is subtitled* Being Further Secrets of a Private Inquiry Office.* *In this collection of stories, the "lady detective" is again Dora White, though she is not the narrator nor does she appear in every tale. What* may *be a different, later collection, ten stories from which appeared in the* Leeds Mercury *in 1892, appears to be called* Experiences of a Lady Detective.† *These stories are narrated by Dora Bell, an agent of Bell & White Agency (suggesting that*

---

* The ten stories were "Fair Deceiver," "Miss Kelmersley's Party and What Became of It," "Breach of Promise," "Birds of a Feather," "Fool and His Money," "The Begging Letter," "Point of Honour," "How We Stimulated Sim Kernahau's Memory," "Who Was the Heir?," and "Between Two Stools." The first appeared in the Saturday, October 31, 1891, issue, and the balance appeared on succeeding Saturdays.

† The first story appeared on Saturday, April 2, 1892, and was "The Gracely Jewels," followed on succeeding Saturdays by "Black Magic, or the Veiled Lady," "Catching a Burglar," "Kleptomaniac and Thief," "Maimed for Life," "The Forged Love Letter," "The Stolen Child," "Levying Blackmail," "Mrs. Bouverie's Will," and "Number 203,421."

these were in fact written after Revelations*), and an example follows. In 1894, a series of twelve stories appeared in the* Adelaide Observer *as* The Adventures of Dora Bell, Detective,* *and these stories are narrated by Dora.† The advertisements for these latter stories mention both* Adventures *and* Revelations *but not* Experiences—*could* Revelations *be merely a reprint of* Adventures of a Lady Detective? *To add to the confusion, the advertisements for neither* Revelations *nor* Experiences *mention any of the other collection titles. Corbett wrote more than two dozen stories about including her lady detective—perhaps more!*

---

* The first story appeared on Saturday, April 14, 1894, and was "SW-E-E-EP," followed on succeeding Saturdays by "Hoist on Her Own Petard," "One of Dora's Failures," "Dora Turns the Tables," "The Acquaintance Dodge," "Broken Trust," "Madame Duchesne's Garden Party," "Pattern of Virtue," "Miss Rankin's Rival," "The Path to Fame," "The Recluse of Hallow Hall," and "The Mysterious Thief."

† In chapter 7 of the *Secrets* volume, Bell expressly states that White's niece Dora assists. However, in the 1892 series, Dora is clearly identified as "Dora Bell." In a story in *The Adventures of Dora Bell, Detective*, Dora notes that White had sold out, and she identifies Mr. Bell (as she consistently refers to him) as her uncle. Thus, unless at some point Mr. Bell married Dora's father's sister, Corbett reinvented her lineage!

CATCHING A BURGLAR

ELIZABETH CORBETT*

D ora," said Mr. Bell, to me one day, "I have a critical piece of work for you. Mr. Blanke, of West Kensington, has been very unfortunate of late. Just before Christmas his house was entered by burglars, who removed plate and valuables worth £300 therefrom. Every effort was made to trace the thief or thieves, and recover the stolen goods, but without the slightest success. This week Mr. Blanke's house has again been robbed, and he vows that if it costs him all he has left, he will bring the offenders to book. He has laid every particular of his case before me, and has empowered us to use whatever means we please, so long as we fathom the mystery. I suggested collusion with the thieves on the part of some of

---

* The story has been transcribed from an appearance in the *Leeds Mercury* weekly supplement for April 16, 1892. The story is headed as Chapter III of the serialized *Experiences of a Lady Detective*.

the domestics, basing my theory on certain details which he gave me. He was somewhat startled at first, for he has deemed his servants incorruptible. His household is not a large one, consisting only of himself and two sisters, and a small staff of servants, who have always given every satisfaction. Nevertheless all other means of detection having failed, he is willing to have our lady detective in the house for a time, but hardly expects any definite results. You are to go in the character of lady's-maid to the Misses Blanke, who will, of course, both be in the secret, and the sooner you begin operations, the better."

A few more somewhat meagre details were submitted to me, and the next day, it being the first of the month, saw me introduced to a new sphere of action. I was very well pleased with my reception, for the ladies had evidently thoroughly entered into the spirit of the thing, and neither the butler-footman, nor any of the other servants, could have the faintest suspicion that I was anything but a "bona fide" lady's-maid. The farce was kept up very gravely until we were all in the privacy of the Misses Blanke's dressing-room, which communicated "en suite" with their bedrooms.

Their stilted ceremony was thrown on one side, and I was fairly besieged with questions. "Oh! You wonderful girl!" exclaimed Miss Ida, who was a bright, charming girl of about my own age. "We expected to receive an elderly, sedate individual, for we never dreamed of finding so young a woman engaged in detective work. Have you ever caught anybody? And do you actually send people to prison, just like a real detective would do?"

"My dear madam," I replied, "the line of demarcation between what you called a 'real' detective and myself is invisible to me. It is my vocation, anomalous as you seem to think it, to frustrate the designs of the wicked, and bring evil-doers to justice. But my plans are not carried out simply by talking, and it is necessary that my assumed work shall bear investigation in a sufficient degree to prevent all suspicion of ulterior design on my part. I would like, therefore, with your permission, to do something in the way of justifying my presence in the house, and we can meanwhile talk things over, as I must, if possible, know all about my 'fellow servants' before I go down to have dinner with them."

"You certainly are very business-like and matter of fact," put in Miss Alice, the younger of the two sisters. "But I have no doubt you are right, so while we are talking you shall plan some fresh mode of putting our hair up—but can you dress hair?"

"Messrs. Bell and White, foreseeing that the art would be useful to us, paid thirty pounds for a course of lessons with Mademoiselle Clair. Suppose I try your hair first, Miss Alice—it is not dressed in harmony with the contour of your face. Splendid—quite a wealth to work upon. And now—while I do my best with it, we will proceed with our real business. Tell me all about the servants."

"There is not much to tell," said Miss Blanke. "Hodgson has been with us fifteen years. He was butler down at Ilvington when our father was still living. When my brother, who is a barrister, found it necessary to come to London, Hodgson came with us. So did Grey, the gardener, who lives in the little lodge with his wife. Pearson, as we still call her, has been with us two years, and was married about twelve months ago to Hodgson. She is our cook. The upper and under housemaids are sisters, who have been in our service six months. They are all careful and attentive, and I really do not think they can possibly be connected with the burglaries."

"Perhaps not—at least not consciously. Have the two housemaids any admirers?"

"I believe they are both 'keeping company,' as they call it."

"With whom?"

"That I cannot say. But of course the young men are respectable, or Hodgson would not permit them to home into the house."

"Have the servants any special evening for receiving visitors?"

"They are allowed to receive a friend on Tuesday evenings, and they have an evening out in turn each week."

"Were they all in the house on the occasions of the robberies?"

"Yes."

"Was their baggage searched?"

"They all insisted on its being done. Pearson was particularly anxious to be 'justified,' as she expressed it, and threatened to leave if her boxes and Hodgson's were not searched. Oh, how beautifully you have done Alice's hair! Why, Alice, you look like a fairy edition of yourself; I only hope mine will be as charming. But it is lunch-time. I hear the bell."

In fact, we all heard the bell, for it made noise enough; and while the young ladies went to the morning-room, where lunch was always laid, I brushed my own hair a little, and washed my hands, preparatory to venturing among the servants. I did not need to introduce myself, for Hodgson, who was now attending to his mistresses' needs, had opened the door for me when I arrived, and had evidently been favourably impressed by my appearance, and by my respectful attitudes towards himself, judging by the warmth with which I was welcomed downstairs.

"Which I am sure you are welcome, Miss—Miss—"

"Jenkins."

"Miss Jenkins, ma'am. As I said to Hodgson—it'll be rele comfort to 'ave a rele lady in the servants' 'all, which I'm sure you looks it, too."

"I'm glad you think so. You see, I've always been very careful to take pattern* quite as much from married ladies, like yourself, as from the young ladies I have had to wait upon—sometimes, in fact, you find the truest ladies in the servants' hall."

This flattery, gross as it was, had its intended effect, and put me at once in the good graces of Mrs. Pearson Hodgson. The housemaids smiled good-humouredly; but the younger one gave me a sly, quizzical glance, which warned me that she had too much common-sense to accept extravagant praise seriously.

I did not make much progress with my case that day, for it was part of my policy not to mention anything about the burglaries until some one else took the initiative. But I made myself very agreeable downstairs, and, while preserving a certain staidness of manner, as became an accomplished lady's-maid, I gave myself no airs of superiority, but became quietly confidential with all the kitcheners.

Neither Miss Ida nor Miss Alice were disposed to work me too hard, and when the first visiting night came round, it was quietly arranged that I should have the time to use as I liked. Mr. Blanke and his sisters were going to a "Patti Concert"† at the Albert Hall. All hands being thus free to follow their own devices, it was resolved to make a merry evening of it.

The first visitors to arrive were Mr. and Mrs. Blandford, brother and sister-in-law of Pearson, who welcomed them very warmly. I noticed,

---

* In the sense of someone to be imitated.

† Adelina Patti (1843–1919) was one of the most famous sopranos of the day, described by Giuseppe Verdi as perhaps the finest singer who ever lived.

however, that Hodgson did not seem to share his wife's enthusiasm, for he frigidly held out the tips of his fingers, by way of shaking hands, and immediately turned to welcome two young men, who came together, on the strength of their acquaintanceship with the two pretty housemaids.

I watched these young men narrowly, for I had held the theory that they knew more about the burglaries than they would like to transpire. But, looking at their fresh, open countenances, and listening to their frank, hearty talk about home affairs, and about their work, I was fain to banish my suspicion. Just before all sat down to a very capital supper, my own "young gentleman" popped in, and certainly no one but myself would have dreamed that he was the smartest private detective our firm had had for many a day. He was very polite to everybody present, and audaciously kissed me before all these people, smilingly apologizing to the others for doing it in their presence.

Of course I dared not resent his impertinence, by seeming really angry, for had I not tacitly pledged myself to receive his attentions by introducing him to these new acquaintances as "my young gentleman"? Such are some of the penalties one has to submit to when one enters the detective business. Still, after all, when the culprit is jolly and good-looking and bright-witted, and—in fact, when he is everything that is nice, it is no very terrible matter to be the object of his salutations, especially if he likes you, and you like him—but that by the way.

"Good evening, sir. Any friends of Miss Jenkins's is welcome. You find us very plain and homely here; but such as we have you are welcome to share."

Mr. Hodgson said this with all the air of one lording it in his own home, and Mr. Adam Henniker at once won his favour by expressing his deep sense of the kindness extended to him—a stranger.

"Pray don't mention it," said Hodgson, loftily; "we never stand on ceremony here, and can at least pride ourselves upon being as hospitable as our poor means will permit. What shall I give you, sir? A little of this game-pie? Or would you prefer some turkey and ham? Yes? Here you are, then, and some of this splendid sausage—my wife defies any one to produce anything daintier. They never tire of the dish upstairs. But it does not do to spoil one's people by over-indulgence."

Thus meandered Mr. Hodgson, while we all did full justice to the ample supply of viands. I noticed that, whether purposely or accidentally,

Hodgson forgot to serve his wife's relations. She, however, amply made up for his neglect by heaping their plates with plenty of good things. I noticed also that Mr. Blandford indulged in an occasional scowl at his sister, which seemed to put that pleasant body into a state of nervousness not quite in keeping with mere sisterly deference. There was something behind, I felt convinced, and of course I resolved to discover what that something was.

Mrs. Blandford, too, appeared very much in awe of her husband, and hardly ventured to speak without casting a glance into his face, as if to ascertain whether she was displeasing him or not.

"Blandford is evidently a domestic tyrant," I thought. "Is he anything worse? I must find out."

Supper over, a round game at cards was proposed and acceded to by nearly all present. The exceptions were Blandford, Pearson, Adam Henniker, and myself. There was a good deal of laughter round the card-table, but Pearson and her brother settled down for a quiet chat. So also, apparently, did "my young gentleman" and myself. Nevertheless, the whole four of us had a keen eye to business, and it did not escape my notice that Pearson, after glancing rapidly round, to make sure she was unobserved, slipped a small piece of paper in her brother's hand. The latter pretended to take up the *Daily News*, and, under its cover, read the note, smiled triumphantly, put the paper, after crumpling it up, into his coat-pocket, and then suddenly bethought him that it was time to be on the move.

"I say, Ann," he called out to his wife, "we mustn't be much longer before we go. You know I have to be up at three o'clock."

Could it be fancy, or did the words, "I must be up at three o'clock," bring an answering gleam of intelligence and satisfaction to the woman's face? And did she really throw a glance of approval at Pearson? And was it also a fact that Pearson was as pale as death, and that she was clutching wildly at her chair, to keep herself from falling?

I certainly thought so. So did Adam Henniker, who was no less observant than myself. Adam bent towards me, and, assuming a very lover-like attitude, whispered, "Something fresh in the wind, eh? I think I could put my hand on the people we are hunting."

As he said this, he gave my hand a squeeze, and as my responses were whispered with a downcast, blushing face, it is not surprising that somebody giggled something about "two spoons." The company would have been very much astonished if they could have guessed the real purport of our conversation.

"Come, Ann! Didn't you hear me say it was time to move?" snarled Blandford; receiving for reply, "Yes, yes, Andrew; in a minute," as the lady hastily rose.

"Oh, dear! Don't go yet!" pleaded the pretty upper-housemaid. "There is only you and me left in the game now, and I don't want to be left an 'old maid.'"

"Neither you shall," exclaimed her admirer, fervently; "we'll be married at Christmas, if you will."

This prompt sally provoked a laugh all round, but did not serve to induce the Blandfords to wait until the game was finished. Indeed, the party was practically broken up, and I heard Hodgson mutter something to the effect that such marplots* should never enter "his house" again. Adam Henniker followed Blandford's lead, saying that as he also had to go to work early in the morning, he had better be moving, too. He was exceedingly polite to his fellow-visitors, even going the length of assisting Blandford to put his topcoat on, and handing Mrs. Blandford her gloves, bonnet, cloak, and umbrella. Then he whispered to me, knowing that his assumed "role" of lover would serve to excuse the want of manners, "Tell Mr. Blanke I will be back at 2:30 A.M. Have picked this fellow's pocket of the note Pearson gave him. New plot under way. Let me in through the drawing-room window."

I nodded my comprehension of all that Adam had said, and then excused myself also, on the plea that the young ladies would be home soon, and that I must be in readiness for them. About an hour later the family returned. Of course, I lost no time in telling Miss Blanke that I had some important information for her brother, and that I was anxious to confer with him without the other servants being cognizant of the fact.

"That is easily managed," said Miss Blanke. "We are all three hungry, and I will ask Sidney to come and have a little refreshment here. Is there anything nice in the larder, do you know?"

---

* "Amarplot" is someone who spoils another's plans.

There were plenty of good things in the larder, I knew, but I thought Hodgson had better answer for himself. I therefore went to the kitchen, to see what there was forthcoming, and surprised Hodgson and Pearson in the middle of a conjugal squabble, which I rightly assumed to refer to the Blandfords.

"The young ladies would like some refreshment, before going to bed. What can you give me for them? I asked.

"Refreshments? At this time of night? Didn't they have a good dinner before they went out? But employers have no consideration now-a-days!"

Thus grumbled Hodgson; but my opinion of him rose a little, when I noticed that he was filling a tray with dainties enough to have done justice to a spread in honour of his own friends, for, from his previous talk, I had almost formed the opinion that he considered the wants of his employers as a very secondary consideration. He then carried the tray to the young ladies' boudoir for me, and was informed that his services were not required any more that night.

Meanwhile Mr. Blanke had joined his sisters, and while the trio warmed themselves, and partook of the food brought for them, I gave them a rapid account of the events of the evening, so far as they appertained to the hunt for the burglars.

"Why, it looks as if Pearson were at the bottom of the mischief," said Mr. Blanke. "I wish this friend of yours would come, for I am all anxiety to learn more."

So said he, and it is not surprising that the young ladies also resolved to wait up, in order to satisfy their natural curiosity. As my services might possibly be required, I was also included among the watchers. When it drew near the appointed time, Mr. Blanke and his sisters, all breathless and on tiptoe, accompanied me to the drawing-room, where Adam could be admitted without the rattling of chains which was inseparable from the opening of outer doors.

A little before half-past two there was a gentle tap at the window, which was immediately opened. We were excited before, but when we saw that Adam was followed into the room by no less than four big policemen, our excitement reached boiling-pitch, though we were all careful to speak in a low tone of voice, the two young ladies showing as much discretion as anybody.

We were soon put into possession of all the facts of the case. The note which Adam had contrived to abstract from Blandford ran as follows:— "The master has bought some beautiful plate. It came home yesterday. I will see that the pantry window is unfastened for you at three o'clock. After this job I have your promise to let me go my own way, and I mean to hold you to your promise, or I, in my turn, will split.* The Police shall know that you are 'Dick the Switcher.' For the last time, three o'clock, and if you lay Jake on to me, I'll lay the police on to you."

There was no signature, but we knew who had written this letter; and it left no doubt on our minds as to who had been accessory to the other burglaries. "Dick the Switcher" was a notorious housebreaker, whom the police had been seeking for some time. The "Jake" mentioned in Pearson's letter was conjectured to be Jake Porter, a bird of the same feather who had recently been doing eighteen months for larceny, and who was already wanted for a still graver offence.

By the time explanations and consultations were over it was time for our men to "plant" themselves. We women retired to the young ladies' boudoir to await events, while the six men posted themselves in readiness for the attack. We all went about our business very cautiously, for we were not sure that Pearson was not intending to afford other aid to her confederates than that of opening the pantry-windows. We sat without a light, to avoid scaring the would-be burglars, and pictured all sorts of horrible scenes going on below.

Apparently the man who called himself Blandford had not imagined that any one had got hold of the incriminatory piece of paper, for shortly after four he appeared at the pantry-window, as arranged with Pearson, and entered the house without much difficulty, followed by another man. The pair were allowed to reach the dining-room sideboard, and to lay their hands upon a handsome case of cutlery, before they were pounced upon from behind, and then they found themselves speedily handcuffed and helpless. I am told they swore awfully, and one of them vowed to murder Pearson, if ever he got the chance.

"I'll learn her to peach on her own husband!" he snarled. By this time bells had been ringing, and the whole household was alarmed. Hodgson

---

* Inform the police.

came running downstairs to see what was the matter, and his consternation was very great when he was told that the reason he had not been roused before was because his own wife was hand and glove with the burglars, and that we feared she would have warned them against venturing in. He alternately raved with anger and cried with dismay at being mixed up with so disreputable a gang. Meanwhile one of the policemen thought he would like to secure Pearson, and ordered Hodgson to show him where she was. That lady, however, had known that the plans of her associates had failed as soon as she heard the uproar caused by their capture. She had promptly lowered herself from her bedroom-window on to an outhouse, and had thence made good her escape through the back garden. Up to the time of writing her whereabouts have not been discovered. But Dick the Switcher, alias Blandford, alias Thompson, is provided with a home for many years to come, as is also Jake Porter, his accomplice, and it is satisfactory to note that Mr. Blanke recovered a great deal of the property stolen from him on former occasions by the same gang.

As for poor Hodgson, he was very thankful to find that he was exonerated from all suspicion of complicity, and even still more thankful to know that some one had a prior claim to the woman he had called his wife. He has foresworn married life for ever, and has even given up his Wednesday receptions, for, as he says, "It behooves one to be careful about who one introduces to one's house."

Catherine Louisa Pirkis (1839–1910) was one of the few British women producing crime writing at the end of the nineteenth century. Pirkis wrote much else as well, but shortly after the appearance of Sherlock Holmes, Pirkis created a true rival to Holmes, Miss Loveday Brooke, who appeared in a series of seven stories in The Ludgate Monthly *magazine, collected as* The Experiences of Loveday Brooke, Lady Detective *in 1894. Brooke, having worked her way up through the "lower ranks" of the profession, came to the attention of Ebenezer Dyer, the head of a detective agency, who appreciated her talents and hired her. Although female private investigators had appeared in fiction previously, their adventures were written by men and seemed to be merely an attempt to fill the public's appetite for new and different detectives. Here, in a story published in July 1893, Brooke breaks up a criminal organization that will seem all too familiar to twenty-first century readers.*

THE GHOST OF
FOUNTAIN LANE

C. L. PIRKIS

"Will you be good enough to tell me how you procured my address?" said Miss Brooke, a little irritably. "I left strict orders that it was to be given to no one."

"I only obtained it with great difficulty from Mr. Dyer; had, in fact, to telegraph three times before I could get it," answered Mr. Clampe, the individual thus addressed. "I'm sure I'm awfully sorry to break into your holiday in this fashion, but—but pardon me if I say that it seems to be one in little more than name." Here he glanced meaningly at the newspapers, memoranda and books of reference with which the table at which Loveday sat was strewn.

She gave a little sigh.

"I suppose you are right," she answered; "it is a holiday in little more than name. I verily believe that we hard workers, after a time, lose our capacity for holiday-keeping. I thought I was pining for a week of perfect laziness and sea-breezes, and so I locked up my desk and fled. No sooner, however, do I find myself in full view of that magnificent sea-and-sky picture than I shut my eyes to it, fasten them instead on the daily papers and set my brains to work, *con amore*, on a ridiculous case that is never likely to come into my hands."

That "magnificent sea-and-sky picture" was one framed by the windows of a room on the fifth floor of the Métropole, at Brighton, whither Loveday, overtaxed in mind and body, had fled for a brief respite from hard work. Here Inspector Clampe, of the Local District Constabulary, had found her out, in order to press the claims of what seemed to him an important case upon her. He was a neat, dapper-looking man, of about fifty, with a manner less brusque and business-like than that of most men in his profession.

"Oh pray drop the ridiculous case," he said earnestly, "and set to work, '*con amore*,' upon another far from ridiculous, and most interesting."

"I'm not sure that it would interest me one quarter so much as the ridiculous one."

"Don't be sure till you've heard the particulars. Listen to this." Here the inspector took a newspaper-cutting from his pocket-book and read aloud as follows:

A cheque, the property of the Rev. Charles Turner, Vicar of East Downes, has been stolen under somewhat peculiar circumstances. It appears that the Rev. gentleman was suddenly called from home by the death of a relative, and thinking he might possibly be away some little time, he left with his wife four blank cheques, signed, for her to fill in as required. They were made payable to self or bearer, and were drawn on the West Sussex Bank. Mrs. Turner, when first questioned on the matter, stated that as soon as her husband had departed, she locked up these cheques in her writing desk. She subsequently, however, corrected this statement, and admitted having left them on the table while she went into the garden to cut some flowers. In all, she was absent, she says, about ten minutes. When she came in from cutting her flowers, she immediately put the cheques away. She had not counted them on receiving them from her husband, and when, as she put them into her Davenport,* she saw there were only three, she concluded that that was the number he had left with her. The loss of the cheque was not discovered until her husband's return, about a week later on. As soon as he was aware of the fact, he tele-graphed to the West Sussex Bank to stop payment, only, how-ever, to make the unpleasant discovery that the cheque, filled in to the amount of six hundred pounds, had been presented and cashed (in gold) two days previously. The clerk who cashed it took no particular notice of the person presenting it, except that he was of gentlemanly appearance, and declares himself to be quite incapable of identifying him. The largeness of the amount raised no suspicion in the mind of the clerk, as Mr. Turner is a man of good means, and since his marriage, about six months back, has been refurnishing the Vicarage, and paying away large sums for old oak furniture and for pictures.

"There, Miss Brooke," said the inspector as he finished reading, "if, in addition to these particulars, I tell you that one or two circumstances that have arisen seem to point suspicion in the direction of the young wife, I feel sure you will admit that a more interesting case, and one more worthy of your talents, is not to be found."

Loveday's answer was to take up a newspaper that lay beside her on the table. "So much for your interesting case," she said; "now listen to my ridiculous one." Then she read aloud as follows:

Authentic Ghost Story. The inhabitants of Fountain Lane, a small turning leading off Ship Street, have been greatly disturbed by the sudden appearance of a ghost in their midst. Last Tuesday night, between ten and eleven o'clock, a little

_____

* An ornamental writing desk with drawers.

girl named Martha Watts, who lives as a help to a shoemaker
and his wife at No. 5 in the lane, ran out into the streets in her
night-clothes in a great state of terror, saying that a ghost had
come to her bedside. The child refused to return to the house
to sleep, and was accordingly taken in by some neighbours. The
shoemaker and his wife, Freer by name, when questioned by the
neighbours on the matter, admitted, with great reluctance, that
they, too, had seen the apparition, which they described as being
a soldier-like individual, with a broad, white forehead and having
his arms folded on his breast. This description is, in all respects
confirmed by the child, Martha Watts, who asserts that the
ghost she saw reminded her of pictures she had seen of the great
Napoleon. The Freers state that it first appeared in the course
of a prayer-meeting held at their house on the previous night,
when it was distinctly seen by Mr. Freer. Subsequently, the wife,
awakening suddenly in the middle of the night, saw the apparition standing at the foot of the bed. They are quite at a loss for an
explanation of the matter. The affair has caused quite a sensation
in the district, and at the time of going to press, the lane is so
thronged and crowded by would-be ghost-seers that the inhabitants have great difficulty in going to and from their houses.

"A scare—a vulgar scare, nothing more," said the inspector as Loveday
laid aside the paper. "Now, Miss Brooke, I ask you seriously, supposing you
get to the bottom of such a stupid, commonplace fraud as that, will you in
any way add to your reputation?"

"And supposing I get to the bottom of such a stupid, commonplace
fraud as a stolen cheque, how much, I should like to know, do I add to my
reputation?"

"Well, put it on other grounds and allow Christian charity to have some
claims. Think of the misery in that gentleman's house unless suspicion can
be lifted from the young wife and directed to the proper quarter."

"Think of the misery of the landlord of the Fountain Lane houses if
all his tenants decamp in a body, as they no doubt will, unless the ghost
mystery is solved."

The inspector sighed. "Well, I suppose I must take it for granted that you will have nothing to do with the case," he said. "I brought the cheque with me, thinking you might like to see it."

"I suppose it's very much like other cheques?" said Loveday indifferently, and turning over her memoranda as if she meant to go back to her ghost again.

"Yes," said Mr. Clampe, taking the cheque from his pocket-book and glancing down at it. "I suppose the cheque is very much like other cheques. This little scribble of figures in pencil at the back—144,000—can scarcely be called a distinguishing mark."

"What's that, Mr. Clampe?" asked Loveday, pushing her memoranda on one side. "144,000 did you say?"

Her whole manner had suddenly changed from apathy to that of keenest interest.

Mr. Clampe, delighted, rose and spread the cheque before her on the table.

"The writing of the words six hundred pounds," he said, "bears so close a resemblance to Mr. Turner's signature, that the gentleman himself told me he would have thought it was his own writing if he had not known that he had not drawn a cheque for that amount on the given date. You see it is that round, school-boy's hand, so easy to imitate, I could write it myself with half-an-hour's practice; no flourishes, nothing distinctive about it."

Loveday made no reply. She had turned the cheque, and was now closely scrutinizing the pencilled figures at the back.

"Of course," continued the inspector, "those figures were not written by the person who wrote the figures on the face of the cheque. That, however, matters but little. I really do not think they are of the slightest importance in the case. They might have been scribbled by some one making a calculation as to the number of pennies in six hundred pounds—there are, as no doubt you know, exactly 144,000."

"Who has engaged your services in this case, the Bank or Mr. Turner?"

"Mr. Turner. When the loss of the cheque was first discovered, he was very excited and irate, and when he came to me the day before yesterday, I had much difficulty in persuading him that there was no need to telegraph to London for half-a-dozen detectives, as we could do the work quite as well as the London men. When, however, I went over to East Downes yesterday to look round and ask a few questions; I found things had altogether changed. He was exceedingly reluctant to answer any questions, lost his temper when I pressed them, and as good as told me that he wished he had not moved in the matter at all. It was this sudden change of demeanour that turned my thoughts in the direction of Mrs. Turner. A man must have a very strong reason for wishing to sit idle under a loss of six hundred pounds, for, of course, under the circumstances, the Bank will not bear the brunt of it."

"Some other motives may be at work in his mind, consideration for old servants, the wish to avoid a scandal in the house."

"Quite so. The fact, taken by itself, would give no ground for suspicion, but certainly looks ugly if taken in connection with another fact which I have since ascertained, namely, that during her husband's absence from home, Mrs. Turner paid off certain debts contracted by her in Brighton before the marriage, and amounting to nearly £500. Paid them off, too, in gold. I think I mentioned to you that the gentleman who presented the stolen cheque at the Bank preferred payment in gold."

"You are supposing not only a confederate, but also a vast amount of cunning as well as of simplicity on the lady's part."

"Quite so. Three parts cunning to one of simplicity is precisely what lady criminals are composed of. And it is, as a rule, that one part of simplicity that betrays them and leads to their detection."

"What sort of woman is Mrs. Turner in other respects?"

"She is young, handsome and of good birth, but is scarcely suited for the position of vicar's wife in a country parish. She has lived a good deal in society and is fond of gaiety, and, in addition, is a Roman Catholic, and, I am told, utterly ignores her husband's church and drives every Sunday to Brighton to attend mass."

"What about the servants in the house? Do they seem steady-going and respectable?"

"There was nothing on the surface to excite suspicion against any one of them. But it is precisely in that quarter than your services would be invaluable. It will, however, be impossible to get you inside the vicarage walls. Mr. Turner, I am confident, would never open his doors to you."

"What do you suggest?"

"I can suggest nothing better than the house of the village schoolmistress, or, rather, of the village schoolmistress's mother, Mrs. Brown. It is only a stone's throw from the vicarage; in fact, its windows overlook the vicarage grounds. It is a four-roomed cottage, and Mrs. Brown, who is a very respectable person, turns over a little money in the summer by receiving lady lodgers desirous of a breath of country air. There would be no difficulty in getting you in there; her spare bedroom is empty now."

"I should have preferred being at the vicarage, but if it cannot be, I must make the most of my stay at Mrs. Brown's. How do we get there?"

"I drove from East Downes here in a trap I hired at the village inn where I put up last night, and where I shall stay tonight. I will drive you, if you will allow me; it is only seven miles off. It's a lovely day for a drive; breezy and not too much dust. Could you be ready in about half an hour's time, say?"

But this, Loveday said, would be an impossibility. She had a special engagement that afternoon; there was a religious service in the town that she particularly wished to attend. It would not be over until three o'clock, and, consequently, not until half-past three would she be ready for the drive to East Downes.

Although Mr. Clampe looked unutterable astonishment at the claims of a religious service being set before those of professional duty, he made no demur to the arrangement, and accordingly half-past three saw Loveday and the inspector in a high-wheeled dog-cart rattling along the Marina in the direction of East Downes.

Loveday made no further allusion to her ghost story, so Mr. Clampe, out of politeness, felt compelled to refer to it.

"I heard all about the Fountain Lane ghost yesterday, before I started for East Downes," he said; "and it seemed to me, with all deference to you, Miss Brooke, an every-day sort of affair, the sort of thing to be explained by a heavy supper or an extra glass of beer."

"There are a few points in this ghost story that separate it from the every-day ghost story," answered Loveday. "For instance, you would expect that such emotionally religious people, as I have since found the Freers to be, would have seen a vision of angels, or at least a solitary saint. Instead, they see a soldier! A soldier, too, in the likeness of a man who is anathema maranatha* to every religious mind—the great Napoleon."

"To what denomination do the Freers belong?"

"To the Wesleyan. Their fathers and mothers before them were Wesleyans; their relatives and friends are Wesleyans, one and all, they say; and, most important item of all, the man's boot and shoe connection lies exclusively among Wesleyan ministers. This, he told me, is the most paying connection that a small boot-maker can have. Half-a-dozen Wesleyan ministers pay better than three times the number of Church clergy, for whereas the Wesleyan minister is always on the tramp among his people, the clergyman generally contrives in the country to keep a horse, or else turns student, and shuts himself up in his study."

"Ha, ha! Capital," laughed Mr. Clampe; "tell that to the Church Defence Society in Wales. Isn't this a first-rate little horse? In another ten minutes we shall be in sight of East Downes."

The long, dusty road down which they had driven was ending now in a narrow, sloping lane, hedged in on either side with hawthorns and wild plum trees. Through these, the August sunshine was beginning to slant now, and from a distant wood there came a faint sound of fluting and piping, as if the blackbirds were thinking of tuning up for their evening carols.

A sudden, sharp curve in this lane brought them in sight of East Downes, a tiny hamlet of about thirty cottages, dominated by the steeple of a church of early English architecture. Adjoining the church was the vicarage, a goodly-sized house, with extensive grounds, and in a lane running alongside these grounds were situated the village schools and the schoolmistress's house. The latter was simply a four-roomed cottage, standing in a pretty garden, with cluster roses and honeysuckle, now in the fullness of their August glory, climbing upwards to its very roof.

Outside this cottage Mr. Clampe drew rein.

---

* While the phrase is used to mean something like "truly accursed," it is actually two distinct words: "anathema," meaning accursed, and "Maranatha," meaning "the Lord is coming." The phrase appears at the end of Paul's first letter to the Corinthians, I Corinthians 16:22.

"If you'll give me five minutes' grace," he said, "I'll go in and tell the good woman that I have brought her, as a lodger, a friend of mine, who is anxious to get away for a time from the noise and glare of Brighton. Of course, the story of the stolen cheque is all over the place, but I don't think anyone has, at present, connected me with the affair. I am supposed to be a gentleman from Brighton, who is anxious to buy a horse the Vicar wishes to sell, and who can't quite arrange terms with him."

While Loveday waited outside in the cart, an open carriage drove past and then in through the vicarage gates. In the carriage were seated a gentleman and lady whom, from the respectful greetings they received from the village children, she conjectured to be the Rev. Charles and Mrs. Turner. Mr. Turner was sanguine-complexioned, red-haired, and wore a distinctly troubled expression of countenance. With Mrs. Turner's appearance Loveday was not favourably impressed. Although a decidedly handsome woman, she was hard-featured and had a scornful curl to her upper lip. She was dressed in the extreme of London fashion.

They threw a look of enquiry at Loveday as they passed, and she felt sure that enquiries as to the latest addition to Mrs. Brown's ménage would soon be afloat in the village.

Mr. Clampe speedily returned, saying that Mrs. Brown was only too delighted to get her spare-room occupied. He whispered a hint as they made their way up to the cottage door between borders thickly planted with stocks and mignonette.

It was:

"Don't ask her any questions, or she'll draw herself up as straight as a ramrod, and say she never listens to gossip of any sort. But just let her alone, and she'll run on like a mill-stream, and tell you as much as you'll want to know about everyone and everything. She and the village postmistress are great friends, and between them they contrive to know pretty much what goes on inside every house in the place."

Mrs. Brown was a stout, rosy-cheeked woman of about fifty, neatly dressed in a dark stuff gown with a big white cap and apron. She welcomed Loveday respectfully, and introduced, evidently with a little pride, her daughter, the village schoolmistress, a well-spoken young woman of about eight-and-twenty.

Mr. Clampe departed with his dog-cart to the village inn, announcing his intention of calling on Loveday at the cottage on the following morning before he returned to Brighton.

Miss Brown also departed, saying she would prepare tea. Left alone with Loveday, Mrs. Brown speedily unloosed her tongue. She had a dozen questions to ask respecting Mr. Clampe and his business in the village. Now, was it true that he had come to East Downes for the whole and sole purpose of buying one of the Vicar's horses? She had heard it whispered that he had been sent by the police to watch the servants at the vicarage. She hoped it was not true, for a more respectable set of servants were not to be met with in any house, far or near. Had Miss Brooke heard about that lost cheque? Such a terrible affair! She had been told that the story of it had reached London. Now, had Miss Brooke seen an account of it in any of the London papers?

Here a reply from Loveday in the negative formed a sufficient excuse for relating with elaborate detail the story of the stolen cheque. Except in its elaborateness of detail, it differed but little from the one Loveday had already heard.

She listened patiently, bearing in mind Mr. Clampe's hint, and asking no questions. And when, in about a quarter of an hour's time, Miss Brown came in with the tea-tray in her hand, Loveday could have passed an examination in the events of the daily family life at the vicarage. She could have answered questions as to the ill-assortedness of the newly-married couple; she knew that they wrangled from morning till night; that the chief subjects of their disagreement were religion and money matters; that the Vicar was hot-tempered, and said whatever came to the tip of his tongue; that the beautiful young wife, though slower of speech, was scathing and sarcastic, and that, in addition, she was wildly extravagant and threw money away in all directions.

In addition to these interesting facts, Loveday could have undertaken to supply information respecting the number of servants at the vicarage, together with their names, ages and respective duties.

During tea, conversation flagged somewhat; Miss Brown's presence evidently acted repressively on her mother, and it was not until the meal was over and Loveday was being shown to her room by Mrs. Brown that opportunity to continue the talk was found.

Loveday opened the ball by remarking on the fact that no Dissenting chapel was to be found in the village.

"Generally, wherever there is a handful of cottages, we find a church at one end and a chapel at the other," she said; "but here, willy-nilly, one must go to church."

"Do you belong to chapel, ma'am?" was Mrs. Brown's reply. "Old Mrs. Turner, the Vicar's mother, who died over a year ago, was so 'low' she was almost chapel, and used often to drive over to Brighton to attend the Countess of Huntingdon's church. People used to say that was bad enough in the Vicar's mother; but what was it compared with what goes on now— the Vicar's wife driving regularly every Sunday into Brighton to a Catholic Church to say her prayers to candles and images? I'm glad you like the room, ma'am. Feather bolster, feather pillows, do you see, ma'am? I've nothing in the way of flock or wool on either of my beds to make people's head ache." Here Mrs. Brown, by way of emphasis, patted and pinched the fat pillows and bolster showing above the spotless white counterpane.

Loveday stood at the cottage window drinking in the sweetness of the country air, laden now with the heavy evening scents of carnation and jessamine. Across the road, from the vicarage, came the loud clanging of a dinner-gong, and almost simultaneously the church clock chimed the hour—seven o'clock.

"Who is that person coming up the lane?" asked Loveday, her attention suddenly attracted by a tall, thin figure, dressed in shabby black, with a large, dowdyish bonnet, and carrying a basket in her hand as if she were returning from some errand. Mrs. Brown peeped over Loveday's shoulder.

"Ah, that's the peculiar young woman I was telling you about, ma'am— Maria Lisle, who used to be old Mrs. Turner's maid. Not that she is over young now; she's five-and-thirty if she's a day. The Vicar kept her on to be his wife's maid after the old lady died, but young Mrs. Turner will have nothing to do with her, she's not good enough for her; so Mr. Turner is just paying her £30 a year for doing nothing. And what Maria does with all that money it would be hard to say. She doesn't spend it on dress, that's certain, and she hasn't kith nor kin, not a soul belonging to her to give a penny to."

"Perhaps she gives it to charities in Brighton. There are plenty of outlets for money there."

"She may," said Mrs. Brown dubiously; "she is always going to Brighton whenever she gets a chance. She used to be a Wesleyan in old Mrs. Turner's time, and went regularly to all the revival meetings for miles round; what she is now, it would be hard to say. Where she goes to church in Brighton, no one knows. She drives over with Mrs. Turner every Sunday, but everyone knows nothing would induce her to go near the candles and images. Thomas—that's the coachman—says he puts her down at the corner of a dirty little street in mid-Brighton, and there he picks her up again after he has fetched Mrs. Turner from her church. No, there's something very queer in her ways."

Maria passed in through the lodge gates of the vicarage. She walked with her head bent, her eyes cast down to the ground.

"Something very queer in her ways," repeated Mrs. Brown. "She never speaks to a soul unless they speak first to her, and gets by herself on every possible opportunity. Do you see that old summer-house over there in the vicarage grounds—it stands between the orchard and kitchen garden—well, every evening at sunset, out comes Maria and disappears into it, and there she stays for over an hour at a time. And what she does there goodness only knows!"

"Perhaps she keeps books there, and studies."

"Studies! My daughter showed her some new books that had come down for the fifth standard the other day, and Maria turned upon her and said quite sharply that there was only one book in the whole world that people ought to study, and that book was the Bible."

"How pretty those vicarage gardens are," said Loveday, a little abruptly. "Does the Vicar ever allow people to see them?"

"Oh, yes, miss; he doesn't at all mind people taking a walk round them. Only yesterday he said to me, 'Mrs. Brown, if ever you feel yourself circumscribed'—yes, 'circumscribed' was the word—'just walk out of your garden-gate and in at mine and enjoy yourself at your leisure among my fruit-trees.' Not that I would like to take advantage of his kindness and make too free; but if you'd care, ma'am, to go for a walk through the grounds, I'll go with you with pleasure. There's a wonderful old cedar hard by the pond people have come ever so far to see."

"It's that old summer-house and little bit of orchard that fascinate me," said Loveday, putting on her hat.

"We shall frighten Maria to death if she sees us so near her haunt," said Mrs. Brown as she led the way downstairs. "This way, if you please, ma'am, the kitchen-garden leads straight into the orchard."

Twilight was deepening rapidly into night now. Bird notes had ceased, the whirr of insects, the croaking of a distant frog were the only sounds that broke the evening stillness.

As Mrs. Brown swung back the gate that divided the kitchen-garden from the orchard, the gaunt, black figure of Maria Lisle was seen approaching in an opposite direction.

"Well, really, I don't see why she should expect to have the orchard all to herself every evening," said Mrs. Brown, with a little toss of her head. "Mind the gooseberry bushes, ma'am, they do catch at your clothes so. My word! what a fine show of fruit the Vicar has this year! I never saw pear trees more laden!"

They were now in the bit of orchard to be seen from the cottage windows. As they rounded the corner of the path in which the old summer-house stood, Maria Lisle turned its corner at the farther end, and suddenly found herself almost face to face with them. If her eyes and not been so persistently fastened on the ground, she would have noted the approach of the intruders as quickly as they had noted hers. Now, as she saw them for the first time, she gave a sudden start, paused for a moment irresolutely, and then turned sharply and walked rapidly away in an opposite direction.

"Maria, Maria!" called Mrs. Brown, "don't run away; we sha'n't stay here for more than a minute or so."

Her words met with no response. The woman did not so much as turn her head.

Loveday stood at the entrance of the old summer-house. It was considerably out of repair, and most probably was never entered by anyone save Maria Lisle, its unswept, undusted condition suggesting colonies of spiders and other creeping things within.

Loveday braved them all and took her seat on the bench that ran round the little place in a semi-circle.

"Do try and overtake the girl, and tell her we shall be gone in a minute," she said, addressing Mrs. Brown. "I will wait here meanwhile. I am so sorry to have frightened her away in that fashion."

Mrs. Brown, under protest, and with a little grumble at the ridiculousness of "people who couldn't look other people in the face," set off in pursuit of Maria.

It was getting dim inside the summer-house now. There was, however, sufficient light to enable Loveday to discover a small packet of books lying in a corner of the bench on which she sat.

One by one she took them in her hand and closely scrutinized them. The first was a much read and pencil-marked Bible; the others were respectively, a congregational hymn-book, a book in a paper cover, on which was printed a flaming picture of a red and yellow angel, pouring blood and fire from out a big black bottle, and entitled *The End of the Age*, and a smaller book, also in a paper cover, on which was depicted a huge black horse, snorting fire and brimstone into ochre-coloured clouds. This book was entitled *The Year Book of the Saints*, and was simply a ruled diary with sensational mottoes for every day in the year. In parts, this diary was filled in with large and very untidy handwriting. In these books seemed to lie the explanation of Maria Lisle's love of evening solitude and the lonely old summer-house.

Mrs. Brown pursued Maria to the servants' entrance to the house, but could not overtake her, the girl making good her retreat there.

She returned to Loveday a little hot, a little breathless, and a little out of temper. It was all so absurd, she said; why couldn't the woman have stayed and had a chat with them? It wasn't as if she would get any harm out of the talk; she knew as well as everyone else in the village that she (Mrs. Brown) was no idle gossip, tittle-tattling over other people's affairs.

But here Loveday, a little sharply, cut short her meanderings.

"Mrs. Brown," she said, and to Mrs. Brown's fancy her voice and manner had entirely changed from that of the pleasant, chatty lady of half-an-hour ago, "I'm sorry to say it will be impossible for me to stay even one night in your pleasant home, I have just recollected some important business that I must transact in Brighton tonight. I haven't unpacked my portmanteau, so if you'll kindly have it taken to your garden-gate, I'll call for it as we drive past—I am going now, at once, to the inn, to see if Mr. Clampe can drive me back into Brighton tonight."

Mrs. Brown had no words ready wherewith to express her astonishment, and Loveday assuredly gave her no time to hunt for them. Ten minutes later saw her rousing Mr. Clampe from a comfortable supper, to which he had just settled himself, with the surprising announcement that she must get back to Brighton with as little delay as possible; now, would he be good enough to drive her there?

"We'll have a pair if they are to be had," she added. "The road is good; it will be moonlight in a quarter of an hour; we ought to do it in less than half the time we took coming."

While a phaeton and pair were being got ready, Loveday had time for a few words of explanation.

Maria Lisle's diary in the old summer-house had given her the last of the links in her chain of evidence that was to bring the theft of the cheque home to the criminal.

"It will be best to drive straight to the police station," she said; "they must take out three warrants, one for Maria Lisle, and two others respectively for Richard Steele, late Wesleyan minister of a chapel in Gordon Street, Brighton, and John Rogers, formerly elder of the same chapel. And let me tell you," she added with a little smile, "that these three worthies would most likely have been left at large to carry on their depredations for some little time to come if it had not been for that ridiculous ghost in Fountain Lane."

More than this there was not time to add, and when, a few minutes later, the two were rattling along the road to Brighton, the presence of the man, whom they were forced to take with them in order to bring back the horses to East Downes, prevented any but the most jerky and fragmentary of additions to this brief explanation.

"I very much fear that John Rogers has bolted," once Loveday whispered under her breath.

And again, a little later, when a smooth bit of road admitted of low-voiced talk, she said:

"We can't wait for the warrant for Steele; they must follow us with it to 15, Draycott Street."

"But I want to know about the ghost," said Mr. Clampe; "I am deeply interested in that ridiculous ghost."

"Wait till we get to 15, Draycott Street," was Loveday's reply; "when you've been there, I feel sure you will understand everything."

Church clocks were chiming a quarter to nine as they drove through Kemp Town at a pace that made the passersby imagine they must be bound on an errand of life and death.

Loveday did not alight at the police station, and five minutes' talk with the inspector in charge there was all that Mr. Clampe required to put things *en train* for the arrest of the three criminals.

It had evidently been an "excursionists' day" at Brighton. The streets leading to the railway station were thronged, and their progress along the bye streets was impeded by the overflow of traffic from the main road.

"We shall get along better on foot; Draycott Street is only a stone's throw from here," said Loveday; "there's a turning on the north side of Western Road that will bring us straight into it."

So they dismissed their trap, and Loveday, acting as cicerone* still, led the way through narrow turnings into the district, half town, half country, that skirts the road leading to the Dyke.

Draycott Street was not difficult to find. It consisted of two rows of newly-built houses of the eight-roomed, lodging-letting order. A dim light shone from the first-floor windows of number fifteen, but the lower window was dark and uncurtained, and a board hanging from its balcony rails proclaimed that it was to let unfurnished. The door of the house stood slightly ajar, and pushing it open, Loveday led the way up a flight of stairs—lighted halfway up with a paraffin lamp—to the first floor.

"I know the way. I was here this afternoon," she whispered to her companion. "This is the last lecture he will give before he starts for Judea; or, in other words, bolts with the money he has managed to conjure from other people's purses into his own."

The door of the room for which they were making, on the first floor, stood open, possibly on account of the heat. It laid bare to view a double row of forms, on which were seated some eight or ten persons in the attitude of all-absorbed listeners. Their faces were upturned, as if fixed on a preacher

---

* Tour guide.

at the farther end of the room, and wore that expression of rapt, painful interest that is sometimes seen on the faces of a congregation of revivalists before the smouldering excitement bursts into flame.

As Loveday and her companion mounted the last of the flight of stairs, the voice of the preacher—full, arrestive, resonant—fell upon their ear; and, standing on the small outside landing, it was possible to catch a glimpse of that preacher through the crack of the half-opened door.

He was a tall, dignified-looking man, of about five-and-forty, with a close crop of white hair, black eye-brows and remarkably luminous and expressive eyes. Altogether his appearance matched his voice: it was emphatically that of a man born to sway, lead, govern the multitude.

A boy came out of an adjoining room and asked Loveday respectfully if she would not like to go in and hear the lecture. She shook her head.

"I could not stand the heat," she said. "Kindly bring us chairs here."

The lecture was evidently drawing to a close now, and Loveday and Mr. Clampe, as they sat outside listening, could not resist an occasional thrill of admiration at the skilful manner in which the preacher led his hearers from one figure of rhetoric to another, until the oratorical climax was reached.

"That man is a born orator," whispered Loveday; "and in addition to the power of the voice has the power of the eye. That audience is as completely hypnotized by him as if they had surrendered themselves to a professional mesmerist."

To judge from the portion of the discourse that fell upon their ear, the preacher was a member of one of the many sects known under the generic name Millenarian. His topic was pollyon* and the great battle of Armageddon. This he described as vividly as if it were being fought out under his very eye, and it would scarcely be an exaggeration to say that he made the cannon roar in the ears of his listeners and the tortured cries of the wounded wail in them. He drew an appalling picture of the carnage of that battlefield, of the blood flowing like a river across the plain, of the mangled men and horses, with the birds of prey swooping down from all quarters,

---

* The Greek name for Abbadon, the "Destroyer," the "Angel of Death," the leader of the army of locusts mentioned in the Book of Revelation.

and the stealthy tigers and leopards creeping out from their mountain lairs. "And all this time," he said, suddenly raising his voice from a whisper to a full, thrilling tone, "gazing calmly down upon the field of slaughter, with bent brows and folded arms, stands the imperial Apollyon. Apollyon did I say? No, I will give him his right name, the name in which he will stand revealed in that dread day, Napoleon! Napoleon it will be who, in that day, will stand as the embodiment of Satanic majesty. Out of the mists suddenly he will walk, a tall, dark figure, with frowning brows and firm-set lips, a man to rule, a man to drive, a man to kill! Apollyon the mighty, Napoleon the imperial, they are one and the same—"

Here a sob and a choking cry from one of the women in the front seats interrupted the discourse and sent the small boy who acted as verger into the room with a glass of water.

"That sermon has been preached before," said Loveday. "Now can you not understand the origin of the ghost in Fountain Lane?"

"Hysterics are catching, there's another woman off now," said Mr. Clampe; "it's high time this sort of thing was put a stop to. Pearson ought to be here in another minute with his warrant."

The words had scarcely passed his lips before heavy steps mounting the stairs announced that Pearson and his warrant were at hand.

"I don't think I can be of any further use," said Loveday, rising to depart. "If you like to come to me tomorrow morning at my hotel at ten o'clock I will tell you, step by step, how I came to connect a stolen cheque with a ridiculous ghost."

"We had a tussle—he showed fight at first," said Mr. Clampe, when, precisely at ten o'clock the next morning, he called upon Miss Brooke at the Métropole. "If he had had time to get his wits together and had called some of the men in that room to the rescue, I verily believe we should have been roughly handled and he might have slipped through our fingers after all. It's wonderful what power these 'born orators,' as you call them, have over minds of a certain order."

"Ah, yes," answered Loveday thoughtfully; "we talk glibly enough about 'magnetic influence,' but scarcely realize how literally true the phrase is. It is my firm opinion that the 'leaders of men,' as they are called, have as absolute and genuine hypnotic power as any modern French expert, although perhaps it may be less consciously exercised. Now tell me about Rogers and Maria Lisle."

"Rogers had bolted, as you expected he would have done, with the six hundred pounds he had been good enough to cash for his reverend colleague. Ostensibly he had started for Judea to collect the elect, as he phrased it, under one banner. In reality, he has sailed for New York, where, thanks to the cable, he will be arrested on his arrival and sent back by return packet. Maria Lisle was arrested this morning on a charge of having stolen the cheque from Mrs. Turner. By the way, Miss Brooke, I think it is almost a pity you didn't take possession of her diary when you had the chance. It would have been invaluable evidence against her and her rascally colleagues."

"I did not see the slightest necessity for so doing. Remember, she is not one of the criminal classes, but a religious enthusiast, and when put upon her defence will at once confess and plead religious conviction as an extenuating circumstance—at least, if she is well advised she will do so. I never read anything that laid bare more frankly than did this diary the mischief that the sensational teaching of these millenarians is doing at the present moment. But I must not take up your time with moralizing. I know you are anxious to learn what, in the first instance, led me to identify a millenarian preacher with a receiver of stolen property."

"Yes, that's it; I want to know about the ghost; that's the point that interests me."

"Very well. As I told you yesterday afternoon, the first thing that struck me as remarkable in this ghost story was the soldierly character of the ghost. One expects emotionally religious people like Freer and his wife to see visions, but one also expects those visions to partake of the nature of those emotions, and to be somewhat shadowy and ecstatic. It seemed to me certain that this Napoleonic ghost must have some sort of religious significance to these people. This conviction it was that set my thoughts running in the direction of the millenarians, who have attached a religious significance (although not a polite one) to the name of Napoleon by embodying the evil Apollyon in the person of a descendant of the great Emperor, and endowing him with all the qualities of his illustrious ancestor. I called upon the Freers, ordered a pair of boots, and while the man was taking my measure, I asked him a few very pointed questions on these millenarian notions. The man prevaricated a good deal at first, but at length was driven to admit that he and his wife were millenarians at heart, that, in fact, the prayer meeting at which the Napoleonic ghost had made its first appearance was a millenarian one, held by a man who had at one time been a Wesleyan preacher in the chapel in Gordon Street, but who had been dismissed from his charge there because his teaching had been held to be unsound. Freer further stated that this man had been so much liked that many members of the congregation seized every opportunity that presented itself of attending his ministrations, some openly, others, like himself and his wife, secretly, lest they might give offence to the elders and ministers of their chapel."

"And the bootmaking connection suffer proportionately," laughed Mr. Clampe.

"Precisely. A visit to the Wesleyan chapel in Gordon Street and a talk with the chapel attendant enabled me to complete the history of this inhibited preacher, the Rev. Richard Steele. From this attendant I ascertained that a certain elder of their chapel, John Rogers by name, had seceded from their communion, thrown in his lot with Richard Steele, and that the two together were now going about the country preaching that the world would come to an end on Thursday, April 11th, 1901, and that five years before this event, viz., on the 5th of March, 1896, one hundred and forty-four thousand living saints would be caught up to heaven. They furthermore announced that this translation would take place in the land of Judea, that, shortly, saints from all parts of the world would be hastening thither, and that in view of this event a society had been formed to provide homes—a series, I suppose—for the multitudes who would otherwise be homeless. Also (a very vital point this), that subscriptions for this society would be gladly received by either gentleman. I had arrived so far in my ghost enquiry when you came to me, bringing the stolen cheque with its pencilled figures, 144,000."

"Ah, I begin to see!" murmured Mr. Clampe.

"It immediately occurred to me that the man who could make persons see an embodiment of his thought at will, would have very little difficulty in influencing other equally receptive minds to a breach of the ten command-ments. The world, it seems to me, abounds in people who are little more than blank sheets of paper, on which a strong hand may transcribe what it will—hysteric subjects, the doctors would call them; hypnotic subjects others would say; really the line that divides the hysteric condition from the hypnotic is a very hazy one. So now, when I saw your stolen cheque, I said to myself, 'there is a sheet of blank paper somewhere in that country vicarage, the thing is to find it out.'"

"Ah, good Mrs. Brown's gossip made your work easy to you there."

"It did. She not only gave me a complete summary of the history of the people within the vicarage walls, but she put so many graphic touches to that history that they lived and moved before me. For instance, she told me that Maria Lisle was in the habit of speaking of Mrs. Turner as a 'Child of the Scarlet Woman,' a 'Daughter of Babylon,' and gave me various other minute particulars, which enabled me, so to speak, to see Maria Lisle going about her daily duties, rendering her mistress reluctant service, hating her in her heart as a member of a corrupt faith, and thinking she was doing God service by despoiling her of some of her wealth, in order to devote it to what seemed to her a holy cause. I would like here to read to you two entries which I copied from her diary under dates respectively August 3rd (the day the cheque was lost) and August 7th (the following Sunday), when Maria no doubt found opportunity to meet Steele at some prayer-meeting in Brighton."

Here Loveday produced her note-book and read from it as follows:

Today I have spoiled the Egyptians! Taken from a Daughter of Babylon that which would go to increase the power of the Beast!

"And again, under date August 7th, she writes:"

I have handed today to my beloved pastor that of which I despoiled at Daughter of Babylon. It was blank, but he told me he would fill it in so that 144,000 of the elect would be each the richer by one penny. Blessed thought! this is the doing of my most unworthy hand.

"A wonderful farrago, that diary of distorted Scriptural phraseology— wild eulogies on the beloved pastor, and morbid ecstatics, such as one would think could be the outcome only of a diseased brain. It seems to me that Portland or Broadmoor, and the ministrations of a sober-minded chaplain, may be about the happiest thing that could befall Maria Lisle at this period of her career. I think I ought to mention in this connection that when at the religious service yesterday afternoon (to attend which I slightly postponed my drive to East Downes), I heard Steele pronounce a fervid eulogy on those who had strengthened his hands for the fight which he knew it would shortly fall to his lot to wage against Apollyon, I did not wonder at weak-minded persons like Maria Lisle, swayed by such eloquence, setting up new standards of right and wrong for themselves."

"Miss Brooke, another question or two. Can you in any way account for the sudden payment of Mrs. Turner's debts—a circumstance that led me a little astray in the first instance?"

"Mrs. Brown explained the matter easily enough. She said that a day or two back, when she was walking on the other side of the vicarage hedge, and the husband and wife in the garden were squabbling as usual over money-matters, she heard Mr. Turner say indignantly, 'only a week or two ago I gave you nearly £500 to pay your debts in Brighton, and now there comes another bill.'"

"Ah, that makes it plain enough. One more question and I have done. I have no doubt there's something in your theory of the hypnotic power (unconsciously exercised) of such men as Richard Steele, although, at the same time, it seems to me a trifle far-fetched and fanciful. But even admitting it, I don't see how you account for the girl, Martha Watts, seeing the ghost. She was not present at the prayer-meeting which called the ghost into being, nor does she appear in any way to have come into contact with the Rev. Richard Steele."

"Don't you think that ghost-seeing is quite as catching as scarlet-fever or measles?" answered Loveday, with a little smile. "Let one member of a family see a much individualized and easily described ghost, such as the one these good people saw, and ten to one others in the same house will see it before the week is over. We are all in the habit of asserting that 'seeing is believing.' Don't you think the converse of the saying is true also, and that 'believing is seeing'?"

Geraldine Bonner (1870–1930) was an American journalist and author, whose father John Bonner was also a journalist and historical writer. By 1899, according to her father's obituary, Geraldine Bonner had already established a reputation as a "well-known" magazine writer and novelist. Though she is best remembered for her Lady Laura, a gentlewoman-burglar featured in her novel The Castlecourt Diamond Case *(1906), the following story features—what else!—an enterprising young journalist who sets out to save a man wrongly accused of murder. The story won a prize in a competition run by* The Black Cat *magazine and first appeared in June 1899.*

THE STATEMENT OF JARED JOHNSON

GERALDINE BONNER

I am going to write my side of the famous Johnson Case.

It's a pretty hard thing to go over in cold blood, but I want the public to hear my version of the story. They know the case against me has been dismissed and they've read in the papers what I said, but it's been so mixed up and so misrepresented that I've decided to make my own state-ment—to write down as simply and as honestly as I can just how it was I came to be suspected.

My name is Jared Johnson and until I was arrested on the 23d of last December, I was the janitor of the Fremont Building, and had been so for two years past.

The Fremont, as people know now, since the trial made it famous, is an old building off Washington Square. It was one of those houses that still exist in that quarter of the city, which used to be the homes of the gentry and gradually got down in the world till they were first sliced off into flats, and then split up into offices.

The Fremont had been a fine, well built house in the beginning, and even when I came into it was in good repair. But it was old-fashioned, without elevators or electric lights, and the offices rented for low prices.

The top story had been used as a photograph gallery, and had long glass skylights in the ceiling. But that was before my time. Ever since I'd been janitor it had been leased by a society of ladies for a studio. One batch painted there all the morning and another all the afternoon. They had models who used to pose for them and who were forever clattering up and down stairs—mostly Italians and generally a pretty tough-looking lot.

This room was a good deal of a charge on me, for I had to keep it heated up to a tremendous temperature, because the models stood up to be painted in their skins as God made them. And, if they were dagoes, I couldn't let them take their deaths. One end of the room, under the corner skylight, was curtained off for them to use as a dressing room.

Below this were four floors of offices and lodgings, and in the basement I and my wife, Rosy, had our rooms. I have to be particular about describing all this, because I want those who read my statement to have everything clear in their minds.

Just about the middle of December there was a great frost, the worst cold snap I remember, and I came to New York from Ohio when I was twelve. On the morning of December 17th Rosy told me that the thermometer outside Miss Maitland, the typewriter's, window, had dropped to 3 above zero. It was mortal cold. I was kept busy building fires and seeing that the steam heat was on full pressure.

I was proud of the old Fremont for not a pipe in her burst or froze. And next door in the Octagon Building, a brand new skyscraper, twelve stories, and with all the modern improvements, the pipes on our side burst and froze so that the ice was clogged down the sides of them in a huge mass with icicles as long as your arm.

I noticed this on the morning of December 17th when I was rubbing off the skylights in the studio. I was standing on a step-ladder when I looked up at the wall of the Octagon rising like a cliff, and just on the angle, a little above our roof, were the pipes with the ice wrapped round them like a winding sheet. I couldn't help laughing for they'd blown so about the Octagon and her modern improvements.

Two days later the black frost broke and there was the biggest thaw that ever was seen. It got soft and warm like Spring, the streets began to swim with water, and all day long the boys were coming down from the offices complaining of the steam heat. I was on the rush all day, for to add to everything else it was Saturday, and Rosy and I have most of the building to ourselves that day and we do the cleaning.

But we didn't do as much as usual that Saturday, for, as I had to tell on the trial, and so must repeat it now, Rosy and I had fallen out. We'd been bickering for quite a while past and Saturday it seemed as if we couldn't meet on the stairs or hand each other a broom or a pail without snapping and nagging. I'm not blaming her, for I was as ugly as she, only my temper is not of that kind. It's the still, sulky sort, and it rises slowly but takes a long time to cool.

The trouble between us was this—Heaven forgive me for raking it all up after Rosy proved herself to be the truest wife a man ever had, but it's part of my statement, and has to go in—Rosy was jealous. She'd always been inclined that way, and when we were first married and everything she did seemed just about right, I tried never to bother or annoy her.

But after five years of marriage I wasn't quite so considerate, and though I swear before Heaven I never did aught that any man mightn't do without shame or blame, I wasn't so mindful of what Rosy liked or disliked. I know now that, without meaning it, I must have provoked her often. I suspect I did it to tease her a little, and I suspect I did it to prove to her that I was my own master and wasn't going to have any woman dictating to me.

It was one of the models up in the ladies' studio that Rosy was jealous about. Most of them being dagoes, as black as mulattoes, and only speaking their own talk, I had no words with them. But there was one of them, Alice Merrion, that was of Irish parentage but American born, and with her I struck up an acquaintance, and we used to stop and pass the time of day when we met on the stairs or in the hall.

Rosy took a dislike to Alice Merrion right from the start. She said she couldn't bear her because she was a model. Nothing that you could say would make Rosy believe that a girl could be honest and earn her living that way.

As for Alice Merrion's looks—she couldn't understand why any one wanted to paint her picture. To tell the truth, I often thought this too, for Alice wasn't what I'd call a pretty girl. She had freckles, yellowish-green eyes and a big bush of red hair that stood out like flames round her head.

I liked the girl and I was sorry for her. She was one of the best I ever knew, honest as a die and straight as a string for all her being a model. She supported her mother, and if ever I was sure of anything in my life, I was sure of Alice Merrion's character. But I wasn't any more taken with her than a married man might be honestly taken with any decent girl.

On Saturday afternoon, the ladies going home early, I made it my business to clean up the studio and lock it till Monday morning. On Saturday, December 19th, the ladies left even earlier than usual, the day settling down dark and threatening rain, and about four I went up with my broom and pail.

I was mightily surprised when I opened the door to see Alice sitting huddled up, cowering over the stove. She was right under the middle skylight and the gray, wintery light fell in on her red hair that was loosely knotted up and looked like a fiery crown. From under her skirt her bare feet were thrust out on the stove ledge, and she had a shawl folded round her shoulders, with her bare arms, white as marble, coming out.

"Why, Alice," said I, "what's up? It's past four and here you are, not even dressed yet."

She looked up at me and I saw that her cheeks were pale and her eyes looked dull and heavy.

"I feel sick," she said, drawing her hand over her forehead, and pushing back her hair. "I've got something sure. A little while ago I was as hot as this stove, and now I'm freezing."

She crouched over it spreading out her hands. I touched one of them; it was like ice. As I stood looking at her I heard the first drops of rain—big, heavy, slow drops—fall on the skylight.

"You've caught a bad cold," I said to her. "You want something to warm you up. Don't you think a cup of tea would do you good?"

Her face brightened directly.

"Oh, Mr. Johnson," she said, "do you think you could get me one? I didn't have a bite of lunch today. I felt so bad. And then I stood here for two hours and that's hard work, even when you're well. I think if I could get something hot I'd feel better."

She looked, up at me with her big, yellowish eyes shining through the gray light, and if ever I was sorry for a woman it was for her. I wished that Rosy wasn't so down on her and I'd have taken her to our rooms and given her a good meal.

"Rest here easy," I said to her, "and I'll get you a bite that will brace you up. I won't be long," and I went out and down the stairs feeling angrier than ever with Rosy for her senseless prejudice.

I hoped and prayed that there might be no one in the kitchen and things went my way for once. Rosy was not there. So I made a little brew of tea, cut some bread and butter, put it on a tray and set off up the stairs.

And it was here that my luck deserted me. For, on the second landing, I met Miss Maitland going out.

"What's the matter?" says she, looking at the tray. "Any one sick?"

It didn't cross my mind not to tell the truth and I answered:

"The model, ma'am, on the top floor, has caught a chill and feels bad."

Miss Maitland laughed and went down the stairs and her testimony in court, if you remember, was pretty damaging for me.

On the fourth floor I ran into Mr. Raymond on the landing. Mr. Raymond is my favorite in the whole Fremont. He is a stenographer and rents all the back rooms on that floor, some of them for offices and the rest for his own lodgings.

"Hullo, Johnson," he says to me in his jolly way, "taking that up to me? Made a mistake this time. That's not my particular tipple."

I laughed, for we all knew that Mr. Raymond's tipple was a pretty strong one.

"No, sir," I said. "It's for Alice Merrion in the studio. She's taken with a chill. She's had nothing to eat since morning and I thought this would warm her up a little."

"Ah, poor girl!" he says, going on down the passage to his own rooms. Then over his shoulder he called: "If you want anything stronger—if she feels faint, or anything—just drop in on me and I'll give it to you."

And he went down the passage. Those two meetings were about as bad for me as they could be, as it turned out afterward.

I went into the studio and found Alice just as I had left her. She drank the tea and ate the bread with a relish and I began to get things ready for my cleaning. Now and then we spoke to each other, and betweenwhiles we could hear the rain drumming on the skylight. It grew dark and leaden, and, as I moved, I could see through the skylights the big wall of the Octagon, with the windows springing out in yellow squares as the gases were lit.

When Alice had finished, I knew she'd want to dress and go home, so I made an excuse to go. She watched me as I set the tea things back on the tray and then said suddenly:

"You're very good to me; let's shake hands."

I was surprised, but took her hand and shook it.

"You're a good girl," I said to her, "mind you remember that I'm always your friend."

"Thanks, Jared Johnson," said she quite solemnly, "I know that. Good-bye."

I turned round and went, some way or other feeling sort of strange and awed. I shut the door behind me and as I was on the stairs I heard her lock it.

In the kitchen I found Rosy. The moment she saw the tray her face darkened, and she pulled up short in her work and eyed me with a sharp look. I was irritable myself, angry with her for her treatment of Alice Merrion, and when she looked at me that way, it made me blaze up. Without waiting for her to ask me, I told her who the tray was for and where I had been.

I don't think it's necessary for me to tell just what we said to each other, but we had a quarrel—a bitter one. Now that both of us have felt what real misery is, we realize with shame what a pair of crazy fools we were.

But we thought of nothing then but our own anger. 1 don't remember all I said. I felt that black rage a man sometimes feels when a woman he loves and honors flings in his teeth low meannesses he never thought of doing. In the middle of it I got up and ran out of the room, banging the door. I went down to the cellar, and stayed there all night sleeping on a pile of gunny sacks in front of the furnace.

The next day Rosy and I were about as stiff to each other as we could be. We hardly spoke at all and ate our meals in a heavy silence. Monday morning broke with a blue sky and sunlight outside, but between us there was still cloudy weather.

I got up early, for I had to build fires in some of the offices, especially in the studio, which, by eight o'clock, was supposed to be warmed and ready for the first class. As I went up the third flight of stairs, Mr. Raymond came out on the landing.

"Hullo! Johnson," says he, "what the devil's the matter with this building? Is she settling?"

"The Fremont's as good as she ever was, sir," I answered. "What's the matter?"

"The ceiling's come down in my bathroom," says he. "Early this morning—whang! bang!—down she came. Come and see the scene of carnage."

I followed him into the bathroom, which opened off the end of the passage, and there, sure enough, the ceiling was down. I picked up a piece of the plaster and felt that it was wet.

"A leak," I said, "the rain's come in above."

Oh, then, he says, suddenly, that explains the crash of glass I heard Saturday evening. There was a tremendous smashing of glass from somewhere up there.

This startled me. I suppose I looked sort of alarmed, for Mr. Raymond said, "I'll go up with you. Probably the skylight's broken."

We ran up the last flight and tried the studio door. It was locked, and when I tried my key I found that there was one already in the keyhole.

I don't know then just what I thought, but I know a deadly feeling of fear took hold of my heart. Mr. Raymond must have seen it in my face.

"Break in the door," says he in a low voice, and, as he spoke, he put his shoulder to the panel and pressed. In a moment we had ripped off the old socket that held the lock and the door burst in.

There was a sudden sharp current of air, cold and wet, and the brown curtain over the models' dressing corner swelled out on the draught. A window was open somewhere and part of the floor was dark with rain stains.

We shut the door with the key still in the lock and ran to where the curtain fell back into its straight folds. Behind it we saw a sight that neither of us will ever forget.

Alice Merrion lay on her face on the floor, the skylight above her broken, and the fragments of glass scattered in every direction.

She was fully dressed, except for her shoes, one of which she held in her hand. Through the broken skylight the rain had beaten upon her till her clothes, the floor, her hair, were oozing moisture. The latter was wet with something else which dyed it a deeper red. The back of her skull was fractured and partly driven in. She was rigid in death, her eyes open, and an expression of strange, terrified surprise stamped upon her features.

That first glimpse impressed every detail of the room upon my mind. Her hat and jacket were hanging from a peg in the wall. On the shelf under the square of looking-glass lay some hair-pins and her purse. All about—on her dress, in her hair, on the floor—shone bits of the shivered skylight. The panes of glass were of a good size and were fitted into light, thin supports of iron. Just in the middle two of these were bowed downward.

We bent over her to see if there were any signs of life, but she was cold and stiff as a marble statue. The physicians afterward said that when we found her she had been dead about thirty-six hours. She had evidently been putting on her shoes when struck down by the terrific blow that killed her.

That is as truthful a description as I can write of the finding of Alice Merrion's body. I ought to know how to do it by this time. I've not only told it so often, but I've dreamed it night after night till I wonder if I'm going to go on dreaming it forever.

The next day I was arrested on suspicion as the murderer and a week later was indicted by the Grand Jury. My trial followed in two months.

I never knew until I was in danger of losing my life on circumstantial evidence how important the most insignificant things can become when people are looking for incriminating actions and words. Foolish things I had said came up against me as black as night. The cup of tea I took the girl was as bad for me as if it had been a cup of poison. But worst of all was the quarrel I had with Rosy. It all had to come out, and the newspapers that were not on my side said it was as bad for me as if I'd been caught red-handed.

I could see as plain as anybody that the case against me was a strong one. It started on the theory that I was in love with Alice Merrion. Both Rosy and I acknowledged that we'd more than once quarreled about her. On the afternoon of December 19th I had had a final interview with her. There were different opinions as to what this had been about. Some had it that she'd threatened to expose me to my wife, who was jealous already; others that she'd given me to understand she wouldn't have anything to do with me. Whatever she'd said, she'd scared or angered me till I'd crept up on her from the back and struck her dead with one—or some thought two—savage blows.

To turn aside suspicion I had then locked the door and left the key in it, had broken the skylight—the noise of which Mr. Raymond had heard at a few minutes after five—and, under cover of the dark, had dropped from the roof to the fire-escapes. When I got to the kitchen my nerves were naturally unstrung and I had quarrelled with my wife, left the room, and had not been seen again until the morning.

The one link in the chain which did not fit was how I had brought the tea tray down with me. The only way I could have done this was to have put it outside the door, and then, after escaping by the fire-ladders, crept back for it and come down again. This, people said, was a proof of my fiendish coolness and cunning.

The fact that the evidence pointed to no one else made it all the worse for me. There did not seem to be a human creature but myself who could be suspected. The girl had no enemies and no followers that anybody knew of. She had led a quiet and perfectly respectable life. That the object was not theft was proved by the fact that her purse, containing twenty dollars, was untouched. There was no doubt that somebody had murdered her, and the murder could be fastened on no one but me.

One of the questions over which there was great argument was what instrument or weapon had been used to deliver the blow. On the upper part of the occiput, just below the crown, the skin and flesh had been cleanly cut as though struck with something sharp-edged or pointed.

There were expert surgeons called up to examine the wounds and they each had their own ideas as to what the murderer had used. One thought a bayonet, or something shaped like a bayonet, such as a pickaxe or an ice-pick. Another said a hatchet or axe. And one—he was the most cel-ebrated of the lot—said he thought that not one but two implements had been employed, a sharp one which cut the scalp, and a heavy one which fractured the skull.

It was this man who said that the murderer had evidently been in a state of frenzy, as the blow or blows must have been of terrific force to so crush the skull. His evidence started the theory that the girl had been killed by a maniac who had entered and come out by the skylight.

The first days of the trial were so terrible I hate to think of them. The whole world seemed against me. The reporters used to come and talk with me and then write me up as "a man with the face of an assassin" or describe me as "the human bloodhound."

Some of them were friendly fellows too—used to clap me on the back and say, "Brace up, old boy, they've not got enough evidence to convict you"; but when it came to believing in me, that was quite another story. I was Jared Johnson The Suspect, as they called me, a good case to make copy out of, and that was all.

There was one of them that I didn't take much notice of or stock in at first. He was the youngest looking chap for his age I ever saw. When I first saw him I thought he was about eighteen. He was a little, thin, smooth-faced, light-haired boy, and new to the business, as you could see by the quiet bashful sort of way he hung round when the others were there.

One day he got at me alone and began to talk to me, easy and natural, as man to man. He told me he was from Ohio, as I was, and that broke the ice right off. Then he said his name was John Paul Hayne, and he was twenty-six years old. He sat quite a while talking of places in the old state we both knew, and I got to feel as if I was a civilized Christian once more, not an Apache Indian that all the world was chasing. When he got up to go, he stood round for a minute in an uneasy sort of way, and then he sud-denly says to me, looking me straight in the eye:

"Jared Johnson, you're not guilty of that murder."

He didn't say it as if he was asking a question, or as if he was trying to persuade himself—he just stated a fact. I looked back at him and I said as quietly as he:

"You're right. But what makes you think so?"

"Oh," says he, speaking in a queer sort of way he had with him, "I can see a church by daylight. I've seen a lot while I've been loafing round here."

The next time he came we had a long talk. He told me he'd viewed the premises and the body the morning the murder was discovered. He was sent by his paper, *The Scoop*. And since then he'd been there several times on his own account.

"And you know," says he, "I've come to a conclusion. The thing that killed Alice Merrion didn't *go* through the skylight, it *came* through it."

"What makes you think that?" I asked.

"The way the iron stanchions were bent. They say the weight of the man hanging to them and pulling himself up bowed them down. Now, I say that's a mistake. To bend those rods that way a man would have to be a giant—a second Sandow.* It was the weight of something that struck them from above—a tremendous weight—that bent and almost broke them."

"What could strike down from there?" I asked. "There's nothing between the roof of the Fremont and Heaven."

"That's the trick," said he. "You tell me what could, and I'll tell you what killed Alice Merrion."

It seemed to me all idle talk, but I couldn't help saying:

"I don't see how you make that out. Alice was struck on the back of the head. If a thing fell on her it would have caught her on the top of her head. She must have been standing right under the skylight."

He leaned forward and put his fingers on my arm, his eyes shining like jewels.

"Johnson," says he, "you're an honest man, I've no doubt, but you've not got much sense. Don't you remember that she was putting on her shoes? Did you ever see a woman put on her shoes? She leans over so that her head's bent forward this way—" and he bent his head far down till the back of his neck was stretched out beyond his collar.

"I guess you and the doctor have got the same idea," said I. "There is nothing that could come down on her from above and strike her dead with one blow but a madman who had been creeping about on the roofs."

---

* Eugen Sandow (1867–1925), a famous German strongman, known as the "father" of bodybuilding.

"I worked over that theory for some time," says he, "but I've come to the conclusion that there's nothing in it. Between the breaking of the glass and the falling of the blow she could have got to the door. No—she was surprised as she was putting on her shoes—surprised and killed in the same instant."

I thought of the expression of her face that morning when we found her dead and stiff, and I looked at John Paul Hayne and nodded without speaking.

After this I saw him every few days. He asked me lots of questions and I got to answering him pretty freely, for I saw that he didn't publish what I said, and I got a great liking for him. He was forever starting theories, but I didn't see that they came to anything.

It was just about this time that the second cold snap struck the city. It was precious cold in my cell and I thought of the old Fremont and Rosy's sitting room with a fire shining through the bars of the grate. Lord! but those times seemed a long way off!

Rosy came to see me with her ears tied up in a worsted scarf. She said it was not as cold as the first snap, but, none the less, the Octagon pipes had frozen and burst again. Some of the Octagon people had come over to the Fremont to ask for rooms. They said the Octagon was a sham, run up by contract and badly built from the curbstone to the chimneys.

Because of these applications the owners of the Fremont were thinking of tearing out the inside of the studio and fitting it up for offices. But, so far, it stood just as it did the morning Alice Merrion's body was found there. The detectives working on the case wouldn't have it touched.

The cold spell was a short one. The back of the winter was broken and it gave way in three days with a big thaw. The sun beat down like Spring and everything ran water.

My trial was going on daily. The evidence for the defense was nearly all in. I was in a strange state of mind—sometimes I felt wild as if I was being smothered; then again I'd be dull and dead-like, not caring what happened.

People kept on saying "They can't convict you on the evidence they've got." But I didn't care much for that. Even if the jury disagreed I was ruined. I'd have to go back to the world and for the rest of my life be pointed out as the man who had brutally murdered a poor, sick, defenseless girl. I'd rather have died, only for Rosy.

It was the afternoon of the third warm day. I'll never forget that day if I live to be two hundred. The window of the cell was open and every now and then a little breath of soft air came in—air full of Spring.

I was alone, sick at heart and dead beat. I'd been in the courtroom since morning. They'd had Rosy on the stand, and the poor girl had got mixed up and made things between us look as bad as could be. Then, seeing what she had done, and being weak and frightened, she'd gone off into hysterics, and they could not get her into any sort of condition to go on. So the case had been called off until Monday and I'd seen Rosy taken out sobbing and half dead, and been brought back to my cell.

I was sitting on the edge of the bed when I heard the rattling of bolts and voices at the door, and in came Hayne. The light from the window fell full on his face and it shone as if there was a lamp lit inside it. The look of him brought me on to my feet as if I'd been yanked up by a derrick. I said something, I don't know what. Maybe I didn't speak at all, but I know I tried to.

Without saying a word he took off his hat and held it out to me. I looked at it stupidly. It was a brown derby, the top broken and split.

"Look at that, Johnson," he said, shaking it under my eyes—"look at it well. It's saved you. Do you understand me? It's saved your life."

I stared at him and tried to say something but my tongue wouldn't work.

He pushed me back on the bed and, holding the hat in front of me, began to talk quick with his breath catching in between like a man who's been running.

"My hat's been ruined in that studio of yours—the studio of the Fremont. Fortunately, Raymond and his assistant stenographer were there and saw the catastrophe. See," he said, thrusting his hand through the hole in the crown. "What a blow!"

"A blow!" I said. "Who struck it?"

"The same person who struck Alice Merrion."

We were silent for a second, staring at each other. I could hear my heart beating like a hammer. Then he began:

"I've been in the studio a good deal lately, studying the place. Today I stopped there at about mid-day, to have another look at those bent rods we've so often spoken of. On the landing I met Raymond and his assistant, and they went in with me, as I wanted to explain to them my idea about the rods. I got on a chair under the broken skylight and they stood below, listening to my explanation. As I stood that way the sun beat down on my head almost as hot as summer and I could hear the dripping of the water from the icicles on the Octagon pipes.

"All of a sudden, without warning, I heard a sharp, snapping sound, there was a crashing noise, and something struck me on the head a stultifying blow. I shouted and struck up, and Raymond and the stenographer caught me as I fell, for I was stunned for a moment. When I pulled myself together I saw that the floor was covered with icicles and chunks of solid ice. Looking up we could see that the great bunch which had been hanging to the pipes had broken off, snapped by its own weight in the thaw."

I fell back on the bed, holding his hand, and stammering something—Heaven knows what.

"Brace up, old man," says he. "You can see daylight now all right. Raymond says that the icicles on the pipes in the last frost were triple that size and weight. *They* bent the iron rods and tore the skylight out. *They* murdered Alice Merrion. All you can say is that they killed her quickly. They must have fallen in two detachments, the vibration of the first break dislodging the second mass, which came almost in the same instant. The glass was broken and the huge, jagged iceberg with its pointed daggers, must have plunged through the opening and in one breath struck the girl senseless and lifeless. Why, pull yourself together old man—you're as white as chalk."

Well, that's all.

The rest of the story is too well known through the papers for me to tell it. The case of the State against Jared Johnson was dismissed. There was a great day when I said good-bye to them all and came out into the daylight again—an innocent man.

But I'm not going to stay here. No. Too many people know me by sight and stare at me, and I can't bear to pass the old Fremont. Rosy and I are going back to Ohio; my brother has a farm there and I'm to help work it with him.

As for John Paul Hayne, I'm glad to say they've raised his salary on *The Scoop*. One of those sensational papers offered him a hundred dollars a week, but he wouldn't take it. He's a fine boy. He's promised to write to me every two weeks.

The American novelist Ellen Glasgow (1873–1945) was primarily known for her writings about the South. Her 1942 novel In This Our Life, *about the contemporary South, won the Pulitzer Prize. She became involved in the women's suffrage movement in the United States in the early twentieth century but dropped out, the activism having come at what she described as the "wrong moment" in her life. Nonetheless, her later work reflects many heroines whose lives embody the virtues of the leaders of the movement. She also published a dozen short stories over her career, and the following, which first appeared in* Harper's New Monthly Magazine *for May 1899, considers the ethical responsibilities of the discoverer of a criminal.*

POINT IN MORALS

ELLEN GLASGOW

T he question seems to be—" began the Englishman. He looked up
and bowed to a girl in a yachting cap who had just come in from
deck and was taking the seat beside him. The question seems to
be—" The girl was having some difficulty in removing her coat, and he
turned to assist her.

"In my opinion," broke in a well-known alienist on his way to a convention in Vienna, "the question is simply whether or not civilization, in
placing an exorbitant value upon human life, is defeating its own aims."
He leaned forward authoritatively, and spoke with a half-foreign preci-
sion of accent."

"You mean that the survival of the fittest is checkmated," remarked a
young journalist travelling in the interest of a New York daily, "that civilization should practice artificial selection, as it were?"

The alienist shrugged his shoulders deprecatingly. "My dear sir," he protested, "I don't mean anything. It is the question that means something."

"Well, as I was saying," began the Englishman again, reaching for the salt and upsetting a spoonful, "the question seems to be whether or not, under any circumstances, the saving of a human life may become positively immoral."

"Upon that point—" began the alienist: but a young lady in a pink blouse who was seated on the Captain's right interrupted him.

"How could it?" she asked. "At least I don't see how it could; do you, Captain?"

"There is no doubt," remarked the journalist, looking up from a conversation he had drifted into with a lawyer from one of the Western States, "that the more humane spirit pervading modern civilization has not worked wholly for good in the development of the species. Probably, for instance, if we had followed the Spartan practice of exposing unhealthy infants, we should have retained something of the Spartan hardihood. Certainly if we had been content to remain barbarians both our digestions and our nerves would have been the better for it, and melancholia would perhaps have been unknown. But, at the same time, the loss of a number of the more heroic virtues is overbalanced by an increase of the softer ones. Notably, human life has never before been regarded so sacredly."

"On the other side," observed the lawyer, lifting his hand to adjust his eye-glasses, and pausing to brush a crumb from his coat, "though it may all be very well to be philanthropic to the point of pauperizing half a community and of growing squeamish about capital punishment, the whole thing sometimes takes a disgustingly morbid turn. Why, it seems as if criminals were the real American heroes! Only last week I visited a man sentenced to death for the murder of his two wives, and, by Jove, the jailer was literally besieged by women sympathizers. I counted six bunches of heliotrope in his cell, and at least fifty notes."

"Oh, but that is a form of nervous hysteria!" said the girl in the yachting cap, "and must be considered separately. Every sentiment has its fanatics— philanthropy as well as religion. But we don't judge a movement by a few overwrought disciples."

"That is true," said the Englishman, quietly. He was a middle-aged man, with an insistently optimistic countenance, and a build suggestive of general solidity. "But to return to the original proposition. I suppose we will all accept as a fundamental postulate the statement that the highest civilization is the one in which the highest value is placed upon individual life—"

"And happiness," added the girl in the yachting cap.

"And happiness," assented the Englishman.

"And yet," commented the lawyer, "I think that most of us will admit that such a society, where life is regarded as sacred because it is valuable to the individual, and not because it is valuable to the state, tends to the non-production of heroes—"

"That the average will be higher and the exception lower," observed the journalist. "In other words, that there will be a general elevation of the mass, accompanied by a corresponding lowering of the few."

"On the whole, I think our system does very well," said the Englishman, carefully measuring the horseradish he was placing upon his oysters. "A mean between two extremes is apt to be satisfactory in results. If we don't produce a Marcus Aurelius or a Seneca, neither do we produce a Nero or a Phocas.* We may have lost patriotism, but we have gained cosmopolitanism, which is better. If we have lost chivalry, we have acquired decency; and if we have ceased to be picturesque, we have become cleanly, which is considerably more to be desired."

"I have never felt the romanticism of the Middle Ages," remarked the girl in the yachting cap. "When I read of the glories of the Crusaders, I can't help remembering that a knight wore a single garment for a lifetime, and hacked his horse to pieces for a whim. Just as I never think of that chivalrous brute, Richard the Lion-Hearted, that I don't see him chopping off the heads of his three thousand prisoners."

"Oh, I don't think that any of us are sighing for a revival of the Middle Ages, returned the journalist. "The worship of the past has usually for its devotees people who have only known the present—"

"Which is as it should be," commented the lawyer. "If man was confined to the worship of the knowable, all the world would lapse into atheism."

"Just as the great lovers of humanity were generally hermits," added the girl in the yachting cap. "I had an uncle who used to say that he never really loved mankind until he went to live in the wilderness."

---

* Poorly regarded Byzantine emperor who ruled from 602 to 610 C.E.

"I think we are drifting from the point," said the alienist, helping himself to potatoes. "Was it not—can the saving of a human life ever prove to be an immoral act? I once held that it could."

"Did you act upon it?" asked the lawyer, with rising interest. "I maintain that no proposition can be said to exist until it is acted upon. Otherwise it is in merely an embryonic state—"

The alienist laid down his fork and leaned forward. He was a notable-looking man of some thirty-odd years, who had made a sudden leap into popularity through several successful cases. He had a nervous, muscular face, with singularly penetrating eyes, and hair of a light sandy color. His hands were white and well shaped.

"It was some years ago," he said, bending a scintillant* glance around the table. "If you will listen—"

There followed a stir of assent, accompanied by a nod from the young lady upon the Captain's right. "I feel as if it would be a ghost story," she declared.

"It is not a story at all," returned the alienist, lifting his wineglass and holding it against the light. "It is merely a fact."

Then he glanced swiftly around the table as if challenging attention.

"As I said," he began, slowly, "it was some few years ago. Just what year does not matter, but at that time I had completed a course at Heidelberg, and expected shortly to set out with an exploring party for South Africa. It turned out afterwards that I did not go, but for the purpose of the present story it is sufficient that I intended to do so, and had made my preparations accordingly. At Heidelberg I had lived among a set of German students who were permeated with the metaphysics of Schopenhauer, von Hartmann, and the rest, and I was pretty well saturated myself. At that age I was an ardent disciple of pessimism. I am still a disciple, but my ardor has abated which is not the fault of pessimism, but the virtue of middle age—"

"A man is usually called conservative when he has passed the twenties," interrupted the journalist, "yet it is not that he grows more conservative, but that he grows less radical."

---

* Sparkling.

"Rather that he grows less in every direction," added the Englishman, "except in physical bulk."

The alienist accepted the suggestions with an inclination, and continued. "One of my most cherished convictions," he said, "was to the effect that every man is the sole arbiter of his fate. As Schopenhauer has it, 'that there is nothing to which a man has a more unassailable title than to his own life and person.' Indeed, that particular sentence had become a kind of motto with our set, and some of my companions even went so far as to preach the proper ending of life with the ending of the power of individual usefulness."

He paused to help himself to salad.

"I was in Scotland at the time, where I had spent a fortnight with my parents, in a small village on the Kyles of Bute. While there I had been treating an invalid cousin who had acquired the morphine habit, and who, under my care, had determined to uproot it. Before leaving I had secured from her the amount of the drug which she had in her possession—some thirty grains—done up in a sealed package, and labelled by a London chemist. As I was in haste, I put it in my bag, thinking that I would add it to my case of medicines when I reached Leicester, where I was to spend the night with an old schoolmate. I took the boat at Tighnabruaich, the small village, found a local train at Gourock to reach Glasgow with one minute in which to catch the first express to London. I made the change and secured a first-class smoking compartment, which I at first thought to be vacant, but when the train had started a man came from the dressing room and took the seat across from me. At first I paid no heed to him, but upon looking up once or twice and finding his eyes upon me, I became unpleasantly conscious of his presence. He was thin almost to emaciation, and yet there was a muscular suggestion of physical force about him which it was difficult to account for, since he was both short and slight. His clothes were shabby, but well made, and his cravat had the appearance of having been tied in haste or by nervous fingers. There was a trace of sensuality about the mouth, over which he wore a drooping yellow mustache tinged with gray, and he was somewhat bald upon the crown of his head, which lent a deceptive hint of intellectuality to his uncovered forehead. As he crossed his legs I saw that his boots were carefully blacked, and that they were long and slender, tapering to a decided point."

"I have always held," interpolated the lawyer, "that to judge a man's character you must read his feet."

The alienist sipped his claret and took up his words:

"After passing the first stop I remembered a book at the bottom of my bag, and, unfastening the strap, in my search for the book I laid a number of small articles upon the seat beside me, among them the sealed package bearing the morphine label and the name of the London chemist. Having found the book, I turned to replace the articles, when I noticed that the man across from me was gazing attentively at the labelled package. For a moment his expression startled me, and I stared back at him from across my open bag, into which I had dropped the articles. There was in his eyes a curious mixture of passion and repulsion, and, beyond it all, the look of a hungry hound when he sees food. Thinking that I had chanced upon a victim of the opium craving, I closed the bag, placed it in the net above my head, and opened my book.

"For a while we rode in silence. Nothing was heard except the noise of the train and the clicking of our bags as they jostled each other in the receptacle above. I remember these details very vividly, because since then I have recalled the slightest fact in connection with the incident. I knew that the man across from me drew a cigar from his case, felt in his pocket for an instant, and then turned to me for a match. At the same time I experienced the feeling that the request veiled a larger purpose, and that there were matches in the pocket into which he thrust his fingers.

"But, as I complied with his request, he glanced indifferently out of the window, and following his gaze, I saw that we were passing a group of low-lying hills flecked with stray patches of heather, and that across the hills a flock of sheep were filing, followed by a peasant girl in a short skirt. It was the last faint suggestion of the Highlands.

"The man across from me leaned out, looking back upon the neutral sky, the sparse patches of heather, and the flock of sheep.

"'What a tone the heather gives to a landscape!' he remarked, and his voice sounded forced and affected.

"I bowed without replying, and as he turned from the window, and I sat upon the back seat in the draught of cinders, I bent forward to lower the sash. In a moment he spoke again:

"'Do you go to London?'

"'To Leicester,' I answered, laying the book aside, impelled by a sudden interest. 'Why do you ask?'

"He flushed nervously.

"'I—Oh, nothing,' he answered, and drew from me.

"Then, as if with swift determination, he reached forward and lifted the book I had laid upon the seat. It was a treatise of von Hartmann's in German.

"'I had judged that you were a physician,' he said, 'a student, perhaps, from a German university?'

"'I am.'

"He paused for an instant, and then spoke in absent-minded reiteration, 'So you don't go on to London?'

"'No,' I returned, impatiently; 'but can I do anything for you?'

"He handed me the book, regarding me resolutely as he did so.

"'Are you a sensible man?'

"I bowed.

"'And a philosopher?'

"'In amateur fashion.'

"With fevered energy he went on more quickly, 'You have in your possession,' he said, 'something for which I would give my whole fortune.' He laid two half-sovereigns and some odd silver in the palm of his hand. 'This is all I possess,' he continued, 'but I would give it gladly.'

"I looked at him curiously.

"'You mean the morphia?' I demanded.

"He nodded. 'I don't ask you to give it to me,' he said; 'I only ask—'

"I interrupted him. 'Are you in pain?'

"He laughed softly, and I really believe he felt a tinge of amusement. 'It is a question of expediency,' he explained. 'If you happen to be a moralist—'

"He broke off. 'What of it?' I inquired.

"He settled himself in his corner, resting his head against the cushions.

"'You get out at Leicester,' he said, recklessly. 'I go on to London, where Providence, represented by Scotland Yard, is awaiting me.'

"I started. 'For what?'

"'They call it murder, I believe,' he returned; 'but what they call it matters very little. I call it justifiable homicide—that also matters very little. The point is—I will arrive, they will be there before me. That is settled. Every station along the road is watched.'

"I glanced out of the window.

"'But you came from Glasgow,' I suggested.

"'Worse luck! I waited in the dressing room until the train started. I hoped to have the compartment alone, but—' He leaned forward and lowered the window shade. 'If you don't object,' he said, apologetically; 'I find the glare trying. It is a question for a moralist,' he repeated. 'Indeed, I may call myself a question for a moralist,' and he smiled again with that ugly humor. 'To begin with the beginning, the question is bred in the bone and it's out in the blood.' He nodded at my look of surprise. 'You are an American,' he continued, 'and so am I. I was born in Washington some thirty years ago. My father was a politician of note, whose honor was held to be unimpeachable—which was a mistake. His name doesn't matter, but he became very wealthy through judicious speculations—in votes and other things. My mother has always suffered from an incipient hysteria, which developed shortly before my birth.' He wiped his forehead with his pocket-handkerchief, and knocked the ashes from his cigar with a flick of his finger. 'The motive for this is not far to seek,' he said, with a glance at my travelling-bag. He had the coolest bravado I have ever met. 'As a child,' he went on, 'I gave great promise. Indeed, we moved to England that I might be educated at Oxford. My father considered the atmospheric ecclesiasticism to be beneficial. But while at college I got into trouble with a woman, and I left. My father died, his fortune burst like a bubble, and my mother moved to the country. I was put into a banking office, but I got into more trouble with women—this time two of them. One was a low variety actress, and I married her. I didn't want to do it. I tried not to, but I couldn't help it, and I did it. A month later I left her. I changed my name and went to Belfast, where I resolved to become an honest man. It was a tough job, but I labored and I succeeded—for a time. The variety actress began looking for me, but I escaped her, and have escaped her so far. That was eight years ago. And several years after reaching Belfast I met another woman. She was different. I fell ill of fever in Ireland, and she nursed me. She was a good woman, with a broad Irish face, strong hands, and motherly shoulders. I was weak and she was strong, and I fell in love with her. I tried to tell her about the variety actress, but somehow I couldn't, and I married her.' He shot the stump of his cigar through the opposite window and lighted another, this time drawing the match from his pocket. 'She is an honest woman,' he said, 'as honest as the day. She believes in me. It would kill her to know about the variety actress—and all the others. There is one child, a girl—a freckle-faced mite just like her mother—and another is coming.'

"'She knows nothing of this affair?'

"'Not a blamed thing. She is the kind of woman who is good because she can't help herself. She enjoys it. I never did. My mother is different, too. She would die if other people knew of this; my wife would die if she knew of it herself. Well, I got tired, and I wanted money, so I left her and went to Dublin. I changed my name and got a clerkship in a shipping office. My wife thinks I went to America to get work, and if she never hears of me she'll probably think no worse. I did intend going to America, but somehow I didn't. I got in with a man who signed somebody's name to a check and got me to present it. Then we quarrelled about the money, and the man threw the job on me and the affair came out. But before they arrested me I ran him down and shot him. I was ridding the world of a damned traitor.'

"He raised the shade with a nervous hand, but the sun flashed into his eyes, and he lowered it.

"'I suppose I'd hang for it,' he said; 'there isn't much doubt of that. If I waited I'd hang for it, but I am not going to wait. I am going to die. It is the only thing left, and I am going to do it.'

"'And how?'

"'Before this train reaches London,' he replied, 'I am a dead man. There are two ways. I might say three, except that a pitch from the carriage might mean only a broken leg. But there is this—' He drew a vial from his pocket and held it to the light. It contained an ounce or so of carbolic acid.

"'One of the most corrosive of irritants,' I observed.

"'And there is your package.'

"My first impulse promised me to force the vial from him. He was a slight man, and I could have overcome him with but little exertion. But the exertion I did not make. I should as soon have thought, when my rational humor reasserted itself, of knocking a man down on Broadway and robbing him of his watch. The acid was as exclusively his property as the clothes he wore, and equally his life was his own. Had he declared his intention to hurl himself from the window I might not have made way for him, but I should certainly not have obstructed his passage.

"But the morphia was mine, and that I should assist him was another matter, so I said,

"'The package belongs to me.'

"'And you will not exchange?'

"'Certainly not.'

"He answered, almost angrily:

"'Why not be reasonable? You admit that I am in a mess of it?'

"'Readily.'

"'You also admit that my life is morally my own?'

"'Equally.'

"'That its continuance could in no wise prove to be of benefit to society?'

"'I do.'

"'That for all connected with me it would be better that I should die unknown and under an assumed name than that I should end upon the scaffold, my wife and mother wrecked for life, my children discovered to be illegitimate?'

"'Yes.'

"'Then you admit also that the best I can do is to kill myself before reaching London?'

"'Perhaps.'

"'So you will leave me the morphine when you get off at Leicester?'

"'No.'

"He struck the windowsill impatiently with the palm of his hand.

"'And why not?'

"I hesitated an instant.

"'Because, upon the whole, I do not care to be the instrument of your self-destruction.'

"'Don't be a fool!' he retorted. 'Speak honestly, and say that because of a little moral shrinkage on your part you prefer to leave a human being to a death of agony. I don't like physical pain. I am like a woman about it, but it is better than hanging, or life-imprisonment, or any jury finding.'

"I became exhortatory.

"'Why not face it like a man and take your chances? Who knows—'

"'I have had my chances,' he returned. 'I have squandered more chances than most men ever lay eyes on—and I don't care. If I had the opportunity, I'd squander them again. It is the only thing chances are made for.'

"'What a scoundrel you are!' I exclaimed.

"'Well, I don't know,' he answered; 'there have been worse men. I never said a harsh word to a woman, and I never hit a man when he was down—'

"I blushed. 'Oh, I didn't mean to hit you,' I responded.

"He took no notice.

"'I like my wife,' he said. 'She is a good woman, and I'd do a good deal to keep her and the children from knowing the truth. Perhaps I'd kill myself even if I didn't want to. I don't know, but I am tired—damned tired.'

"'And yet you deserted her.'

"'I did. I tried not to, but I couldn't help it. If I was free to go back to her tomorrow, unless I was ill and wanted nursing, I'd see that she had grown shapeless, and that her hands were coarse.' He stretched out his own, which were singularly white and delicate. 'I believe I'd leave her in a week,' he said.

"Then with an eager movement he pointed to my bag.

"'That is the ending of the difficulty,' he added, 'otherwise I swear that before the train gets to London I will swallow this stuff, and die like a rat.'

"'I admit your right to die in any manner you choose, but I don't see that it is my place to assist you. It is an ugly job.'

"'So am I,' he retorted, grimly. 'At any rate, if you leave the train with that package in your bag it will be cowardice—sheer cowardice. And for the sake of your cowardice you will damn me to this—' He touched the vial.

"'It won't be pleasant,' I said, and we were silent.

"I knew that the man had spoken the truth. I was accustomed to lies, and had learned to detect them. I knew, also, that the world would be well rid of him and his kind. Why I should preserve him for death upon the gallows I did not see. The majesty of the law would be in no way ruffled by his premature departure; and if I could trust that part of his story, the lives of innocent women and children would, in the other case, suffer considerably. And even if I and my unopened bag alighted at Leicester, I was sure that he would never reach London alive. He was a desperate man, this I read in his set face, his dazed eyes, his nervous hands. He was a poor devil, and I was sorry for him as it was. Why, then, should I contribute, by my refusal to comply with his request, an additional hour of agony to his existence? Could I, with my pretence of philosophic latitudinarianism, alight at my station, leaving him to swallow the acid and die like a rat in a cage before the journey was over? I remembered that I had once seen a guinea pig die from the effects of carbolic acid, and the remembrance sickened me suddenly.

"As I sat there listening to the noise of the slackening train, which was nearing Leicester, I thought of a hundred things. I thought of Schopenhauer and von Hartmann. I thought of the dying guinea pig. I thought of the broad-faced Irish wife and the two children.

"Then 'Leicester' flashed before me, and the train stopped. I rose, gathered my coat and rug, and lifted the volume of von Hartmann from the seat. The man remained motionless in the corner of the compartment, but his eyes followed me.

"I stooped, opened by bag, and laid the chemist's package upon the seat. Then I stepped out, closing the door after me."

As the speaker finished, he reached forward, selected an almond from the stand of nuts, fitted it carefully between the crackers, and cracked it slowly.

The young lady upon the Captain's right shook herself with a shudder.

"What a horrible story!" she exclaimed; "for it is a story, after all, and not a fact."

"A point, rather," suggested the Englishman; "but is that all?"

"All of the point," returned the alienist. "The next day I saw in the *Times* that a man, supposed to be James Morganson, who was wanted for murder, was found dead in a first-class smoking compartment of the Midland Railway, Coroner's verdict, 'Death resulting from an overdose of morphia, taken with suicidal intent.'"

The journalist dropped a lump of sugar in his cup and watched it attentively.

"I don't think I could have done it," he said. "I might have left him with his carbolic. But I couldn't have deliberately given him his death-potion."

"But as long as he was going to die," responded the girl in the yachting cap, "it was better to let him die painlessly."

The Englishman smiled. "Can a woman ever consider the ethical side of a question when the sympathetic one is visible?" he asked.

The alienist cracked another almond. "I was sincere," he said. "Of that there is no doubt. I thought I did right. The question is—did I do right?"

"It would have been wiser," began the lawyer, argumentatively, "since you were stronger than he, to take the vial from him, and to leave him to the care of the law."

"But the wife and children," replied the girl in the yachting cap. "And hanging is so horrible!"

"So is murder," responded the lawyer, dryly.

The young lady on the Captain's right laid her napkin upon the table and rose. "I don't know what was right," she said, "but I do know that in your place I should have felt like a murderer."

The alienist smiled half cynically. "So I did," he answered; "but there is such a thing, my dear young lady, as a conscientious murderer."

Elizabeth Thomasina Meade Smith (1844–1914) wrote over 300 books under the name L. T. Meade. Born in Ireland, she moved to London in 1879. While many of her works were "girls' stories," she was also a prolific author of sensational, mystery, adventure, and crime tales. She often collaborated with male co-authors, first with Dr. Clifford Hallifax in producing a series of mystery-adventures known as Stories from a Doctor's Diary, *then with Robert Eustace, the pen name of Dr. Eustace Robert Barton (1854–1953). Eustace collaborated with other writers as well, including Dorothy Sayers. Meade and Eustace created two notable female villains, Madame Koluchy, the leader of a gang of criminals, depicted in ten short stories collected as* The Brotherhood of the Seven Kings *(1899), and the murderous Madame Sara, who was featured in six short stories collected as* The Sorceress of the Strand *(1903). Here, the Madame Sara duels with her nemeses, the police-surgeon detective Eric Vandeleur and his "Watson," Robert Druce. The story first appeared in the* Strand Magazine *for November 1902.*

THE BLOOD-RED CROSS

L. T. MEADE AND ROBERT EUSTACE

I n the month of November in the year 1899 I found myself a guest in the house of one of my oldest friends—George Rowland. His beautiful place in Yorkshire was an ideal holiday resort. It went by the name of Rowland's Folly, and had been built on the site of a former dwelling in the reign of the first George. The house was now replete with every modern luxury. It, however, very nearly cost its first owner, if not the whole of his fortune, yet the most precious heirloom of the family. This was a pearl necklace of almost fabulous value. It had been secured as booty by a certain Geoffrey Rowland at the time of the Battle of Agincourt, had originally been the property of one of the Dukes of Genoa, and had even for a short time been in the keeping of the Pope. From the moment that Geoffrey Rowland took possession of the necklace there had been several attempts made to deprive him of it. Sword, fire, water, poison, had all been used, but ineffectually. The necklace with its eighty pearls, smooth, symmetrical, pear-shaped, of a translucent white colour and with a subdued iridescent sheen, was still in the possession of the family, and was likely to remain there, as George Rowland told me, until the end of time. Each bride wore the necklace on her wedding-day, after which it was put into the strong-room and, as a rule, never seen again until the next bridal occasion. The pearls were roughly estimated as worth from two to three thousand pounds each, but the historical value of the necklace put the price almost beyond the dreams of avarice.

It was reported that in the autumn of that same year an American millionaire had offered to buy it from the family at their own price, but as no terms would be listened to the negotiations fell through.

George Rowland belonged to the oldest and proudest family in the West Riding, and no man looked a better gentleman or more fit to uphold ancient dignities than he. He was proud to boast that from the earliest days no stain of dishonour had touched his house, that the women of the family were as good as the men, their blood pure, their morals irreproachable, their ideas lofty.

I went to Rowland's Folly in November, and found a pleasant, hospitable, and cheerful hostess in Lady Kennedy, Rowland's only sister. Antonia Ripley was, however, the centre of all interest. Rowland was engaged to Antonia, and the history was romantic. Lady Kennedy told me all about it.

"She is a penniless girl without family," remarked the good woman, somewhat snappishly. "I can't imagine what George was thinking of."

"How did your brother meet her?" I asked.

"We were both in Italy last autumn; we were staying in Naples, at the Vesuve. An English lady was staying there of the name of Studley. She died while we were at the hotel. She had under her charge a young girl, the same Antonia who is now engaged to my brother. Before her death she begged of us to befriend her, saying that the child was without money and without friends. All Mrs. Studley's money died with her. We promised, not being able to do otherwise. George fell in love almost at first sight. Little Antonia was provided for by becoming engaged to my brother. I have nothing to say against the girl, but I dislike this sort of match very much. Besides, she is more foreign than English."

"Cannot Miss Ripley tell you anything about her history?"

"Nothing, except that Mrs. Studley adopted her when she was a tiny child. She says, also, that she has a dim recollection of a large building crowded with people, and a man who stretched out his arms to her and was taken forcibly away. That is all. She is quite a nice child, and amiable, with touching ways and a pathetic face; but no one knows what her ancestry was. Ah, there you are, Antonia! What is the matter now?"

The girl tripped across the room. She was like a young fawn; of a smooth, olive complexion—dark of eye and mysteriously beautiful, with the graceful step which is seldom granted to an English girl.

"My lace dress has come," she said. "Markham is unpacking it—but the bodice is made with a low neck."

Lady Kennedy frowned.

"You are too absurd, Antonia," she said. "Why won't you dress like other girls? I assure you that peculiarity of yours of always wearing your dress high in the evening annoys George."

"Does it?" she answered, and she stepped back and put her hand to her neck just below the throat—a constant habit of hers, as I afterwards had occasion to observe.

"It disturbs him very much," said Lady Kennedy. "He spoke to me about it only yesterday. Please understand, Antonia, that at the ball you cannot possibly wear a dress high to your throat. It cannot be permitted."

"I shall be properly dressed on the night of the ball," replied the girl.

Her face grew crimson, then deadly pale.

"It only wants a fortnight to that time, but I shall be ready."

There was a solemnity about her words. She turned and left the room.

"Antonia is a very trying character," said Lady Kennedy. "Why won't she act like other girls? She makes such a fuss about wearing a proper evening dress that she tries my patience—but she is all crotchets."

"A sweet little girl for all that," was my answer.

"Yes; men like her."

Soon afterwards, as I was strolling, on the terrace, I met Miss Ripley. She was sitting in a low chair. I noticed how small, and slim, and young she looked, and how pathetic was the expression of her little face. When she saw me she seemed to hesitate; then she came to my side.

"May I walk with you, Mr. Druce?" she asked.

"I am quite at your service," I answered. "Where shall we go?"

"It doesn't matter. I want to know if you will help me."

"Certainly, if I can, Miss Ripley."

"It is most important. I want to go to London."

"Surely that is not very difficult?"

"They won't allow me to go alone, and they are both very busy. I have just sent a telegram to a friend. I want to see her. I know she will receive me. I want to go tomorrow. May I venture to ask that you should be my escort?"

"My dear Miss Ripley, certainly," I said. "I will help you with pleasure."

"It must be done," she said, in a low voice. "I have put it off too long. When I marry him he shall not be disappointed."

"I do not understand you, I said, but I will go with you with the greatest willingness."

She smiled; and the next day, much to my own amazement, I found myself travelling first-class up to London, with little Miss Ripley as my companion. Neither Rowland nor his sister had approved; but Antonia had her own way, and the fact that I would escort her cleared off some difficulties.

During our journey she bent towards me and said, in a low tone:—

"Have you ever heard of that most wonderful, that great woman, Madame Sara?"

I looked at her intently.

"I have certainly heard of Madame Sara," I said, with emphasis, "but I sincerely trust that you have nothing to do with her."

"I have known her almost all my life," said the girl. "Mrs. Studley knew her also. I love her very much. I trust her. I am going to see her now."

"What do you mean?"

"It was to her I wired yesterday. She will receive me; she will help me. I am returning to the Folly tonight. Will you add to your kindness by escorting me home?"

"Certainly."

At Euston I put my charge into a hansom, arranging to meet her on the departure platform at twenty minutes to six that evening, and then taking another hansom drove as fast as I could to Vandeleur's address. During the latter part of my journey to town a sudden, almost unaccountable, desire to consult Vandeleur had taken possession of me. I was lucky enough to find this busiest of men at home and at leisure. He gave an exclamation of delight when my name was announced, and then came towards me with outstretched hand.

"I was just about to wire to you, Druce," he said. "From where have you sprung?"

"From no less a place than Rowland's Folly," was my answer.

"More and more amazing. Then you have met Miss Ripley, George Rowland's fiancée?"

"You have heard of the engagement, Vandeleur?"

"Who has not? What sort is the young lady?"

"I can tell you all you want to know, for I have travelled up to town with her."

"Ah!"

He was silent for a minute, evidently thinking hard; then drawing a chair near mine he seated himself.

"How long have you been at Rowland's Folly?" he asked.

"Nearly a week. I am to remain until after the wedding. I consider Rowland a lucky man. He is marrying a sweet little girl."

"You think so? By the way, have you ever noticed any peculiarity about her?"

"Only that she is singularly amiable and attractive."

"But any habit—pray think carefully before you answer me."

"Really, Vandeleur, your questions surprise me. Little Miss Ripley is a person with ideas and is not ashamed to stick to her principles. You know, of course, that in a house like Rowland's Folly it is the custom for the ladies to come to dinner in full dress. Now, Miss Ripley won't accommodate herself to this fashion, but will wear her dress high to the throat, however gay and festive the occasion."

"Ah! There doesn't seem to be much in that, does there?"

"I don't quite agree with you. Pressure has been brought to bear on the girl to make her conform to the usual regulations, and Lady Kennedy, a woman old enough to be her mother, is quite disagreeable on the point."

"But the girl sticks to her determination?"

"Absolutely, although she promises to yield and to wear the conventional dress at the ball given in her honour a week before the wedding."

Vandeleur was silent for nearly a minute; then dropping his voice he said, slowly:—

"Did Miss Ripley ever mention in your presence the name of our mutual foe—Madame Sara?"

"How strange that you should ask! On our journey to town today she told me that she knew the woman—she has known her for the greater part of her life—poor child, she even loves her. Vandeleur, that young girl is with Madame Sara now."

"Don't be alarmed, Druce; there is no immediate danger; but I may as well tell you that through my secret agents I have made discoveries which show that Madame has another iron in the fire, that once again she is preparing to convulse Society, and that little Miss Ripley is the victim."

"You must be mistaken."

"So sure am I, that I want your help. You are returning to Rowland's Folly?"

"Tonight."

"And Miss Ripley?"

"She goes with me. We meet at Euston for the six o'clock train."

"So far, good. By the way, has Rowland spoken to you lately about the pearl necklace?"

"No; why do you ask?"

"Because I understand that it was his intention to have the pearls slightly altered and reset in order to fit Miss Ripley's slender throat; also to have a diamond clasp affixed in place of the somewhat insecure one at present attached to the string of pearls. Messrs. Theodore and Mark, of Bond Street, were to undertake the commission. All was in preparation, and a messenger, accompanied by two detectives, was to go to Rowland's Folly to fetch the treasure, when the whole thing was countermanded, Rowland having changed his mind and having decided that the strong-room at the Folly was the best place in which to keep the necklace."

"He has not mentioned the subject to me," I said. "How do you know?"

"I have my emissaries. One thing is certain—little Miss Ripley is to wear the pearls on her wedding-day—and the Italian family, distant relatives of the present Duke of Genoa, to whom the pearls belonged, and from whom they were stolen shortly before the Battle of Agincourt, are again taking active steps to secure them. You have heard the story of the American millionaire? Well, that was a blind—the necklace was in reality to be delivered into the hands of the old family as soon as he had purchased it. Now, Druce, this is the state of things: Madame Sara is an adventuress, and the cleverest woman in the world—Miss Ripley is very young and ignorant. Miss Ripley is to wear the pearls on her wedding-day and Madame wants them. You can infer the rest."

"What do you want me to do?" I asked.

"Go back and watch. If you see anything to arouse suspicion, wire to me."

"What about telling Rowland?"

"I would rather not consult him. I want to protect Miss Ripley, and at the same time to get Madame into my power. She managed to elude us last time, but she shall not this. My idea is to inveigle her to her ruin. Why, Druce, the woman is being more trusted and run after and admired day by day. She appeals to the greatest foibles of the world. She knows some valuable secrets, and is an adept in the art of restoring beauty and to a certain extent conquering the ravages of time. She is at present aided by an Arab, one of the most dangerous men I have ever seen, with the subtlety of a serpent, and legerdemain in every one of his ten fingers. It is not an easy thing to entrap her."

"And yet you mean to do it?"

"Some day, some day. Perhaps now."

His eyes were bright. I had seldom seen him look more excited.

After a short time I left him. Miss Ripley met me at Euston. She was silent and unresponsive and looked depressed. Once I saw her put her hand to her neck.

"Are you in pain?" I asked.

"You might be a doctor, Mr. Druce, from your question."

"But answer me," I said.

She was silent for a minute; then she said, slowly:—

"You are good, and I think I ought to tell you. But will you regard it as a secret? You wonder, perhaps, how it is that I don't wear a low dress in the evening. I will tell you why. On my neck, just below the throat, there grew a wart or mole—large, brown, and ugly. The Italian doctors would not remove it on account of the position. It lies just over what they said was an aberrant artery, and the removal might cause very dangerous haemorrhage. One day Madame saw it; she said the doctors were wrong, and that she could easily take it away and leave no mark behind. I hesitated for a long time, but yesterday, when Lady Kennedy spoke to me as she did, I made up my mind. I wired to Madame and went to her today. She gave me chloroform and removed the mole. My neck is bandaged up and it smarts a little. I am not to remove the bandage until she sees me again. She is very pleased with the result, and says that my neck will now be beautiful like other women's, and that I can on the night of the ball wear the lovely Brussels lace dress that Lady Kennedy has given me. That is my secret. Will you respect it?"

I promised, and soon afterwards we reached the end of our journey.

A few days went by. One morning at breakfast I noticed that the little signora only played with her food. An open letter lay by her plate. Rowland, by whose side she always sat, turned to her.

"What is the matter, Antonia?" he said. "Have you had an unpleasant letter?"

"It is from—"

"From whom, dear?"

"Madame Sara."

"What did I hear you say?" cried Lady Kennedy.

"I have had a letter from Madame Sara, Lady Kennedy."

"That shocking woman in the Strand—that adventuress? My dear, is it possible that you know her? Her name is in the mouth of everyone. She is quite notorious."

Instantly the room became full of voices, some talking loudly, some gently, but all praising Madame Sara. Even the men took her part; as to the women, they were unanimous about her charms and her genius.

In the midst of the commotion little Antonia burst into a flood of tears and left the room. Rowland followed her. What next occurred I cannot tell, but in the course of the morning I met Lady Kennedy.

"Well," she said, "that child has won, as I knew she would. Madame Sara wishes to come here, and George says that Antonia's friend is to be invited. I shall be glad when the marriage is over and I can get out of this. It is really detestable that in the last days of my reign I should have to give that woman the entrée to the house."

She left me, and I wandered into the entrance hall. There I saw Rowland. He had a telegraph form in his hands, on which some words were written.

"Ah, Druce!" he said. "I am just sending a telegram to the station. What! do you want to send one too?"

For I had seated myself by the table which held the telegraph forms.

"If you don't think I am taking too great a liberty, Rowland," I said, suddenly, "I should like to ask a friend of mine here for a day or two."

"Twenty friends, if you like, my dear Druce. What a man you are to apologize about such a trifle! Who is the special friend?"

"No less a person than Eric Vandeleur, the police-surgeon for Westminster."

"What! Vandeleur—the gayest, jolliest man I have ever met! Would he care to come?"

Rowland's eyes were sparkling with excitement.

"I think so; more especially if you will give me leave to say that you would welcome him."

"Tell him he shall have a thousand welcomes, the best room in the house, the best horse. Get him to come by all means, Druce."

Our two telegrams were sent off. In the course of the morning replies in the affirmative came to each.

That evening Madame Sara arrived. She came by the last train. The brougham was sent to meet her. She entered the house shortly before midnight. I was standing in the hall when she arrived, and I felt a momentary sense of pleasure when I saw her start as her eyes met mine. But she was not a woman to be caught off her guard. She approached me at once with outstretched hand and an eager voice.

"This is charming, Mr. Druce," she said. "I do not think anything pleases me more." Then she added, turning to Rowland, "Mr. Dixon Druce is a very old friend of mine."

Rowland gave me a bewildered glance. Madame turned and began to talk to her hostess. Antonia was standing near one of the open drawing-rooms. She had on a soft dress of pale green silk. I had seldom seen a more graceful little creature. But the expression of her face disturbed me. It wore now the fascinated look of a bird when a snake attracts it. Could Madame Sara be the snake? Was Antonia afraid of this woman?

The next day Lady Kennedy came to me with a confidence.

"I am glad your police friend is coming," she said. "It will be safer."

"Vandeleur arrives at twelve o'clock," was my answer.

"Well, I am pleased. I like that woman less and less. I was amazed when she dared to call you her friend."

"Oh, we have met before on business," I answered, guardedly.

"You won't tell me anything further, Mr. Druce?"

"You must excuse me, Lady Kennedy."

"Her assurance is unbounded," continued the good lady. "She has brought a maid or nurse with her—a most extraordinary-looking woman. That, perhaps, is allowable; but she has also brought her black servant, an Arabian, who goes by the name of Achmed. I must say he is a picturesque creature with his quaint Oriental dress. He was all in flaming yellow this morning, and the embroidery on his jacket was worth a small fortune. But it is the daring of the woman that annoys me. She goes on as though she were somebody."

"She is a very emphatic somebody," I could not help replying. "London Society is at her feet."

"I only hope that Antonia will take her remedies and let her go. The woman has no welcome from me," said the indignant mistress of Rowland's Folly.

I did not see anything of Antonia that morning, and at the appointed time I went down to the station to meet Vandeleur. He arrived in high spirits, did not ask a question with regard to Antonia, received the information that Madame Sara was in the house with stolid silence, and seemed intent on the pleasures of the moment.

"Rowland's Folly!" he said, looking round him as we approached one of the finest houses in the whole of Yorkshire. "A folly, truly, and yet a pleasant one, Druce, eh? I fancy," he added, with a slight smile, "that I am going to have a good time here."

"I hope you will disentangle a most tangled skein," was my reply.

He shrugged his shoulders. Suddenly his manner altered.

"Who is that woman?" he said, with a strain of anxiety quite apparent in his voice.

"Who?" I asked.

"That woman on the terrace in nurse's dress."

"I don't know. She has been brought here by Madame Sara—a sort of maid and nurse as well. I suppose poor little Antonia will be put under her charge."

"Don't let her see me, Druce, that's all. Ah, here is our host."

Vandeleur quickened his movements, and the next instant was shaking hands with Rowland.

The rest of the day passed without adventure. I did not see Antonia. She did not even appear at dinner. Rowland, however, assured me that she was taking necessary rest and would be all right on the morrow. He seemed inclined to be gracious to Madame Sara, and was annoyed at his sister's manner to their guest.

Soon after dinner, as I was standing in one of the smoking-rooms, I felt a light hand on my arm, and, turning, encountered the splendid pose and audacious, bright, defiant glance of Madame herself.

"Mr. Druce," she said, "just one moment. It is quite right that you and I should be plain with each other. I know the reason why you are here. You have come for the express purpose of spying upon me and spoiling what you consider my game. But understand, Mr. Druce, that there is danger to yourself when you interfere with the schemes of one like me. Forewarned is forearmed."

Someone came into the room and Madame left it.

The ball was but a week off, and preparations for the great event were taking place. Attached to the house at the left was a great room built for this purpose.

Rowland and I were walking down this room on a special morning; he was commenting on its architectural merits and telling me what band he intended to have in the musicians' gallery, when Antonia glided into the room.

"How pale you are, little Tonia!" he said.

This was his favourite name for her. He put his hand under her chin, raised her sweet, blushing face, and looked into her eyes.

"Ah, you want my answer. What a persistent little puss it is! You shall have your way, Tonia—yes, certainly. For you I will grant what has never been granted before. All the same, what will my lady say?"

He shrugged his shoulders.

"But you will let me wear them whether she is angry or not?" persisted Antonia.

"Yes, child, I have said it."

She took his hand and raised it to her lips, then, with a curtsy, tripped out of the room.

"A rare, bright little bird," he said, turning to me. "Do you know, I feel that I have done an extraordinarily good thing for myself in securing little Antonia. No troublesome mamma-in-law—no brothers and sisters, not my own and yet emphatically mine to consider—just the child herself. I am very happy and a very lucky fellow. I am glad my little girl has no past history. She is just her dear little, dainty self, no more and no less."

"What did she want with you now?" I asked.

"Little witch," he said, with a laugh. "The pearls, the pearls. She insists on wearing the great necklace on the night of the ball. Dear little girl. I can fancy how the baubles will gleam and shine on her fair throat."

I made no answer, but I was certain that little Antonia's request did not emanate from herself. I thought that I would search for Vandeleur and tell him of the circumstance, but the next remark of Rowland's nipped my project in the bud.

"By the way, your friend has promised to be back for dinner. He left here early this morning."

"Vandeleur?" I cried.

"Yes, he has gone to town. What a first-rate fellow he is!"

"He tells a good story," I answered.

"Capital. Who would suspect him of being the greatest criminal expert of the day? But, thank goodness, we have no need of his services at Rowland's Folly."

Late in the evening Vandeleur returned. He entered the house just before dinner. I observed by the brightness of his eyes and the intense gravity of his manner that he was satisfied with himself. This in his case was always a good sign. At dinner he was his brightest self, courteous to everyone, and to Madame Sara in particular.

Late that night, as I was preparing to go to bed, he entered my room without knocking.

"Well, Druce," he said, "it is all right."

"All right!" I cried; "what do you mean?"

"You will soon know. The moment I saw that woman I had my suspicions. I was in town today making some very interesting inquiries. I am primed now on every point. Expect a *dénouement* of a startling character very soon, but be sure of one thing—however black appearances may be the little bride is safe, and so are the pearls."

He left me without waiting for my reply.

The next day passed, and the next. I seemed to live on tenter-hooks. Little Antonia was gay and bright like a bird. Madame's invitation had been extended by Lady Kennedy at Rowland's command to the day after the ball—little Antonia skipped when she heard it.

"I love her," said the girl.

More and more guests arrived—the days flew on wings—the evenings were lively. Madame was a power in herself. Vandeleur was another. These two, sworn foes at heart, aided and abetted each other to make things go brilliantly for the rest of the guests. Rowland was in the highest spirits.

At last the evening before the ball came and went. Vandeleur's grand coup had not come off. I retired to bed as usual. The night was a stormy one—rain rattled against the window-panes, the wind sighed and shuddered. I had just put out my candle and was about to seek forgetfulness in sleep when once again in his unceremonious fashion Vandeleur burst into my room.

"I want you at once, Druce, in the bedroom of Madame Sara's servant. Get into your clothes as fast as you possibly can and join me there."

He left the room as abruptly as he had entered it. I hastily dressed, and with stealthy steps, in the dead of night, to the accompaniment of the ever-increasing tempest, sought the room in question.

I found it brightly lighted; Vandeleur pacing the floor as though he himself were the very spirit of the storm; and, most astonishing sight of all, the nurse whom Madame Sara had brought to Rowland's Folly, and whose name I had never happened to hear, gagged and bound in a chair drawn into the centre of the room.

"So I think that is all, nurse," said Vandeleur, as I entered. "Pray take a chair, Druce. We quite understand each other, don't we, nurse, and the facts are wonderfully simple. Your name as entered in the archives of crime at Westminster is not as you have given out, Mary Jessop, but Rebecca Curt. You escaped from Portland prison on the night of November 30th, just a year ago. You could not have managed your escape but for the connivance of the lady in whose service you are now. Your crime was forgery, with a strong and very daring attempt at poisoning. Your victim was a harmless invalid lady. Your knowledge of crime, therefore, is what may be called extensive. There are yet eleven years of your sentence to run. You have doubtless served Madame Sara well—but perhaps you can serve me better. You know the consequence if you refuse, for I explained that to you frankly and clearly before this gentleman came into the room. Druce, will you oblige me—will you lock the door while I remove the gag from the prisoner's mouth?"

I hurried to obey. The woman breathed more freely when the gag was removed. Her face was a swarthy red all over. Her crooked eyes favoured us with many shifty glances.

"Now, then, have the goodness to begin, Rebecca Curt," said Vandeleur. "Tell us everything you can."

She swallowed hard, and said:—

"You have forced me—"

"We won't mind that part," interrupted Vandeleur. "The story, please, Mrs. Curt."

If looks could kill, Rebecca Curt would have killed Vandeleur then. He gave her in return a gentle, bland glance, and she started on her narrative.

"Madame knows a secret about Antonia Ripley."

"Of what nature?"

"It concerns her parentage."

"And that is?"

The woman hesitated and writhed.

"The names of her parents, please," said Vandeleur, in a voice cold as ice and hard as iron.

"Her father was Italian by birth."

"His name?"

"Count Gioletti. He was unhappily married, and stabbed his English wife in an access of jealousy when Antonia was three years old. He was executed for the crime on the 20th of June, 18——. The child was adopted and taken out of the country by an English lady who was present in court— her name was Mrs. Studley. Madame Sara was also present. She was much interested in the trial, and had an interview afterwards with Mrs. Studley. It was arranged that Antonia should be called by the surname of Ripley— the name of an old relative of Mrs. Studley's—and that her real name and history were never to be told to her."

"I understand," said Vandeleur, gently. "This is of deep interest, is it not, Druce?"

I nodded, too much absorbed in watching the face of the woman to have time for words.

"But now," continued Vandeleur, "there are reasons why Madame should change her mind with regard to keeping the matter a close secret—is that not so, Mrs. Curt?"

"Yes," said Mrs. Curt.

"You will have the kindness to continue."

"Madame has an object she blackmails the signora. She wants to get the signora completely into her power."

"Indeed! Is she succeeding?"

"Yes."

"How has she managed? Be very careful what you say, please."

"The mode is subtle—the young lady had a disfiguring mole or wart on her neck, just below the throat. Madame removed the mole."

"Quite a simple process, I doubt not," said Vandeleur, in a careless tone.

"Yes, it was done easily—I was present. The young lady was conducted into a chamber with a red light."

Vandeleur's extraordinary eyes suddenly leapt into fire. He took a chair and drew it so close to Mrs. Curt's that his face was within a foot or two of hers.

"Now, you will be very careful what you say," he remarked. "You know the consequence to yourself unless this narrative is absolutely reliable."

She began to tremble, but continued:

"I was present at the operation. Not a single ray of ordinary light was allowed to penetrate. The patient was put under chloroform. The mole was removed. Afterwards Madame wrote something on her neck. The words were very small and neatly done—they formed a cross on the young lady's neck. Afterwards I heard what they were."

"Repeat them."

"I can't. You will know in the moment of victory."

"I choose to know now. A detective from my division at Westminster comes here early tomorrow morning—he brings handcuffs—and—"

"I will tell you," interrupted the woman. "The words were these:—

"'I AM THE DUGHTER OF PAOLO GIOLETTI, WHO WAS EXECUTED FOR THE MURDER OF MY MOTHER, JUNE 20TH, 18—.'"

"How were the words written?"

"With nitrate of silver."

"Fiend!" muttered Vandeleur.

He jumped up and began to pace the room. I had never seen his face so black with ungovernable rage.

"You know what this means?" he said at last to me. "Nitrate of silver eats into the flesh and is permanent. Once exposed to the light the case is hopeless, and the helpless child becomes her own executioner."

The nurse looked up restlessly.

"The operation was performed in a room with a red light," she said, "and up to the present the words have not been seen. Unless the young lady exposes her neck to the blue rays of ordinary light they never will be. In order to give her a chance to keep her deadly secret Madame has had a large carbuncle of the deepest red cut and prepared. It is in the shape of a cross, and is suspended to a fine gold, almost invisible, thread. This the signora is to wear when in full evening dress. It will keep in its place, for the back of the cross will be dusted with gum."

"But it cannot be Madame's aim to hide the fateful words," said Vandeleur. "You are concealing something, nurse."

Her face grew an ugly red. After a pause the following words came out with great reluctance:—

"The young lady wears the carbuncle as a reward."

"Ah," said Vandeleur, "now we are beginning to see daylight. As a reward for what?"

"Madame wants something which the signora can give her. It is a case of exchange; the carbuncle which hides the fatal secret is given in exchange for that which the signora can transfer to Madame."

"I understand at last," said Vandeleur. "Really, Druce, I feel myself privileged to say that of all the malevolent—" he broke off abruptly. "Never mind," he said, "we are keeping nurse. Nurse, you have answered all my questions with praiseworthy exactitude, but before you return to your well-earned slumbers I have one more piece of information to seek from you. Was it entirely by Miss Ripley's desire, or was it in any respect owing to Madame Sara's instigations, that the young lady is permitted to wear the pearl necklace on the night of the dance? You have, of course, nurse, heard of the pearl necklace?"

Rebecca Curt's face showed that she undoubtedly had.

"I see you are acquainted with that most interesting story. Now, answer my question. The request to wear the necklace tomorrow night was suggested by Madame, was it not?"

"Ah, yes—yes!" cried the woman, carried out of herself by sudden excitement. "It was to that point all else tended—all, all!"

"Thank you, that will do. You understand that from this day you are absolutely in my service. As long as you serve me faithfully you are safe."

"I will do my best, sir," she replied, in a modest tone, her eyes seeking the ground.

The moment we were alone Vandeleur turned to me.

"Things are simplifying themselves," he said.

"I fail to understand," was my answer. "I should say that complications, and alarming ones, abound."

"Nevertheless, I see my way clear. Druce, it is not good for you to be so long out of bed, but in order that you may repose soundly when you return to your room I will tell you frankly what my mode of operations will be tomorrow. The simplest plan would be to tell Rowland everything, but for various reasons that does not suit me. I take an interest in the little girl, and if she chooses to conceal her secret (at present, remember, she does not know it, but the poor child will certainly be told everything tomorrow) I don't intend to interfere. In the second place, I am anxious to lay a trap for Madame. Now, two things are evident. Madame Sara's object in coming here is to steal the pearls. Her plan is to terrify the little signora into giving them to her in order that the fiendish words written on the child's neck may not be seen. As the signora must wear a dress with a low neck tomorrow night, she can only hide the words by means of the red carbuncle. Madame will only give her the carbuncle if she, in exchange, gives Madame the pearls. You see?"

"I do," I answered, slowly.

He drew himself up to his slender height, and his eyes became full of suppressed laughter.

"The child's neck has been injured with nitrate of silver. Nevertheless, until it is exposed to the blue rays of light the ominous, fiendish words will not appear on her white throat. Once they do appear they will be indelible. Now, listen! Madame, with all her cunning, forgot something. To the action of nitrate of silver there is an antidote. This is nothing more or less than our old friend cyanide of potassium. Tomorrow nurse, under my instructions, will take the little patient into a room carefully prepared with the hateful red light, and will bathe the neck just where the baleful words are written with a solution of cyanide of potassium. The nitrate of silver will then become neutralized and the letters will never come out."

"But the child will not know that. The terror of Madame's cruel story will be upon her, and she will exchange the pearls for the cross."

"I think not, for I shall be there to prevent it. Now, Druce, I have told you all that is necessary. Go to bed and sleep comfortably."

The next morning dawned dull and sullen, but the fierce storm of the night before was over. The ravages which had taken place, however, in the stately old park were very manifest, for trees had been torn up by their roots and some of the stateliest and largest of the oaks had been deprived of their best branches.

Little Miss Ripley did not appear at all that day. I was not surprised at her absence. The time had come when doubtless Madame found it necessary to divulge her awful scheme to the unhappy child. In the midst of that gay houseful of people no one specially missed her; even Rowland was engaged with many necessary matters, and had little time to devote to his future wife. The ballroom, decorated with real flowers, was a beautiful sight.

Vandeleur, our host, and I paced up and down the long room. Rowland was in great excitement, making many suggestions, altering this decoration and the other. The flowers were too profuse in one place, too scanty in another. The lights, too, were not bright enough.

"By all means have the ballroom well lighted," said Vandeleur. "In a room like this, so large, and with so many doors leading into passages and sitting-out rooms, it is well to have the light as brilliant as possible. You will forgive my suggestion, Mr. Rowland, when I say I speak entirely from the point of view of a man who has some acquaintance with the treacherous dealings of crime."

Rowland started.

"Are you afraid that an attempt will be made here tonight to steal the necklace?" he asked, suddenly.

"We won't talk of it," replied Vandeleur. "Act on my suggestion and you have nothing to fear."

Rowland shrugged his shoulders, and crossing the room gave some directions to several men who were putting in the final touches.

Nearly a hundred guests were expected to arrive from the surrounding country, and the house was as full as it could possibly hold. Rowland was to open the ball with little Antonia.

There was no late dinner that day, and as evening approached Vandeleur sought me.

"I say, Druce, dress as early as you can, and come down and meet me in our host's study."

I looked at him in astonishment, but did not question him. I saw that he was intensely excited. His face was cold and stern; it invariably wore that expression when he was most moved.

I hurried into my evening clothes and came down again. Vandeleur was standing in the study talking to Rowland. The guests were beginning to arrive. The musicians were tuning up in the adjacent ballroom, and signs of hurry and festival pervaded the entire place. Rowland was in high spirits and looked very handsome. He and Vandeleur talked together, and I stood a little apart. Vandeleur was just about to make a light reply to one of our host's questions when we heard the swish of drapery in the passage outside, and little Antonia, dressed for her first ball, entered. She was in soft white lace, and her neck and arms were bare. The effect of her entrance was somewhat startling and would have arrested attention even were we not all specially interested in her. Her face, neck, and arms were nearly as white as her dress, her dark eyes were much dilated, and her soft black hair surrounded her small face like a shadow. In the midst of the whiteness a large red cross sparkled on her throat like living fire. Rowland uttered an exclamation and then stood still; as for Vandeleur and myself, we held our breath in suspense. What might not the next few minutes reveal?

It was the look on Antonia's face that aroused our fears. What ailed her? She came forward like one blind, or as one who walks in her sleep. One hand was held out slightly in advance, as though she meant to guide herself by the sense of touch. She certainly saw neither Vandeleur nor me, but when she got close to Rowland the blind expression left her eyes. She gave a sudden and exceedingly bitter cry, and ran forward, flinging herself into his arms.

"Kiss me once before we part for ever. Kiss me just once before we part," she said.

"My dear little one," I heard him answer, "what is the meaning of this? You are not well. There, Antonia, cease trembling. Before we part, my dear? But there is no thought of parting. Let me look at you, darling. Ah!"

He held her at arm's length and gazed at her critically.

"No girl could look sweeter, Antonia," he said, "and you have come now for the finishing touch—the beautiful pearls. But what is this, my dear? Why should you spoil your white neck with anything so incongruous? Let me remove it."

She put up her hand to her neck, thus covering the crimson cross. Then her wild eyes met Vandeleur's. She seemed to recognise his presence for the first time.

"You can safely remove it," he said to her, speaking in a semi-whisper.

Rowland gave him an astonished glance. His look seemed to say, "Leave us," but Vandeleur did not move.

"We must see this thing out," he said to me.

Meanwhile Rowland's arm encircled Antonia's neck, and his hand sought for the clasp of the narrow gold thread that held the cross in place.

"One moment," said Antonia.

She stepped back a pace; the trembling in her voice left it, it gathered strength, her fear gave way to dignity. This was the hour of her deepest humiliation, and yet she looked noble.

"My dearest," she said, "my kindest and best of friends. I had yielded to temptation, terror made me weak, the dread of losing you unnerved me, but I won't come to you charged with a sin on my conscience; I won't conceal anything from you. I know you won't wish me now to become your wife; nevertheless, you shall know the truth."

"What do you mean, Antonia? What do your strange words signify? Are you mad?" said George Rowland.

"No, I wish I were; but I am no mate for you; I cannot bring dishonour to your honour. Madame said it could be hidden, that this"—she touched the cross—"would hide it. For this I was to pay—yes, to pay a shameful price. I consented, for the terror was so cruel. But I—I came here and looked into your face and I could not do it. Madame shall have her blood-red cross back and you shall know all. You shall see."

With a fierce gesture she tore the cross from her neck and flung it on the floor.

"The pearls for this," she cried; "the pearls were the price; but I would rather you knew. Take me up to the brightest light and you will see for yourself."

Rowland's face wore an expression impossible to fathom. The red cross lay on the floor; Antonia's eyes were fixed on his. She was no child to be humoured; she was a woman and despair was driving her wild. When she said, "Take me up to the brightest light," he took her hand without a word and led her to where the full rays of a powerful electric light turned the place into day.

"Look!" cried Antonia, "look! Madame wrote it here—here."

She pointed to her throat.

"The words are hidden, but this light will soon cause them to appear. You will see for yourself, you will know the truth. At last you will understand who I really am."

There was silence for a few minutes. Antonia kept pointing to her neck. Rowland's eyes were fixed upon it. After a breathless period of agony Vandeleur stepped forward.

"Miss Antonia," he cried, "you have suffered enough. I am in a position to relieve your terrors. You little guessed, Rowland, that for the last few days I have taken an extreme liberty with regard to you. I have been in your house simply and solely in the exercise of my professional qualities. In the exercise of my manifest duties I came across a ghastly secret. Miss Antonia was to be subjected to a cruel ordeal. Madame Sara, for reasons of her own, had invented one of the most fiendish plots it has ever been my unhappy lot to come across. But I have been in time. Miss Antonia, you need fear nothing. Your neck contains no ghastly secret. Listen! I have saved you. The nurse whom Madame believed to be devoted to her service considered it best for prudential reasons to transfer herself to me. Under my directions she bathed your neck today with a preparation of cyanide of potassium. You do not know what that is, but it is a chemical preparation which neutralizes the effect of what that horrible woman has done. You have nothing to fear—your secret lies buried beneath your white skin."

"But what is the mystery?" said Rowland. "Your actions, Antonia, and your words, Vandeleur, are enough to drive a man mad. What is it all about? I will know."

"Miss Ripley can tell you or not, as she pleases," replied Vandeleur. "The unhappy child was to be blackmailed, Madame Sara's object being to secure the pearl necklace worth a King's ransom. The cross was to be given in exchange for the necklace. That was her aim, but she is defeated. Ask me no questions, sir. If this young lady chooses to tell you, well and good, but if not the secret is her own."

Vandeleur bowed and backed towards me.

"The secret is mine," cried Antonia, "but it also shall be yours, George. I will not be your wife with this ghastly thing between us. You may never speak to me again, but you shall know all the truth."

"Upon my word, a brave girl, and I respect her," whispered Vandeleur. Come, Druce, our work so far as Miss Antonia is concerned is finished."

We left the room.

"Now to see Madame Sara," continued my friend. "We will go to her rooms. Walls have ears in her case; she doubtless knows the whole *dénouement* already; but we will find her at once, she can scarcely have escaped yet."

He flew upstairs. I followed him. We went from one corridor to another. At last we found Madame's apartments. Her bedroom door stood wide open. Rebecca Curt was standing in the middle of the room. Madame herself was nowhere to be seen, but there was every sign of hurried departure.

"Where is Madame Sara?" inquired Vandeleur, in a peremptory voice.

Rebecca Curt shrugged her shoulders.

"Has she gone down? Is she in the ballroom? Speak!" said Vandeleur.

The nurse gave another shrug.

"I only know that Achmed the Arabian rushed in here a few minutes ago," was her answer. "He was excited. He said something to Madame. I think he had been listening—eavesdropping, you call it. Madame was convulsed with rage. She thrust a few things together and she's gone. Perhaps you can catch her."

Vandeleur's face turned white.

"I'll have a try," he said. "Don't keep me, Druce."

He rushed away. I don't know what immediate steps he took, but he did not return to Rowland's Folly. Neither was Madame Sara captured.

But notwithstanding her escape and her meditated crime, notwithstanding little Antonia's hour of terror, the ball went on merrily, and the bride-elect opened it with her future husband. On her fair neck gleamed the pearls, lovely in their soft lustre. What she told Rowland was never known; how he took the news is a secret between Antonia and himself. But one thing is certain: no one was more gallant in his conduct, more ardent in his glances of love, than was the master of Rowland's Folly that night. They were married on the day fixed, and Madame Sara was defeated.

The Baroness Emma Magdolna Rozália Mária Jozefa Borbála "Emmuska" Orczy de Orci, who wrote as the Baroness Orczy (1865–1947), was a prolific Hungarian-born British writer of adventures and crime. She is best remembered as the creator of Sir Percy Blakeney, the English fop who was secretly the Scarlet Pimpernel, the scourge of the French revolutionaries. In 1903, Orczy wrote a hugely successful stage play about Blakeney, based on one of her short stories, and subsequently produced thirteen books featuring the Scarlet Pimpernel. She also wrote two separate series of compelling, clever stories of detection. Lady Molly of Scotland Yard *(1910) collected a dozen tales about a Molly Robertson-Kirk, who joined Scotland Yard to save her fiancé from a false accusation, building a fine career, only to quit when she has saved her man. Orczy also wrote thirty-eight stories featuring a near-anonymous armchair detective, the "Old Man in the Corner," whose deductions are recorded by Miss Polly Burton, a journalist. Six stories appeared in 1901 as "Mysteries of London," followed a year later by seven "Mysteries of Great Cities" and collected in 1908 as* The Old Man in the Corner. *Two other volumes,* The Case of Miss Elliott *(1905) and* Unravelled Knots *(1925) round out the complete tales of the Old Man in the Corner. The series spawned twelve silent films in 1924, and some of the stories have been adapted for radio and television. The following first appeared in* The Royal Magazine *for September 1901.*

THE REGENT'S PARK MURDER

BARONESS ORCZY

I

By this time Miss Polly Burton had become quite accustomed to her extraordinary vis-á-vis* in the corner.

He was always there, when she arrived, in the selfsame corner, dressed in one of his remarkable check tweed suits; he seldom said good morning, and invariably when she appeared he began to fidget with increased nervousness, with some tattered and knotty piece of string.

"Were you ever interested in the Regent's Park murder?" he asked her one day.

---

* Literally, "face-to-face," here meaning a person sitting across from Miss Burton.

Polly replied that she had forgotten most of the particulars connected with that curious murder, but that she fully remembered the stir and flutter it had caused in a certain section of London Society.

"The racing and gambling set, particularly, you mean," he said. "All the persons implicated in the murder, directly or indirectly, were of the type commonly called 'Society men,' or 'men about town,' whilst the Harewood Club in Hanover Square, round which centred all the scandal in connection with the murder, was one of the smartest clubs in London.

"Probably the doings of the Harewood Club, which was essentially a gambling club, would for ever have remained 'officially' absent from the knowledge of the police authorities but for the murder in the Regent's Park and the revelations which came to light in connection with it.

"I dare say you know the quiet square which lies between Portland Place and the Regent's Park and is called Park Crescent at its south end, and subsequently Park Square East and West. The Marylebone Road, with all its heavy traffic, cuts straight across the large square and its pretty gardens, but the latter are connected together by a tunnel under the road; and of course you must remember that the new tube station in the south portion of the Square had not yet been planned.

"February 6th, 1907, was a very foggy night, nevertheless Mr. Aaron Cohen, of 30, Park Square West, at two o'clock in the morning, having finally pocketed the heavy winnings which he had just swept off the green table of the Harewood Club, started to walk home alone. An hour later most of the inhabitants of Park Square West were aroused from their peaceful slumbers by the sounds of a violent altercation in the road. A man's angry voice was heard shouting violently for a minute or two, and was followed immediately by frantic screams of 'Police' and 'Murder.' Then there was the double sharp report of firearms, and nothing more.

"The fog was very dense, and, as you no doubt have experienced yourself, it is very difficult to locate sound in a fog. Nevertheless, not more than a minute or two had elapsed before Constable F 18, the point policeman at the corner of Marylebone Road, arrived on the scene, and, having first of all whistled for any of his comrades on the beat, began to grope his way about in the fog, more confused than effectually assisted by contradictory directions from the inhabitants of the houses close by, who were nearly falling out of the upper windows as they shouted out to the constable.

"'By the railings, policeman.'

"'Higher up the road.'

"'No, lower down.'

"'It was on this side of the pavement I am sure.'

"'No, the other.'

"At last it was another policeman, F 22, who, turning into Park Square West from the north side, almost stumbled upon the body of a man lying on the pavement with his head against the railings of the Square. By this time quite a little crowd of people from the different houses in the road had come down, curious to know what had actually happened.

"The policeman turned the strong light of his bull's-eye lantern on the unfortunate man's face.

"'It looks as if he had been strangled, don't it?' he murmured to his comrade.

"And he pointed to the swollen tongue, the eyes half out of their sockets, bloodshot and congested, the purple, almost black, hue of the face.

"At this point one of the spectators, more callous to horrors, peered curiously into the dead man's face. He uttered an exclamation of astonishment.

"'Why, surely, it's Mr. Cohen from No. 30!'

"The mention of a name familiar down the length of the street had caused two or three other men to come forward and to look more closely into the horribly distorted mask of the murdered man.

"'Our next-door neighbour, undoubtedly,' asserted Mr. Ellison, a young barrister, residing at No. 31.

"'What in the world was he doing this foggy night all alone, and on foot?' asked somebody else.

"'He usually came home very late. I fancy he belonged to some gambling club in town. I dare say he couldn't get a cab to bring him out here. Mind you, I don't know much about him. We only knew him to nod to.'

"'Poor beggar! it looks almost like an old-fashioned case of garroting.'

"Anyway, the blackguardly murderer, whoever he was, wanted to make sure he had killed his man!' added Constable F 18, as he picked up an object from the pavement. 'Here's the revolver, with two cartridges missing. You gentlemen heard the report just now?'

"'He don't seem to have hit him though. The poor bloke was strangled, no doubt.'

"'And tried to shoot at his assailant, obviously,' asserted the young barrister with authority.

"'If he succeeded in hitting the brute, there might be a chance of tracing the way he went.'

"'But not in the fog.'

"Soon, however, the appearance of the inspector, detective, and medical officer, who had quickly been informed of the tragedy, put an end to further discussion.

"The bell at No. 30 was rung, and the servants—all four of them women—were asked to look at the body.

"Amidst tears of horror and screams of fright, they all recognized in the murdered man their master, Mr. Aaron Cohen. He was therefore conveyed to his own room pending the coroner's inquest.

"The police had a pretty difficult task, you will admit; there were so very few indications to go by, and at first literally no clue.

"The inquest revealed practically nothing. Very little was known in the neighbourhood about Mr. Aaron Cohen and his affairs. His female servants did not even know the name or whereabouts of the various clubs he frequented.

"He had an office in Throgmorton Street and went to business every day. He dined at home, and sometimes had friends to dinner. When he was alone he invariably went to the club, where he stayed until the small hours of the morning.

"The night of the murder he had gone out at about nine o'clock. That was the last his servants had seen of him. With regard to the revolver, all four servants swore positively that they had never seen it before, and that, unless Mr. Cohen had bought it that very day, it did not belong to their master.

"Beyond that, no trace whatever of the murderer had been found, but on the morning after the crime a couple of keys linked together by a short metal chain were found close to a gate at the opposite end of the Square, that which immediately faced Portland Place. These were proved to be, firstly, Mr. Cohen's latch-key, and, secondly, his gate-key of the Square.

"It was therefore presumed that the murderer, having accomplished his fell design and ransacked his victim's pockets, had found the keys and made good his escape by slipping into the Square, cutting under the tunnel, and out again by the further gate. He then took the precaution not to carry the keys with him any further, but threw them away and disappeared in the fog.

"The jury returned a verdict of wilful murder against some person or persons unknown, and the police were put on their mettle to discover the unknown and daring murderer. The result of their investigations, conducted with marvellous skill by Mr. William Fisher, led, about a week after the crime, to the sensational arrest of one of London's smartest young bucks.

"The case Mr. Fisher had got up against the accused briefly amounted to this:

"On the night of February 6th, soon after midnight, play began to run very high at the Harewood Club, in Hanover Square. Mr. Aaron Cohen held the bank at roulette against some twenty or thirty of his friends, mostly young fellows with no wits and plenty of money. 'The Bank' was winning heavily, and it appears that this was the third consecutive night on which Mr. Aaron Cohen had gone home richer by several hundreds than he had been at the start of play.

"Young John Ashley, who is the son of a very worthy county gentleman who is M.F.H.* somewhere in the Midlands, was losing heavily, and in his case also it appears that it was the third consecutive night that Fortune had turned her face against him.

"Remember," continued the man in the corner, "that when I tell you all these details and facts, I am giving you the combined evidence of several witnesses, which it took many days to collect and to classify.

"It appears that young Mr. Ashley, though very popular in society, was generally believed to be in what is vulgarly termed 'low water'; up to his eyes in debt, and mortally afraid of his dad, whose younger son he was, and who had on one occasion threatened to ship him off to Australia with

* Master of Fox Hounds.

a £5 note in his pocket if he made any further extravagant calls upon his paternal indulgence.

"It was also evident to all John Ashley's many companions that the worthy M.F.H. held the purse-strings in a very tight grip. The young man, bitten with the desire to cut a smart figure in the circles in which he moved, had often recourse to the varying fortunes which now and again smiled upon him across the green tables in the Harewood Club.

"Be that as it may, the general consensus of opinion at the Club was that young Ashley had changed his last 'pony'* before he sat down to a turn of roulette with Aaron Cohen on that particular night of February 6th.

"It appears that all his friends, conspicuous among whom was Mr. Walter Hatherell, tried their very best to dissuade him from pitting his luck against that of Cohen, who had been having a most unprecedented run of good fortune. But young Ashley, heated with wine, exasperated at his own bad luck, would listen to no one; he tossed one £5 note after another on the board, he borrowed from those who would lend, then played on parole† for a while. Finally, at half-past one in the morning, after a run of nineteen on the red, the young man found himself without a penny in his pockets, and owing a debt—gambling debt—a debt of honour of £1500 to Mr. Aaron Cohen.

"Now we must render this much maligned gentleman that justice which was persistently denied to him by press and public alike; it was positively asserted by all those present that Mr. Cohen himself repeatedly tried to induce young Mr. Ashley to give up playing. He himself was in a delicate position in the matter, as he was the winner, and once or twice the taunt had risen to the young man's lips, accusing the holder of the bank of the wish to retire on a competence before the break in his luck.

"Mr. Aaron Cohen, smoking the best of Havanas, had finally shrugged his shoulders and said: 'As you please!'

"But at half-past one he had had enough of the player, who always lost and never paid—never could pay, so Mr. Cohen probably believed. He therefore at that hour refused to accept Mr. John Ashley's 'promissory' stakes any longer. A very few heated words ensued, quickly checked by

---

* £25.

† Pledge of honor—borrowing on one's mere promise to repay.

the management, who are ever on the alert to avoid the least suspicion of scandal.

"In the meanwhile Mr. Hatherell, with great good sense, persuaded young Ashley to leave the Club and all its temptations and go home; if possible to bed.

"The friendship of the two young men, which was very well known in society, consisted chiefly, it appears, in Walter Hatherell being the willing companion and helpmeet of John Ashley in his mad and extravagant pranks. But tonight the latter, apparently tardily sobered by his terrible and heavy losses, allowed himself to be led away by his friend from the scene of his disasters. It was then about twenty minutes to two.

"Here the situation becomes interesting," continued the man in the corner in his nervous way. "No wonder that the police interrogated at least a dozen witnesses before they were quite satisfied that every statement was conclusively proved.

"Walter Hatherell, after about ten minutes' absence, that is to say at ten minutes to two, returned to the club room. In reply to several inquiries, he said that he had parted with his friend at the corner of New Bond Street, since he seemed anxious to be alone, and that Ashley said he would take a turn down Piccadilly before going home—he thought a walk would do him good.

"At two o'clock or thereabouts Mr. Aaron Cohen, satisfied with his evening's work, gave up his position at the bank and, pocketing his heavy winnings, started on his homeward walk, while Mr. Walter Hatherell left the club half an hour later.

"At three o'clock precisely the cries of 'Murder' and the report of fire-arms were heard in Park Square West, and Mr. Aaron Cohen was found strangled outside the garden railings."

II. THE MOTIVE

"Now at first sight the murder in the Regent's Park appeared both to police and public as one of those silly, clumsy crimes, obviously the work of a novice, and absolutely purposeless, seeing that it could but inevitably lead its perpetrators, without any difficulty, to the gallows.

"You see, a motive had been established. 'Seek him whom the crime benefits,' say our French *confrères*. But there was something more than that.

"Constable James Funnell, on his beat, turned from Portland Place into Park Crescent a few minutes after he had heard the clock at Holy Trinity Church, Marylebone, strike half-past two. The fog at that moment was perhaps not quite so dense as it was later on in the morning, and the policeman saw two gentlemen in overcoats and top-hats leaning arm in arm against the railings of the Square, close to the gate. He could not, of course, distinguish their faces because of the fog, but he heard one of them saying to the other:

"'It is but a question of time, Mr. Cohen. I know my father will pay the money for me, and you will lose nothing by waiting.'

"To this the other apparently made no reply, and the constable passed on; when he returned to the same spot, after having walked over his beat, the two gentlemen had gone, but later on it was near this very gate that the two keys referred to at the inquest had been found.

"Another interesting fact," added the man in the corner, with one of those sarcastic smiles of his which Polly could not quite explain, "was the finding of the revolver upon the scene of the crime. That revolver, shown to Mr. Ashley's valet, was sworn to by him as being the property of his master.

"All these facts made, of course, a very remarkable, so far quite unbroken, chain of circumstantial evidence against Mr. John Ashley. No wonder, therefore, that the police, thoroughly satisfied with Mr. Fisher's work and their own, applied for a warrant against the young man, and arrested him in his rooms in Clarges Street exactly a week after the committal of the crime.

"As a matter of fact, you know, experience has invariably taught me that when a murderer seems particularly foolish and clumsy, and proofs against him seem particularly damning, that is the time when the police should be most guarded against pitfalls.

"Now in this case, if John Ashley had indeed committed the murder in Regent's Park in the manner suggested by the police, he would have been a criminal in more senses than one, for idiocy of that kind is to my mind worse than many crimes.

"The prosecution brought its witnesses up in triumphal array one after another. There were the members of the Harewood Club—who had seen the prisoner's excited condition after his heavy gambling losses to Mr. Aaron Cohen; there was Mr. Hatherell, who, in spite of his friendship for Ashley, was bound to admit that he had parted from him at the corner of Bond Street at twenty minutes to two, and had not seen him again till his return home at five A.M.

"Then came the evidence of Arthur Chipps, John Ashley's valet. It proved of a very sensational character.

"He deposed that on the night in question his master came home at about ten minutes to two. Chipps had then not yet gone to bed. Five minutes later Mr. Ashley went out again, telling the valet not to sit up for him. Chipps could not say at what time either of the young gentlemen had come home.

"That short visit home—presumably to fetch the revolver—was thought to be very important, and Mr. John Ashley's friends felt that his case was practically hopeless.

"The valet's evidence and that of James Funnell, the constable, who had overheard the conversation near the park railings, were certainly the two most damning proofs against the accused. I assure you I was having a rare old time that day. There were two faces in court to watch which was the greatest treat I had had for many a day. One of these was Mr. John Ashley's.

"Here's his photo—short, dark, dapper, a little 'racy' in style, but otherwise he looks a son of a well-to-do farmer. He was very quiet and placid in court, and addressed a few words now and again to his solicitor. He listened gravely, and with an occasional shrug of the shoulders, to the recital of the crime, such as the police had reconstructed it, before an excited and horrified audience.

"Mr. John Ashley, driven to madness and frenzy by terrible financial difficulties, had first of all gone home in search of a weapon, then waylaid Mr. Aaron Cohen somewhere on that gentleman's way home. The young man had begged for delay. Mr. Cohen perhaps was obdurate; but Ashley followed him with his importunities almost to his door.

"There, seeing his creditor determined at last to cut short the painful interview, he had seized the unfortunate man at an unguarded moment from behind, and strangled him; then, fearing that his dastardly work was not fully accomplished, he had shot twice at the already dead body, missing it both times from sheer nervous excitement. The murderer then must have emptied his victim's pockets, and, finding the key of the garden, thought that it would be a safe way of evading capture by cutting across the squares, under the tunnel, and so through the more distant gate which faced Portland Place.

"The loss of the revolver was one of those unforeseen accidents which a retributive Providence places in the path of the miscreant, delivering him by his own act of folly into the hands of human justice.

"Mr. John Ashley, however, did not appear the least bit impressed by the recital of his crime. He had not engaged the services of one of the most eminent lawyers, expert at extracting contradictions from witnesses by skilful cross-examinations—oh, dear me, no! he had been contented with those of a dull, prosy, very second-rate limb of the law, who, as he called his witnesses, was completely innocent of any desire to create a sensation.

"He rose quietly from his seat, and, amidst breathless silence, called the first of three witnesses on behalf of his client. He called three—but he could have produced twelve—gentlemen, members of the Ashton Club in Great Portland Street, all of whom swore that at three o'clock on the morning of February 6th, that is to say, at the very moment when the cries of 'Murder' roused the inhabitants of Park Square West, and the crime was being committed, Mr. John Ashley was sitting quietly in the club-rooms of the Ashton playing bridge with the three witnesses. He had come in a few minutes before three—as the hall porter of the Club testified—and stayed for about an hour and a half.

"I need not tell you that this undoubted, this fully proved, alibi was a positive bombshell in the stronghold of the prosecution. The most accomplished criminal could not possibly be in two places at once, and though the Ashton Club transgresses in many ways against the gambling laws of our very moral country, yet its members belong to the best, most unimpeachable classes of society. Mr. Ashley had been seen and spoken to at the very moment of the crime by at least a dozen gentlemen whose testimony was absolutely above suspicion.

"Mr. John Ashley's conduct throughout this astonishing phase of the inquiry remained perfectly calm and correct. It was no doubt the consciousness of being able to prove his innocence with such absolute conclusion that had steadied his nerves throughout the proceedings.

"His answers to the magistrate were clear and simple, even on the ticklish subject of the revolver.

"'I left the club, sir,' he explained, 'fully determined to speak with Mr. Cohen alone in order to ask him for a delay in the settlement of my debt to him. You will understand that I should not care to do this in the presence of other gentlemen. I went home for a minute or two—not in order to fetch a revolver, as the police assert, for I always carry a revolver about with me in foggy weather—but in order to see if a very important business letter had come for me in my absence.

"'Then I went out again, and met Mr. Aaron Cohen not far from the Harewood Club. I walked the greater part of the way with him, and our conversation was of the most amicable character. We parted at the top of Portland Place, near the gate of the Square, where the policeman saw us. Mr. Cohen then had the intention of cutting across the Square, as being a shorter way to his own house. I thought the Square looked dark and dangerous in the fog, especially as Mr. Cohen was carrying a large sum of money.

"'We had a short discussion on the subject, and finally I persuaded him to take my revolver, as I was going home only through very frequented streets, and moreover carried nothing that was worth stealing. After a little demur Mr. Cohen accepted the loan of my revolver, and that is how it came to be found on the actual scene of the crime; finally I parted from Mr. Cohen a very few minutes after I had heard the church clock striking a quarter before three. I was at the Oxford Street end of Great Portland Street at five minutes to three, and it takes at least ten minutes to walk from where I was to the Ashton Club.'

"This explanation was all the more credible, mind you, because the question of the revolver had never been very satisfactorily explained by the prosecution. A man who has effectually strangled his victim would not discharge two shots of his revolver for, apparently, no other purpose than that of rousing the attention of the nearest passerby. It was far more likely that it was Mr. Cohen who shot—perhaps wildly into the air, when suddenly attacked from behind. Mr. Ashley's explanation therefore was not only plausible, it was the only possible one.

"You will understand therefore how it was that, after nearly half an hour's examination, the magistrate, the police, and the public were alike pleased to proclaim that the accused left the court without a stain upon his character."

III. FRIENDS

"Yes," interrupted Polly eagerly, since, for once, her acumen had been at least as sharp as his, "but suspicion of that horrible crime only shifted its taint from one friend to another, and, of course, I know—"

"But that's just it," he quietly interrupted, "you don't know—Mr. Walter Hatherell, of course, you mean. So did every one else at once. The friend, weak and willing, committing a crime on behalf of his cowardly, yet more assertive friend who had tempted him to evil. It was a good theory; and was held pretty generally, I fancy, even by the police.

"I say 'even' because they worked really hard in order to build up a case against young Hatherell, but the great difficulty was that of time. At the hour when the policeman had seen the two men outside Park Square together, Walter Hatherell was still sitting in the Harewood Club, which he never left until twenty minutes to two. Had he wished to waylay and rob Aaron Cohen he would not have waited surely till the time when presumably the latter would already have reached home.

"Moreover, twenty minutes was an incredibly short time in which to walk from Hanover Square to Regent's Park without the chance of cutting across the squares, to look for a man, whose whereabouts you could not determine to within twenty yards or so, to have an argument with him, murder him, and ransack his pockets. And then there was the total absence of motive."

"But," said Polly meditatively, for she remembered now that the Regent's Park murder, as it had been popularly called, was one of those which had remained as impenetrable a mystery as any other crime had ever been in the annals of the police.

The man in the corner cocked his funny birdlike head well on one side and looked at her, highly amused evidently at her perplexity.

"You do not see how that murder was committed?" he asked with a grin.

Polly was bound to admit that she did not.

"If you had happened to have been in Mr. John Ashley's predicament," he persisted, "you do not see how you could conveniently have done away with Mr. Aaron Cohen, pocketed his winnings, and then led the police of your country entirely by the nose, by proving an indisputable alibi?"

"I could not arrange conveniently," she retorted, "to be in two different places half a mile apart at one and the same time."

"No! I quite admit that you could not do this unless you also had a friend—"

"A friend? But you say—"

"I say that I admired Mr. John Ashley, for his was the head which planned the whole thing, but he could not have accomplished the fascinating and terrible drama without the help of willing and able hands."

"Even then—" she protested.

"Point number one," he began excitedly, fidgeting with his inevitable piece of string. "John Ashley and his friend Walter Hatherell leave the club together, and together decide on the plan of campaign. Hatherell returns to the club, and Ashley goes to fetch the revolver—the revolver which played such an important part in the drama, but not the part assigned to it by the police. Now try to follow Ashley closely, as he dogs Aaron Cohen's footsteps. Do you believe that he entered into conversation with him? That he walked by his side? That he asked for delay? No! He sneaked behind him and caught him by the throat, as the garroters used to do in the fog. Cohen was apoplectic, and Ashley is young and powerful. Moreover, he meant to kill—"

"But the two men talked together outside the Square gates," protested Polly, "one of whom was Cohen, and the other Ashley."

"Pardon me," he said, jumping up in his seat like a monkey on a stick, "there were not two men talking outside the Square gates. According to the testimony of James Funnell, the constable, two men were leaning arm in arm against the railings and one man was talking."

"Then you think that—"

"At the hour when James Funnell heard Holy Trinity clock striking half-past two Aaron Cohen was already dead. Look how simple the whole thing is," he added eagerly, "and how easy after that—easy, but oh, dear me! how wonderfully, how stupendously clever. As soon as James Funnell has passed on, John Ashley, having opened the gate, lifts the body of Aaron Cohen in his arms and carries him across the Square. The Square is deserted, of course, but the way is easy enough, and we must presume that Ashley had been in it before. Anyway, there was no fear of meeting any one.

"In the meantime Hatherell has left the club: as fast as his athletic legs can carry him he rushes along Oxford Street and Portland Place. It had been arranged between the two miscreants that the Square gate should be left on the latch.

"Close on Ashley's heels now, Hatherell too cuts across the Square, and reaches the further gate in good time to give his confederate a hand in disposing the body against the railings. Then, without another instant's delay, Ashley runs back across the gardens, straight to the Ashton Club, throwing away the keys of the dead man, on the very spot where he had made it a point of being seen and heard by a passerby.

"Hatherell gives his friend six or seven minutes' start, then he begins the altercation which lasts two or three minutes, and finally rouses the neighbourhood with cries of 'Murder' and report of pistol in order to establish that the crime was committed at the hour when its perpetrator has already made out an indisputable alibi."

"I don't know what you think of it all, of course," added the funny creature as he fumbled for his coat and his gloves, "but I call the planning of that murder—on the part of novices, mind you—one of the cleverest pieces of strategy I have ever come across. It is one of those cases where there is no possibility whatever now of bringing the crime home to its perpetrator or his abettor. They have not left a single proof behind them; they foresaw everything, and each acted his part with a coolness and courage which, applied to a great and good cause, would have made fine statesmen of them both.

"As it is, I fear, they are just a pair of young blackguards, who have escaped human justice, and have only deserved the full and ungrudging admiration of yours very sincerely."

He had gone. Polly wanted to call him back, but his meagre person was no longer visible through the glass door. There were many things she would have wished to ask of him—what were his proofs, his facts? His were theories, after all, and yet, somehow, she felt that he had solved once again one of the darkest mysteries of great criminal London.

Augusta Groner (1850–1929), who also wrote under several masculine pseudonyms, including August or Auguste Groner and Olaf Björnson, is known as the "mother" of Austrian crime writing. She wrote an extensive series of stories that appeared from 1890 to 1922 about an Austrian police detective, Inspector Joseph Muller, many of which have appeared in English and Scandinavian translations. Yet Groner's contribution to crime writing is little known outside Austria (where "The Golden Augusta" award is presented to outstanding female mystery writers), perhaps as a result of the aftermath of the first World War. Neither Groner nor Muller is listed in any of the encyclopedias of crime writing. Muller was in many ways an antidote to Sherlock Holmes. The New York Times *observed in its review of the first collection,* Joe Muller: Detective, *"He differs so much, in personality and endowments, from other famous detectives of fiction that Frau Groner must be credited with the creation of a new character. Unlike Sherlock Holmes, he does not reason out his conclusions, but seems rather to be forced into them by instinct, to be impelled along his course from one discovery to another by inspiration. Unlike Monsieur Lecocq, in his methods he is neither brilliant, startling or melodramatic."*

THE CASE OF THE REGISTERED LETTER

AUGUSTA GRONER[*]

O h, sir, save him if you can—save my poor nephew! I know he is innocent!"

The little old lady sank back in her chair, gazing up at Commissioner von Riedau with tear-dimmed eyes full of helpless appeal. The commissioner looked thoughtful. "But the case is in the hands of the local authorities, Madam," he answered gently, a strain of pity in his voice. "I don't exactly see how we could interfere."

"But they believe Albert guilty! They haven't given him a chance!"

---

[*] A collection of six of the Muller stories, translated by Grace Isabel Colbron, was published in English in 1910 by Duffield & Co.

"He cannot be sentenced without sufficient proof of his guilt."

"But the trial, the horrible trial—it will kill him—his heart is weak. I thought—I thought you might send some one some one of your detectives—to find out the truth of the case. You must have the best people here in Vienna. Oh, my poor Albert—"

Her voice died away in a suppressed sob, and she covered her face to keep back the tears.

The commissioner pressed a bell on his desk. "Is Detective Joseph Muller anywhere about the building?" he asked of the attendant who appeared at the door.

"I think he is, sir. I saw him come in not long ago."

"Ask him to come up to this room. Say I would like to speak to him." The attendant went out.

"I have sent for one of the best men on our force, Madam," continued the commissioner, turning back to the pathetic little figure in the chair. "We will go into this matter a little more in detail and see if it is possible for us to interfere with the work of the local, authorities in G—."

The little old lady gave her eyes a last hasty dab with a dainty handkerchief and raised her head again, fighting for self-control. She was a quaint little figure, with soft grey hair drawn back smoothly from a gentle-featured face in which each wrinkle seemed the seal of some loving thought for others. Her bonnet and gown were of excellent material in delicate soft colours, but cut in the style of an earlier decade. The capable lines of her thin little hands showed through the fabric of her grey gloves. Her whole attitude bore the impress of one who had adventured far beyond the customary routine of her home circle, adventured out into the world in fear and trembling, impelled by the stress of a great love.

A knock was heard at the door, and a small, slight man, with a kind, smooth-shaven face, entered at the commissioner's call. "You sent for me, sir?" he asked.

"Yes, Muller, there is a matter here in which I need your advice, your assistance, perhaps. This is Detective Muller, Miss—" (the commissioner picked up the card on his desk) "Miss Graumann. If you will tell us now, more in detail, all that you can tell us about this case, we may be able to help you."

"Oh, if you would," murmured Miss Graumann, with something more of hope in her voice. The expression of sympathetic interest on the face of the newcomer had already won her confidence for him. Her slight figure straightened up in the chair, and the two men sat down opposite her, prepared to listen to her story.

"I will tell you all I know and understand about this matter, gentlemen," she began. "My name is Babette Graumann, and I live with my nephew, Albert Graumann, engineering expert, in the village of Grunau, which is not far from the city of G—. My nephew Albert, the dearest, truest—" sobs threatened to overcome her again, but she mastered them bravely. "Albert is now in prison, accused of the murder of his friend, John Siders, in the latter's lodgings in G—."

"Yes, that is the gist of what you have already told me," said the commissioner. "Muller, Miss Graumann believes her nephew innocent, contrary to the opinion of the local authorities in G—. She has come to ask for some one from here who could ferret out the truth of this matter. You are free now, and if we find that it can be done without offending the local authorities—"

"Who is the commissioner in charge of the case in G—?" asked Muller.

"Commissioner Lange is his name, I believe," replied Miss Graumann.

"H'm!" Muller and the commissioner exchanged glances.

"I think we can venture to hear more of this," said the commissioner, as if in answer to their unspoken thought. "Can you give us the details now, Madam? Who is, or rather who was, this John Siders?"

"John Siders came to our village a little over a year ago," continued Miss Graumann. "He came from Chicago; he told us, although he was evidently a German by birth. He bought a nice little piece of property, not far from our home, and settled down there. He was a quiet man and made few friends, but he seemed to take to Albert and came to see us frequently. Albert had spent some years in America, in Chicago, and Siders liked to talk to him about things and people there. But one day Siders suddenly sold his property and moved to G—. Two weeks later he was found dead in his lodgings in the city, murdered, and now—now they have accused Albert of the crime."

"On what grounds?—Oh, I beg your pardon, sir; I did not mean—"

"That's all right, Muller," said the commissioner. "As you may have to undertake the case, you might as well begin to do the questioning now."

"They say"—Miss Graumann's voice quavered—"they say that Albert was the last person known to have been in Siders' room; they say that it was his revolver, found in the room. That is the dreadful part of it—it was his revolver. He acknowledges it, but he did not know, until the police showed it to him, that the weapon was not in its usual place in his study. They tell me that everything speaks for his guilt, but I cannot believe it—I cannot. He says he is innocent in spite of everything. I believe him. I brought him up, sir; I was like his own mother to him. He never knew any other mother. He never lied to me, not once, when he was a little boy, and I don't believe he'd lie to me now, now that he's a man of forty-five. He says he did not kill John Siders. Oh, I know, even without his saying it, that he would not do such a thing."

"Can you tell us anything more about the murder itself?" questioned Muller gently. "Is there any possibility of suicide? Or was there a robbery?"

"They say it was no suicide, sir, and that there was a large sum of money missing. But why should Albert take any one else's money? He has money of his own, and he earns a good income besides—we have all that we need. Oh, it is some dreadful mistake! There is the newspaper account of the discovery of the body. Perhaps Mr. Muller might like to read that." She pointed to a sheet of newspaper on the desk. The commissioner handed it to Muller. It was an evening paper, dated G—, September 24th, and it gave an elaborate account, in provincial journalese, of the discovery that morning of the body of John Siders, evidently murdered, in his lodgings. The main facts to be gathered from the long-winded story were as follows:

John Siders had rented the rooms in which he met his death about ten days before, paying a month's rent in advance. The lodgings consisted of two rooms in a little house in a quiet street. It was a street of simple two-story, one and two family dwellings, occupied by artisans and small tradespeople. There were many open spaces, gardens and vacant lots in the street. The house in which Siders lodged belonged to a travelling salesman by the name of Winter. The man was away from home a great deal, and his wife, with her child and an old servant, lived in the lower part of the house, while the rooms occupied by Siders were in the upper story. Siders lived very quietly, going out frequently in the afternoon, but returning early in the evening. He had said to his landlady that he had many friends in G—. But during the time of his stay in the house he had had but one caller, a gentleman who came on the evening of the 23rd of September. The old maid had opened the door for him and showed him to Mr. Siders' rooms. She described this visitor as having a full black beard, and wearing a broad-brimmed grey felt hat. Nobody saw the man go out, for the old maid, the only person in the house at the time, had retired early. Mrs. Winter and her little girl were spending the night with the former's mother in a distant part of the city. The next morning the old servant, taking the lodger's coffee up to him at the usual hour, found him dead on the floor of his sitting-room, shot through the heart. The woman ran screaming from the house and alarmed the neighbours. A policeman at the corner heard the noise, and led the crowd up to the room where the dead man lay. It was plain to be seen that this was not a case of suicide. Everywhere were signs of a terrible struggle. The furniture was overturned, the dressing-table and the cupboard were open and their contents scattered on the floor, one of the window curtains was torn into strips, as if the victim had been trying to escape by way of the window, but had been dragged back into the room by his murderer. An overturned ink bottle on the table had spattered wide, and added to the general confusion. In the midst of the disorder lay the body of the murdered man, now cold in the rigour of death.

The police commissioner arrived soon, took possession of the rooms, and made a thorough examination of the premises. A letter found on the desk gave another proof, if such were needed, that this was not a case of suicide. This letter was in the handwriting of the dead man, and read as follows:

> *Dear Friend:*
>
> *I appreciate greatly all the kindness shown me by yourself and your good wife. I have been more successful than I thought possible in overcoming the obstacles you know of. Therefore, I shall be very glad to join you day after tomorrow, Sunday, in the proposed excursion. I will call for you at 8 A.M.—the cab and the champagne will be my*

share of the trip. We'll have a jolly day and drink a glass or two to
our plans for the future.
    With best greetings for both of you,
    Your old friend,
    John

    G—, Friday, Sept. 23rd.

An envelope, not yet addressed, lay beside this letter. It was clear that the man who penned these words had no thought of suicide. On the contrary, he was looking forward to a day of pleasure in the near future, and laying plans for the time to come. The murderer's bullet had pierced a heart pulsing with the joy of life.

This was the gist of the account in the evening paper. Muller read it through carefully, lingering over several points which seemed to interest him particularly. Then he turned to Miss Babette Graumann. "And then what happened?" he asked.

"Then the Police Commissioner came to Grunau and questioned my nephew. They had found out that Albert was Mr. Siders' only friend here. And late that evening the Mayor and the Commissioner came to our house with the revolver they had found in the room in G—, and they—they—" her voice trembled again, "they arrested my dear boy and took him away."

"Have you visited him in prison? What does he say about it himself?"

"He seems quite hopeless. He says that he is innocent—oh, I know he is—but everything is against him. He acknowledges that it was he who was in Mr. Siders' room the evening before the murder. He went there because Siders wrote him to come. He says he left early, and that John acted queerly. He knows they will not believe his story. This worry and anxiety will kill him. He has a serious heart trouble; he has suffered from it for years, and it has been growing steadily worse. I dare not think what this excitement may do for him." Miss Graumann broke down again and sobbed aloud. Muller laid his hands soothingly on the little old fingers that gripped the arm of the chair.

"Did your nephew send you here to ask for help?" he inquired very gently.

"Oh, no." The old lady looked up at him through her tears. "No, he would not have done that. I'm afraid that he'll be angry if he knows that I have come. He seemed so hopeless, so dazed. I just couldn't stand it. It seemed to me that the police in G— were taking things for granted, and just sitting there waiting for an innocent man to confess, instead of looking for the real murderer, who may be gone, the Lord knows where, by now!" Miss Graumann's faded cheeks flushed a delicate pink, and she straightened up in her chair again, while her eyes snapped defiance through the tears that hung on their lashes.

A faint gleam twinkled up in Muller's eyes, and he did not look at his chief. Doctor von Riedau's own face glowed in a slowly mounting flush, and his eyes drooped in a moment of conscious embarrassment at some recollection, the sting of which was evidently made worse by Muller's presence. But Commissioner von Riedau had brains enough to acknowledge his mistakes and to learn from them. He looked across the desk at Miss Graumann. "You are right, Madam, the police have made that mistake more than once. And a man with a clear record deserves the benefit of the doubt. We will take up this case. Detective Muller will be put in charge of it. And that means, Madam, that we are giving you the very best assistance the Imperial Police Force affords."

Miss Babette Graumann did not attempt to speak. In a wave of emotion she stretched out both little hands to the detective and clasped his warmly. "Oh, thank you," she said at last. "I thank you. He's just like my own boy to me; he's all the child I ever had, you know."

"But there are difficulties in the way," continued the commissioner in a business-like tone. "The local authorities in G— have not asked for our assistance, and we are taking up the case over their heads, as it were. I shall have to leave that to Muller's diplomacy. He will come to G— and have an interview with your nephew. Then he will have to use his own judgment as to the next steps, and as to how far he may go in opposition to what has been done by the police there."

"And then I may go back home?" asked Miss Graumann. "Go home with the assurance that you will help my poor boy?"

"Yes, you may depend on us, Madam. Is there anything we can do for you here? Are you alone in the city?"

"No, thank you. There is a friend here who will take care of me. She will put me on the afternoon express back to G—."

"It is very likely that I will take that train myself," said Muller. "If there is anything that you need on the journey, call on me."

"Oh, thank you, I will indeed! Thank you both, gentlemen. And now good-bye, and God bless you!"

The commissioner bowed and Muller held the door open for Miss Graumann to pass out. There was silence in the room, as the two men looked after the quaint little figure slowly descending the stairs.

"A brave little woman," murmured the commissioner.

"It is not only the mother in the flesh who knows what a mother's love is," added Muller.

Next morning Joseph Muller stood in the cell of the prison in G— confronting Albert Graumann, accused of the murder of John Siders.

The detective had just come from a rather difficult interview with Commissioner Lange. But the latter, though not a brilliant man, was at least good-natured. He acknowledged the right of the accused and his family to ask for outside assistance, and agreed with Muller that it was better to have some one in the official service brought in, rather than a private detective whose work, in its eventual results, might bring shame on the police. Muller explained that Miss Graumann did not want her nephew to know that it was she who had asked for aid in his behalf, and that it could only redound to his, Lange's, credit if it were understood that he had sent to Vienna for expert assistance in this case. It would be a proof of his conscientious attention to duty, and would insure praise for him, whichever way the case turned out. Commissioner Lange saw the force of this argument, and finally gave Muller permission to handle the case as he thought best, rather relieved than otherwise for his own part. The detective's next errand was to the prison, where he now stood looking up into the deep-set, dark eyes of a tall, broad-shouldered, black-bearded man, who had arisen from the cot at his entrance. Albert Graumann had a strong, self-reliant face and bearing. His natural expression was somewhat hard and stern, but it was the expression of a man of integrity and responsibility. Muller had already made some inquiries as to the prisoner's reputation and business standing in the community, and all that he had heard was favourable. A certain hardness and lack of amiability in Graumann's nature made it difficult for him to win the hearts of others, but although he was not generally loved, he was universally respected. Through the signs of nagging fear, sorrow, and ill-health, printed clearly on the face before him, Muller's keen eyes looked down into the soul of a man who might be overbearing, pitiless even, if occasion demanded, but who would not murder—at least not for the sake of gain. This last possibility Muller had dismissed from his mind, even before he saw the prisoner. The man's reputation was sufficient to make the thought ridiculous. But he had not made up his mind whether it might not be a case of a murder after a quarrel. Now he began to doubt even this when he looked into the intelligent, harsh-featured face of the man in the cell. But Muller had the gift of putting aside his own convictions, when he wanted his mind clear to consider evidence before him.

Graumann had risen from his sitting position when he saw a stranger. His heavy brows drew down over his, eyes, but he waited for the other to speak.

"I am Detective Joseph Muller, from Vienna," began the newcomer, when he had seen that the prisoner did not intend to start the conversation.

"Have you come to question me again?" asked Graumann wearily. "I can say no more than I have already said to the Police Commissioner. And no amount of cross-examination can make me confess a crime of which I am not guilty—no matter what evidence there may be against me." The prisoner's voice was hard and determined in spite of its note of physical and mental weariness.

"I have not come to extort a confession from you, Mr. Graumann," Muller replied gently, "but to help you establish your innocence, if it be possible."

A wave of colour flooded the prisoner's cheek. He gasped, pressed his hand to his heard and dropped down on his cot. "Pardon me," he said finally, hesitating like a man who is fighting for breath. "My heart is weak; any excitement upsets me. You mean that the authorities are not convinced of my guilt, in spite of the evidence? You mean that they will give me the benefit of the doubt—that they will give me a chance for life?"

"Yes, that is the reason for my coming here. I am to take this case in hand. If you will talk freely to me, Mr. Graumann, I may be able to help you. I have seen too many mistakes of justice because of circumstantial evidence to lay any too great stress upon it. I have waited to hear your side of the story from yourself. I did not want to hear it from others. Will you tell it to me now? No, do not move, I will get the stool myself."

Graumann sat back on the cot, his head resting against the wall. His eyes had closed while Muller was speaking, but his quieter breathing showed that he was mastering the physical attack which had so shaken him at the first glimpse of hope. He opened his eyes now and looked at Muller steadily for a moment. Then he said: "Yes, I will tell you: my life and my work have taught me to gauge men. I will tell you everything I know about this sad affair. I will tell you the absolute truth, and I think you will believe me."

"I will believe you," said Muller simply.

"You know the details of the murder, of course, and why I was arrested?"

"You were arrested because you were the last person seen in the company of the murdered man?"

"Exactly. Then I may go back and tell you something of my connection with John Siders?"

"It would be the very best thing to do."

"I live in Grunau, as you doubtless know, and am the engineering expert of large machine works there. My father before me held an important position in the factory, and my family have always lived in Grunau. I have traveled a great deal myself. I am forty-five years old, a childless widower, and live with my old aunt, Miss Babette Graumann, and my ward, Miss Eleonora Roemer, a young lady of twenty-two." Muller looked up with a slight start of surprise, but did not say anything. Graumann continued:

"A little over a year ago, John Siders, who signed himself as coming from Chicago, bought a piece of property in our town and came to live there. I made his acquaintance in the cafe and he seemed to take a fancy to me. I also had spent several years in Chicago, and we naturally came to speak of the place. We discovered that we had several mutual acquaintances there, and enjoyed talking over the old times. Otherwise I did not take particularly to the man, and as I came to know him better I noticed that he never mentioned that part of his life which lay back of the years in Chicago. I asked a casual question once or twice as to his home and family, but he evaded me every time, and would not give a direct answer. He was evidently a German by birth and education, a man with university training, and one who knew life thoroughly. He had delightful manners, and when he could forget his shyness for a while, he could be very agreeable. The ladies of my family came to like him, and encouraged him to call frequently. Then the thing happened that I should not have believed possible. My ward, Miss Roemer, a quiet, reserved girl, fell in love with this man about whom none of us knew anything, a man with a past of which he did not care to speak.

"I was not in any way satisfied with the match, and they seemed to realise it. For Siders managed to persuade the girl to a secret engagement. I discovered it a month or two ago, and it made me very angry. I did not let them see how badly I felt, but I warned Lora not to have too much to do with the boy, and I set about finding out something regarding his earlier life. It was my duty to do this, as I was the girl's guardian. She has no other relative living, and no one to turn to except my aunt and myself. I wrote to Mr. Richard Tressider in Chicago, the owner of the factory in which I had been employed while there. John had told me that Tressider had been his client during the four years in which he practiced law in Chicago. I received an answer about the middle of August. Mr. Tressider had been able to find out only that John was born in the town of Hartberg in a certain year. This was enough. I took leave of absence for a few days and went to Hartberg, which, as you know, is about 140 miles from here. Three days later I knew all that I wanted to know. John Siders was not the man's real name, or, rather, it was only part of his name. His full name was Theodor John Bellmann, and his mother was an Englishwoman whose maiden name was Siders. His father was a county official who died at an early age, leaving his widow and the boy in deepest poverty. Mrs. Bellmann moved to G— to give music lessons. Theodor went to school there, then finally to college, and was an excellent pupil everywhere. But one day it was discovered that he had been stealing money from the banker in whose house he was serving as private tutor to the latter's sons. A large sum of money was missing, and every evidence pointed to young Bellmann as the thief. He denied strenuously that he was guilty, but the District Judge (it was the present Prosecuting Attorney Schmidt in G—) sentenced him. He spent eight months in prison, during which time his mother died of grief at the disgrace. There must have been something good in the boy, for he had never forgotten that it was his guilt that struck down his only relative, the mother who had worked so hard for him. He had atoned for this crime of his youth, and during the years that have passed since then, he had been an honest, upright man."

Graumann paused a moment and pressed his hand to his heart again. His voice had grown weaker, and he breathed hard. Finally he continued: "I commanded my ward to break off her engagement, as I could not allow her to marry a man who was a freed convict. Siders sold his property some few weeks after that and moved to G—. Eleonora acquiesced in my commands, but she was very unhappy and allowed me to see very little of her. Then came the events of the evening of September 23rd, the events which have turned out so terribly. I will try to tell you the story just as it happened, so far as I am concerned. I had seen nothing of John since he left this town. He had made several attempts before his departure for G— to change my opinion, and my decision as to his marriage to my ward. But I let him see plainly that it was impossible for him to enter our family with such a past behind him. He asserted his innocence of the charges against him, and declared that he had been unjustly accused and imprisoned. I am afraid that I was hard towards him. I begin to understand now, as I never thought I should, what it means to be accused of crime. I begin to realise that it is possible for every evidence to point to a man who is absolutely innocent of the deed in question. I begin to think now that John may have been right, that possibly he also may have been accused and sentenced on circumstantial evidence alone. I have thought much, and I have learned much in these terrible days."

The prisoner paused again and sat brooding, his eyes looking out into space. Muller respected his suffering and sat in equal silence, until Graumann raised his eyes to his again. "Then came the evening of the 23rd of September?"

"Yes, that evening—it's all like a dream to me." Graumann began again. "John wrote me a letter asking me to come to see him on that evening. I tore up the letter and threw it away—or perhaps, yes, I remember now, I did not wish Eleonora to see that he had written me. He asked me to come to see him, as he had something to say to me, something of the greatest importance for us both. He asked me not to mention to any one that I was to see him, as it would be wiser no one should know that we were still in communication with each other. There was a strain of nervous excitement visible in his letter. I thought it better to go and see him as he requested; I felt that I owed him some little reparation for having denied him the great wish of his heart. It was my duty to make up to him in other ways for what I had felt obliged to do. I knew him for a nervous, high-strung man, overwrought by brooding for years on what he called his wrongs, and I did not know what he might do if I refused his request. It was not of myself I thought in this connection, but of the girl at home who looked to me for protection.

"I had no fear for myself; it never occurred to me to think of taking a weapon with me. How my revolver—and it is undoubtedly my revolver, for there was a peculiar break in the silver ornamentation on the handle which is easily recognizable—how this revolver of mine got into his room, is more than I can say. Until the Police Commissioner showed it to me two or three days ago, I had no idea that it was not in the box in my study where it is ordinarily kept." Graumann paused again and looked about him as if searching for something. He rose and poured himself out a glass of water. "Let me put some of this in it," said Muller. "It will do you good." From a flask in his pocket he poured a few drops of brandy into the water. Graumann drank it and nodded gratefully. Then he took up his story again.

"I never discovered why Siders had sent for me. When I arrived at the appointed time I found the door of the house closed. I was obliged to ring several times before an old servant opened the door. She seemed surprised that it had been locked. She said that the door was always unlatched, and that Mr. Siders himself must have closed it, contrary to all custom, for she had not done it, and there was no one else in the house but the two of them. Siders was waiting for me at the top of the stairs, calling down a noisy welcome.

"When I asked him finally what it was so important that he wanted to say to me, he evaded me and continued to chatter on about commonplace things. Finally I insisted upon knowing why he had wanted me to come, and he replied that the reason for it had already been fulfilled, that he had nothing more to say, and that I could go as soon as I wanted to. He appeared quite calm, but he must have been very nervous. For as I stood by the desk, telling him what I thought of his actions, he moved his hand hastily among the papers there and upset the ink stand. I jumped back, but not before I had received several large spots of ink on my trousers. He was profuse in his apologies for the accident, and tried to take out the spots with blotting paper. Then at last, when I insisted upon going, he looked out to see whether there was still a light on the stairs, and led me down to the door himself, standing there for some time looking after me.

"I was slightly alarmed as well as angry at his actions. I believe that he could not have been quite in his right mind, that the strain of nervousness which was apparent in his nature had really made him ill. For I remember several peculiar incidents of my visit to him. One of these was that he almost insisted upon my taking away with me, ostensibly to take care of them, several valuable pieces of jewelry which he possessed. He seemed almost offended when I refused to do anything of the kind. Then, as I parted from him at the door, not in a very good humour I will acknowledge, he said to me: 'You will think of me very often in the future—more often than you would believe now!'

"This is all the truth, and nothing but the truth, about my visit to John Siders on the evening of September 23rd. As it had been his wish I said nothing to the ladies at home, or to any one else about the occurrence. And as I have told you, I destroyed his letter asking me to come to him.

"The following day about noon, the Commissioner of Police from G— called at my office in the factory, and informed me bluntly that John Siders had been found shot dead in his lodgings that morning. I was naturally shocked, as one would be at such news, in spite of the fact that I had parted from the man in anger, and that I had no reason to be particularly fond of him. What shocked me most of all was the sudden thought that John had taken his own life. It was a perfectly natural thought when I considered his nervousness, and his peculiar actions of the evening before. I believe I exclaimed, 'It was a suicide!' almost without realising that I was doing so. The commissioner looked at me sharply and said that suicide was out of the question, that it was an evident case of murder. He questioned me as to Siders' affairs, of which I told only what every one here in the village knew. I did not consider it incumbent upon me to disclose to the police the disgrace of the man's early life. I had been obliged to hurt him cruelly enough because of that, and I saw no necessity for blackening his name, now that he was dead. Also, as according to what the commissioner said, it was a case of murder for robbery, I did not wish to go into any details of our connection with Siders that would cause the name of my ward to be mentioned. After a few more questions the commissioner left me. I was busy all the afternoon, and did not return to my home until later than usual. I found my aunt somewhat worried because Miss Roemer had left the house immediately after our early dinner, and had not yet returned. We both knew the girl to be still grieving over her broken engagement, and we dreaded the effect this last dreadful news might have on her. We supposed, however, that she had gone to spend the afternoon with a friend, and were rather glad to be spared the necessity of telling her at once what had happened. I had scarcely finished my supper, when the door bell rang, and to my astonishment the Mayor of Grunau was announced, accompanied by the same Police Commissioner who had visited me in my office that morning. The Mayor was an old friend of mine and his deeply grave face showed me that something serious had occurred. It was indeed serious! and for some minutes I could not grasp the meaning of the commissioner's questions. Finally I realised with a tremendous shock that I—I myself was under suspicion of the murder of John Siders. The description given by the old servant of the man who had visited Siders the evening before, the very clothes that I wore, my hat and the trousers spotted by the purple ink, led to my identification as this mysterious visitor. The servant had let me in but she had not seen me go out.

"Then I discovered—when confronted suddenly with my own revolver which had been found on the floor of the room, some distance from the body of the dead man, that this same revolver had been identified as mine by my ward, Eleonora Roemer, who had been to the police station at G— in the early afternoon hours. Some impulse of loyalty to her dead lover, some foolish feminine fear that I might have spoken against him in my earlier interviews with the commissioner had driven the girl to this step. A few questions sufficed to draw from her the story of her secret engagement, of its ending, and of my quarrel with John. I will say for her that I am certain she did not realise that all these things were calculated to cast suspicion on me. The poor girl is too unused to the ways of police courts, to the devious ways of the law, to realise what she was doing. The sight of my revolver broke her down completely and she acknowledged that it was mine. That is all. Except that I was arrested and brought here as you see. I told the commissioner the story of my visit to John Siders exactly as I told it to you, but it was plain to be seen that he did not believe me. It is plain to be seen also, that he is firmly convinced of my guilt and that he is greatly satisfied with himself at having traced the criminal so soon."

"And yet he was not quite satisfied," said Muller gently. "You see that he has sent to the Capital for assistance on the case." Muller felt this little untruth to be justified for the sake of the honour of the police force.

"Yes, I'm surprised at that," said Graumann in his former tone of weariness. "What do you think you will be able to do about it?"

"I must ask questions here and there before I can form a plan of campaign," replied Muller. "What do you think about it yourself? Who do you think killed Siders?"

"How can I know who it was? I only know it is not I," answered Graumann.

"Did he have any enemies?"

"No, none that I knew of, and he had few friends either."

"You knew there was a sum of money missing from his rooms?"

"Yes, the sum they named to me was just about the price that he had received for the sale of his property here. They did me the honour to believe that if I had taken the money at all, I had done so merely as a blind. At least they did not take me for a thief as well as a murderer. If the money is really missing, it was for its sake he was murdered I suppose."

"Yes, that would be natural," said Muller. "And you know nothing of any other relations or connections that the man may have had? Anything that might give us a clue to the truth?"

"No, nothing. He stood so alone here, as far as I knew. Of course, as I told you, his actions of the evening before having been so peculiar—and as I knew that he was not in the happiest frame of mind—I naturally thought of suicide at once, when they told me that he had been found shot dead.

Then they told me that the appearance of the room and many other things, proved suicide to have been out of the question. I know nothing more about it. I cannot think any more about it. I know only that I am here in danger of being sentenced for the crime that I never committed—that is enough to keep any man's mind busy." He leaned back with an intense fatigue in every line of his face and figure.

Muller rose from his seat. "I am afraid I have tired you, Mr. Graumann," he said, "but it was necessary that I should know all that you had to tell me. Try and rest a little now and meanwhile be assured that I am doing all I can to find out the truth of this matter. As far as I can tell now I do not believe that you have killed John Siders. But I must find some further proofs that will convince others as well as myself. If it is of any comfort to you, I can tell you that during a long career as police detective I have been most astonishingly fortunate in the cases I have undertaken. I am hoping that my usual good luck will follow me here also. I am hoping it for your sake."

The man on the cot took the hand the detective offered him and pressed it firmly. "You will let me know as soon as you have found anything—anything that gives me hope?"

"I will indeed. And now save your strength and do not worry. I will help you if it is in my power."

After leaving the prison, Muller took the train for the village of Grunau, about half an hour distant from the city. He found his way easily to Graumann's home, an attractive old house set in a large garden amid groups of beautiful old trees. When he sent up his card to Miss Graumann, the old lady tripped down stairs in a flutter of excitement.

"Did you see him?" she asked. "You have been to the prison? What do you think? How does he seem?"

"He seems calm today," replied Muller, "although the confinement and the anxiety are evidently wearing on him."

"And you heard his story? And you believe him innocent?"

"I am inclined to do so. But there is more yet for me to investigate in this matter. It is certainly not as simple as the police here seem to believe. May I speak to your ward, Miss Roemer? She is at home now?"

"Yes, Lora is at home. If you will wait here a moment I will send her in."

Muller paced up and down the large sunny room, casting a glance over the handsome old pieces of furniture and the family portraits on the wall. It was evidently the home of generations of well-to-do, well-bred people, the narrow circle of whose life was made rich by congenial duties and a comfortable feeling of their standing in the community.

While he was studying one of the portraits more carefully, he became aware that there was some one in the room. He turned and saw a tall blond girl standing by the door. She had entered so softly that even Muller's quick ear had not heard the opening of the door.

"Do you wish to speak to me?" she said, coming down into the room. "I am Eleonora Roemer."

Her face, which could be called handsome in its even regularity of feature and delicate skin, was very pale now, and around her eyes were dark rings that spoke of sleepless nights. Grief and mental shock were preying upon this girl's mind. "She is not the one to make a confidant of those around her," thought Muller to himself. Then he added aloud: "If it does not distress you too much to talk about this sad affair, I will be very grateful if you will answer a few questions."

"I will tell you whatever I can," said the girl in the same low even tone in which she had first spoken. "Miss Graumann tells me that you have come from Vienna to take up this case. It is only natural that we should want to give you every assistance in our power."

"What is your opinion about it?" was Muller's next remark, made rather suddenly after a moment's pause.

The directness of the question seemed to shake the girl out of her enforced calm. A slow flush mounted into her pale cheeks and then died away, again leaving them whiter than before. "I do not know—oh, I do not know what to believe."

"But you do not think Mr. Graumann capable of such a crime, do you?"

"Not of the robbery, of course not; that would be absurd! But has it been clearly proven that there is a robbery? Might it not have been—might they not have—"

"You mean, might they not have quarreled? Of course there is that possibility. And that is why I wanted to speak to you. You are the one person who could possibly throw light on this subject. Was there any other reason beyond the dead man's past that would render your guardian unwilling to have you marry him?"

Again the slow flush mounted to Eleonora Roemer's cheeks and her head drooped.

"I fear it may be painful for you to answer this," said Muller gently, "and yet I must insist on it in the interest of justice."

"He—my guardian—wished to marry me himself," the girl's words came slowly and painfully.

Muller drew in his breath so sharply that it was almost like a whistle. "He did not tell me that; it might make a difference."

"That . . . that is . . . what I fear," said the girl, her eyes looking keenly into those of the man who sat opposite. "And then, it was his revolver."

"Then you do believe him guilty?"

"It would be horrible, horrible—and yet I do not know what to think."

There was silence in the room for a moment. Miss Roemer's head drooped again and her hands twisted nervously in her lap. Muller's brain was very busy with this new phase of the problem. Finally he spoke.

"Let us dismiss this side of the question and talk of another phase of it, a phase of which it is necessary for me to know something. You would naturally be the person nearest the dead man, the one, the only one, perhaps, to whom he had given his confidence. Do you know of any enemies he might have had in the city?"

"No, I do not know of any enemies, or even of any friends he had there. When the terrible thing happened that clouded his past, when he had regained his freedom, after his term of imprisonment, there was no one left whom he cared to see again. He does not seem to have borne any malice towards the banker who accused him of the theft. The evidence was so strong against him that he felt the suspicion was justified. But there was hatred in his heart for one man, for the Justice who sentenced him, Justice Schmidt, who is now Attorney General in G—."

"The man who, in the name of the State, will conduct this case?" asked Muller quickly.

"Yes, I believe it is so. Is it not an irony that this man, the only one whom John really hated, should be the one to avenge him now?"

"H'm! yes. But did you know of any friends in G—?"

"No, none at all."

"No friends whom he might have made while he was in America and then met again in Germany?"

"No, he never spoke of any such to me. He told me that he made few friends. He did not seek them for he was afraid that they might find out what had happened and turn from him. He was morbidly sensitive and could not bear the disappointment."

"Why did he return to Germany?"

"He was lonely and wanted to come home again. He had made money in America—John was very clever and highly educated—but his heart longed for his own tongue and his own people."

Muller took a folded piece of paper from his pocket. "Do you know this handwriting?"

Miss Roemer read the few lines hastily and her voice trembled as she said: "This is John's handwriting. I know it well. This is the letter that was found on the table?"

"Yes, this letter appears to be the last he had written in life. Do you know to whom it could have been written? The envelope, as I suppose you know from the newspaper reports, was not addressed. Do you know of any friends with whom he could have been on terms of sufficient intimacy to write such a letter? Do you know what these plans for the future could have been? It would certainly be natural that he should have spoken to you first about them."

"No; I cannot understand this letter at all," replied the girl. "I have thought of it frequently these terrible days. I have wondered why it was that if he had friends in the city, he did not speak to me of them. He repeatedly told me that he had no friends there at all, that his life should begin anew after we were married."

"And did he have any particular plans, in a business way, perhaps?"

"No; he had a comfortable little income and need have no fear for the future. John was, of course, too young a man to settle down and do nothing. But the only definite plans he had made were that we should travel a little at first, and then he would look about him for a congenial occupation. I always thought it likely he would resume a law practice somewhere. I cannot understand in the slightest what the plans are to which the letter referred."

"And do you think, from what you know of his state of mind when you saw him last, that he would be likely so soon to be planning pleasures like this?"

"No, no indeed! John was terribly crushed when my guardian insisted on breaking off our engagement. Until my twenty-fourth birthday I am still bound to do as my guardian says, you know. John's life and early misfortune made him, as I have already said, morbidly sensitive and the thought that it would be a bar to anything we might plan in the future, had rendered him so depressed that—and it was not the least of my anxieties and my troubles—that I feared . . . I feared anything might happen."

"You feared he might take his own life, do you mean?"

"Yes, yes, that is what I feared. But is it not terrible to think that he should have died this way—by the hand of a murderer?"

"H'm! And you cannot remember any possible friend he may have found—some schoolboy friend of his youth, perhaps, with whom he had again struck up an acquaintance."

"Oh, no, no, I am positive of that. John could not bear to hear the names even of the people he had known before his misfortune. Still, I do remember his once having spoken of a man, a German he had met in Chicago and rather taken a fancy to, and who had also returned to Germany."

"Could this possibly have been the man to whom the letter is addressed?"

"No, no. This friend of John's was not married; I remember his saying that. And he lived in Germany somewhere—let me think—yes, in Frankfort-on-Main."

"And do you remember the man's name?"

"No, I cannot, I am sorry to say. John only mentioned it once. It was only by a great effort that I could remember the incident at all."

"And has it not struck you as rather peculiar that this friend, the one to whom the cordial letter was addressed, did not come forward and make his identity known? G— is a city, it is true, but it is not a very large city, and any man being on terms of intimate acquaintance with one who was murdered would be apt to come forward in the hope of throwing some light on the mystery."

"Why, yes, I had not thought of that. It is peculiar, is it not? But some people are so foolishly afraid of having anything to do with the police, you know."

"That is very true, Miss Roemer. Still it is a queer incident and something that I must look into."

"What do you believe?" asked the girl tensely.

"I am not in a position to say as yet. When I am, I will come to you and tell you."

"Then you do not think that my guardian killed John—that there was a quarrel between the men?"

"There is, of course, a possibility that it may have been so. You know your guardian better than I do, naturally. Our knowledge of a man's character is often a far better guide than any circumstantial evidence."

"My guardian is a man of the greatest uprightness of character. But he can be very hard and pitiless sometimes. And he has a violent temper which his weak heart has forced him to keep in control of late years."

"All this speaks for the possibility that there may have been a quarrel ending in the fatal shot. But what I want to know from you is this—do you think it possible, that, this having happened, Albert Graumann would not have been the first to confess his unpremeditated crime? Is not this the most likely thing for a man of his character to do? Would he so stubbornly deny it, if it had happened?"

The girl started. "I had not thought of that! Why, why, of course, he might have killed John in a moment of temper, but he was never a man to conceal a fault. He is as pitiless towards his own weakness, as towards that of others. You are right, oh, you must be right. Oh, if you could take this awful fear from my heart! Even my grief for John would be easier to bear then."

Muller rose from his chair. "I think I can promise you that this load will be lifted from your heart, Miss Roemer."

"Then you believe—that it was just a case of murder for robbery? For the money? And John had some valuable jewelry, I know that."

"I do not know yet," replied Muller slowly, "but I will find out, I generally do."

"Oh, to think that I should have done that poor man such an injustice! It is terrible, terrible! This house has been ghastly these days. His poor aunt knows that he is innocent—she could never believe otherwise—she has felt the hideous suspicion in my mind—it has made her suffering worse—will they ever forgive me?"

"Her joy, if I can free her nephew, will make her forget everything. Go to her now, Miss Roemer, comfort her with the assurance that you also believe him to be innocent. I must hasten back to G— and go on with this quest."

The girl stood at the doorway shaded by the overhanging branches of two great trees, looking down the street after the slight figure of the detective. "Oh, it is all easier to hear, hard as it is, easier now that this horrible suspicion has gone from my mind—why did I not think of that before?"

Alone in the corner of the smoking compartment in the train to G—, Muller arranged in his mind the facts he had already gathered. He had questioned the servants of John Siders' former household, had found that the dead man received very few letters, only an occasional business communication from his bank. Of the few others, the servants knew nothing except that he had always thrown the envelopes carelessly in the waste paper basket and had never seemed to have any correspondence which he cared to conceal. No friend from elsewhere had ever visited him in Grunau, and he had made few friends there except the Graumann family.

The facts of the case, as he knew them now, were such as to make it extremely doubtful that Graumann was the murderer. Muller himself had been inclined to believe in the possibility of a quarrel between the two men, particularly when he had heard that Graumann himself was in love with his handsome ward. But the second thought that came to him then, impelled by the unerring instinct that so often guided him to the truth, was the assurance that in a case of this kind, in a case of a quarrel terminating fatally, a man like Albert Graumann would be the very first to give himself up to the police and to tell the facts of the case. Albert Graumann was a man of honour and unimpeachable integrity. Such a man would not persist in a foolish denial of the deed which he had committed in a moment of temper. There would be nothing to gain from it, and his own conscience would be his severest judge. "The disorder in the room?" thought Muller. "It'll be too late for that now. I suppose they have rearranged the place. I can only go by what the local detectives have seen, by the police reports. But I do not understand this extreme disorder. There is no reason why there should be a struggle when the robber was armed with a pistol. If Siders was supposed to have been interrupted when writing a letter, interrupted by a thief come with intent to steal, a thief armed with a revolver, the sight of this weapon alone would be sufficient to insure his not moving from his seat. I can understand the open drawers and cupboard; that is explained by the thief's hasty search for booty. But the torn window curtain and the overturned chairs are peculiar.

"Of course there is always a possibility that the thief might have entered one room while Siders was in the other; that the latter might have surprised the robber in his search for money or valuables, and that there might have been a hand-to-hand struggle before the intruder could pull out his revolver. Oh, if I could only have seen the body! This is working under terrific difficulties. The marks of a hand-to-hand struggle would have been very plain on the clothes and on the person of the murdered man. But this letter? I do not understand this letter at all. It is the dead man's handwriting, that we know, but why did not the friend to whom it was addressed come forward and make himself known? As far as I can learn from the police reports in G—, there was no personal interest shown, no personal inquiries made about the dead man. There was only the natural excitement that a murder would create. Now a family, expecting to make a pleasure excursion with a friend in a day or two and suddenly hearing that this friend had been found murdered in his lodgings, would be inclined to take some little personal interest in the matter. These people must have been in town and at home, for the excursion spoken of in the letter was to occur two days after the murder. Miss Roemer's remark about the dread that some people have as to any connection with the police, is true to a limited extent only. It is true only of the ignorant mind, not of a man presumably well-to-do and properly educated. I do not understand why the man to whom this letter was addressed has not made himself known. The only explanation is—that there was no such man! A sudden sharp whistle broke from the detective's lips.

"I must examine the dead man's personal effects, his baggage, his papers; there may be something there. His queer letter to Graumann—his desire that the latter's visit should be kept secret—a visit which apparently had no cause at all, except to get Graumann to the house, to get him to the house in a way that he should be seen coming, but should not be seen going away. What does this mean?

"Graumann was the only person against whom Siders had an active cause of quarrel for the moment. There was one other man whom he hated, and this other man was the prosecuting attorney who would conduct any case of murder that came up in the town of G—.

"Now John Siders is found murdered—is found killed, in his lodgings, the morning after he has arranged things so that his antagonist, his rival in love, Albert Graumann, shall come under suspicion of having murdered him.

"What evidence have we that this man did not commit suicide? We have the evidence of the disorder in the room, a disorder that could have been made just as well by the man himself before he ended his own life. We have the evidence of a letter to some unknown, making plans for pleasure during the next days, and speaking of further plans, presumably concerning business, for the future. In a town the size of G—, where every one must have read of the murder, no one has come forward claiming to be the friend for whom this letter was written. Until this Unknown makes himself known, the letter as an evidence points rather to premeditated suicide than to the contrary. Oh, if I could only have seen the body! They tell me the pistol was found some little distance from the body. Is it at all likely that a murderer would go away leaving such evidence behind him? If Graumann had killed Siders in a hasty quarrel, he might possibly, in his excitement, have left his revolver. But I have already disposed of this possibility. A man of sufficient brains to so carefully plan his suicide as to conceal every trace of it and cast suspicion upon the man who had made him unhappy, such a one would be quite clever enough to throw the pistol far away from his body and to leave no traces of powder on his coat or any such other evidence.

"If I were to say now what I think, I would say that John Siders deliberately took his own life and planned it in such a way as to cast suspicion upon Albert Graumann. But that would indeed be a terrible revenge. And I must have some tangible proof of it before any court will accept my belief. This proof must be hidden somewhere. The thing for me to do is to find it."

The evidence gathered at the time of the death went to show that Siders had been paid a considerable sum in cash for the sale of his property at Grunau. And there was no trace of his having deposited this sum in any bank in G— or in Grunau, in both of which places he had deposited other securities. Therefore the money had presumably been in his room at the time of his death. A search had been made for this money in every possible place of concealment among the dead man's belongings, and it had not been found. Muller asked the Police Commissioner to give him the key to the rooms, which were still officially closed, and also the keys to the dead man's pieces of baggage. Commissioner Lange seemed to think all this extra search quite unnecessary, as it did not occur to him that anything else was to be looked for except the money.

It was quite late when Muller began his examination of the dead man's effects. He was struck by the fact that there was scarcely a bit of paper to be found anywhere, no letters, no business papers, except bank books showing the amount of his securities in the bank in G— and in Grunau, and giving facts about some investments in Chicago. There was nothing of more recent date and no personal correspondence whatever. The same was true of the pockets of the suit Siders had been wearing at the time of his death. A man of any property or position at all in the world gathers about him so much of this kind of material that its absence shows premeditation. The suit Siders had been wearing when he was killed was lying on the table in the room. It was a plain grey business suit of good cut and material. The body had been prepared for burial in a beseeming suit of black. Muller made a careful examination of the clothes, and found only what the police reports showed him had already been found by the examination made by the local authorities. Upon a second careful examination, however, he found that in one of the vest pockets there was a little extra pocket, like a change pocket, and in it he found a crumpled piece of paper. He took it out, smoothed and read it. It was a post office receipt for a registered letter. The date was still clear, but the name of the person to whom the letter had been addressed was illegible. The creases of the paper and a certain dampness, as if it had been inadvertently touched by a wet finger, had smeared the writing. But the letter had been sent the day before the death of John Siders, and it had been registered from the main post office in G—. This was sufficient for Muller. Then he turned to the desk. Here also there was nothing that could help him. But a sudden thought, came to him, and he took up the blotting pad. This, to his delight, was in the form of a book with a handsome embroidered cover. It looked comparatively new and was, as Muller surmised, a gift from Miss Roemer to her betrothed. But few of the pages had been used, and on two of them a closely written letter had been blotted several times, showing that there had been several sheets of the letter. Muller held it up to the looking-glass, but the repeated blotting had blurred the writing to such an extent that it was impossible to decipher any but a few disconnected words, which gave no clue. On a page further along on the blotter, however, he saw what appeared to be the impression of an address. He held it up to the glass and gave a whistle of delight. The words could be plainly deciphered here:

> *MR. LEO PERNBURG,*
>
> *FRANKFURT AM MAIN,*
>
> *MAINZER LANDSTRASSE.*

and above the name was a smear which, after a little study, could be deciphered as the written word "Registered."

With this page of the blotter carefully tucked away in his pocketbook, Muller hurried to the post office, arriving just at closing hour. He made himself known at once to the postmaster, and asked to be shown the records of registered letters sent on a certain date. Here he found scheduled a letter addressed to Mr. Leo Pernburg, Frankfurt am Main, sent by John Siders, G—, Josef Street 7.

Muller then hastened to the telegraph office and despatched a lengthy telegram to the postal authorities in Frankfurt am Main. When the answer came to him next morning, he packed his grip and took the first express train leaving G—. He first made a short visit, however, to Albert Graumann's cell in the prison. Muller was much too kind-hearted not to relieve the anxiety of this man, to whom such mental strain might easily prove fatal. He told Graumann that he was going in search of evidence which might throw light on the death of Siders, and comforted the prisoner with the assurance that he, Muller, believed Graumann innocent, and believed also that within a day or two he would return to G— with proofs that his belief was the right one.

Three days later Muller returned to Grunau and went at once to the Graumann home. It was quite late when he arrived, but he had already notified Miss Roemer by telegram as to his coming, with a request that she should be ready to see him. He found her waiting for him, pale and anxious-eyed, when he arrived. "I have been to Frankfurt am Main," he said, "and I have seen Mr. Pernburg—"

"Yes, yes, that is the name; now I remember," interrupted the girl eagerly. "That is the name of John's friend there."

"I have seen Mr. Pernburg and he gave me this letter." Muller laid a thick envelope on the girl's lap.

She looked down at it, her eyes widening as if she had seen a ghost. "That—that is John's writing," she exclaimed in a hoarse whisper. "Where did it come from?"

"Pernburg gave it to me. The day before his death John Siders sent him this letter, requesting that Pernburg forward it to you before a certain date. When I explained the circumstances to Mr. Pernburg, he gave me the letter at once. I feel that this paper holds the clue to the mystery. Will you open it?"

With trembling hands the girl tore open the envelope. It enclosed still another sealed envelope, without an address. But there was a sheet of paper around this letter, on which was written the following:

My beloved Eleonore:

Before you read what I have to say to you here I want you to promise me, in memory of our love and by your hope of future salvation, that you will do what I ask you to do.

I ask you to give the enclosed letter, although it is addressed to you, to the Judge who will preside in the trial against Graumann. The letter is written to you and will be given back to you. For you, the beloved of my soul, you are the only human being with whom I can still communicate, to whom I can still express my wishes. But you must not give the letter to the Judge until you have assured yourself that the prosecuting attorney insists upon Graumann's guilt. In case he is acquitted, which I do not think probable, then open this letter in the presence of Graumann himself and one or two witnesses. For I wish Graumann, who is innocent, to be able to prove his innocence.

You will know by this time that I have determined to end my life by my own hand. Forgive me, beloved. I cannot live on without you—without the honour of which I was robbed so unjustly.

God bless you.

One who will love you even beyond the grave, Remember your promise. It was given to the dead. JOHN.

"Oh, what does it all mean?" asked Eleonora, dropping the letter in her lap.

"It is as I thought," replied Muller. "John Siders took his own life, but made every arrangement to have suspicion fall upon Graumann."

"But why? oh, why?"

"It was a terrible revenge. But perhaps—perhaps it was just retribution. Graumann would not understand that Siders could have been suspected of, and imprisoned for, a theft he had not committed. He must know now that it is quite possible for a man to be in danger of sentence of death even, for a crime of which he is innocent."

"Oh, my God! It is terrible." The girl's head fell across her folded arms on the table. Deep shuddering sobs shook her frame.

Muller waited quietly until the first shock had passed. Finally her sobs died away and she raised her head again. "What am I to do?" she asked.

"You must open this letter tomorrow in the presence of the Police Commissioner and Graumann."

"But this promise? This promise that he asks of me—that I should wait until the trial?"

"You have not given this promise. Would you take it upon yourself to endanger your guardian's life still more? Every further day spent in his prison, in this anxiety, might be fatal."

"But this promise? The promise demanded of me by the man to whom I had given my love? Is it not my duty to keep it?"

Muller rose from his chair. His slight figure seemed to grow taller, and the gentleness in his voice gave way to a commanding tone of firm decision.

"Our duty is to the living, not to the dead. The dead have no right to drag down others after them. Believe me, Miss Roemer, the purpose that was in your betrothed's mind when he ended his own life, has been fulfilled.

Albert Graumann knows now what are the feelings of a man who bears the prison stigma unjustly. He will never again judge his fellow-men as harshly as he has done until now. His soul has been purged in these terrible days; have you the right to endanger his life needlessly?"

"Oh, I do not know! I do not know what to do."

"I have no choice," said Muller firmly. "It is my duty to make known the fact to the Police Commissioner that there is such a letter in existence. The Police Commissioner will then have to follow his duty in demanding the letter from you. Mr. Pernburg, Sider's friend, saw this argument at once. Although he also had a letter from the dead man, asking him to send the enclosure to you, registered, on a certain date, he knew that it was his duty to give all the papers to the authorities. Would it not be better for you to give them up of your own free will?" Muller took a step nearer the girl and whispered: "And would it not be a noble revenge on your part? You would be indeed returning good for evil."

Eleonora clasped her hands and her lips moved as if in silent prayer. Then she rose slowly and held out the letters to Muller. "Do what you will with them," she said. "My strength is at an end."

The next day, in the presence of Commissioner Lange and of the accused Albert Graumann, Muller opened the letter which he had received from Miss Roemer and read it aloud. The girl herself, by her own request, was not present. Both Muller and Graumann understood that the strain of this message from the dead would be too much for her to bear. This was the letter:

G— September 21st.

My beloved:

When you put this letter in the hands of the Judge, I will have found in death the peace that I could never find on earth. There was no chance of happiness for me since I have realised that I love you, that you love me, and that I must give you up if I am to remain what I have always been—in spite of everything—a man of honour.

Albert Graumann would keep his word, this I know. Wherever you might follow me as my wife, there his will would have been before us, blasting my reputation, blackening the flame which you were to bear.

I could not have endured it. My soul was sick of all this secrecy, sick at the injustice of mankind. In spite of worldly success, my life was cold and barren in the strange land to which I had fled. My home called to me and I came back to it.

I kissed the earth of my own country, and I wept at my mother's grave. I was happy again under the skies which had domed above my childhood. For I am an honest man, beloved, and I always have been.

One day I sat at table beside the man—the Judge who condemned me, here in G— in those terrible days. He naturally did not know me again. I, myself, brought the conversation around to a professional subject. I asked him if it were not possible that circumstantial evidence could lie; if the entire past, the reputation of the accused would not be a factor in his favour. The Judge denied it. It was his opinion, beyond a doubt, that circumstantial evidence was sufficient to convict anyone.

My soul rose within me. This infallibility, this legal arrogance, aroused my blood. "That man should have a lesson!" I said to myself.

But I had forgotten it all—all my anger, all my hatred and bitterness, when I met you. I dare not trust myself to think of you too much, now that everything is arranged for the one last step. It takes all my control to keep my decision unwavering while I sit here and tell you how much your love, your great tenderness, your sweet trust in me, meant to me.

Let me talk rather of Albert Graumann. I will forgive him for believing in my guilt, but I cannot forgive him that he, the man of cultivation and mental grasp, could not believe it possible for a convicted thief to have repented and to have lived an honest life after the atonement of his crime. I still cannot believe that this was Graumann's opinion. I am forced to think that it was an excuse only on his part, an excuse to keep us apart, an excuse to keep you for himself.

You are lost to me now. There is nothing more in life for me. If the injustice of mankind has stained my honour beyond repair, has robbed me of every chance of happiness at any time and in any place, then I die easily, beloved, for there is little charm in such a life as would be mine after this.

But I do not wish to die quite in vain. There are two men who have touched my life, who need the lesson my death can teach them. These men are Albert Graumann and the prosecuting attorney Gustav Schmidt, the man who once condemned me so cruelly. His present position would make him the representative of the state in a murder trial, and I know his opinions too well not to foresee that he would declare Graumann guilty because of the circumstantial evidence which will be against him. My letter, given to the Presiding Judge after the Attorney has made his speech, will cause him humiliation, will ruin his brilliant arguments and cast ridicule upon him.

Do not think me hard or revengeful. I do not hate anyone now that death is so near. But is it inhuman that I should want to teach these two men a lesson? a lesson which they need, believe me, and it is such a slight compensation for the torture these last eight years have been to me!

And now I will explain in detail all the circumstances. I have arranged that Albert Graumann shall come to me on the evening of September 23rd between 7 and 8 o'clock. I asked him to do so by letter, asking him also to keep the fact of his visit to me a secret. Tonight, the 22nd of September, I received his answer promising that he would come. Therefore I can look upon everything that is to happen, as having already happened, for now there need be no further change in my plans. I will send this letter this evening to my friend Pernburg in Frankfurt am Main. In case anything should happen that would render impossible for me to carry out my plans, I will send Pernburg another letter asking him not to carry out the instructions of the first.

I can now proceed to tell you what will happen here tomorrow evening, the 23rd of September.

Albert Graumann will come to me, unknown to his family or friends, as I have asked him to come. I will so arrange it that the *old servant will see him come in but will not see him go out. My landlady will not be in my way, for she has already told me that she will spend the night of the 23rd with her mother, in another part of the city. It is to be a birthday celebration I believe, so that I can be certain her plans will not be changed.*

Graumann and I will be alone, therefore, with no reliable witnesses near. I will keep him there for a little while with commonplace conversation, for I have nothing to say to him. If he moves near the desk I will upset the inkbottle. The spots on his clothes will be another evidence against him. I will endeavour to get him to keep my jewelry which is, as you know, of considerable value. I will tell him that I am going away for a while and ask him to take charge of it for me. I, myself, will take him down to the door and let him out, when I have satisfied myself that the old servant is in bed or at least at the back of the house. The revolver which shall end my misery is Graumann's property. I took it from its place without his knowledge.

The 10,000 gulden which I told my landlady were still in the house, and which would therefore be thought missing after my death, I have deposited in a bank in Frankfort in your name. Here is the certificate of deposit.

I will endeavour not to hold the revolver sufficiently close to have the powder burn my clothes. And I will exert every effort of mind and body to throw it far from me after I have fired the fatal shot. I think that I will be able to do this, for I am a very good shot and I have no fear of death. One thing more I will do, to turn aside all suspicion of suicide. I will write a letter to some person who does not exist, a letter which will make it appear as if I were in excellent humour and planning for the future.

And now, good-bye to life. People have called me eccentric, they may be right. This last deed of mine at least, is out of the ordinary. No one will say now that ended my life in a moment of darkened mind, in a rush of despair. My brain is perfectly clear, my heart beats calmly, now that I have arranged everything for my departure from this world of falsehood and unreality. My last deed shall go to prove to the world how little actual, apparent facts can be trusted.

The one thing real, the one thing true in all this world of false-hood was your love and your trust. I thank you for it.

THEODOR BELLMNN, KNOWN AS JOHN SIDERS.

Joseph Muller refuses to take any particular credit for this case. The letter would have come in time to prevent Graumann's conviction without his assistance, he says. The only person whose gratitude he has a right to is Prosecuting Attorney Gustav Schmidt. He managed to have the Police Commissioner in G— read the letter in detail to the attorney. But Muller himself knows that it failed of its effect, so far as that dignitary was concerned. For nothing but open ridicule could ever convince a man of such decided opinions that he is not the one infallible person in the world.

But Albert Graumann had learned his lesson. And he told Muller himself that the few days of life which might remain to him were a gift to him from the detective. He felt that his weak heart would not have stood the strain and the disgrace of an open trial, even if that trial ended in acquittal. Two months later he was found dead in his bed, a calm smile on his lips.

Before he died he had learned that it was the undaunted courage of his timid little old aunt that had brought Muller to take charge of the case and to free her beloved nephew from the dreaded prison. And the last days that these two passed together were very happy.

But as aforesaid, Muller refuses to have this case included in the list of his successes. He did not change the ultimate result, he merely anticipated it, he says.

Mary Elizabeth Braddon (1835–1915), after a brief career as an actress, became a very popular writer of the Victorian and early Edwardian period. She is best remembered for her enormously popular sensational novel Lady Audley's Secret *(1862). While this work certainly deals with crimes, with themes partially based on the Road Hill House murder of 1860 which also inspired Wilkie Collins and Charles Dickens, it is not crime fiction in any modern sense. However, her earlier work,* Trail of the Serpent *(1860), has been called the first English detective novel. Elements include boy assistants for the detectives (not unlike Holmes's Irregulars), evidence planted on a corpse, and the detective's use of disguise. The principal detective, Joseph Peters, is also quite unusual: Not only is he mute, he is lower-class. Although Braddon wrote eighty novels, she also wrote numerous short stories. The following, which first appeared in* Lloyd's Weekly Newspaper *for December 27, 1896, combines a ghost story with a sad tale of a crime gone badly wrong.*

THE WINNING SEQUENCE

M. E. BRADDON

THE PROLOGUE

The house is silent. A roomy, old-fashioned house—in the Royal village, that old-world Richmond to which King and Queen, and dukes and duchesses, and loose-lived ladies used to come a century and a half ago, and where Royalty still inhabits and loyal joy-bells ring loud.

The house is silent in the quiet, grey hour betwixt night and morning. Through the tall window on the staircase, a horizontal rift in the sky, a streak of pale light beneath a ridge of black cloud, tells that day is near.

Not a sound but the faint patter of mice, like the trickling of water, behind the worm-eaten panelling. Not a sound? Yes; there is a sound—a sound which has been heard often in that house—on that landing, at just that grey hour which is neither night nor morning. The sound of a footfall that is lighter than tread of a human foot; the sound of a sigh that reaches from the far distance of an unknown grave.

A door opens gently, slowly, and a scared face looks out into the dimness. It is the mistress of the house, who has heard that footfall before tonight, and who knows the story of it, and wants to see and hear more than mortal lips can tell her. She steps softly in slippered feet, as if her footsteps would disturb a ghost. She sees, or fancies she sees, in that grey twilight—first a pair of slippers, standing on the threshold of the door opposite her own door— embroidered velvet slippers, with red heels; next, turning her eyes towards the staircase, she sees, or fancies she sees, a figure slowly descending—the figure of a woman, handsome, past her first youth, but still young; tall, commanding; dressed in a loose gown of Indian silk, curiously patterned, a dull red, with a yellow scroll figured over it. The woman of the house sees, or believes she sees, all this—every particular of the tall figure, the loose flowing hair, the bare white arms, even to the delicate modelling of the hand which lightly touches the stout oak banister-rail.

Slowly, softly, she follows that silent figure, treading so stealthily with its bare feet, slowly, stair by stair, with cautious pauses and lingering movements to the hall below, which is darker than that upper corridor; and, after gentlest opening of a door, into the dark drawing-room, where the woman of the house sees—or thinks she sees—that shadow woman strike a light with flint and steel and clumsy process of burning tinder, and so light a candle.

Then the shadow-woman sets down the tall silver candlestick on a phantasmal card-table. And the house-mistress sees that other woman who has been dead a century and a half kneel on the carpeted floor, which is scattered with cards thick as fallen leaves in November woods—kings and queens and aces, cards that turn the fortune of the game. She gathers them up in heaps, and kneeling by the table in the dim candlelight, she sorts pack after pack with infinite pains, assures herself with earnest eyes and puckered brows of numbers and of suits, each pack complete, and with nothing to spare; and then after this patient labour, which lasts a long time, lays one small pack of cards on the table, and flings all the rest about the floor around the card-table. The little pack of selected cards she thrusts into the bosom of her red and yellow bedgown; and then she blows out the candle and creeps out of the room and across the hall, and upstairs again, her figure lighted by an unearthly light—a bluish glimmer, faint and dim and fitful, which the woman of the house fancies must be the light that hangs above an unhallowed grave—a light whereof the shadow-woman is unconscious, and so must needs grope for a candle to light her stealthy search.

Slowly and softly she steps, with pale, naked foot, from stair to stair, and at the top of the staircase melts and is absorbed into the growing dawn; and, lo! when the living woman looks at the ground by the door of the empty bed-chamber the velvet shoes are gone. There is nothing left but a fancy or a dream. The old eight-day clock ticks in the dark hall below; the mice scamper, a bird sings on the little suburban garden outside, a cool breath of the morning blows in at an open window. The new-born day has begun in all its freshness of awaking bird and opening flower.

This is the story of the ghost.

Now for the story of the woman who lived and sinned and suffered in that house a century and a half ago.

THE STORY

"Dearest, if you would make me happy, you would give up high play," said the Colonel.

"I would go further than that," answered Mrs. Fermor; "if it would make you happy, I would give up cards altogether. What are they worth? An hour's excitement, the triumph of a winning hand, the misery of losing more than one can afford to lose, and make light of one's losses and sit smiling, while one thinks of servants' wages overdue, and black looks from one's milliner."

"Indeed, my love, this passion for play, so common in your charming sex nowadays, is a folly that touches near the edge of sin. And if you could make such a sacrifice for my sake, abandon a practice which fashion has made almost a necessity."

"What trumpery, worldly pleasure would I not sacrifice for you? Why I would give up more than cards. I would give up eating and drinking, and starve to death smiling in your face all the time, were we shipwrecked on a desert island. I would give up friends and home—change my religion."

"Thou shalt give up nothing but a passion which verges on vice. I know your losses at cards have vexed you."

"Yes! But I have been luckier lately. I won enough last week to pay all my little domestic debts. You will see only smiling faces among my household."

"My dear Sybilla, to my mind it is more degrading to win than to lose, and I doubt that good luck, as you call it, exercises a worse influence on a woman-gamester than ill-fortune."

"Yet, severely as you condemn the passion, you sometimes play yourself."

"I never venture more than I can afford to lose. I am a man, and I cannot always refuse to share the amusements of my friends."

They were in the first raptures of affianced love. She was young and beautiful—a widow who had married a man considerably her senior, and whose marriage had proved a disappointment, since the husband's fortune was less than people thought when the matrimonial bargain was struck. She had been left with an income just large enough to make a show with, and insufficient for comfort and show. She might have lived comfortably and avoided debt had she consented to exist without a couple of footmen and to ride in a hired coach. But the coach and footmen seemed to her as essential as the air she breathed, and when she played high it was with the hope of supplementing her income by a run of luck at quadrille or faro.

She had been a gamester for years, and with varying fortunes, now lifted to the Empyrean, now sunk low as Hades, hourly expecting to be hauled off to the Sponging House, and to see dress, coach, and gilded chair, abigail* and footman, vanish like Cinderella's cavalcade at the stroke of midnight.

For this season, since her engagement to Ralph Challoner, her star had been in the ascendant, and she had enjoyed a run of luck, at which her friends began to wonder, not without an occasional curled lip and shrugged shoulder, not without an occasional inuendo.

It was one of these inuendos, carelessly uttered in a crowded card-room, and overheard by Colonel Challoner, which had made him urge her to play no more. Not for worlds would he have repeated the sneer, the scornful hint,

---

* A lady's personal maid (the term is based on the name of a servant in a 1616 play).

which, had it not fallen from a woman's lips, would have been accounted for with blood. He told her only that he had observed the pernicious influence of the gaming-table. He had seen her feverish and excited at cards, ennuied, and absent-minded when she was away from the card-table. He had seen her haggard countenance and worried aspect, even during a run of luck which her friends had called miraculous.

He was a poor man—a soldier in a line regiment; but he had fought with Wolfe at Quebec, and his name had appeared advantageously in the Gazette. He knew that to marry the beautiful widow would be to hazard the peace and happiness of his future life; but he was still young enough to be desperately in love, and he turned a deaf ear to the whispers of prudence, when asked, "What have you, with scarce two hundred a year beyond a lieutenant-colonel's pay, to do with an expensive wife?"

He knew that the lady was living beyond her means, and had ventured to expostulate with her upon her extravagance, but she put him off with a kiss.

"When I am your wife I will live as you bid me," she said. "In a cottage by Kensington gravel-pits, with one red-elbowed servant-wench. Do you remember the cottage we passed that day we rode out westwards after we had visited the Princess—a wooden hovel, smothered with roses and honeysuckle? Well, Ralph, I would be content to live there—with you."

"Why your hoop would not pass through the doorway, love."

"I would live without a hoop; without fine clothes, or jewels"—with a sigh at the thought of jewels which might be seized by her creditors tomorrow, were they ill-natured enough to take the law of her.

"Then live without cards, Sybilla. Make that sacrifice, and I will hold myself the happiest of men."

"Let me get out of debt first," she urged.

"What? Are you so sure of winning?" His head was bent low to kiss the small hand that he was wont to clasp and fondle throughout their confidential talk, seated side by side on the Louis Quatorze sofa. Had he been looking at her he must have seen the sudden terror in her eyes, and the sickly whiteness under her rouge as he asked that question.

"Sure? No, of course not," she answered, fretfully; "who can be *sure* of winning? Only I believe in luck; and it seems foolish to leave off play until my luck changes."

His prayers prevailed, and she gave him her promise. But she did not give up her card-parties. She had her "day" and her "night"; and once a week the tables in her spacious drawing-room were going all day and all night; and she insisted upon Colonel Challoner's playing for at least an hour or so at her parties. "My future husband has puritanical ideas about women gamesters," she said, lightly; "and I am his obedient slave; so he must take my place and help to amuse my friends."

She would hang over his shoulder sometimes as he played, and her flashing eyes and flushed cheeks showed that she had lost none of her interest in the game. The perfume of her hair, the soft touch of her cheek as it brushed against his, even the light pressure of the restless hand which fluttered and trembled on his shoulder, distracted his attention from the cards in his hand, and his play would have been careless and automatic had she not advised and even commanded him.

He usually sat in her favorite place, at an oblong table that stood in front of two long, narrow windows. Voluminous curtains of gold and amber brocade covered the windows and the wall space between them, and these rich draperies made a splendid background for powder and diamonds, brilliant eyes and complexion; and her visitors, who noted Mrs. Fermor's preference for this particular table, were wont to ascribe the choice to vanity.

The game affected at that time, and in that particular circle, was a development, or at least a modification, of faro. Challoner, as deputy host, took the bank, and did his utmost to keep the play low; such play as would have provoked the scorn of those fine gentlemen Horace Walpole writes about, who could make love at the end of the room, while they were risking thousands on the turn of a card at the other end. Sybilla's luck seemed to have passed to her lover. Moderate as the play was, his winnings were not altogether despicable. He handed them to his mistress to dispose of among those insatiable creditors who made her life a burden.

"Another sop for Cerberus," she would say, laughingly, as she put his money in her apron pocket. "You really ought to play a bolder game, since Fortune is so kind to you."

"I doubt I am unwise to play at all, Sybilla; for, after all, it is only letting you gamble behind a mask."

"Pshaw, child, somebody must play for politeness sake; or people will leave off coming to my house. They would fancy themselves reproved by my self-denial. No, so long as I have my day and my evening in this court suburb, somebody must make my house pleasant."

She teased her lover until one night he consented to play high, still at her favourite table, with the background of voluminous brocade. A circular mirror, surmounted by a brazen eagle, occupied the only wall-space between the amplitude of the curtains, but the candles in the brazen sconces, on either side of the glass, were never lighted. Mrs. Fermor declared they threw the players' cards into shadow. There were only a pair of candles on each card-table, and people often complained to one another that Mrs. Fermor's drawing-room was too ill lighted for anything but a camera obscura.*

"If the play is to be serious, love, you had best seek some other amusement than to watch my cards." Challoner said, before he took his seat. "Your presence makes all other things seem trivial."

"What! May I not be your adviser?" she asked.

"I would rather play my own hand."

"As you will," she said, and turned from him with a vexed air, to lavish her attentions upon a wit of 70, whose conversation so amused her that a ripple of youthful and aged laughter was wafted to Colonel Challoner's ear as he sat at cards, and distracted him greatly. Indeed, he soon found he was no better off for having got rid of his adviser, since his glances were continually wandering towards that distant corner where the ancient jest-maker was lolling across the spinet, looking up at Mrs. Fermor, and where a brace of younger sparks had joined them.

He knew that he was playing wildly—backing weak cards, doubling the stakes, just when he ought not. His luck had turned.

"She is my luck," he thought, "and without her I am nothing."

He tried to catch her eye; but she did not look his way—till the end of the hand, when, as he flung his losses on the table, she turned suddenly and looked at him across all the length of the room as if the jingle of his guineas had attracted her.

---

* A darkened enclosure in which images of objects might be projected through a pinhole—a form of entertainment among the rich.

He beckoned her with a glance. She left her friends instantly and came gliding to his elbow.

"Well," she whispered, "have you lost much?"

"Only a month's pay. Not worth speaking of, so long as you are pleased."

"I am not pleased. You should let me advise you. Fairy Goodluck was not at your christening."

She established herself in her old place, hung over his chair, cut the cards for him; and with pretty impetuous movement flung the cards that were done with from the table to the floor. The perfume that hung about her lace and frippery, the ivory whiteness, of her arm, the tapering hand, the music of her *sotto voce* speech, these were the ingredients in the intoxicating cup which she brewed for him nightly. He was not master of his wits, he was not master of himself, when she hung over him, when her hair touched his brow and her breath fluttered on his cheek, and he scarcely knew what he dealt, or to whom he dealt, scarcely knew whether he was winning or losing, had but one desire, one impulse—to draw the lovely head down to his breast, and lose himself in the witchcraft of her kisses.

The game was played with two packs shuffled together, and the banker might have the cards cut by whomsoever he chose; by the black footman handing chocolate if he thought blackie would bring him luck. Colonel Challoner's luck was at his elbow in the dazzling white hand, which scarce needed the sparkle of diamonds—the restless impetuous hand, which swooped upon the cards like a white bird, quick and eager. It was growing late, and pack after pack had been thrown down since the game began, until the floor about the table was scattered thick with cards. The losers had begun to look at their watches and yawn ostentatiously. The bank was winning steadily, when one of the men who had been losing, cried out:—

"I protest against that Queen of Hearts. It is the third that has been played since the pack was cut? And 'tis not the first time I have suspected an interloping honour. No wonder you are so fortunate a banker, Colonel Challoner. Some good fairy doctors your cards. I'll wager that previous packs would prove as rich in winning cards as the last Mrs. Fermor flung on the floor, if anyone would take the trouble to hunt for them."

If anyone would take the trouble? All the seven players were down on their knees within the next minute, gathering up the scattered cards, counting, sorting, arranging, and oh! that terrible array of honors, damning evidence of somebody's dishonour, which Sir Lomax Treherne, the man who had given the alarm, laid out on the card-table. A king of spades not accounted for; ace of diamonds, not accounted for; and so on, and so on. The packs which had been gathered up and sorted were complete without those cards.

Colonel Challoner stood in the midst of the excited babblers, white as marble, silent, till the last card had been picked up.

"This matter concerns you and me primarily, Sir Lomax," he said; "and I think we can settle it without any fuss. My friend shall wait upon you."

He walked out of the room without another word, without one look at the woman who stood with her powdered head against the blue and gold brocade, her tall slim figure leaning against the curtained wall, smiling at the company with tremulous lips, that convulsive smile accentuated by carmine, fanning herself, and saying over and over again: "'Tis all vastly absurd. I protest not one of you knows how to count a pack of cards."

Mrs. Fermor's black footman had little rest that night, but was kept trudging about upon his lady's service. He carried a letter to Colonel Challoner's suburban lodging; and was told there was no answer, but on going back to his mistress she stormed at him, wrote another letter, longer, more passionate than the last, and despatched him again, bidding him not to return to her without Colonel Challoner's reply, if he valued his life.

"I shall kill you if you come back empty handed," she cried. Day was dawning when he brought his mistress Challoner's letter, for which he had waited more than an hour, sitting in darkness on a bench in the entrance hall. Mrs. Fermor's hands shook as broke the seal, and her scowling brow told poor Scipio that she was not much better pleased with her lover's letter than she had been by his silence. She stared at the letter with heaving breast and quivering lips, then crushed the paper suddenly, and turned on the weary African as if he had offended her.

"Go to bed, fool," she said; "but be sure you are up and dressed before 8 o'clock, and ready to go on an errand."

It was now five, a summer morning, and the birds were singing in the hawthorns and lilacs that screened Mrs. Fermor's garden from the high road. She snatched up her hood, with a sudden design of going to her lover's lodgings, to fling her arms about his neck and hold him back from death, as Circe might have held him; for, though his letter contained nothing but an icy farewell, she knew that a duel between him and Treherne was inevitable. She would have gone to him, secure in her power to mould him to her will, but, as she stopped automatically before her looking-glass to put on her hood, the reflection she saw there in the clear morning light made her change her mind. Was that haggard countenance, plastered with white lead and ceruse, with drawn features and purple lips, a face to work Circean spells. To see her as she looked this morning in the searching eastern light, would be enough to break love's spell at its strongest. No, she would not try to see him. She would write to him again and again, passionate protestations of love, piteous entreaties, fevered words blotted with tears. Could he resist such an appeal?

"For my sake—for my sake—refuse to meet the man. Tell him that I, and I alone, was the cheat; that you have done with me for ever. I care not what shame I have to endure. I can hide myself from the world, turn Catholic, and bury myself alive in a convent; but, oh, if you have a spark of mercy in your nature, let me not suffer the agony of knowing that I killed you—that you flung away your life because of my sin. My love—my husband that was to be—have pity upon me. I will never ask to see you again, if you would have it so. Live a stranger to me, if you will; only live, live, live; and save the woman who adores you from madness."

Those were the closing sentences of a long letter—a letter of passionate recapitulation—such a letter as distracted women write, drowning meaning in a torrent of words. A letter which generally fails in its purpose.

Scipio carried the letter to Challoner's lodgings at 8 o'clock, and brought home the fatal news. Colonel Challoner had left the house in a coach at half-past 7, with two other gentlemen. He had been heard to tell the coachman to drive to Ham-common.

Mrs. Fermor went about the house all day, smiling, and talking to herself, as she had talked to her departing guests the previous night. "So vastly absurd! Was there ever such a ridiculous mistake?" Dear Lady Sarah could not conceive that she tampered with the cards. If there were too many honours it was the cardmaker's error. The cards came into her house in sealed packets, and she never touched them till the game began. She still smiled her strange artificial smile, still talked to herself or to any rare visitor in the same strain, long after Colonel Challoner had been lying in Petersham churchyard, shot through the heart by Sir Lomax Treherne.

She was quite mad, but quite harmless. She lived for many years in this piteous condition, and used to walk about Richmond with an attendant, pointed out as the poor lady that had lost her wits after the tragical death of her lover, who had been discovered cheating at cards, and had been killed in the duel which followed that discovery.

Anna Katharine Green is often called "the mother of the detective novel" (though that laurel should properly be worn by the little-remembered Seeley Regester). Her first ambition was to write romantic verse. However, Green achieved immediate success with her first novel, The Leavenworth Case: A Lawyer's Story, *published in 1868, featuring New York police detective Ebenezer Gryce. The book was not only popular but well-received critically; Agatha Christie herself later expressed that the book influenced her writing. In three later novels, Gryce is joined by a nosy spinster named Amelia Butterworth. Green produced almost forty books, and she was highly regarded for her ingenious plots and careful use of evidence. Green's father was a lawyer, and her understanding of criminal law is well in evidence throughout her work. Green also wrote nine stories about a young female detective, Violet Strange, who is a debutante and secretly works with a detective agency. These were collected in* The Golden Slipper, and Other Problems for Violet Strange, *first published in 1915.*

MISSING: PAGE THIRTEEN

ANNA KATHARINE GREEN

I.

O ne more! just one more well-paying affair, and I promise to stop; really and truly to stop."

"But, Puss, why one more? You have earned the amount you set for yourself,—or very nearly,—and though my help is not great, in three months I can add enough—"

"No, you cannot, Arthur. You are doing well; I appreciate it; in fact, I am just delighted to have you work for me in the way you do, but you cannot, in your position, make enough in three months, or in six, to meet the situation as I see it. Enough does not satisfy me. The measure must be full, heaped up, and running over. Possible failure following promise must be provided for. Never must I feel myself called upon to do this kind of thing again. Besides, I have never got over the Zabriskie tragedy. It haunts me continually. Something new may help to put it out of my head. I feel guilty. I was responsible—"

"No, Puss. I will not have it that you were responsible. Some such end was bound to follow a complication like that. Sooner or later he would have been driven to shoot himself—"

"But not her."

"No, not her. But do you think she would have given those few minutes of perfect understanding with her blind husband for a few years more of miserable life?"

Violet made no answer; she was too absorbed in her surprise. Was this Arthur? Had a few weeks' work and a close connection with the really serious things of life made this change in him? Her face beamed at the thought, which seeing, but not understanding what underlay this evidence of joy, he bent and kissed her, saying with some of his old nonchalance:

"Forget it, Violet; only don't let anyone or anything lead you to interest yourself in another affair of the kind. If you do, I shall have to consult a certain friend of yours as to the best way of stopping this folly. I mention no names. Oh! you need not look so frightened. Only behave; that's all."

"He's right," she acknowledged to herself, as he sauntered away; "altogether right."

Yet because she wanted the extra money—

The scene invited alarm,—that is, for so young a girl as Violet, surveying it from an automobile some time after the stroke of midnight. An unknown house at the end of a heavily shaded walk, in the open doorway of which could be seen the silhouette of a woman's form leaning eagerly forward with arms outstretched in an appeal for help! It vanished while she looked, but the effect remained, holding her to her seat for one startled moment. This seemed strange, for she had anticipated adventure. One is not summoned from a private ball to ride a dozen miles into the country on an errand of investigation, without some expectation of encountering the mysterious and the tragic. But Violet Strange, for all her many experiences, was of a most susceptible nature, and for the instant in which that door stood open, with only the memory of that expectant figure to disturb the faintly lit vista of the hall beyond, she felt that grip upon the throat which comes from an indefinable fear which no words can explain and no plummet sound.

But this soon passed. With the setting of her foot to ground, conditions changed and her emotions took on a more normal character. The figure of a man now stood in the place held by the vanished woman, and it was not only that of one she knew but that of one whom she trusted—a friend whose very presence gave her courage. With this recognition came a better understanding of the situation, and it was with a beaming eye and unclouded features that she tripped up the walk to meet the expectant figure and outstretched hand of Roger Upjohn.

"You here!" she exclaimed, amid smiles and blushes, as he drew her into the hall.

He at once launched forth into explanations mingled with apologies for the presumption he had shown in putting her to this inconvenience. There was trouble in the house—great trouble. Something had occurred for which an explanation must be found before morning, or the happiness and honour of more than one person now under this unhappy roof would be wrecked. He knew it was late—that she had been obliged to take a long and dreary ride alone, but her success with the problem which had once come near wrecking his own life had emboldened him to telephone to the office and—"But you are in ball-dress," he cried in amazement. "Did you think—"

"I came from a ball. Word reached me between the dances. I did not go home. I had been bidden to hurry."

He looked his appreciation, but when he spoke it was to say:

"This is the situation. Miss Digby—"

"The lady who is to be married tomorrow?"

"Who *hopes* to be married tomorrow."

"How, *hopes*?"

"Who *will* be married tomorrow, if a certain article lost in this house tonight can be found before any of the persons who have been dining here leave for their homes."

Violet uttered an exclamation.

"Then, Mr. Cornell—" she began.

"Mr. Cornell has our utmost confidence," Roger hastened to interpose. "But the article missing is one which he might reasonably desire to possess and which he alone of all present had the opportunity of securing. You can therefore see why he, with his pride—the pride of a man not rich, engaged to marry a woman who is—should declare that unless his innocence is established before daybreak, the doors of St. Bartholomew will remain shut tomorrow."

"But the article lost—what is it?"

"Miss Digby will give you the particulars. She is waiting to receive you," he added with a gesture towards a half-open door at their right.

Violet glanced that way, then cast her looks up and down the hall in which they stood.

"Do you know that you have not told me in whose house I am? Not hers, I know. She lives in the city."

"And you are twelve miles from Harlem. Miss Strange, you are in the Van Broecklyn mansion, famous enough you will acknowledge. Have you never been here before?"

"I have been by here, but I recognized nothing in the dark. What an exciting place for an investigation!"

"And Mr. Van Broecklyn? Have you never met him?"

"Once, when a child. He frightened me *then*."

"And may frighten you now; though I doubt it. Time has mellowed him. Besides, I have prepared him for what might otherwise occasion him some astonishment. Naturally he would not look for just the sort of lady investigator I am about to introduce to him."

She smiled. Violet Strange was a very charming young woman, as well as a keen prober of odd mysteries.

The meeting between herself and Miss Digby was a sympathetic one. After the first inevitable shock which the latter felt at sight of the beauty and fashionable appearance of the mysterious little being who was to solve her difficulties, her glance, which under other circumstances might have lingered unduly upon the piquant features and exquisite dressing of the fairy-like figure before her, passed at once to Violet's eyes in whose steady depths beamed an intelligence quite at odds with the coquettish dimples which so often misled the casual observer in his estimation of a character singularly subtle and well-poised.

As for the impression she herself made upon Violet, it was the same she made upon everyone. No one could look long at Florence Digby and not recognize the loftiness of her spirit and the generous nature of her impulses. In person she was tall, and as she leaned to take Violet's hand, the difference between them brought out the salient points in each, to the great admiration of the one onlooker.

Meantime for all her interest in the case in hand, Violet could not help casting a hurried look about her, in gratification of the curiosity incited by her entrance into a house signalized from its foundation by such a series of tragic events. The result was disappointing. The walls were plain, the furniture simple. Nothing suggestive in either, unless it was the fact that nothing was new, nothing modern. As it looked in the days of Burr and Hamilton so it looked today, even to the rather startling detail of candles which did duty on every side in place of gas.

As Violet recalled the reason for this, the fascination of the past seized upon her imagination. There was no knowing where this might have carried her, had not the feverish gleam in Miss Digby's eyes warned her that the present held its own excitement. Instantly, she was all attention and listening with undivided mind to that lady's disclosures.

They were brief and to the following effect:

The dinner which had brought some half-dozen people together in this house had been given in celebration of her impending marriage. But it was also in a way meant as a compliment to one of the other guests, a Mr. Spielhagen, who, during the week, had succeeded in demonstrating to a few experts the value of a discovery he had made which would transform a great industry.

In speaking of this discovery, Miss Digby did not go into particulars, the whole matter being far beyond her understanding; but in stating its value she openly acknowledged that it was in the line of Mr. Cornell's own work, and one which involved calculations and a formula which, if prematurely disclosed, would invalidate the contract Mr. Spielhagen hoped to make, and thus destroy his present hopes.

Of this formula but two copies existed. One was locked up in a safe-deposit vault in Boston, the other he had brought into the house on his person, and it was the latter which was now missing, it having been abstracted during the evening from a manuscript of sixteen or more sheets, under circumstances which he would now endeavour to relate.

Mr. Van Broecklyn, their host, had in his melancholy life but one interest which could be called at all absorbing. This was for explosives. As a consequence, much of the talk at the dinner-table had been on Mr. Spielhagen's discovery, and the possible changes it might introduce into this especial industry. As these, worked out from a formula kept secret from the trade, could not but affect greatly Mr. Cornell's interests, she found herself listening intently, when Mr. Van Broecklyn, with an apology for his interference, ventured to remark that if Mr. Spielhagen had made a valuable discovery in this line, so had he, and one which he had substantiated by many experiments. It was not a marketable one, such as Mr. Spielhagen's was, but in his work upon the same, and in the tests which he had been led to make, he had discovered certain instances he would gladly name, which demanded exceptional procedure to be successful. If Mr. Spielhagen's method did not allow for these exceptions, nor make suitable provision for them, then Mr. Spielhagen's method would fail more times than it would succeed. Did it so allow and so provide? It would relieve him greatly to learn that it did.

The answer came quickly. Yes, it did. But later and after some further conversation, Mr. Spielhagen's confidence seemed to wane, and before they left the dinner-table, he openly declared his intention of looking over his manuscript again that very night, in order to be sure that the formula therein contained duly covered all the exceptions mentioned by Mr. Van Broecklyn.

If Mr. Cornell's countenance showed any change at this moment, she for one had not noticed it; but the bitterness with which he remarked upon the other's good fortune in having discovered this formula of whose entire success he had no doubt, was apparent to everybody, and naturally gave point to the circumstances which a short time afterward associated him with the disappearance of the same.

The ladies (there were two others besides herself) having withdrawn in a body to the music-room, the gentlemen all proceeded to the library to smoke. Here, conversation loosed from the one topic which had hitherto engrossed it, was proceeding briskly, when Mr. Spielhagen, with a nervous gesture, impulsively looked about him and said:

"I cannot rest till I have run through my thesis again. Where can I find a quiet spot? I won't be long; I read very rapidly."

It was for Mr. Van Broecklyn to answer, but no word coming from him, every eye turned his way, only to find him sunk in one of those fits of abstraction so well known to his friends, and from which no one who has this strange man's peace of mind at heart ever presumes to rouse him.

What was to be done? These moods of their singular host sometimes lasted half an hour, and Mr. Spielhagen had not the appearance of a man of patience. Indeed he presently gave proof of the great uneasiness he was labouring under, for noticing a door standing ajar on the other side of the room, he remarked to those around him:

"A den! and lighted! Do you see any objection to my shutting myself in there for a few minutes?"

No one venturing to reply, he rose, and giving a slight push to the door, disclosed a small room exquisitely panelled and brightly lighted, but without one article of furniture in it, not even a chair.

"The very place," quoth Mr. Spielhagen, and lifting a light cane-bottomed chair from the many standing about, he carried it inside and shut the door behind him.

Several minutes passed during which the man who had served at table entered with a tray on which were several small glasses evidently containing some choice liqueur. Finding his master fixed in one of his strange moods, he set the tray down and, pointing to one of the glasses, said:

"That is for Mr. Van Broecklyn. It contains his usual quieting powder." And urging the gentlemen to help themselves, he quietly left the room.

Mr. Upjohn lifted the glass nearest him, and Mr. Cornell seemed about to do the same when he suddenly reached forward and catching up one farther off started for the room in which Mr. Spielhagen had so deliberately secluded himself.

Why he did all this—why, above all things, he should reach across the tray for a glass instead of taking the one under his hand, he can no more explain than why he has followed many another unhappy impulse. Nor did he understand the nervous start given by Mr. Spielhagen at his entrance, or the stare with which that gentleman took the glass from his hand and mechanically drank its contents, till he saw how his hand had stretched itself across the sheet of paper he was reading, in an open attempt to hide the lines visible between his fingers. Then indeed the intruder flushed and withdrew in great embarrassment, fully conscious of his indiscretion but not deeply disturbed till Mr. Van Broecklyn, suddenly arousing and glancing down at the tray placed very near his hand, remarked in some surprise: "Dobbs seems to have forgotten me." Then indeed, the unfortunate Mr. Cornell realized what he had done. It was the glass intended for his host which he had caught up and carried into the other room—the glass which he had been told contained a drug. Of what folly he had been guilty, and how tame would be any effort at excuse!

Attempting none, he rose and with a hurried glance at Mr. Upjohn who flushed in sympathy at his distress, he crossed to the door he had so lately closed upon Mr. Spielhagen. But feeling his shoulder touched as his hand pressed the knob, he turned to meet the eye of Mr. Van Broecklyn fixed upon him with an expression which utterly confounded him.

"Where are you going?" that gentleman asked.

The questioning tone, the severe look, expressive at once of displeasure and astonishment, were most disconcerting, but Mr. Cornell managed to stammer forth:

"Mr. Spielhagen is in here consulting his thesis. When your man brought in the cordial, I was awkward enough to catch up your glass and carry it in to Mr. Spielhagen. He drank it and I—I am anxious to see if it did him any harm."

As he uttered the last word he felt Mr. Van Broecklyn's hand slip from his shoulder, but no word accompanied the action, nor did his host make the least move to follow him into the room.

This was a matter of great regret to him later, as it left him for a moment out of the range of every eye, during which he says he simply stood in a state of shock at seeing Mr. Spielhagen still sitting there, manuscript in hand, but with head fallen forward and eyes closed; dead, asleep or—he hardly knew what; the sight so paralyzed him.

Whether or not this was the exact truth and the whole truth, Mr. Cornell certainly looked very unlike himself as he stepped back into Mr.

Van Broecklyn's presence; and he was only partially reassured when that gentleman protested that there was no real harm in the drug, and that Mr. Spielhagen would be all right if left to wake naturally and without shock. However, as his present attitude was one of great discomfort, they decided to carry him back and lay him on the library lounge. But before doing this, Mr. Upjohn drew from his flaccid grasp the precious manuscript, and carrying it into the larger room placed it on a remote table, where it remained undisturbed till Mr. Spielhagen, suddenly coming to himself at the end of some fifteen minutes, missed the sheets from his hand, and bounding up, crossed the room to repossess himself of them.

His face, as he lifted them up and rapidly ran through them with ever-accumulating anxiety, told them what they had to expect.

The page containing the formula was gone!

Violet now saw her problem.

II

There was no doubt about the loss I have mentioned; all could see that page 13 was not there. In vain a second handling of every sheet, the one so numbered was not to be found. Page 14 met the eye on the top of the pile, and page 12 finished it off at the bottom, but no page 13 in between, or anywhere else.

Where had it vanished, and through whose agency had this misadventure occurred? No one could say, or, at least, no one there made any attempt to do so, though everybody started to look for it.

But where look? The adjoining small room offered no facilities for hiding a cigar-end, much less a square of shining white paper. Bare walls, a bare floor, and a single chair for furniture, comprised all that was to be seen in this direction. Nor could the room in which they then stood be thought to hold it, unless it was on the person of some one of them. Could this be the explanation of the mystery? No man looked his doubts; but Mr. Cornell, possibly divining the general feeling, stepped up to Mr. Van Broecklyn and in a cool voice, but with the red burning hotly on either cheek, said so as to be heard by everyone present:

"I demand to be searched—at once and thoroughly."

A moment's silence, then the common cry:

"We will all be searched."

"Is Mr. Spielhagen sure that the missing page was with the others when he sat down in the adjoining room to read his thesis?" asked their perturbed host.

"Very sure," came the emphatic reply. "Indeed, I was just going through the formula itself when I fell asleep."

"You are ready to assert this?"

"I am ready to swear it."

Mr. Cornell repeated his request.

"I demand that you make a thorough search of my person. I must be cleared, and instantly, of every suspicion, he gravely asserted, or how can I marry Miss Digby tomorrow?"

After that there was no further hesitation. One and all subjected themselves to the ordeal suggested; even Mr. Spielhagen. But this effort was as futile as the rest. The lost page was not found.

What were they to think? What were they to do?

There seemed to be nothing left to do, and yet some further attempt must be made towards the recovery of this important formula. Mr. Cornell's marriage and Mr. Spielhagen's business success both depended upon its being in the latter's hands before six in the morning, when he was engaged to hand it over again to a certain manufacturer sailing for Europe on an early steamer.

Five hours!

Had Mr. Van Broecklyn a suggestion to offer? No, he was as much at sea as the rest.

Simultaneously look crossed look. Blankness was on every face.

"Let us call the ladies," suggested one.

It was done, and however great the tension had been before, it was even greater when Miss Digby stepped upon the scene. But she was not a woman to be shaken from her poise even by a crisis of this importance. When the dilemma had been presented to her and the full situation grasped, she looked first at Mr. Cornell and then at Mr. Spielhagen, and quietly said:

"There is but one explanation possible of this matter. Mr. Spielhagen will excuse me, but he is evidently mistaken in thinking that he saw the lost page among the rest. The condition into which he was thrown by the unaccustomed drug he had drank, made him liable to hallucinations. I have not the least doubt he thought he had been studying the formula at the time he dropped off to sleep. I have every confidence in the gentleman's candour. But so have I in that of Mr. Cornell," she supplemented, with a smile.

An exclamation from Mr. Van Broecklyn and a subdued murmur from all but Mr. Spielhagen testified to the effect of this suggestion, and there is no saying what might have been the result if Mr. Cornell had not hurriedly put in this extraordinary and most unexpected protest:

"Miss Digby has my gratitude," said he, "for a confidence which I hope to prove to be deserved. But I must say this for Mr. Spielhagen. He was correct in stating that he was engaged in looking over his formula when I stepped into his presence with the glass of cordial. If you were not in a position to see the hurried way in which his hand instinctively spread itself over the page he was reading, I was; and if that does not seem conclusive to you, then I feel bound to state that in unconsciously following this movement of his, I plainly saw the number written on the top of the page, and that number was—13."

Aloud exclamation, this time from Spielhagen himself, announced his gratitude and corresponding change of attitude toward the speaker.

"Wherever that damned page has gone," he protested, advancing towards Cornell with outstretched hand, "you have nothing to do with its disappearance."

Instantly all constraint fled, and every countenance took on a relieved expression. *But the problem remained.*

Suddenly those very words passed someone's lips, and with their utterance Mr. Upjohn remembered how at an extraordinary crisis in his own life, he had been helped and an equally difficult problem settled, by a little lady secretly attached to a private detective agency. If she could only be found and hurried here before morning, all might yet be well. He would make the effort. Such wild schemes sometimes work. He telephoned to the office and—

Was there anything else Miss Strange would like to know?

III

Miss Strange, thus appealed to, asked where the gentlemen were now.

She was told that they were still all together in the library; the ladies had been sent home.

"Then let us go to them," said Violet, hiding under a smile her great fear that here was an affair which might very easily spell for her that dismal word, *failure*.

So great was that fear that under all ordinary circumstances she would have had no thought for anything else in the short interim between this stating of the problem and her speedy entrance among the persons involved. But the circumstances of this case were so far from ordinary, or rather let me put it in this way, the setting of the case was so very extraordinary, that she scarcely thought of the problem before her, in her great interest in the house through whose rambling halls she was being so carefully guided. So much that was tragic and heartrending had occurred here. The Van Broecklyn name, the Van Broecklyn history, above all the Van Broecklyn tradition, which made the house unique in the country's annals, all made an appeal to her imagination, and centred her thoughts on what she saw about her. There was a door which no man ever opened— had never opened since Revolutionary times—should she see it? Should she know it if she did see it? Then Mr. Van Broecklyn himself! Just to meet him, under any conditions and in any place, was an event. But to meet him here, under the pall of his own mystery! No wonder she had no words for her companions, or that her thoughts clung to this anticipation in wonder and almost fearsome delight.

His story was a well-known one. A bachelor and a misanthrope, he lived absolutely alone save for a large entourage of servants, all men and elderly ones at that. He never visited. Though he now and then, as on this occasion, entertained certain persons under his roof, he declined every invitation for himself, avoiding even, with equal strictness, all evening amusements of whatever kind, which would detain him in the city after ten at night. Perhaps this was to ensure no break in his rule of life never to sleep out of his own bed. Though he was a man well over fifty he had not spent, according to his own statement, but two nights out of his own bed since his return from Europe in early boyhood, and those were in obedience to a judicial summons which took him to Boston.

This was his main eccentricity, but he had another which is apparent enough from what has already been said. He avoided women. If thrown in with them during his short visits into town, he was invariably polite and at all times companionable, but he never sought them out, nor had gossip, contrary to its usual habit, ever linked his name with one of the sex.

Yet he was a man of more than ordinary attraction. His features were fine and his figure impressive. He might have been the cynosure of all eyes had he chosen to enter crowded drawing-rooms, or even to frequent public assemblages, but having turned his back upon everything of the kind in his youth, he had found it impossible to alter his habits with advancing years; nor was he now expected to. The position he had taken was respected. Leonard Van Broecklyn was no longer criticized.

Was there any explanation for this strangely self-centred life? Those who knew him best seemed to think so. In the first place he had sprung from an unfortunate stock. Events of an unusual and tragic nature had marked the family of both parents. Nor had his parents themselves been exempt from this seeming fatality. Antagonistic in tastes and temperament, they had dragged on an unhappy existence in the old home, till both natures rebelled, and a separation ensued which not only disunited their lives but sent them to opposite sides of the globe never to return again. At least, that was the inference drawn from the peculiar circumstances attending the event. On the morning of one never-to-be-forgotten day, John Van Broecklyn, the grandfather of the present representative of the family, found the following note from his son lying on the library table:

FATHER:
   Life in this house, or any house, with *her* is no longer endurable. One of us must go. The mother should not be separated from her child. Therefore it is I whom you will never see again. Forget me, but be considerate of her and the boy.
                                        WILLIAM.

Six hours later another note was found, this time; from the wife:

FATHER:

Tied to a rotting corpse what does one do? Lop off one's arm if necessary to rid one of the contact. As all love between your son and myself is dead, I can no longer live within the sound of his voice. As this is his home, he is the one to remain in it. May our child reap the benefit of his mother's loss and his father's affection.

RHODA.

Both were gone, and gone forever. Simultaneous in their departure, they preserved each his own silence and sent no word back. If the one went East and the other West, they may have met on the other side of the globe, but never again in the home which sheltered their boy. For him and for his grandfather they had sunk from sight in the great sea of humanity, leaving them stranded on an isolated and mournful shore. The grandfather steeled himself to the double loss, for the child's sake; but the boy of eleven succumbed. Few of the world's great sufferers, of whatever age or condition, have mourned as this child mourned, or shown the effects of his grief so deeply or so long. Not till he had passed his majority did the line, carved in one day in his baby forehead, lose any of its intensity; and there are those who declare that even later than that, the midnight stillness of the house was disturbed from time to time by his muffled shriek of "Mother! Mother!" sending the servants from the house, and adding one more horror to the many which clung about this accursed mansion.

Of this cry Violet had heard, and it was that and the door—But I have already told you about the door which she was still looking for, when her two companions suddenly halted, and she found herself on the threshold of the library, in full view of Mr. Van Broecklyn and his two guests.

Slight and fairy-like in figure, with an air of modest reserve more in keeping with her youth and dainty dimpling beauty than with her errand, her appearance produced an astonishment which none of the gentlemen were able to disguise. This the clever detective, with a genius for social problems and odd elusive cases! This darling of the ball-room in satin and pearls! Mr. Spielhagen glanced at Mr. Carroll, and Mr. Carroll at Mr. Spielhagen, and both at Mr. Upjohn, in very evident distrust. As for Violet, she had eyes only for Mr. Van Broecklyn who stood before her in a surprise equal to that of the others but with more restraint in its expression.

She was not disappointed in him. She had expected to see a man, reserved almost to the point of austerity. And she found his first look even more awe-compelling than her imagination had pictured; so much so indeed, that her resolution faltered, and she took a quick step backward; which seeing, he smiled and her heart and hopes grew warm again. That he could smile, and smile with absolute sweetness, was her great comfort when later—But I am introducing you too hurriedly to the catastrophe. There is much to be told first.

I pass over the preliminaries, and come at once to the moment when Violet, having listened to a repetition of the full facts, stood with downcast eyes before these gentlemen, complaining in some alarm to herself:

"They expect me to tell them now and without further search or parley just where this missing page is. I shall have to balk that expectation without losing their confidence. But how?"

Summoning up her courage and meeting each inquiring eye with a look which seemed to carry a different message to each, she remarked very quietly:

"This is not a matter to guess at. I must have time and I must look a little deeper into the facts just given me. I presume that the table I see over there is the one upon which Mr. Upjohn laid the manuscript during Mr. Spielhagen's unconsciousness."

All nodded.

"Is it—I mean the table—in the same condition it was then? Has nothing been taken from it except the manuscript?"

"Nothing."

"Then the missing page is not there," she smiled, pointing to its bare top. A pause, during which she stood with her gaze fixed on the floor before her. She was thinking and thinking hard.

Suddenly she came to a decision. Addressing Mr. Upjohn she asked if he were quite sure that in taking the manuscript from Mr. Spielhagen's hand he had neither disarranged nor dropped one of its pages.

The answer was unequivocal.

"Then," she declared, with quiet assurance and a steady meeting with her own of every eye, "as the thirteenth page was not found among the others when they were taken from this table, nor on the persons of either Mr. Carroll or Mr. Spielhagen, it is still in that inner room."

"Impossible!" came from every lip, each in a different tone. "That room is absolutely empty."

"May I have a look at its emptiness?" she asked, with a naïve glance at Mr. Van Broecklyn.

"There is positively nothing in the room but the chair Mr. Spielhagen sat on," objected that gentleman with a noticeable air of reluctance.

"Still, may I not have a look at it?" she persisted, with that disarming smile she kept for great occasions.

Mr. Van Broecklyn bowed. He could not refuse a request so urged, but his step was slow and his manner next to ungracious as he led the way to the door of the adjoining room and threw it open.

Just what she had been told to expect! Bare walls and floors and an empty chair! Yet she did not instantly withdraw, but stood silently contemplating the panelled wainscoting surrounding her, as though she suspected it of containing some secret hiding-place not apparent to the eye.

Mr. Van Broecklyn, noting this, hastened to say:

"The walls are sound, Miss Strange. They contain no hidden cupboards."

"And that door?" she asked, pointing to a portion of the wainscoting so exactly like the rest that only the most experienced eye could detect the line of deeper colour which marked an opening.

For an instant Mr. Van Broecklyn stood rigid, then the immovable pallor, which was one of his chief characteristics, gave way to a deep flush, as he explained:

"There was a door there once; but it has been permanently closed. With cement," he forced himself to add, his countenance losing its evanescent colour till it shone ghastly again in the strong light.

With difficulty Violet preserved her show of composure. "*The* door!" she murmured to herself. "I have found it. The great historic door!" But her tone was light as she ventured to say:

"Then it can no longer be opened by your hand or any other?"

"It could not be opened with an axe."

Violet sighed in the midst of her triumph. Her curiosity had been satisfied, but the problem she had been set to solve looked inexplicable. But she was not one to yield easily to discouragement. Marking the disappointment approaching to disdain in every eye but Mr. Upjohn's, she drew herself up—(she had not far to draw) and made this final proposal.

"A sheet of paper," she remarked, "of the size of this one cannot be spirited away, or dissolved into thin air. It exists; it is here; and all we want is some happy thought in order to find it. I acknowledge that that happy thought has not come to me yet, but sometimes I get it in what may seem to you a very odd way. Forgetting myself, I try to assume the individuality of the person who has worked the mystery. If I can think with his thoughts, I possibly may follow him in his actions. In this case I should like to make believe for a few moments that I am Mr. Spielhagen" (with what a delicious smile she said this). "I should like to hold his thesis in my hand and be interrupted in my reading by Mr. Cornell offering his glass of cordial; then I should like to nod and slip off mentally into a deep sleep. Possibly in that sleep the dream may come which will clarify the whole situation. Will you humour me so far?"

A ridiculous concession, but finally she had her way; the farce was enacted and they left her as she had requested them to do, alone with her dreams in the small room.

Suddenly they heard her cry out, and in another moment she appeared before them, the picture of excitement.

"Is this chair standing exactly as it did when Mr. Spielhagen occupied it?" she asked.

"No," said Mr. Upjohn, "it faced the other way."

"She stepped back and twirled the chair about with her disengaged hand. "So?"

Mr. Upjohn and Mr. Spielhagen both nodded, so did the others when she glanced at them.

With a sign of ill-concealed satisfaction, she drew their attention to herself; then eagerly cried:

"Gentlemen, look here!"

Seating herself, she allowed her whole body to relax till she presented the picture of one calmly asleep. Then, as they continued to gaze at her with fascinated eyes, not knowing what to expect, they saw something white escape from her lap and slide across the floor till it touched and was stayed by the wainscot. It was the top page of the manuscript she held, and as some inkling of the truth reached their astonished minds, she sprang impetuously to her feet and, pointing to the fallen sheet, cried:

"Do you understand now? Look where it lies, and then look here!"

She had bounded toward the wall and was now on her knees pointing to the bottom of the wainscot, just a few inches to the left of the fallen page.

"A crack!" she cried, "under what was once the door. It's a very thin one, hardly perceptible to the eye. But see!" Here she laid her finger on the fallen paper and drawing it towards her, pushed it carefully against the lower edge of the wainscot. Half of it at once disappeared.

"I could easily slip it all through," she assured them, withdrawing the sheet and leaping to her feet in triumph. "You know now where the missing page lies, Mr. Spielhagen. All that remains is for Mr. Van Broecklyn to get it for you."

IV

The cries of mingled astonishment and relief which greeted this simple elucidation of the mystery were broken by a curiously choked, almost unintelligible, cry. It came from the man thus appealed to, who, unnoticed by them all, had started at her first word and gradually, as action followed action, withdrawn himself till he now stood alone and in an attitude almost of defiance behind the large table in the centre of the library.

"I am sorry," he began, with a brusqueness which gradually toned down into a forced urbanity as he beheld every eye fixed upon him in amazement, "that circumstances forbid my being of assistance to you in this unfortunate matter. If the paper lies where you say, and I see no other explanation of its loss, I am afraid it will have to remain there for this night at least. The cement in which that door is embedded is thick as any wall; it would take men with pickaxes, possibly with dynamite, to make a breach there wide enough for anyone to reach in. And we are far from any such help."

In the midst of the consternation caused by these words, the clock on the mantel behind his back rang out the hour. It was but a double stroke, but that meant two hours after midnight and had the effect of a knell in the hearts of those most interested.

"But I am expected to give that formula into the hands of our manager before six o'clock in the morning. The steamer sails at a quarter after."

"Can't you reproduce a copy of it from memory?" someone asked; "and insert it in its proper place among the pages you hold there?"

"The paper would not be the same. That would lead to questions and the truth would come out. As the chief value of the process contained in that formula lies in its secrecy, no explanation I could give would relieve me from the suspicions which an acknowledgment of the existence of a third copy, however well hidden, would entail. I should lose my great opportunity."

Mr. Cornell's state of mind can be imagined. In an access of mingled regret and despair, he cast a glance at Violet, who, with a nod of understanding, left the little room in which they still stood, and approached Mr. Van Broecklyn.

Lifting up her head,—for he was very tall,—and instinctively rising on her toes the nearer to reach his ear, she asked in a cautious whisper:

"Is there no other way of reaching that place?"

She acknowledged afterwards, that for one moment her heart stood still from fear, such a change took place in his face, though she says he did not move a muscle. Then, just when she was expecting from him some harsh or forbidding word, he wheeled abruptly away from her and crossing to a window at his side, lifted the shade and looked out. When he returned, he was his usual self so far as she could see.

"There is a way," he now confided to her in a tone as low as her own, "but it can only be taken by a child."

"Not by me?" she asked, smiling down at her own childish proportions.

For an instant he seemed taken aback, then she saw his hand begin to tremble and his lips twitch. Somehow—she knew not why—she began to pity him, and asked herself as she felt rather than saw the struggle in his mind, that here was a trouble which if once understood would greatly dwarf that of the two men in the room behind them.

"I am discreet," she whisperingly declared. "I have heard the history of that door—how it was against the tradition of the family to have it opened. There must have been some very dreadful reason. But old superstitions do not affect me, and if you will allow me to take the way you mention, I will follow your bidding exactly, and will not trouble myself about anything but the recovery of this paper, which must lie only a little way inside that blocked-up door."

Was his look one of rebuke at her presumption, or just the constrained expression of a perturbed mind? Probably, the latter, for while she watched him for some understanding of his mood, he reached out his hand and touched one of the satin folds crossing her shoulder.

"You would soil this irretrievably," said he.

"There is stuff in the stores for another," she smiled. Slowly his touch deepened into pressure. Watching him she saw the crust of some old fear or dominant superstition melt under her eyes, and was quite prepared, when he remarked, with what for him was a lightsome air:

"I will buy the stuff, if you will dare the darkness and intricacies of our old cellar. I can give you no light. You will have to feel your way according to my direction."

"I am ready to dare anything."

He left her abruptly.

"I will warn Miss Digby," he called back. "She shall go with you as far as the cellar."

V

Violet in her short career as an investigator of mysteries had been in many a situation calling for more than womanly nerve and courage. But never—or so it seemed to her at the time—had she experienced a greater depression of spirit than when she stood with Miss Digby before a small door at the extreme end of the cellar, and understood that here was her road—a road which once entered, she must take alone.

First, it was such a small door! No child older than eleven could possibly squeeze through it. But she was of the size of a child of eleven and might possibly manage that difficulty.

Secondly: there are always some unforeseen possibilities in every situation, and though she had listened carefully to Mr. Van Broecklyn's directions and was sure that she knew them by heart, she wished she had kissed her father more tenderly in leaving him that night for the ball, and that she had not pouted so undutifully at some harsh stricture he had made. Did this mean fear? She despised the feeling if it did.

Thirdly: She hated darkness. She knew this when she offered herself for this undertaking; but she was in a bright room at the moment and only imagined what she must now face as a reality. But one jet had been lit in the cellar and that near the entrance. Mr. Van Broecklyn seemed not to need light, even in his unfastening of the small door which Violet was sure had been protected by more than one lock.

Doubt, shadow, and a solitary climb between unknown walls, with only a streak of light for her goal, and the clinging pressure of Florence Digby's hand on her own for solace—surely the prospect was one to tax the courage of her young heart to its limit. But she had promised, and she would fulfill. So with a brave smile she stooped to the little door, and in another moment had started on her journey.

For journey the shortest distance may seem when every inch means a heart-throb and one grows old in traversing a foot. At first the way was easy; she had but to crawl up a slight incline with the comforting consciousness that two people were within reach of her voice, almost within sound of her beating heart. But presently she came to a turn, beyond which her fingers failed to reach any wall on her left. Then came a step up which she stumbled, and farther on a short flight, each tread of which she had been told to test before she ventured to climb it, lest the decay of innumerable years should have weakened the wood too much to bear her weight. One, two, three, four, five steps! Then a landing with an open space beyond. Half of her journey was done. Here she felt she could give a minute to drawing her breath naturally, if the air, unchanged in years, would allow her to do so. Besides, here she had been enjoined to do a certain thing and to do it according to instructions. Three matches had been given her and a little night candle. Denied all light up to now, it was at this point she was to light her candle and place it on the floor, so that in returning she should not miss the staircase and get a fall. She had promised to do this, and was only too happy to see a spark of light scintillate into life in the immeasurable darkness.

She was now in a great room long closed to the world, where once officers in Colonial wars had feasted, and more than one council had been held. A room, too, which had seen more than one tragic happening, as its almost unparalleled isolation proclaimed. So much Mr. Van Broecklyn had told her, but she was warned to be careful in traversing it and not upon any pretext to swerve aside from the right-hand wall till she came to a huge mantelpiece. This passed, and a sharp corner turned, she ought to see somewhere in the dim spaces before her a streak of vivid light shining through the crack at the bottom of the blocked-up door. The paper should be somewhere near this streak.

All simple, all easy of accomplishment, if only that streak of light were all she was likely to see or think of. If the horror which was gripping her throat should not take shape! If things would remain shrouded in impenetrable darkness, and not force themselves in shadowy suggestion upon her excited fancy! But the blackness of the passageway through which she had just struggled, was not to be found here. Whether it was the effect of that small flame flickering at the top of the staircase behind her, or of some change in her own powers of seeing, surely there was a difference in her present outlook. Tall shapes were becoming visible—the air was no longer blank—she could see—Then suddenly she saw why. In the wall high up on her right was a window. It was small and all but invisible, being covered on the outside with vines, and on the inside with the cobwebs of a century. But some small gleams from the starlight night came through, making phantasms out of ordinary things, which unseen were horrible enough, and half seen choked her heart with terror.

"I cannot bear it," she whispered to herself even while creeping forward, her hand upon the wall. "I will close my eyes" was her next thought. "I will make my own darkness," and with a spasmodic forcing of her lids together, she continued to creep on, passing the mantelpiece, where she knocked against something which fell with an awful clatter.

This sound, followed as it was by that of smothered voices from the excited group awaiting the result of her experiment from behind the impenetrable wall she should be nearing now if she had followed her instructions aright, freed her instantly from her fancies; and opening her eyes once more, she cast a look ahead, and to her delight, saw but a few steps away, the thin streak of bright light which marked the end of her journey.

It took her but a moment after that to find the missing page, and picking it up in haste from the dusty floor, she turned herself quickly about and joyfully began to retrace her steps. Why, then, was it that in the course of a few minutes more her voice suddenly broke into a wild, unearthly shriek, which ringing with terror burst the bounds of that dungeon-like room, and sank, a barbed shaft, into the breasts of those awaiting the result of her doubtful adventure, at either end of this dread no-thoroughfare.

What had happened?

If they had thought to look out, they would have seen that the moon—held in check by a bank of cloud occupying half the heavens—had suddenly burst its bounds and was sending long bars of revealing light into every uncurtained window.

VI

Florence Digby, in her short and sheltered life, had possibly never known any very great or deep emotion. But she touched the bottom of extreme terror at that moment, as with her ears still thrilling with Violet's piercing cry, she turned to look at Mr. Van Broecklyn, and beheld the instantaneous wreck it had made of this seemingly strong man. Not till he came to lie in his coffin would he show a more ghastly countenance; and trembling herself almost to the point of falling, she caught him by the arm and sought to read in his face what had happened. Something disastrous she was sure; something which he had feared and was partially prepared for, yet which in happening had crushed him. Was it a pitfall into which the poor little lady had fallen? If so—But he is speaking—mumbling low words to himself. Some of them she can hear. He is reproaching himself—repeating over and over that he should never have taken such a chance; that he should have remembered her youth—the weakness of a young girl's nerve. He had been mad, and now—and now—

With the repetition of this word his murmuring ceased. All his energies were now absorbed in listening at the low door separating him from what he was agonizing to know—a door impossible to enter, impossible to enlarge—a barrier to all help—an opening whereby sound might pass but nothing else save her own small body, now lying—where?

"Is she hurt?" faltered Florence, stooping, herself, to listen. "Can you hear anything—anything?"

For an instant he did not answer; every faculty was absorbed in the one sense; then slowly and in gasps he began to mutter:

"I think—I hear—*something*. Her step—no, no, no step. All is as quiet as death; not a sound,—not a breath—she has fainted. O God! O God! Why this calamity on top of all!"

He had sprung to his feet at the utterance of this invocation, but next moment was down on his knees again, listening—listening.

Never was silence more profound; they were hearkening for murmurs from a tomb. Florence began to sense the full horror of it all, and was swaying helplessly when Mr. Van Broecklyn impulsively lifted his hand in an admonitory Hush! and through the daze of her faculties a small far sound began to make itself heard, growing louder as she waited, then becoming faint again, then altogether ceasing only to renew itself once more, till it resolved into an approaching step, faltering in its course, but coming ever nearer and nearer.

"She's safe! She's not hurt!" sprang from Florence's lips in inexpressible relief; and expecting Mr. Van Broecklyn to show an equal joy, she turned toward him, with the cheerful cry.

"Now if she has been so fortunate as to find that missing page, we shall all be repaid for our fright."

A movement on his part, a shifting of position which brought him finally to his feet, but he gave no other proof of having heard her, nor did his countenance mirror her relief. "It is as if he dreaded, instead of hailed, her return," was Florence's inward comment as she watched him involuntarily recoil at each fresh token of Violet's advance.

Yet because this seemed so very unnatural, she persisted in her efforts to lighten the situation, and when he made no attempt to encourage Violet in her approach, she herself stooped and called out a cheerful welcome which must have rung sweetly in the poor little detective's ears.

A sorry sight was Violet, when, helped by Florence she finally crawled into view through the narrow opening and stood once again on the cellar floor. Pale, trembling, and soiled with the dust of years, she presented a helpless figure enough, till the joy in Florence's face recalled some of her spirit, and, glancing down at her hand in which a sheet of paper was visible, she asked for Mr. Spielhagen.

"I've got the formula," she said. "If you will bring him, I will hand it over to him here."

Not a word of her adventure; nor so much as one glance at Mr. Van Broecklyn, standing far back in the shadows.

Nor was she more communicative, when, the formula restored and everything made right with Mr. Spielhagen, they all came together again in the library for a final word.

"I was frightened by the silence and the darkness, and so cried out," she explained in answer to their questions. "Anyone would have done so who found himself alone in so musty a place," she added, with an attempt at lightsomeness which deepened the pallor on Mr. Van Broecklyn's cheek, already sufficiently noticeable to have been remarked upon by more than one.

"No ghosts?" laughed Mr. Cornell, too happy in the return of his hopes to be fully sensible of the feelings of those about him. "No whispers from impalpable lips or touches from spectre hands? Nothing to explain the mystery of that room so long shut up that even Mr. Van Broecklyn declares himself ignorant of its secret?"

"Nothing," returned Violet, showing her dimples in full force now.

"If Miss Strange had any such experiences—if she has anything to tell worthy of so marked a curiosity, she will tell it now," came from the gentleman just alluded to, in tones so stern and strange that all show of frivolity ceased on the instant. "Have you anything to tell, Miss Strange?"

Greatly startled, she regarded him with widening eyes for a moment, then with a move towards the door, remarked, with a general look about her:

"Mr. Van Broecklyn knows his own house, and doubtless can relate its histories if he will. I am a busy little body who having finished my work am now ready to return home, there to wait for the next problem which an indulgent fate may offer me."

She was near the threshold—she was about to take her leave, when suddenly she felt two hands fall on her shoulder, and turning, met the eyes of Mr. Van Broecklyn burning into her own.

"You saw!" dropped in an almost inaudible whisper from his lips.

The shiver which shook her answered him better than any word.

With an exclamation of despair, he withdrew his hands, and facing the others now standing together recovered some of his self-possession:

"I must ask for another hour of your company. I can no longer keep my sorrow to myself. A dividing line has just been drawn across my life, and I must have the sympathy of someone who knows my past, or I shall go mad in my self-imposed solitude. Come back, Miss Strange. You of all others have the prior right to hear."

VII

"I shall have to begin," said he, when they were all seated and ready to listen, "by giving you some idea, not so much of the family tradition, as of the effect of this tradition upon all who bore the name of Van Broecklyn. This is not the only house, even in America, which contains a room shut away from intrusion. In England there are many. But there is this difference between most of them and ours. No bars or locks forcibly held shut the door we were forbidden to open. The command was enough; that and the superstitious fear which such a command, attended by a long and unquestioning obedience, was likely to engender.

"I know no more than you do why some early ancestor laid his ban upon this room. But from my earliest years I was given to understand that there was one latch in the house which was never to be lifted; that any fault would be forgiven sooner than that; that the honour of the whole family stood in the way of disobedience, and that I was to preserve that honour to my dying day. You will say that all this is fantastic, and wonder that sane people in these modern times should subject themselves to such a ridiculous restriction, especially when no good reason was alleged, and the very source of the tradition from which it sprung forgotten. You are right; but if you look long into human nature, you will see that the bonds which hold the firmest are not material ones—that an idea will make a man and mould a character—that it lies at the source of all heroisms and is to be courted or feared as the case may be.

"For me it possessed a power proportionate to my loneliness. I don't think there was ever a more lonely child. My father and mother were so unhappy in each other's companionship that one or other of them was almost always away. But I saw little of either even when they were at home. The constraint in their attitude toward each other affected their conduct toward me. I have asked myself more than once if either of them had any real affection for me. To my father I spoke of her; to her of him; and never pleasurably. This I am forced to say, or you cannot understand my story. Would to God I could tell another tale! Would to God I had such memories as other men have of a father's clasp, a mother's kiss—but no! my grief, already profound, might have become abysmal. Perhaps it is best as it is; only, I might have been a different child, and made for myself a different fate—who knows.

"As it was, I was thrown almost entirely upon my own resources for any amusement. This led me to a discovery I made one day. In a far part of the cellar behind some heavy casks, I found a little door. It was so low—so exactly fitted to my small body, that I had the greatest desire to enter it. But I could not get around the casks. At last an expedient occurred to me. We had an old servant who came nearer loving me than anyone else. One day when I chanced to be alone in the cellar, I took out my ball and began throwing it about. Finally it landed behind the casks, and I ran with a beseeching cry to Michael, to move them.

"It was a task requiring no little strength and address, but he managed, after a few herculean efforts, to shift them aside and I saw with delight my way opened to that mysterious little door. But I did not approach it then; some instinct deterred me. But when the opportunity came for me to venture there alone, I did so, in the most adventurous spirit, and began my operations by sliding behind the casks and testing the handle of the little door. It turned, and after a pull or two the door yielded. With my heart in my mouth, I stooped and peered in. I could see nothing—a black hole and nothing more. This caused me a moment's hesitation. I was afraid of the dark—had always been. But curiosity and the spirit of adventure triumphed. Saying to myself that I was Robinson Crusoe exploring the cave, I crawled in, only to find that I had gained nothing. It was as dark inside as it had looked to be from without.

"There was no fun in this, so I crawled back and when I tried the experiment again, it was with a bit of candle in my hand, and a surreptitious match or two. What I saw, when with a very trembling little hand I had lighted one of the matches, would have been disappointing to most boys, but not to me. The litter and old boards I saw in odd corners about me were full of possibilities, while in the dimness beyond I seemed to perceive a sort of staircase which might lead—I do not think I made any attempt to answer that question even in my own mind, but when, after some hesitation and a sense of great daring, I finally crept up those steps, I remember very well my sensation at finding myself in front of a narrow closed door. It suggested too vividly the one in Grandfather's little room—the door in the wainscot which we were never to open. I had my first real trembling fit here, and at once fascinated and repelled by this obstruction I stumbled and lost my candle, which, going out in the fall, left me in total darkness and a very frightened state of mind. For my imagination, which had been greatly stirred by my own vague thoughts of the forbidden room, immediately began to people the space about me with ghoulish figures. How should I escape them, how ever reach my own little room again, undetected and in safety?

"But these terrors, deep as they were, were nothing to the real fright which seized me when, the darkness finally braved, and the way found back into the bright, wide-open halls of the house, I became conscious of having dropped something besides the candle. My matchbox was gone—not *my* match-box, but my grandfather's which I had found lying on his table and carried off on this adventure, in all the confidence of irresponsible youth. To make use of it for a little while, trusting to his not missing it in the confusion I had noticed about the house that morning, was one thing; to lose it was another. It was no common box. Made of gold and cherished for some special reason well known to himself, I had often heard him say that some day I would appreciate its value and be glad to own it. And I had left it in that hole and at any minute he might miss it—possibly ask for it! The day was one of torment. My mother was away or shut up in her room. My father—I don't know just what thoughts I had about him. He was not to be seen either, and the servants cast strange looks at me when I spoke his name. But I little realized the blow which had just fallen upon the house in his definite departure, and only thought of my own trouble, and of how I should meet my grandfather's eye when the hour came for him to draw me to his knee for his usual good-night.

"That I was spared this ordeal for the first time this very night first comforted me, then added to my distress. He had discovered his loss and was angry. On the morrow he would ask me for the box and I would have to lie, for never could I find the courage to tell him where I had been. Such an act of presumption he would never forgive, or so I thought as I lay and shivered in my little bed. That his coldness, his neglect, sprang from the discovery just made that my mother as well as my father had just fled the house forever was as little known to me as the morning calamity. I had been given my usual tendance and was tucked safely into bed; but the gloom, the silence which presently settled upon the house had a very different explanation in my mind from the real one. My sin (for such it loomed large in my mind by this time) coloured the whole situation and accounted for every event.

"At what hour I slipped from my bed on to the cold floor, I shall never know. To me it seemed to be in the dead of night; but I doubt if it were more than ten. So slowly creep away the moments to a wakeful child. I had made a great resolve. Awful as the prospect seemed to me,—frightened as I was by the very thought,—I had determined in my small mind to go down into the cellar, and into that midnight hole again, in search of the lost box. I would take a candle and matches, this time from my own mantel-shelf, and if everyone was asleep, as appeared from the deathly quiet of the house, I would be able to go and come without anybody ever being the wiser.

"Dressing in the dark, I found my matches and my candle and, putting them in one of my pockets, softly opened my door and looked out. Nobody was stirring; every light was out except a solitary one in the lower hall. That this still burned conveyed no meaning to my mind. How could I know that the house was so still and the rooms so dark because everyone was out searching for some clue to my mother's flight? If I had looked at the clock—but I did not; I was too intent upon my errand, too filled with the fever of my desperate undertaking, to be affected by anything not bearing directly upon it.

"Of the terror caused by my own shadow on the wall as I made the turn in the hall below, I have as keen a recollection today as though it happened yesterday. But that did not deter me; nothing deterred me, till safe in the cellar I crouched down behind the casks to get my breath again before entering the hole beyond.

"I had made some noise in feeling my way around these casks, and I trembled lest these sounds had been heard upstairs! But this fear soon gave place to one far greater. Other sounds were making themselves heard. A din of small skurrying feet above, below, on every side of me! Rats! rats in the wall! rats on the cellar bottom! How I ever stirred from the spot I do not know, but when I did stir, it was to go forward, and enter the uncanny hole.

"I had intended to light my candle when I got inside; but for some reason I went stumbling along in the dark, following the wall till I got to the steps where I had dropped the box. Here a light was necessary, but my hand did not go to my pocket. I thought it better to climb the steps first, and softly one foot found the tread and then another. I had only three more to climb and then my right hand, now feeling its way along the wall, would be free to strike a match. I climbed the three steps and was steadying myself against the door for a final plunge, when something happened—something so strange, so unexpected, and so incredible that I wonder I did not shriek aloud in my terror. The door was moving under my hand. It was slowly opening inward. I could feel the chill made by the widening crack. Moment by moment this chill increased; the gap was growing—a presence was there—a presence before which I sank in a small heap upon the landing. Would it advance? Had it feet—hands? Was it a presence which could be felt?

"Whatever it was, it made no attempt to pass, and presently I lifted my head only to quake anew at the sound of a voice—a human voice—my mother's voice—so near me that by putting out my arms I might have touched her.

"She was speaking to my father. I knew it from the tone. She was saying words which, little understood as they were, made such a havoc in my youthful mind that I have never forgotten them.

"'I have come!' she said. 'They think I have fled the house and are looking far and wide for me. We shall not be disturbed. Who would think of looking here for either you or me?'

"*Here!* The word sank like a plummet in my breast. I had known for some few minutes that I was on the threshold of the forbidden room; but they were *in* it. I can scarcely make you understand the tumult which this awoke in my brain. Somehow, I had never thought that any such braving of the house's law would be possible.

"I heard my father's answer, but it conveyed no meaning to me. I also realized that he spoke from a distance,—that he was at one end of the room while we were at the other. I was presently to have this idea confirmed, for while I was striving with all my might and main to subdue my very heart-throbs so that she would not hear me or suspect my presence, the darkness—I should rather say the blackness of the place yielded to a flash of lightning—heat lightning, all glare and no sound—and I caught an instantaneous vision of my father's figure standing with gleaming things about him, which affected me at the moment as supernatural, but which, in later years, I decided to have been weapons hanging on a wall.

"She saw him too, for she gave a quick laugh and said they would not need any candles; and then, there was another flash and I saw something in his hand and something in hers, and though I did not yet understand, I felt myself turning deathly sick and gave a choking gasp which was lost in the rush she made into the centre of the room, and the keenness of her swift low cry.

"'*Garde toi!* for only one of us will ever leave this room alive!'

"A duel! a duel to the death between this husband and wife—this father and mother—in this hole of dead tragedies and within the sight and hearing of their child! Has Satan ever devised a scheme more hideous for ruining the life of an eleven-year-old boy!

"Not that I took it all in at once. I was too innocent and much too dazed to comprehend such hatred, much less the passions which engendered it. I only knew that something horrible—something beyond the conception of my childish mind—was going to take place in the darkness before me; and the terror of it made me speechless; would to God it had made me deaf and blind and dead!

"She had dashed from her corner and he had slid away from his, as the next fantastic gleam which lit up the room showed me. It also showed the weapons in their hands, and for a moment I felt reassured when I saw these were swords, for I had seen them before with foils in their hands practising for exercise, as they said, in the great garret. But the swords had buttons on them, and this time the tips were sharp and shone in the keen light.

"An exclamation from her and a growl of rage from him were followed by movements I could scarcely hear, but which were terrifying from their very quiet. Then the sound of a clash. The swords had crossed.

"Had the lightning flashed forth then, the end of one of them might have occurred. But the darkness remained undisturbed, and when the glare relit the great room again, they were already far apart. This called out a word from him; the one sentence he spoke—I can never forget it:

"Rhoda, there is blood on your sleeve; I have wounded you. Shall we call it off and fly, as the poor creatures in there think we have, to the opposite ends of the earth?"

"I almost spoke; I almost added my childish plea to his for them to stop—to remember me and stop. But not a muscle in my throat responded to my agonized effort. Her cold, clear 'No!' fell before my tongue was loosed or my heart freed from the ponderous weight crushing it.

"'I have vowed and *I* keep my promises,' she went on in a tone quite strange to me. 'What would either's life be worth with the other alive and happy in this world?'

"He made no answer; and those subtle movements—shadows of movements I might almost call them—recommenced. Then there came a sudden cry, shrill and poignant—had Grandfather been in his room he would surely have heard it—and the flash coming almost simultaneously with its utterance, I saw what has haunted my sleep from that day to this, my father pinned against the wall, sword still in hand, and before him my mother, fiercely triumphant, her staring eyes fixed on his and—

"Nature could bear no more; the band loosened from my throat; the oppression lifted from my breast long enough for me to give one wild wail and she turned, saw (heaven sent its flashes quickly at this moment) and recognizing my childish form, all the horror of her deed (or so I have fondly hoped) rose within her, and she gave a start and fell full upon the point upturned to receive her.

"A groan; then a gasping sigh from him, and silence settled upon the room and upon my heart and so far as I knew upon the whole created world."

"That is my story, friends. Do you wonder that I have never been or lived like other men?"

After a few moments of sympathetic silence, Mr. Van Broecklyn went on to say:

"I don't think I ever had a moment's doubt that my parents both lay dead on the floor of that great room. When I came to myself—which may have been soon, and may not have been for a long while—the lightning had ceased to flash, leaving the darkness stretching like a blank pall between me and that spot in which were concentrated all the terrors of which my imagination was capable. I dared not enter it. I dared not take one step that way. My instinct was to fly and hide my trembling body again in my own bed; and associated with this, in fact dominating it and making me old before my time, was another—never to tell; never to let anyone, least of all my grandfather—know what that forbidden room now contained. I felt in an irresistible sort of way that my father's and mother's honour was at stake. Besides, terror held me back; I felt that I should die if I spoke. Childhood has such terrors and such heroisms. Silence often covers in such, abysses of thought and feeling which astonish us in later years. There is no suffering like a child's, terrified by a secret it dare not for some reason disclose.

"Events aided me. When, in desperation to see once more the light and all the things which linked me to life—my little bed, the toys on the windowsill, my squirrel in its cage—I forced myself to retraverse the empty house, expecting at every turn to hear my father's voice or come upon the image of my mother—yes, such was the confusion of my mind, though I knew well enough even then that they were dead and that I should never hear the one or see the other. I was so benumbed with the cold in my half-dressed condition, that I woke in a fever next morning after a terrible dream which forced from my lips the cry of 'Mother! Mother!'—only that.

"I was cautious even in delirium. This delirium and my flushed cheeks and shining eyes led them to be very careful to me. I was told that my mother was away from home; and when after two days of search they were quite sure that all efforts to find either her or my father were likely to prove fruitless, that she had gone to Europe where we would follow her as soon as I was well. This promise, offering as it did, a prospect of immediate release from the terrors which were consuming me, had an extraordinary effect upon me. I got up out of my bed saying that I was well now and ready to start on the instant. The doctor, finding my pulse equable, and my whole condition wonderfully improved, and attributing it, as was natural, to my hope of soon joining my mother, advised my whim to be humoured and this hope kept active till travel and intercourse with children should give me strength and prepare me for the bitter truth ultimately awaiting me. They listened to him and in twenty-four hours our preparations were made. We saw the house closed—with what emotions surging in one small breast, I leave you to imagine—and then started on our long tour. For five years we wandered over the continent of Europe, my grandfather finding distraction, as well as myself, in foreign scenes and associations.

"But return was inevitable. What I suffered on re-entering this house, God and my sleepless pillow alone know. Had any discovery been made in our absence; or would it be made now that renovation and repairs of all kinds were necessary? Time finally answered me. My secret was safe and likely to continue so, and this fact once settled, life became endurable, if not cheerful. Since then I have spent only two nights out of this house, and they were unavoidable. When my grandfather died I had the wainscot door cemented in. It was done from this side and the cement painted to match the wood. No one opened the door nor have I ever crossed its threshold. Sometimes I think I have been foolish; and sometimes I know that I have been very wise. My reason has stood firm; how do I know that it would have done so if I had subjected myself to the possible discovery that one or both of them might have been saved if I had disclosed instead of concealed my adventure."

A pause during which white horror had shone on every face; then with a final glance at Violet, he said:

"What sequel do you see to this story, Miss Strange? I can tell the past, I leave you to picture the future."

Rising, she let her eye travel from face to face till it rested on the one awaiting it, when she answered dreamily: "If some morning in the news column there should appear an account of the ancient and historic home of the Van Broecklyns having burned to the ground in the night, the whole country would mourn, and the city feel defrauded of one of its treasures. But there are five persons who would see in it the sequel which you ask for."

When this happened, as it did happen, some few weeks later, the astonishing discovery was made that no insurance had been put upon this house. Why was it that after such a loss Mr. Van Broecklyn seemed to renew his youth? It was a constant source of comment among his friends.

Carolyn Wells (1870–1942) was an American writer, poet, and critic. Despite being deaf from early childhood, Wells wrote more than 170 books of crime fiction, parodies, and humorous verse. She penned sixty-one titles about a detective named Fleming Stone and created the American series of "year's best mystery stories" in 1931. Among her titles is The Technique of the Mystery Story: Complete Practical Study of the Theory and Structure of the Form with Examples from the Best Mystery Writers, *first published in 1913, which includes numerous examples from the Sherlock Holmes canon. Wells was a devotee of the Master. She befriended Harry Thurston Peck and Arthur Bartlett Maurice, respectively the senior and junior editors of the influential* Bookman *magazine in the early twentieth century, and the three friends celebrated their love of all things Sherlockian in numerous essays, reviews, and poems in early issues of the* Bookman.* *However, the following first appeared in the* Century Magazine *for May 1915 with illustrations by Frederic Dorr Steele, who regularly illustrated the American publications of the Holmes stories beginning in 1903.*

---

* See S.E. Dahlinger and Leslie S. Klinger, eds., *Sherlock Holmes and the Bookman: An Anthology of Literary Treasures (1895–1933)* (Indianapolis: Wessex Press, 2010).

THE ADVENTURE OF
THE CLOTHES-LINE

CAROLYN WELLS

T he members of the Society of Infallible Detectives* were just sitting around and being socially infallible in their rooms in Fakir Street, when President Holmes strode in. He was much saturniner than usual, and the others at once deduced there was something toward.

"And it's this," said Holmes, perceiving that they had perceived it. "A reward is offered for the solution of a great mystery—so great, my colleagues, that I fear none of you will be able to solve it, or even to help me in the marvelous work I shall do when ferreting it out."

"Humph!" grunted the Thinking Machine,* riveting his steel-blue eyes upon the speaker.

"He voices all our sentiments, said Raffles,† with his winning smile. "Fire away, Holmes. What's the prob?"

"To explain a most mysterious proceeding down on the East Side."

Though a tall man, Holmes spoke shortly, for he was peeved at the inattentive attitude of his collection of colleagues. But of course he still had his Watson, so he put up with the indifference of the rest of the cold world.

"Aren't all proceedings down on the East Side mysterious?" asked Arsène Lupin‡ with an aristocratic look.

Holmes passed his brow wearily under his hand.

"Inspector Spyer," he said, "was riding on the Elevated Road—one of the small numbered Avenues—when, as he passed a tenement-house district, he saw a clothes-line strung from one high window to another across a courtyard."

"Was it Monday?" asked the Thinking Machine, who for the moment was thinking he was a washing machine.

"That doesn't matter. About the middle of the line was suspended—"

"By clothes-pins?" asked two or three of the Infallibles at once.

"Was suspended a beautiful woman."

"Hanged?"

"No. *Do listen!* She hung by her hands and was evidently trying to cross from one house to the other. By her exhausted and agonized face, the inspector feared she could not hold on much longer. He sprang from his seat to rush to her assistance, but the train had already started, and he was too late to get off."

---

* Jacque Futrelle recorded this detective's tales, in *The Thinking Machine* (1907).

† The stories of A. J. Raffles, the gentleman thief, and his companion Bunny Manders were told by E. W. Hornung, the brother-in-law of Arthur Conan Doyle, between 1898 and 1909.

‡ The biographer of the thief Arsène Lupin is Maurice LeBlanc.

"What was she doing there?" "Did she fall?" "What did she look like?" and various similar nonsensical queries fell from the lips of the great detectives.

"Be silent, and I will tell you all the known facts. She was a society woman, it is clear, for she was robed in a chiffon evening gown, one of those roll-top things. She wore rich jewelry and dainty slippers with jeweled buckles. Her hair, unloosed from its moorings, hung in heavy masses far down her back."

"How extraordinary! What does it all mean?" asked M. Dupin,* ever straightforward of speech.

"I don't know yet," answered Holmes, honestly. "I've studied the matter only a few months. But I will find out, if I have to raze the whole tenement block. There *must* be a clue somewhere."

"Marvelous! Holmes, marvelous!" said a phonograph in the corner, which Watson had fixed up, as he had to go out.

"The police have asked us to take up the case and have offered a reward for its solution. Find out who was the lady, what she was doing, and why she did it."

"Are there any clues?" asked M. Vidocq,† while M. Lecoq‡ said simultaneously, "Any footprints?"

"There is one footprint; no other clue."

"Where is the footprint?"

"On the ground, right under where the lady was hanging."

"But you said the rope was high from the ground."

"More than a hundred feet."

"And she stepped down and made a single footprint. Strange! Quite strange!" and the Thinking Machine shook his yellow old head.

"She did nothing of the sort," said Holmes, petulantly. "If you fellows would listen, you might hear something. The occupants of the tenement

---

* Edgar Allan Poe wrote three stories about the amateur detective, the Chevalier Auguste Dupin, whom Holmes regards as a "very inferior fellow."

† Eugène Vidocq was a thief-taker and head of the Sûreté in Paris. His memoirs, published in 1828, were extremely popular and led the way for the growth of detective fiction.

‡ Monsieur Lecoq was a police detective whose cases were written up by Émile Gaboriau. Lecoq first appeared in 1866. Holmes called him a "miserable bungler."

houses have been questioned. But, as it turns out, none of them chanced to be at home at the time of the occurrence. There was a parade in the next street, and they had all gone to see it."

"Had a light snow fallen the night before?" asked Lecoq, eagerly.

"Yes, of course," answered Holmes. "How could we know anything, else? Well, the lady had dropped her slipper, and although the slipper was not found, it having been annexed by the tenement people who came home first, I had a chance to study the footprint. The slipper was a two and a half D. It was too small for her."

"How do you know?"

"Women always wear slippers too small for them."

"Then how did she come to drop it off?" This from Raffles, triumphantly.

Holmes looked at him pityingly.

"She kicked it off because it was too tight. Women always kick off their slippers when playing bridge or in an opera box or at a dinner."

"And always when they're crossing a clothes-line?" This in Lupin's most sarcastic vein.

"Naturally," said Holmes, with a taciturnine frown. "The footprint clearly denotes a lady of wealth and fashion, somewhat short of stature, and weighing about one hundred and sixty. She was of an animated nature—"

"Suspended animation," put in Luther Trant,[*] wittily, and Scientific Sprague[†] added, "Like the Coffin of Damocles, or whoever it was."

But Holmes frowned on their light-headedness.

"We must find out what it all means," he said in his gloomiest way. "I have a tracing of the footprint."

"I wonder if my seismospygmograph would work on it," mused Trant.

"I am the Prince of Footprints," declared Lecoq, pompously. "I will solve the mystery."

"Do your best, all of you," said their illustrious president. "I fear you can do little; these things are unintelligible to the unintelligent. But study on it, and meet here again one week from tonight, with your answers neatly typewritten on one side of the paper."

---

* *The Achievements of Luther Trant* by Edwin Ballmer and William MacHarg appeared in 1910.

† A detective whose adventures are recorded by Francis Lynde in an eponymous 1912 book.

The Infallible Detectives started off, each affecting a jaunty sanguineness of demeanor, which did not in the least impress their president, who was used to sanguinary impressions.

They spent their allotted seven days in the study of the problem; and a lot of the seven nights, too, for they wanted to delve into the baffling secret by sun or candlelight, as dear Mrs. Browning so poetically puts it.

And when the week had fled, the Infallibles again gathered in the Fakir Street sanctum, each face wearing the smug smirk and smile of one who had quested a successful quest and was about to accept his just reward.

"And now," said President Holmes, "as nothing can be hid from the Infallible Detectives, I assume we have all discovered *why* the lady hung from the clothes-line above that deep and dangerous chasm of a tenement courtyard."

"We have," replied his colleagues, in varying tones of pride, conceit, and mock modesty.

"I cannot think," went on the hawk-like voice, "that you have, any of you, stumbled upon the real solution of the mystery; but I will listen to your amateur attempts."

"As the oldest member of our organization, I will tell my solution first," said Vidocq, calmly. "I have not been able to find the lady, but I am convinced that she was merely an expert trapezist or tight-rope walker, practising a new trick to amaze her Coney Island audiences."

"Nonsense!" cried Holmes. "In that case the lady would have worn tights or fleshings. We are told she was in full evening dress of the smartest set."

Arsène Lupin spoke next.

"It's too easy," he said boredly; "she was a typist or stenographer who had been annoyed by attentions from her employer, and was trying to escape from the brute."

"Again I call your attention to her costume," said Holmes, with a look of intolerance on his finely cold-chiseled face.

"That's all right," returned Lupin, easily. "Those girls dress every old way! I've seen 'em. They don't think anything of evening clothes at their work."

"He was much saturniner than usual, and the others at once deduced
there was something toward"

"Humph!" said the Thinking Machine, and the others all agreed with him.

"Next," said Holmes, sternly.

"I'm next," said Lecoq. "I submit that the lady escaped from a nearby lunatic asylum. She had the illusion that she was an old overcoat and the moths had got at her. So of course she hung herself on the clothes-line. This theory of lunacy also accounts for the fact that the lady's hair was down—like *Ophelia's*, you know."

"It would have been easier for her to swallow a few good moth balls," said Holmes, looking at Lecoq in stormy silence. "Mr. Gryce,* you are an experienced deducer; what did *you* conclude?"

Mr. Gryce glued his eyes to his right boot toe, after his celebrated habit. "I make out she was a-slumming. You know, all the best ladies are keen about it. And I feel that she belonged to the Cult for the Betterment of Clothes-lines. She was by way of being a tester. She had to go across them hand over hand, and if they bore her weight, they were passed by the censor."

"And if they didn't?"

"Apparently that predicament had not occurred at the time of our problem, and so cannot be considered."

---

* Ebenezer Gryce, the hero of a series of stories by Anna Katharine Green. See page 247, above.

" The lady had dropped her slipper "

"I think Gryce is right about the slumming," remarked Luther Trant, "but the reason for the lady hanging from the clothes-line is the imperative necessity she felt for a thorough airing, after her tenemental visitations; there is a certain tenement scent, if I may express it, that requires ozone in quantities."

"You're too material," said the Thinking Machine, with a faraway look in his weak, blue eyes. "This lady was a disciple of New Thought. She had to go into the silence, or concentrate, or whatever they call it. And they always choose strange places for these thinking spells. They have to have solitude, and, as I understand it, the clothes-line was not crowded?"

Rouletabille* laughed right out.

"You're way off, Thinky," he said. "What ailed that dame was just that she wanted to reduce. I've read about it in the women's journals. They all want to reduce. They take all sorts of crazy exercises, and this crossing clothes-lines hand over hand is the latest. I'll bet it took off twenty of those avoirdupois with which old Sherly credited her."

"Pish and a few tushes!" remarked Raffles, in his smart society jargon. "You don't fool me. That clever little bear was making up a new dance to thrill society next winter. You'll see. Sunday-paper headlines: 'Stunning

* Joseph Rouletabille was a reporter-detective whose adventures were recorded by Gaston Leroux, beginning in 1908.

New Dance! The Clothes-Line Cling! Caught on Like Wildfire!' *That's* what it's all about. What do you know, eh?"

"Go take a walk, Raffles," said Holmes, not unkindly; "you're sleepy yet. Scientific Sprague, you sometimes put over an abstruse theory, what do you say?"

"I didn't need science," said Sprague, carelessly. "As soon as I heard she had her hair down, I jumped to the correct conclusion. She had been washing her hair, and was drying it. My sister always sticks her head out of the skylight; but this lady's plan is, I should judge, a more all-round success."

As they had now all voiced their theories, President Holmes rose to give them the inestimable benefit of his own views.

"Your ideas are not without some merit," he conceded, "but you have over-looked the eternal-feminine element in the problem. As soon as I tell you the real solution, you will each wonder why it escaped your notice. The lady thought she heard a mouse, so she scrambled out of the window, preferring to risk her life on the perilous clothes-line rather than stay in the dwelling where the mouse was also. It is all very simple. She was doing her hair, threw her head over forward to twist it, as they always do, and so espied the mouse sitting in the corner."

"Marvelous! Holmes, marvelous!" exclaimed Watson, who had just come back from his errand.

Even as they were all pondering on Holmes's superior wisdom, the telephone bell rang.

"Are you there?" said President Holmes, for he was ever English of speech.

"' Marvelous ! Holmes, marvelous !' said Watson "

"Yes, yes," returned the impatient voice of the chief of police. "Call off your detective workers. We have discovered who the lady was who crossed the clothes-line and why she did it."

"I can't imagine you really know," said Holmes into the transmitter; "but tell me what you think."

"A-r-r-rh! Of course I know! It was just one of those confounded moving-picture stunts!"

"Indeed! And why did the lady kick off her slipper?"

"A-r-r-r-h! It was part of the fool plot. She's Miss Flossy Flicker of the Flim-Flam Film Company, doin' the six-reel thriller, *At the End of Her Rope*."

"Ah," said Holmes suavely, "my compliments to Miss Flicker on her good work."

"Marvelous, Holmes, marvelous!" said Watson.

Susan Glaspell (1876–1948) was an American writer of note, who produced nine novels, fourteen plays, more than fifty short stories, and a biography. Hailed by British critics as a "genius" for her work in the theater, she discovered the plays of Eugene O'Neill and became associated with Edna St. Vincent Millay and Theodore Dreiser. Her 1931 play Alison's House *won the Pulitzer Prize for Drama. Today she is regarded as a pioneer of feminist writing and the first important American female playwright. In 1916, after co-writing a play with her husband George Cram Cook, Glaspell wrote a searing one-act drama titled* Trifles *based on a murder trial she had covered in Des Moines, Iowa, in 1900. The play was highly successful (Glaspell played the character of Mrs. Hale in the first performance), and it has been regularly anthologized as one of the great American dramas. Glaspell subsequently turned the play into the powerful story, first published in* Every Week *magazine for March 5, 1917, that follows.*

JURY OF HER PEERS

SUSAN GLASPELL

When Martha Hale opened the storm door and got a cut of the north wind, she ran back for her big woolen scarf. As she hurriedly wound that round her head her eye made a scandalized sweep of her kitchen. It was no ordinary thing that called her away—it was probably farther from ordinary than anything that had ever happened in Dickson County. But what her eye took in was that her kitchen was in no shape for leaving; her bread all ready for mixing, half the flour sifted and half unsifted.

She hated to see things half done; but she had been at that when the team from town stopped to get Mr. Hale, and then the sheriff came running in to say his wife wished Mrs. Hale would come too—adding, with a grin, that he guessed she was getting scary and wanted another woman along. So she had dropped everything right where it was.

"Martha!" now came her husband's impatient voice. "Don't keep folks waiting out here in the cold."

She again opened the storm-door, and this time joined the three men and the one woman waiting for her in the big two-seated buggy.

After she had the robes tucked around her she took another look at the woman who sat beside her on the back seat. She had met Mrs. Peters the year before at the county fair, and the thing she remembered about her was that she didn't seem like a sheriff's wife. She was small and thin and didn't have a strong voice. Mrs. Gorman, sheriff's wife before Gorman went out and Peters came in, had a voice that somehow seemed to be backing up the law with every word. But if Mrs. Peters didn't look like a sheriff's wife, Peters made it up in looking like a sheriff. He was to a dot the kind of man who could get himself elected sheriff—a heavy man with a big voice, who was particularly genial with the law-abiding, as if to make it plain that he knew the difference between criminals and non-criminals. And right there it came into Mrs. Hale's mind, with a stab, that this man who was so pleasant and lively with all of them was going to the Wrights' now as a sheriff.

"The country's not very pleasant this time of year," Mrs. Peters at last ventured, as if she felt they ought to be talking as well as the men.

Mrs. Hale scarcely finished her reply, for they had gone up a little hill and could see the Wright place now, and seeing it did not make her feel like talking. It looked very lonesome this cold March morning. It had always been a lonesome-looking place. It was down in a hollow, and the poplar trees around it were lonesome-looking trees. The men were looking at it and talking about what had happened. The county attorney was bending to one side of the buggy, and kept looking steadily at the place as they drew up to it.

"I'm glad you came with me," Mrs. Peters said nervously, as the two women were about to follow the men in through the kitchen door.

Even after she had her foot on the door-step, her hand on the knob, Martha Hale had a moment of feeling she could not cross that threshold. And the reason it seemed she couldn't cross it now was simply because she hadn't crossed it before. Time and time again it had been in her mind, "I ought to go over and see Minnie Foster"—she still thought of her as Minnie

Foster, though for twenty years she had been Mrs. Wright. And then there was always something to do and Minnie Foster would go from her mind. But *now* she could come.

The men went over to the stove. The women stood close together by the door. Young Henderson, the county attorney, turned around and said, "Come up to the fire, ladies."

Mrs. Peters took a step forward, then stopped. "I'm not—cold," she said.

And so the two women stood by the door, at first not even so much as looking around the kitchen.

The men talked for a minute about what a good thing it was the sheriff had sent his deputy out that morning to make a fire for them, and then Sheriff Peters stepped back from the stove, unbuttoned his outer coat, and leaned his hands on the kitchen table in a way that seemed to mark the beginning of official business. "Now, Mr. Hale," he said in a sort of semi-official voice, "before we move things about, you tell Mr. Henderson just what it was you saw when you came here yesterday morning."

The county attorney was looking around the kitchen.

"By the way," he said, "has anything been moved?" He turned to the sheriff. "Are things just as you left them yesterday?"

Peters looked from cupboard to sink; from that to a small worn rocker a little to one side of the kitchen table.

"It's just the same."

"Somebody should have been left here yesterday," said the county attorney.

"Oh—yesterday," returned the sheriff, with a little gesture as of yesterday having been more than he could bear to think of. "When I had to send Frank to Morris Center for that man who went crazy—let me tell you, I had my hands full *yesterday*. I knew you could get back from Omaha by today, George, and as long as I went over everything here myself—"

"Well, Mr. Hale," said the county attorney, in a way of letting what was past and gone go, "tell just what happened when you came here yesterday morning."

Mrs. Hale, still leaning against the door, had that sinking feeling of the mother whose child is about to speak a piece. Lewis often wandered along and got things mixed up in a story. She hoped he would tell this straight and plain, and not say unnecessary things that would just make things harder for Minnie Foster. He didn't begin at once, and she noticed that he looked queer—as if standing in that kitchen and having to tell what he had seen there yesterday morning made him almost sick.

"Yes, Mr. Hale?" the county attorney reminded.

"Harry and I had started to town with a load of potatoes," Mrs. Hale's husband began.

Harry was Mrs. Hale's oldest boy. He wasn't with them now, for the very good reason that those potatoes never got to town yesterday and he was taking them this morning, so he hadn't been home when the sheriff stopped to say he wanted Mr. Hale to come over to the Wright place and tell the county attorney his story there, where he could point it all out. With all Mrs. Hale's other emotions came the fear now that maybe Harry wasn't dressed warm enough—they hadn't any of them realized how that north wind did bite.

"We come along this road," Hale was going on, with a motion of his hand to the road over which they had just come, "and as we got in sight of the house I says to Harry, 'I'm goin' to see if I can't get John Wright to take a telephone.' You see, he explained to Henderson, unless I can get somebody to go in with me they won't come out this branch road except for a price *I* can't pay. I'd spoke to Wright about it once before; but he put me off, saying folks talked too much anyway, and all he asked was peace and quiet—guess you know about how much he talked himself. But I thought maybe if I went to the house and talked about it before his wife, and said all the women-folks liked the telephones, and that in this lonesome stretch of road it would be a good thing—well, I said to Harry that that was what I was going to say—though I said at the same time that I didn't know as what his wife wanted made much difference to John—"

Now, there he was!—saying things he didn't need to say. Mrs. Hale tried to catch her husband's eye, but fortunately the county attorney interrupted with:

"Let's talk about that a little later, Mr. Hale. I do want to talk about that, but I'm anxious now to get along to just what happened when you got here.

When he began this time, it was very deliberately and carefully:

"I didn't see or hear anything. I knocked at the door. And still it was all quiet inside. I knew they must be up—it was past eight o'clock. So I knocked again, louder, and I thought I heard somebody say, 'Come in.' I wasn't sure—I'm not sure yet. But I opened the door—this door, jerking a hand toward the door by which the two women stood, and there, in that rocker—pointing to it—sat Mrs. Wright."

Every one in the kitchen looked at the rocker. It came into Mrs. Hale's mind that that rocker didn't look in the least like Minnie Foster—the Minnie Foster of twenty years before. It was a dingy red, with wooden rungs up the back, and the middle run was gone, and the chair sagged to one side.

"How did she—look?" the county attorney was inquiring.

"Well," said Hale, "she looked—queer."

"How do you mean—queer?"

As he asked it he took out a notebook and pencil. Mrs. Hale did not like the sight of that pencil. She kept her eye fixed on her husband, as if to keep him from saying unnecessary things that would go into that notebook and make trouble.

Hale did speak guardedly, as if the pencil had affected him too.

"Well, as if she didn't know what she was going to do next. And kind of—done up."

"How did she seem to feel about your coming?"

"Why, I don't think she minded—one way or other. She didn't pay much attention. I said, 'Ho' do, Mrs. Wright? It's cold, ain't it?' And she said, 'Is it?'—and went on pleatin' at her apron.

"Well, I was surprised. She didn't ask me to come up to the stove, or to sit down, but just set there, not even lookin' at me. And so I said: 'I want to see John.'

"And then she—laughed. I guess you would call it a laugh.

"I thought of Harry and the team outside, so I said, a little sharp, 'Can I see John?' 'No,' says she kind of dull like. 'Ain't he home?' says I. Then she looked at me. 'Yes,' says she, 'he's home.' 'Then why can't I see him?' I asked her, out of patience with her now. 'Cause he's dead,' says she, just as quiet and dull—and fell to pleatin' her apron. 'Dead?' says I, like you do when you can't take in what you've heard.

"She just nodded her head, not getting a bit excited, but rockin' back and forth.

"'Why—where is he?' says I, not knowing *what* to say.

"She just pointed upstairs—like this"—pointing to the room above.

"I got up, with the idea of going up there myself. By this time I—didn't know what to do. I walked from there to here; then I says: 'Why, what did he die of?'

"'He died of a rope round his neck,' says she; and just went on pleatin' at her apron.

Hale stopped speaking, and stood staring at the rocker, as if he were still seeing the woman who had sat there the morning before. Nobody spoke; it was as if every one were seeing the woman who had sat there the morning before.

"And what did you do then?" the county attorney at last broke the silence.

"I went out and called Harry. I thought I might—need help. I got Harry in, and we went upstairs." His voice fell almost to a whisper. "There he was—lying over the—"

"I think I'd rather have you go into that upstairs," the county attorney interrupted, "where you can point it all out. Just go on now with the rest of the story."

"Well, my first thought was to get that rope off. It looked—"

He stopped, his face twitching.

"But Harry, he went up to him, and he said, 'No, he's dead all right, and we'd better not touch anything.' So we went downstairs.

"She was still sitting that same way. 'Has anybody been notified?' I asked. 'No,' says she, unconcerned.

"'Who did this, Mrs. Wright?' said Harry. He said it businesslike, and she stopped pleatin' at her apron. 'I don't know,' she says. 'You don't *know*?' says Harry. 'Weren't you sleepin' in the bed with him?' 'Yes,' says she, 'but I was on the inside.' 'Somebody slipped a rope round his neck and strangled him, and you didn't wake up?' says Harry. 'I didn't wake up,' she said after him.

"We may have looked as if we didn't see how that could be, for after a minute she said, 'I sleep sound.'

"Harry was going to ask her more questions, but I said maybe that weren't our business; maybe we ought to let her tell her story first to the coroner or the sheriff. So Harry went fast as he could over to High Road—the Rivers' place, where there's a telephone."

"And what did she do when she knew you had gone for the coroner?" The attorney got his pencil in his hand all ready for writing.

"She moved from that chair to this one over here"—Hale pointed to a small chair in the corner—and just sat there with her hands held together and looking down. I got a feeling that I ought to make some conversation, so I said I had come in to see if John wanted to put in a telephone; and at that she started to laugh, and then she stopped and looked at me—scared."

At sound of a moving pencil the man who was telling the story looked up.

"I dunno—maybe it wasn't scared, he hastened; I wouldn't like to say it was. Soon Harry got back, and then Dr. Lloyd came, and you, Mr. Peters, and so I guess that's all I know that you don't."

He said that last with relief, and moved a little, as if relaxing. Every one moved a little. The county attorney walked toward the stair door.

"I guess we'll go upstairs first—then out to the barn and around there."

He paused and looked around the kitchen.

"You're convinced there was nothing important here?" he asked the sheriff. "Nothing that would point—to any motive?"

The sheriff too looked all around, as if to re-convince himself.

"Nothing here but kitchen things," he said, with a little laugh for the insignificance of kitchen things.

The county attorney was looking at the cupboard—a peculiar, ungainly structure, half closet and half cupboard, the upper part of it being built in the wall, and the lower part just the old-fashioned kitchen cupboard. As if its queerness attracted him, he got a chair and opened the upper part and looked in. After a moment he drew his hand away sticky.

"Here's a nice mess," he said resentfully.

The two women had drawn nearer, and now the sheriff's wife spoke.

"Oh—her fruit," she said, looking to Mrs. Hale for sympathetic understanding. She turned back to the county attorney and explained: "She worried about that when it turned so cold last night. She said the fire would go out and her jars might burst."

Mrs. Peters' husband broke into a laugh.

"Well, can you beat the women! Held for murder, and worrying about her preserves!"

The young attorney set his lips.

"I guess before we're through with her she may have something more serious than preserves to worry about."

"Oh, well," said Mrs. Hale's husband, with good-natured superiority, "women are used to worrying over trifles."

The two women moved a little closer together. Neither of them spoke. The county attorney seemed suddenly to remember his manners—and think of his future.

"And yet," said he, with the gallantry of a young politician, "for all their worries, what would we do without the ladies?"

The women did not speak, did not unbend. He went to the sink and began washing his hands. He turned to wipe them on the roller towel— whirled it for a cleaner place.

"Dirty towels! Not much of a housekeeper, would you say, ladies?"

He kicked his foot against some dirty pans under the sink.

"There's a great deal of work to be done on a farm," said Mrs. Hale stiffly.

"To be sure. And yet"—with a little bow to her—"I know there are some Dickson County farm-houses that do not have such roller towels." He gave it a pull to expose its full length again.

"Those towels get dirty awful quick. Men's hands aren't always as clean as they might be."

"Ah, loyal to your sex, I see," he laughed. He stopped and gave her a keen look. "But you and Mrs. Wright were neighbors. I suppose you were friends, too."

Martha Hale shook her head.

"I've seen little enough of her of late years. I've not been in this house— it's more than a year.

"And why was that? You didn't like her?"

"I liked her well enough," she replied with spirit. "Farmers' wives have their hands full, Mr. Henderson. And then—" She looked around the kitchen.

"Yes?" he encouraged.

"It never seemed a very cheerful place," said she, more to herself than to him.

"No," he agreed; "I don't think any one would call it cheerful. I shouldn't say she had the home-making instinct."

"Well, I don't know as Wright had, either," she muttered.

"You mean they didn't get on very well?" he was quick to ask.

"No; I don't mean anything," she answered, with decision. As she turned a little away from him, she added: "But I don't think a place would be any the cheerfuler for John Wright's bein' in it."

"I'd like to talk to you about that a little later, Mrs. Hale," he said. "I'm anxious to get the lay of things upstairs now."

He moved toward the stair door, followed by the two men.

"I suppose anything Mrs. Peters does'll be all right?" the sheriff inquired. "She was to take in some clothes for her, you know—and a few little things. We left in such a hurry yesterday."

The county attorney looked at the two women whom they were leaving alone there among the kitchen things.

"Yes—Mrs. Peters," he said, his glance resting on the woman who was not Mrs. Peters, the big farmer woman who stood behind the sheriff's wife. "Of course Mrs. Peters is one of us," he said, in a manner of entrusting responsibility. "And keep your eye out, Mrs. Peters, for anything that might be of use. No telling; you women might come upon a clue to the motive—and that's the thing we need."

Mr. Hale rubbed his face after the fashion of a showman getting ready for a pleasantry.

"But would the women know a clue if they did come upon it?" he said; and, having delivered himself of this, he followed the others through the stair door.

The women stood motionless and silent, listening to the footsteps, first upon the stairs, then in the room above them.

Then, as if releasing herself from something strange, Mrs. Hale began to arrange the dirty pans under the sink, which the county attorney's disdainful push of the foot had deranged.

"I'd hate to have men comin' into my kitchen," she said testily—"snoopin' round and criticizing."

"Of course it's no more than their duty," said the sheriff's wife, in her manner of timid acquiescence.

"Duty's all right," replied Mrs. Hale bluffly; "but I guess that deputy sheriff that come out to make the fire might have got a little of this on." She gave the roller towel a pull. "Wish I'd thought of that sooner! Seems mean to talk about her for not having things slicked up, when she had to come away in such a hurry."

She looked around the kitchen. Certainly it was not "slicked up." Her eye was held by a bucket of sugar on a low shelf. The cover was off the wooden bucket, and beside it was a paper bag—half full.

Mrs. Hale moved toward it.

"She was putting this in there," she said to herself—slowly.

She thought of the flour in her kitchen at home—half sifted, half not sifted. She had been interrupted, and had left things half done. What had interrupted Minnie Foster? Why had that work been left half done? She made a move as if to finish it,—unfinished things always bothered her,—and then she glanced around and saw that Mrs. Peters was watching her—and she didn't want Mrs. Peters to get that feeling she had got of work begun and then—for some reason—not finished.

"It's a shame about her fruit," she said, and walked toward the cupboard that the county attorney had opened, and got on the chair, murmuring: "I wonder if it's all gone."

It was a sorry enough looking sight, but "Here's one that's all right," she said at last. She held it toward the light. "This is cherries, too." She looked again. "I declare I believe that's the only one."

With a sigh, she got down from the chair, went to the sink, and wiped off the bottle.

"She'll feel awful bad, after all her hard work in the hot weather. I remember the afternoon I put up my cherries last summer."

She set the bottle on the table, and, with another sigh, started to sit down in the rocker. But she did not sit down. Something kept her from sitting down in that chair. She straightened—stepped back, and, half turned away, stood looking at it, seeing the woman who had sat there "pleatin' at her apron."

The thin voice of the sheriff's wife broke in upon her: "I must be getting those things from the front room closet." She opened the door into the other room, started in, stepped back. "You coming with me, Mrs. Hale?" she asked nervously. "You—you could help me get them."

They were soon back—the stark coldness of that shut-up room was not a thing to linger in.

"My!" said Mrs. Peters, dropping the things on the table and hurrying to the stove.

Mrs. Hale stood examining the clothes the woman who was being detained in town had said she wanted.

"Wright was close!" she exclaimed, holding up a shabby black skirt that bore the marks of much making over. "I think maybe that's why she kept so much to herself. I s'pose she felt she couldn't do her part; and then, you don't enjoy things when you feel shabby. She used to wear pretty clothes and be lively—when she was Minnie Foster, one of the town girls, singing in the choir. But that—oh, that was twenty years ago."

With a carefulness in which there was something tender, she folded the shabby clothes and piled them at one corner of the table. She looked up at Mrs. Peters, and there was something in the other woman's look that irritated her.

"She don't care," she said to herself. "Much difference it makes to her whether Minnie Foster had pretty clothes when she was a girl."

Then she looked again, and she wasn't so sure; in fact, she hadn't at any time been perfectly sure about Mrs. Peters. She had that shrinking manner, and yet her eyes looked as if they could see a long way into things.

"This all you was to take in?" asked Mrs. Hale.

"No," said the sheriff's wife; "she said she wanted an apron. Funny thing to want," she ventured in her nervous little way, "for there's not much to get you dirty in jail, goodness knows. But I suppose just to make her feel more natural. If you're used to wearing an apron—She said they were in the bottom drawer of this cupboard. Yes—here they are. And then her little shawl that always hung on the stair door."

She took the small gray shawl from behind the door leading upstairs, and stood a minute looking at it.

Suddenly Mrs. Hale took a quick step toward the other woman.

"Mrs. Peters!"

"Yes, Mrs. Hale?"

"Do you think she—did it?"

A frightened look blurred the other thing in Mrs. Peters' eyes.

"Oh, I don't know," she said, in a voice that seemed to shrink away from the subject.

"Well, I don't think she did," affirmed Mrs. Hale stoutly. "Asking for an apron, and her little shawl. Worryin' about her fruit."

"Mr. Peters says—" Footsteps were heard in the room above; she stopped, looked up, then went on in a lowered voice: "Mr. Peters says—it looks bad for her. Mr. Henderson is awful sarcastic in a speech, and he's going to make fun of her saying she didn't—wake up."

For a moment Mrs. Hale had no answer. Then, "Well, I guess John Wright didn't wake up—when they was slippin' that rope under his neck," she muttered.

"No, it's *strange*," breathed Mrs. Peters. "They think it was such a—funny way to kill a man.

She began to laugh; at sound of the laugh, abruptly stopped.

"That's just what Mr. Hale said," said Mrs. Hale, in a resolutely natural voice. "There was a gun in the house. He says that's what he can't understand."

"Mr. Henderson said, coming out, that what was needed for the case was a motive. Something to show anger—or sudden feeling."

"Well, I don't see any signs of anger around here," said Mrs. Hale. "I don't—"

She stopped. It was as if her mind tripped on something. Her eye was caught by a dish-towel in the middle of the kitchen table. Slowly she moved toward the table. One half of it was wiped clean, the other half messy. Her eyes made a slow, almost unwilling turn to the bucket of sugar and the half empty bag beside it. Things begun—and not finished.

After a moment she stepped back, and said, in that manner of releasing herself:

"Wonder how they're finding things upstairs? I hope she had it a little more red up up there. You know,"—she paused, and feeling gathered,—"it seems kind of *sneaking*: locking her up in town and coming out here to get her own house to turn against her!"

"But, Mrs. Hale," said the sheriff's wife, "the law is the law."

"I s'pose 'tis," answered Mrs. Hale shortly.

She turned to the stove, saying something about that fire not being much to brag of. She worked with it a minute, and when she straightened up she said aggressively:

"The law is the law—and a bad stove is a bad stove. How'd you like to cook on this?"—pointing with the poker to the broken lining. She opened the oven door and started to express her opinion of the oven; but she was swept into her own thoughts, thinking of what it would mean, year after year, to have that stove to wrestle with. The thought of Minnie Foster trying to bake in that oven—and the thought of her never going over to see Minnie Foster—

She was startled by hearing Mrs. Peters say: "A person gets discouraged—and loses heart."

The sheriff's wife had looked from the stove to the sink—to the pail of water which had been carried in from outside. The two women stood there silent, above them the footsteps of the men who were looking for evidence against the woman who had worked in that kitchen. That look of seeing into things, of seeing through a thing to something else, was in the eyes of the sheriff's wife now. When Mrs. Hale next spoke to her, it was gently:

"Better loosen up your things, Mrs. Peters. We'll not feel them when we go out."

Mrs. Peters went to the back of the room to hang up the fur tippet she was wearing. A moment later she exclaimed, "Why, she was piecing a quilt," and held up a large sewing basket piled high with quilt pieces.

Mrs. Hale spread some of the blocks out on the table.

"It's log-cabin pattern," she said, putting several of them together. "Pretty, isn't it?"

They were so engaged with the quilt that they did not hear the footsteps on the stairs. Just as the stair door opened Mrs. Hale was saying:

"Do you suppose she was going to quilt it or just knot it?"

The sheriff threw up his hands.

"They wonder whether she was going to quilt it or just knot it!"

There was a laugh for the ways of women, a warming of hands over the stove, and then the county attorney said briskly:

"Well, let's go right out to the barn and get that cleared up."

"I don't see as there's anything so strange," Mrs. Hale said resentfully, after the outside door had closed on the three men—"our taking up our time with little things while we're waiting for them to get the evidence. I don't see as it's anything to laugh about."

"Of course they've got awful important things on their minds," said the sheriff's wife apologetically.

They returned to an inspection of the block for the quilt. Mrs. Hale was looking at the fine, even sewing, and preoccupied with thoughts of the woman who had done that sewing, when she heard the sheriff's wife say, in a queer tone:

"Why, look at this one."

She turned to take the block held out to her.

"The sewing," said Mrs. Peters, in a troubled way. "All the rest of them have been so nice and even—but—this one. Why, it looks as if she didn't know what she was about!"

Their eyes met—something flashed to life, passed between them; then, as if with an effort, they seemed to pull away from each other. A moment Mrs. Hale sat there, her hands folded over that sewing which was so unlike all the rest of the sewing. Then she had pulled a knot and drawn the threads.

"Oh, what are you doing, Mrs. Hale?" asked the sheriff's wife, startled.

"Just pulling out a stitch or two that's not sewed very good," said Mrs. Hale mildly.

"I don't think we ought to touch things," Mrs. Peters said, a little helplessly.

"I'll just finish up this end," answered Mrs. Hale, still in that mild, matter-of-fact fashion.

She threaded a needle and started to replace bad sewing with good. For a little while she sewed in silence. Then, in that thin, timid voice, she heard:

"Mrs. Hale!"

"Yes, Mrs. Peters?"

"What do you suppose she was so—nervous about?"

"Oh, *I* don't know," said Mrs. Hale, as if dismissing a thing not important enough to spend much time on. "I don't know as she was—nervous. I sew awful queer sometimes when I'm just tired."

She cut a thread, and out of the corner of her eye looked up at Mrs. Peters. The small, lean face of the sheriff's wife seemed to have tightened up. Her eyes had that look of peering into something. But next moment she moved, and said in her thin, indecisive way:

"Well, I must get those clothes wrapped. They may be through sooner than we think. I wonder where I could find a piece of paper—and string."

"In that cupboard, maybe," suggested Mrs. Hale, after a glance around.

One piece of the crazy sewing remained unripped. Mrs. Peters' back turned, Martha Hale now scrutinized that piece, compared it with the dainty, accurate sewing of the other blocks. The difference was startling. Holding this block made her feel queer, as if the distracted thoughts of the woman who had perhaps turned to it to try and quiet herself were communicating themselves to her.

Mrs. Peters' voice roused her.

"Here's a bird-cage," she said. "Did she have a bird, Mrs. Hale?"

"Why, I don't know whether she did or not." She turned to look at the cage Mrs. Peters was holding up. "I've not been here in so long." She sighed. "There was a man round last year selling canaries cheap—but I don't know as she took one. Maybe she did. She used to sing real pretty herself."

Mrs. Peters looked around the kitchen.

"Seems kind of funny to think of a bird here." She half laughed—an attempt to put up a barrier. "But she must have had one—or why would she have a cage? I wonder what happened to it."

"I suppose maybe the cat got it," suggested Mrs. Hale, resuming her sewing.

"No; she didn't have a cat. She's got that feeling some people have about cats—being afraid of them. When they brought her to our house yesterday, my cat got in the room, and she was real upset and asked me to take it out."

"My sister Bessie was like that," laughed Mrs. Hale.

The sheriff's wife did not reply. The silence made Mrs. Hale turn round. Mrs. Peters was examining the bird-cage.

"Look at this door," she said slowly. "It's broke. One hinge has been pulled apart."

Mrs. Hale came nearer.

"Looks as if some one must have been—rough with it."

Again their eyes met—startled, questioning, apprehensive. For a moment neither spoke nor stirred. Then Mrs. Hale, turning away, said brusquely:

"If they're going to find any evidence, I wish they'd be about it. I don't like this place."

"But I'm awful glad you came with me, Mrs. Hale." Mrs. Peters put the bird-cage on the table and sat down. "It would be lonesome for me—sitting here alone."

"Yes, it would, wouldn't it?" agreed Mrs. Hale, a certain determined naturalness in her voice. She had picked up the sewing, but now it dropped in her lap, and she murmured in a different voice: "But I tell you what I *do* wish, Mrs. Peters. I wish I had come over sometimes when she was here. I wish—I had."

"But of course you were awful busy, Mrs. Hale. Your house—and your children."

"I could've come," retorted Mrs. Hale shortly. "I stayed away because it weren't cheerful—and that's why I ought to have come. I"—she looked around—"I've never liked this place. Maybe because it's down in a hollow and you don't see the road. I don't know what it is, but it's a lonesome place, and always was. I wish I had come over to see Minnie Foster sometimes. I can see now—" She did not put it into words.

"Well, you mustn't reproach yourself," counseled Mrs. Peters. "Somehow, we just don't see how it is with other folks till—something comes up."

"Not having children makes less work," mused Mrs. Hale, after a silence, "but it makes a quiet house—and Wright out to work all day—and no company when he did come in. Did you know John Wright, Mrs. Peters?"

"Not to know him. I've seen him in town. They say he was a good man."

"Yes—good," conceded John Wright's neighbor grimly. "He didn't drink, and kept his word as well as most, I guess, and paid his debts. But he was a hard man, Mrs. Peters. Just to pass the time of day with him—" She stopped, shivered a little. "Like a raw wind that gets to the bone." Her eye fell upon the cage on the table before her, and she added, almost bitterly: "I should think she would've wanted a bird!"

Suddenly she leaned forward, looking intently at the cage. "But what do you s'pose went wrong with it?"

"I don't know," returned Mrs. Peters; "unless it got sick and died."

But after she said it she reached over and swung the broken door. Both women watched it as if somehow held by it.

"You didn't know—her?" Mrs. Hale asked, a gentler note in her voice.

"Not till they brought her yesterday," said the sheriff's wife.

"She—come to think of it, she was kind of like a bird herself. Real sweet and pretty, but kind of timid and—fluttery. How—she—did—change."

That held her for a long time. Finally, as if struck with a happy thought and relieved to get back to everyday things, she exclaimed:

"Tell you what, Mrs. Peters, why don't you take the quilt in with you? It might take up her mind."

"Why, I think that's a real nice idea, Mrs. Hale," agreed the sheriff's wife, as if she too were glad to come into the atmosphere of a simple kindness. "There couldn't possibly be any objection to that, could there? Now, just what will I take? I wonder if her patches are in here—and her things."

They turned to the sewing basket.

"Here's some red," said Mrs. Hale, bringing out a roll of cloth. Underneath that was a box. "Here, maybe her scissors are in here—and her things." She held it up. "What a pretty box! I'll warrant that was something she had a long time ago—when she was a girl."

She held it in her hand a moment; then, with a little sigh, opened it.

Instantly her hand went to her nose.

"Why—!"

Mrs. Peters drew nearer—then turned away.

"There's something wrapped up in this piece of silk," faltered Mrs. Hale.

"This isn't her scissors," said Mrs. Peters, in a shrinking voice.

Her hand not steady, Mrs. Hale raised the piece of silk. "Oh, Mrs. Peters!" she cried. "It's—"

Mrs. Peters bent closer.

"It's the bird," she whispered.

"But, Mrs. Peters!" cried Mrs. Hale. "*Look* at it! Its *neck*—look at its neck! It's all—other side *to*."

She held the box away from her.

The sheriff's wife again bent closer.

"Somebody wrung its neck," said she, in a voice that was slow and deep.

And then again the eyes of the two women met—this time clung together in a look of dawning comprehension, of growing horror. Mrs. Peters looked from the dead bird to the broken door of the cage. Again their eyes met. And just then there was a sound at the outside door.

Mrs. Hale slipped the box under the quilt pieces in the basket, and sank into the chair before it. Mrs. Peters stood holding to the table. The county attorney and the sheriff came in from outside.

"Well, ladies," said the county attorney, as one turning from serious things to little pleasantries, "have you decided whether she was going to quilt it or knot it?"

"We think," began the sheriff's wife in a flurried voice, "that she was going to—knot it."

He was too preoccupied to notice the change that came in her voice on that last.

"Well, that's very interesting, I'm sure," he said tolerantly. He caught sight of the bird-cage. "Has the bird flown?"

"We think the cat got it," said Mrs. Hale in a voice curiously even.

He was walking up and down, as if thinking something out.

"Is there a cat?" he asked absently.

Mrs. Hale shot a look up at the sheriff's wife.

"Well, not *now*, said Mrs. Peters. "They're superstitious, you know; they leave."

She sank into her chair.

The county attorney did not heed her.

"No sign at all of any one having come in from the outside," he said to Peters, in the manner of continuing an interrupted conversation. "Their own rope. Now let's go upstairs again and go over it, piece by piece. It would have to have been someone who knew just the—"

The stair door closed behind them and their voices were lost.

The two women sat motionless, not looking at each other, but as if peering into something and at the same time holding back. When they spoke now it was as if they were afraid of what they were saying, but as if they could not help saying it.

"She liked the bird," said Martha Hale, low and slowly. "She was going to bury it in that pretty box."

"When I was a girl," said Mrs. Peters, under her breath, "my kitten—there was a boy took a hatchet, and before my eyes—before I could get there—" She covered her face an instant. "If they hadn't held me back I would have"—she caught herself, looked upstairs where footsteps were heard, and finished weakly—"hurt him."

Then they sat without speaking or moving.

"I wonder how it would seem," Mrs. Hale at last began, as if feeling her way over strange ground—"never to have had any children around?" Her eyes made a slow sweep of the kitchen, as if seeing what that kitchen had meant through all the years. "No, Wright wouldn't like the bird," she said after that—"a thing that sang. She used to sing. He killed that too." Her voice tightened.

Mrs. Peters moved uneasily.

"Of course we don't know who killed the bird."

"I knew John Wright," was Mrs. Hale's answer.

"It was an awful thing was done in this house that night, Mrs. Hale," said the sheriff's wife. "Killing a man while he slept—slipping a thing round his neck that choked the life out of him."

Mrs. Hale's hand went out to the bird-cage.

"His neck. Choked the life out of him."

"We don't *know* who killed him," whispered Mrs. Peters wildly. "We don't *know*."

Mrs. Hale had not moved. "If there had been years and years of—nothing, then a bird to sing to you, it would be awful—still—after the bird was still."

It was as if something within her not herself had spoken, and it found in Mrs. Peters something she did not know as herself.

"I know what stillness is," she said, in a queer, monotonous voice. "When we homesteaded in Dakota, and my first baby died—after he was two years old—and me with no other then—"

Mrs. Hale stirred.

"How soon do you suppose they'll be through looking for the evidence?"

"I know what stillness is," repeated Mrs. Peters, in just that same way. Then she too pulled back. "The law has got to punish crime, Mrs. Hale," she said in her tight little way.

"I wish you'd seen Minnie Foster," was the answer, "when she wore a white dress with blue ribbons, and stood up there in the choir and sang."

The picture of that girl, the fact that she had lived neighbor to that girl for twenty years, and had let her die for lack of life, was suddenly more than she could bear.

"Oh, I *wish* I'd come over here once in a while!" she cried. "That was a crime! That was a crime! Who's going to punish that?"

"We mustn't take on," said Mrs. Peters, with a frightened look toward the stairs.

"I might a' *known* she needed help! I tell you, it's *queer*, Mrs. Peters. We live close together, and we live far apart. We all go through the same things—it's all just a different kind of the same thing! If it weren't—why do you and I understand? Why do we know—what we know this minute?"

She dashed her hand across her eyes. Then, seeing the jar of fruit on the table, she reached for it and choked out:

"If I was you I wouldn't *tell* her her fruit was gone! Tell her it *ain't*. Tell her it's all right—all of it. Here—take this in to prove it to her! She—she may never know whether it was broke or not."

She turned away.

Mrs. Peters reached out for the bottle of fruit as if she were glad to take it—as if touching a familiar thing, having something to do, could keep her from something else. She got up, looked about for something to wrap the fruit in, took a petticoat from the pile of clothes she had brought from the front room, and nervously started winding that round the bottle.

"My!" she began, in a high, false voice, "it's a good thing the men couldn't hear us! Getting all stirred up over a little thing like a—dead canary." She hurried over that. "As if that could have anything to do with—with—My, wouldn't they *laugh*?"

Footsteps were heard on the stairs.

"Maybe they would," muttered Mrs. Hale—"maybe they wouldn't."

"No, Peters," said the county attorney incisively; "it's all perfectly clear, except the reason for doing it. But you know juries when it comes to women. If there was some definite thing—something to show. Something to make a story about. A thing that would connect up with this clumsy way of doing it."

In a covert way Mrs. Hale looked at Mrs. Peters. Mrs. Peters was looking at her. Quickly they looked away from each other. The outer door opened and Mr. Hale came in.

"I've got the team round now," he said. "Pretty cold out there."

"I'm going to stay here awhile by myself," the county attorney suddenly announced. "You can send Frank out for me, can't you?" he asked the sheriff. "I want to go over everything. I'm not satisfied we can't do better."

Again, for one brief moment, the two women's eyes found one another. The sheriff came up to the table.

"Did you want to see what Mrs. Peters was going to take in?"

The county attorney picked up the apron. He laughed.

"Oh, I guess they're not very dangerous things the ladies have picked out."

Mrs. Hale's hand was on the sewing basket in which the box was concealed. She felt that she ought to take her hand off the basket. She did not seem able to. He picked up one of the quilt blocks which she had piled on to cover the box. Her eyes felt like fire. She had a feeling that if he took up the basket she would snatch it from him.

But he did not take it up. With another little laugh, he turned away, saying:

"No; Mrs. Peters doesn't need supervising. For that matter, a sheriff's wife is married to the law. Ever think of it that way, Mrs. Peters?"

Mrs. Peters was standing beside the table. Mrs. Hale shot a look up at her; but she could not see her face. Mrs. Peters had turned away. When she spoke, her voice was muffled.

"Not—just that way," she said.

"Married to the law!" chuckled Mrs. Peters' husband. He moved toward the door into the front room, and said to the county attorney:

"I just want you to come in here a minute, George. We ought to take a look at these windows."

"Oh—windows," said the county attorney scoffingly.

"We'll be right out, Mr. Hale," said the sheriff to the farmer, who was still waiting by the door.

Hale went to look after the horses. The sheriff followed the county attorney into the other room. Again—for one final moment—the two women were alone in that kitchen.

Martha Hale sprang up, her hands tight together, looking at that other woman, with whom it rested. At first she could not see her eyes, for the sheriff's wife had not turned back since she turned away at that suggestion of being married to the law. But now Mrs. Hale made her turn back. Her eyes made her turn back. Slowly, unwillingly, Mrs. Peters turned her head until her eyes met the eyes of the other woman. There was a moment when they held each other in a steady, burning look in which there was no evasion nor flinching. Then Martha Hale's eyes pointed the way to the basket in which was hidden the thing that would make certain the conviction of the other woman—that woman who was not there and yet who had been there with them all through that hour.

For a moment Mrs. Peters did not move. And then she did it. With a rush forward, she threw back the quilt pieces, got the box, tried to put it in her hand-bag. It was too big. Desperately she opened it, started to take the bird out. But there she broke—she could not touch the bird. She stood there helpless, foolish.

There was the sound of a knob turning in the inner door. Martha Hale snatched the box from the sheriff's wife, and got it in the pocket of her big coat just as the sheriff and the county attorney came back into the kitchen.

"Well, Henry," said the county attorney facetiously, "at least we found out that she was not going to quilt it. She was going to—what is it you call it, ladies?"

Mrs. Hale's hand was against the pocket of her coat.

"Knot it," was her low reply.

He did not see her eyes.

BIBLIOGRAPHY

Bonner; Geraldine. *The Castlecourt Diamond Case.* New York: Funk & Wagnalls (1906).

Brunsdale, Mitzi M. *Icons of Mystery and Crime Detection.* Santa Barbara, CA: ABC-CLIO (2010).

Clark, Sandra. *Women and Crime in the Street Literature of Early Modern England.* Basingstoke, Hampshire: Palgrave Macmillan (2004).

Cohen, Daniel A. *Pillars of Salt, Monuments of Grace.* New York: Oxford University Press (1992).

Craig, Patricia, and Mary Cadogan. *The Lady Investigates: Women Detectives and Spies in Fiction.* New York: St. Martins Press (1981).

Crowe, Catherine. *Susan Hopley or, The Adventures of a Maid Servant.* London: G. Routledge (1852).

Curran, John. *Agatha Christie: Murder in the Making*. New York: HarperCollins (2011).

Gaskell, Elizabeth Cleghorn. *Gothic Tales*. New York: Penguin Books (2000).

Green, Anna Katharine. *Masterpieces of Mystery*. Indianapolis: Dodd, Mead and Company (1913).

———. *The Golden Slipper: And Other Problems for Violet Strange*. San Bernardino, CA : World Library Classics (2017).

———. *The Leavenworth Case*. Edited by Michael Sims. New York: Penguin Group USA (2010).

Groner, Augusta. *Detective Joe Muller Five Mysteries*. Translated by Grace Isabel Colbron. N.p.: Mcallister Editions (2015).

Haining, Peter. *The Classic Era of Crime Fiction*. Chicago: Chicago Review Press (2002).

Janik, Erika. *Pistols and Petticoats: 175 Years of Lady Detectives in Fact and Fiction*. Boston: Beacon Press (2016).

Kestner, Joseph A. *Sherlock's Sisters: British Female Detectives, 1864–1913*. Aldershot, Hampshire: Ashgate (2003).

Knight, Stephen Thomas. *Crime Fiction since 1800*. Basingstoke, Hampshire: Palgrave Macmillan (2010).

———. *Towards Sherlock Holmes: A Thematic History of Crime Fiction in the 19th Century World*. Jefferson, NC: McFarland and Co. (2017).

Nickerson, Catherine Ross. *The Web of Iniquity: Early Detective Fiction by American Women*. Durham, NC: Duke University Press (1998).

Queen, Ellery. *The Female of the Species: The Great Women Detectives and Criminals*. Boston: Little, Brown (1943).

Rielly, Edward J. *Murder 101: Essays on the Teaching of Detective Fiction*. Jefferson, NC: McFarland & Co. (2009).

Rzepka, Charles J. *Detective Fiction (Cultural History of Literature).* Cambridge: Polity (2005).

Sims, George Robert. *Dorcas Dene, Detective.* New York: F. V. White & Co. (1897).

Sims, Michael, ed. *The Penguin Book of Victorian Women in Crime.* New York: Penguin Classics (2011).

———. *The Dead Witness: A Connoisseur's Collection of Victorian Detective Stories.* New York: Walker & Company (2012).

Slung, Michele B. *Crime on Her Mind: Fifteen Stories of Female Sleuths from the Victorian Era to the Forties.* New York: Pantheon Books (1975).

Sussex, Lucy. *Women Writers and Detectives in Nineteenth-Century Crime Fiction.* Basingstoke, Hampshire: Palgrave Macmillan (2010).

Van Deventer, Emma Murdoch. *Shadowed by Three.* Chicago: Donnelly, Gassette & Lloyd (1883).

Victor, Metta Victoria Fuller. *The Dead Letter: An American Romance.* New York: Beadle & Co. (1866).

Watson, Kate. *Women Writing Crime Fiction, 1860–1880.* Jefferson, NC: McFarland and Co. (2012).

Wood, Mrs. Henry. *Johnny Ludlow.* London: Richard Bentley & Son (1874).

ACKNOWLEDGMENTS

Many thanks to the terrific team at Pegasus Books: Claiborne Hancock, Iris Blasi, and Maria Fernandez. This is our fourth book together, and I look forward to many more. No book is the product of a single person, and every writer relies on a "village." Mine is populated with the greatest people: my agent, Don Maass; my lawyer and friend Jonathan Kirsch; my longtime Sherlockian friends Andy Peck, Jerry Margolin, and Mike Whelan, constant cheerleaders; my frequent collaborator Laurie R. King, whom I adore and admire; my friend and colleague Neil Gaiman, who always reaches for the stars and shows us how to follow; my dear friend and writing partner Laura Caldwell, who has read and criticized more of my work than I ever had any right to ask; my children and grandchildren; and especially, as always, *the* woman, my wife, Sharon, who made me become a writer.

Very special thanks to my friend Sara Paretsky, who inspired me both generally and specifically to write this book. Sara's career, and her indomitable pursuit of truth and justice, are shining examples of how I and many others want to live our lives. I was privileged to hear Sara give a talk on forgotten Victorian women crime writers, and it gave me the idea for this anthology. I hope that Sara regards it as a grateful appreciation for the writers included in the book as well as those discussed in the introduction. We must not forget the giants on whose shoulders we stand.

ABOUT THE EDITOR

Leslie S. Klinger is considered to be one of the world's foremost authorities on Sherlock Holmes, Dracula, H. P. Lovecraft, Frankenstein, and nineteenth-century genre fiction and has annotated or edited more than thirty books. Klinger is a long-time member of the Baker Street Irregulars, and served as the series editor for the Manuscript Series of the Baker Street Irregulars; he is currently the series editor for the BSI's Biography Series. He served three terms as chapter president of the SoCal chapter of the Mystery Writers of America and on its national board. He is also the treasurer of the Horror Writers Association. He lectures frequently on Holmes, Dracula, Lovecraft, Frankenstein, and their worlds, including frequent panels at the Los Angeles Times Festival of Books, Bouchercon, StokerCon, NecronomiCon, the World Horror Convention, World Fantasy Convention, VampireCon, Comicpalooza, WonderCon, and San Diego Comic-Con, and he has taught courses on Holmes and Dracula at UCLA Extension.

Klinger's work has received numerous awards and nominations, including the Edgar for Best Critical-Biographical Book in 2005 for *The New Annotated Sherlock Holmes: The Complete Short Stories* and the Anthony and Silver Falchion awards for Best Anthology in 2015 for *In the Company of Sherlock Holmes* (co-edited with Laurie R. King), as well as nominations for the Bram Stoker Award for Best Nonfiction book for *New Annotated H. P. Lovecraft* and *Annotated Sandman*. His introductions and essays have appeared in numerous books, graphic novels, academic journals, newspapers, the *Los Angeles Review of Books*, and *Playboy Magazine*; he also reviews books for the *Los Angeles Times* and other periodicals. He was the technical advisor for Warner Bros. on the film *Sherlock Holmes: A Game of Shadows* (2011) and served (without credit) in that role for Warner Bros.' earlier hit *Sherlock Holmes* (2009). He has consulted on a number of novels, comic books, graphic novels, and other films featuring Holmes and Dracula.

Klinger received an A.B. in English from the University of California; he also received a J.D. degree from the University of California School of Law (Boalt Hall). He and his wife, Sharon, have five adult children, and six grandchildren, and they live in Malibu with their dog and cat. By day, Klinger practices law in Westwood, specializing in tax, estate planning, and business law.